ALSO BY MEGHAN QUINN

BRIDESMAID
UNDERCOVER

MEGHAN QUINN

Bloom books

P.O. Box 4410, Naperville, Illinois 60567-4410
(630) 961-3900
sourcebooks.com

Cataloging-in-Publication data is on file with the Library of Congress.

Printed and bound in Canada.
MBP 10 9 8 7 6 5 4 3 2 1

PROLOGUE
HARDY

MY PENIS FEELS PHENOMENAL.

Like it's floating on a puffy white cloud being blown around by whispers of "you had sex" last night.

Not just any kind of sex, but mind-altering sex.

Sex that made me see stars.

As if my head was stuck in an erotic wormhole where luminous spheroids were glittering all around me.

To keep it simple for you…I am not the same man that I was before last night.

A new standard has been set, an impossible standard, and there's only one person to blame…well, not blame, but celebrate.

Fucking Everly Plum.

Not to be corny, but she took my breath away last night.

Stole it.

Made me believe that I'd actually died of asphyxiation and risen to orgasmic heaven.

And before you say I'm being a bit overdramatic about a night of sex, I swear on my left nut that I've never felt this way before.

Ever.

Also, and this is very, very important…I never saw this dark mistress of the night coming.

A total wild card.

A loop that was thrown my way and I took it.

Sure, yes, we're friends.

And, of course, I've always thought she was beautiful.

But did I think when looking at her, "Oh hey, there's coupling in our future"?

Never.

But hell, just look at her peacefully sleeping, her nearly pitch-black hair strewn across the white of her pillow, creating a stark contrast of innocence and sin. Beard burn mars the soft, silky skin on her cheeks, neck, and chest. Yeah, I was feral over the feel of her beneath me. And those lips, which drove me absolutely insane last night, are puffy, pink, and swollen.

I can see myself all over her.

I can recall the feel of her hands caressing my back, her nails digging into my skin.

I can smell her sweet perfume surrounding us like an erotic cloud of mischief.

And if I hold my breath, I can faintly still hear the way she gasped when I entered her.

Fuck...I can still feel it...

I drag my hands over my face as I roll to my back, very unfamiliar with my surroundings but feeling comfortable at the same time. I prop myself up on my elbows and glance around her studio apartment. It's tiny compared to the farmhouse I have outside of San Francisco and my apartment here in town. Pretty sure the primary bedroom in my farmhouse is bigger than her studio. But whereas my place feels starkly decorated by someone I paid, Everly's apartment is full of warmth and character.

Velvet curtains drape the exposed brick wall that offers a rather large window and view of the bay. Gold-framed black and white pictures hang around her apartment, while an impressive ficus soaks up the sun from the corner of her apartment. Across from the bedroom space, she's created a dining nook right next to the kitchen with a wood table that is flawed with imperfections but decorated with a smooth, matte black vase. Her apartment is a combination of old world and modern functionality, something I didn't get to appreciate last night as I was pushing her up against the door and mauling her mouth.

Or when I had her legs wrapped around my face.

Or when I was rocking her bed like a madman against the wall with my uncontrolled and wild thrusts.

Christ.

When I got dressed last night, I had no intention of ending up naked and in bed with Everly, but thanks to a decent consumption of heavy-handed Moscow mules, Jell-O shots, and a persistent ex-girlfriend, I ended the night tearing Everly's clothes off with zero patience.

And as I glance over at her beautiful face again, I realize that I want a repeat. I want a lot of repeats. I want all of the fucking repeats until—

Bzzzz.

Brows knitted together, I glance to the floor where my pants are bunched up, my phone sticking out of the back pocket. *Why's he texting me?*

The only time Hudson, my older brother, would ever text me this early is if it's urgent.

Groaning quietly to myself, I snag my phone. With my back toward Everly, I open the text message.

Hudson: Please, for the love of God, tell me you didn't sleep with Everly last night.

Fear prickles the back of my neck as I try to figure out how the hell he'd even know what happened. I didn't accidentally call him in the middle of…everything…did I? I exit out of the text message and go to my recent calls in my phone. There's nothing.

But then…

I notice the texts above the one from this morning.

Hardy: Everly is so hot. Such a good kisser.

Hudson: What? Are you fucking serious right now?

Hudson: Hardy, pick up your phone.

Hudson: What the hell is going on? Are you with her right now?

Hudson: Hardy!

Oh shit.

I have a feeling this won't be good. I can go about this two ways: I can tell him the truth, or I can possibly go about this conversation in a roundabout way to see how much trouble I might be in.

Obviously, I choose the latter.

Hardy: And if I did sleep with her…that would be…?

He texts back immediately.

Hudson: Bad, you moron! That would be very bad.

I twist my lips to the side, trying to understand why sleeping with Everly would be a bad thing, because from personal experience, it was a good thing.

A very good thing.

Easily the best decision I've ever made.

Hardy: Just for reference, could you explain why sleeping with her would be a bad thing?

Hudson: Because she's working with your sister! And don't you remember what happened a few years ago, when I happened to ask if I could date one of her employees?

Hardy: Attempting to remember, but the brain is a bit foggy at the moment.

Hudson: She freaked out, said there were millions of women to choose from, don't dip in her pond.

Hmm, I have a distant memory of such a thing.

Hardy: So you think she would be mad?

Hudson: Are you saying you had sex with Everly last night?

Hardy: I'm not confirming anything.

Hudson: Well, I'm at your apartment and you're not here, so you tell me what the hell you did last night.

Jesus, this guy.

Hardy: Fine, we slept together.

Hudson: Fucking Christ, Hardy.

Hardy: It was the Moscow mules!

Hudson: Are you at her place now?

Hardy: Yes. She's sleeping and I'm trying not to wake her up for another round.

Hudson: Don't even fucking look at her. Get up, grab your clothes, and leave. I'm not kidding, Hardy, this won't go over well.

Hardy: I understand why this might not go well, but also…maybe she would be happy for me?

Hudson: She won't be.

Hardy: But maybe she will…

Hudson: SHE WON'T! Haisley is very protective of her business, you and I know that. If you date someone she's working with, and you ruin that relationship, Haisley is going to be pissed.

> The relationship she has with Dad is severed, so don't taint
> the relationship she has with you.

And that right there, that's all he has to say, because he's right.

After Haisley married Jude, we found out some things about our father that, well, let's just say they didn't settle well, so as a group we decided to part ways with him and his billion-dollar hotel chain business. We started our own cooperative with our dad's direct competitors, the Cane brothers, and we have multiple ventures now under the cooperative, including Haisley's business, which also involves Everly...

> **Hudson:** Not to mention, Everly is an employee under the cooperative, in a way, and we've been strict about not dating employees.

Once again, the fucker is right.

> **Hudson:** So get out. Now.

Internally I groan because the last thing I want to do is leave this bed.

It's warm.

Naked Everly is next to me.

And I had plans. Wonderful, amazing, throbbing plans. Yes... throbbing.

I was going to make some coffee, maybe order some breakfast, and then wake Everly up with my tongue.

What I wouldn't give for another taste.

But Hudson is right. He's really right. I crossed a line last night, a line that could hurt my sister. And Haisley is not someone I ever want to hurt. She's been through enough in her life and, if anything, I'll do whatever it takes to protect her, which means...I need to bolt.

I glance over my shoulder just to make sure Everly is not awake and when I see her still peacefully sleeping, the covers nearly exposing her spectacular chest, I internally weep inside and then turn away. I slip out of bed, completely naked, and grab my clothes before I move to her bathroom.

I quietly shut the door and start dressing.

My dick that was once feeling phenomenal is now on a watchlist for murder. The broken dream of another round with Everly fills me with such deep sorrow that I feel it all the way to the tips of my goddamn toes.

I don't even bother to check out my disappointed expression in the mirror as I quickly slip on my clothes—I know what it looks like.

Depressed.

Deprived.

Defeated.

I stick my phone in my back pocket, run my hand through my hair, and then on a depleted sigh, I exit the bathroom, just in time to see Everly sit up from the bed and stretch her arms over her head, showing off her beautiful beard burn-covered chest.

Fuck.

Me.

When she sees me out of the corner of her eye, she quickly scrambles for the sheets to cover herself up.

Babe, I sucked on your tits last night, several times, so no need to cover up.

"Oh…hi," she says cutely as she wets her lips, taking me in with her eyes.

I scratch the back of my head as I mentally tell myself to stay away. "Hey," I say, my voice coming out all scratchy.

"Are you, uh…leaving?"

I thumb toward the door and say, "Yeah, was going to take off."

"Oh, sure, yeah." She worries at her lower lip.

"Have an early start to the day," I add.

"Of course. Work, work, work," she says awkwardly.

"Yup, got to love that work."

"So much work," she says.

"All the work," I mumble.

Any other ways we can say work? Because I'm here for the sweat-inducing conversation.

She glances at the sheets, silence falling between us before she says, "Yeah." When she lifts her eyes to me, vulnerability laces through them. "I, uh, hope I didn't do anything wrong."

Fuck, she's second-guessing herself, and that's the last thing I want her to do when she was the best sex of my goddamn life.

"No, you didn't," I say. "It was…last night was…phenomenal. Really fucking great."

I catch the blush in her cheeks. "Yeah, it was."

"The best," I say.

"Easily," she replies.

"Like, my world is different now." Her brows lift, and I feel like I've said too much. Time to shift gears. I take a step toward the door. "Well, I should be going."

Her expression falls. "You don't, uh…you don't want any coffee or anything?"

I shake my head as I find my shoes on the floor and slip those on quickly. "Nah, I'll pick something up. But thanks."

"Okay." She worries that lip again. I *want* to walk up to her, push her back on the bed, and make out with her…for hours.

"So, yeah, thanks for last night, but I'll, uh, I'll see you around, I'm sure."

"Yeah." She diverts her eyes to the bundled-up sheets in front of her. "Um, before you leave, not sure how much alcohol took over last night, but…you said some things…"

Oh, I'm sure I did.

I'm sure I said a lot of things.

Hell, I'm worried what came out of my mouth last night after experiencing what I can only describe as the purest form of ecstasy.

I wouldn't be surprised if there was a *yahoo* thrown out.

A *hurray*.

A *blessed be to God*.

"Yeah, there was lots of alcohol, huh?" I say, trying not to be awkward, but also…hating myself. "People say weird things when alcohol is involved."

She slowly nods. "Okay, yeah, I get it." She softly smiles and then meets my eyes, a distance forming in them. "You know, I still think you have a chance with Maple. I saw you guys talking, so, you know, if you want me to still try to make that happen, I can."

I want to squeeze my eyes shut in irritation because after last night, the last thing I want is for Everly to think she still needs to help me out with my ex. I want nothing to do with Maple romantically.

Maple wants nothing to do with me.

We're friends.

The persistent ex-girlfriend I mentioned? That was Maple. She was the one pushing me toward Everly last night.

And I freely went with the flow.

But…fuck, after what Hudson said, maybe…maybe agreeing with Everly might be the easy sidestep to avoid any confusion and awkwardness.

"That, uh, that would be awesome," I say as a tight ball forms in my throat.

No, it would not be awesome. What would be awesome is if I could climb back in bed with you, if we could share a coffee while you curl into my chest, if we could not leave your apartment all day and just get lost in each other.

She demurely pushes her hair behind her ear, avoiding all eye contact with me as her shoulders turn in. "Okay, well, see you."

I lift my hand up to her and offer her a wave. "See ya."

And with that, I exit her apartment, shutting the door behind me. I walk a few feet away, pause, and then lean against the wall of her apartment building, letting my head fall back to the hard surface.

Fuck me.

How did this even happen?

I'll tell you how…I was desperate to find a relationship. So desperate that I asked the wrong person to help me—well, maybe they *were* the right person.

And how does Everly fit into all of that? Well…it's quite the fucking story and, after last night, it just became a complicated one.

I glance back at her door, the gears in my head spinning.

This. Is. Not. Right.

Fuck, I have to go back in…

CHAPTER ONE
HARDY

"HARDY, MAN!" I HEAR KEN say right before his arms wrap around me from behind as he pulls me into a tight hug.

I turn around and return the hug. "Ken Doll, congrats, dude."

Ken's face beams at me as he adjusts his tie. Ken, my best friend from college, has always felt uncomfortable in a suit—a tie especially—and it's something we bonded over since I prefer a pair of jeans and a plaid shirt over a suit and tie just like him. But when we need to, we know how to clean up. Like for his swanky engagement party. Having gold-rimmed tumblers with custom ice cubes for whiskey seems a bit much, something my rich-as-shit father would do to impress the people around him.

"Can you believe she said yes?" Ken asks.

"I can." I chuckle. "Polly loves you, man."

"I know, but, fuck, that was nerve-wracking. I wish you could have been there."

"I'm sorry." I grip his shoulder. "I wish I was there too, but this bullshit happening with my father has really tied me up lately."

Ken winces, knowing exactly what I'm talking about.

Let me lay it out for you.

My dad: Reginald Hopper, CEO and owner of Hopper Industries.

He's put me and my two siblings, Hudson and Haisley, through a roller coaster of fatherhood.

Whether it's a heavy dose of guilt for not performing the way he prefers, or a mountain of praise for making a cutthroat decision under his umbrella of employment, his feelings toward his children have been up and down, never satisfied.

And this past summer, everything imploded. Spectacularly.

You see, Haisley left the family business to pursue her own aspirations. Our prideful father wasn't happy about it and has been gunning for her to bring her business to Hopper Industries, to the point that he was willing to walk over whoever he could to make that happen. Well, Hudson and I weren't going to tolerate that. If our dad taught us one thing growing up, purposefully or not, it was that we siblings needed to stick together. So we came up with a plan to part ways with Hopper Industries.

Since the company has multiple branches of business, one being Hopper Almonds—what I'm in charge of—I used my trust fund to buy it out, and my dad had no problem parting ways. Moron. It's worth more than he realized, and Hudson and I joined forces with our dad's competitor to do right in the world.

But it's been a long-ass process.

It's taken a toll on us.

On our personal lives.

And on our relationship with our dad.

Let's just say he didn't take the news well.

"Yeah, how's everything going with your dad?" Ken asks.

I take a sip of my drink and say, "Well, Dad is furious, as you can imagine, and has a vendetta against us. Pretty sure he wants to file a lawsuit against his own children, but he doesn't have any justification. So that's where we stand."

"Yikes. And how is the business going?"

I smirk at him. "Amazing."

"Yeah?" Ken's expression turns into excitement.

"Yeah, the farms are flourishing. We restructured a bit and increased pay, which has improved morale, made a better working environment, and has increased production. We've had some of the biggest harvests we've ever had and are growing with some purchases of other almond farms, but maintaining staff loyalty. We invested in a wedding business and are almost done with the storefront, which is—"

"Wedding business?" Ken says with a raised brow. "How the hell did you go from almonds to a wedding business? That doesn't seem like you."

I chuckle. "I told you about Maggie, right?"

"Who's Maggie?" Ken asks, elbowing me like an idiot.

"Nothing like that, dude. She's engaged to Brody, one of our investors, who used to work for my dad. Maggie was a savior at Haisley's wedding. Haisley's maid of honor couldn't be there because of her pregnancy, and during the welcome reception Brody introduced Maggie to us. We quickly found out she's a wedding planner and, well, long story short, she filled in as a bridesmaid and helped out with the wedding. In the end, we wanted to help her expand her business, and we needed an event planner on staff for the charity and partner events we're planning, so it all worked out."

"Huh, interesting. She filled in as a bridesmaid?"

"Yeah. Maggie and her assistant Everly expanded on that idea and started a 'Bridesmaid for Hire' service that falls under the umbrella of their business."

"Bridesmaid for hire?" I hear Polly say as she comes up next to Ken. "What's that?"

Strapped into a flowy, sparkly gold dress, Polly, another one of my best friends from college, looks breathtaking and just as uncomfortable as Ken and me. There is no doubt in my mind that her mom picked out the dress and forced her to wear it since Polly is more of a casual girl. Either way, she looks stunning.

We hug, and when I step away, I say, "Congrats, Polly. I'm really happy for the both of you."

She rubs my arm. "Thanks, Hardy. We're pretty excited. Only took a decade, but hey, sometimes the best things are worth waiting for."

"Didn't help that you broke up with me two years ago," Ken says in a teasing tone.

"Maybe because you weren't proposing, you moron," I say, which causes Polly to laugh.

"And this is why you should always listen to your best friend." Polly presses a kiss to Ken's lips and for a moment, a strong moment, a bout of jealousy strikes me.

Fresh from witnessing my madly in love sister marry, to hearing about the romantic proposal between two of my best friends, and struggling with feelings of loneliness when I finish work and get home to my apartment every night…my mind has been swirling with thoughts recently.

Romantic thoughts.

Like maybe it's about damn time I start thinking about the future of my personal life and not just my career.

The business is running well—I'm almost redundant if I'm honest—my bank account looks extremely healthy, and yet I have no one to share it with. Haisley and Hudson are both the epitome of success, and I've been feeling that familiar sense of *unsettled* again as of late. As if I don't have a grand purpose.

Back in college, I enjoyed being in a relationship. But that relationship ran its course, and once Hudson and I started taking over certain aspects of Dad's business—long before we parted ways with him—I just never found time to even consider dating someone else.

Now that I feel solid in my schedule and my job—despite the possible looming lawsuit—I feel the need to perhaps find a relationship of my own, especially now, being surrounded by couples.

Haisley and Jude.

Maggie and Brody.

Ken and Polly.

Fuck, if Hudson finds someone, I'm screwed.

"You okay over there, big man?" Ken asks. "You're staring."

"Oh, sorry," I say, shaking my head. "Just caught up in the love."

Polly links her arm through Ken's. "Wishing you had someone standing next to you?" she asks playfully. "Possibly a date?"

"Maybe," I say as I sip my drink.

Polly chuckles. "You've always loved being in a relationship."

"I have," I say as I look around the room, my thoughts falling to the one person who I shared a relationship with in college. It was sweet, stable. She has to be here—she's Polly's best friend.

"She's not here," Polly says, seeing right through me.

"What? Who? I wasn't looking for anyone," I say, feigning ignorance.

"Liar," Ken says on a boisterous laugh.

"Don't even think about it," Polly says, pointing her finger at me. "She is off limits."

I raise a brow. "Why…is she with someone?"

Polly shakes her head. "No, but she is my maid of honor, and she's already worried about taking on the role—she doesn't need to worry about you sniffing around with those hearts in your eyes. Which, by the way, did you ask him?" Polly nudges Ken.

"Oh, right." Ken meets my gaze. "Want to be my best man?"

"Oh, my God, that's how you're going to ask him?" Polly jabs Ken in the arm.

He chuckles and shrugs. "I'm not about to propose to him like you did to Maple. This is how guys do it." He looks at me again. "So, will you?"

I laugh and nod. "Would be honored, man." And I am honored, despite feeling like a third wheel in the love. We share a quick bro hug and then I glance at Polly and say, "So, where is Maple, if she's your maid of honor?"

Polly's eyes narrow. "I told you. Do not even go near her."

"She was my girlfriend for three years, Polly. I can at least say hi to her."

"Is that all you're going to do?" Polly asks, folding her arms now.

"I might ask how she's doing, as that would be the polite thing to do. Maybe see if she wants to grab some coffee and catch up."

"No," Polly replies. "No coffee."

"You're acting like I was the one who broke up with her," I reply.

"I know how it went down," Polly says. "I was there. And you and I both know *why* she broke up with you."

I sigh and tilt my head to the side. "We were both going our separate ways. It would have been too hard."

"Yes, but this was after you told her that you'd follow her."

I push my hand through my hair. I'd just felt so untethered back then. I needed to start my career, to prove to my dad that I was capable. Family focused. *Business* focused. Leaving my family to follow Maple to a job in Denver just didn't make sense. And strangely, my life has felt a little like that lately. *Untethered.* "It was complicated, Polly. You know that."

Ken puts his arm around his fiancée. "It was, babe."

She sighs. "You're right. I'm sorry. I just…She's moving back here, finally, after ten years away. She's nervous, she's not accustomed to the city life anymore, and she's starting a new job. I don't want anything to scare her off and, unfortunately, I think you coming back in her life would do that."

Now it's my turn to be surprised. "She's moving back to San Francisco?"

Polly slowly nods. "She is, and she's very wary. She lived in a hut in the wetlands of Peru for several years while studying animal patterns. Returning to San Francisco means she'll be living in a big city with trolleys, and cars, and tourists. She's nervous and scared and, now that I asked her to be my maid of honor, she's overwhelmed. The last thing she wants is an ex coming back into her life."

"She said that to you?"

"Yes," Polly replies while crossing her arms.

Holy shit though. Maple's going to be back in San Francisco. I was thinking about just reconnecting—I didn't know she was going to be back here for good. That changes everything.

"But maybe…maybe I'm supposed to come back into her life," I say, hope lifting in my chest.

"Oh, Jesus," Ken mutters.

"Shut up, man. I'm serious." I let out a deep sigh. "Listen, I'm…I'm ready to start dating. To find someone to settle down with. I've realized that after watching Haisley and you guys. I'm missing something in my life, and I think that something is…well…a *someone*. Maple and I were great together. Don't you think we should give it another shot? I mean, you guys got back together after breaking up, so why can't I have that with Maple?"

"He has a point," Ken says.

Polly looks between the two of us and then points her finger at me. "No."

"Come on, Polly," I drag out.

"I said no, and what the bride says goes. Understood?"

"Yes," I grumble even though in the back of my mind I don't agree with that one bit, but that's a bridge I can cross later.

"Now…back to what you first said. What is this 'bridesmaid for hire' thing you were talking about?" She looks over my shoulder and adds, "And hurry up because my mom is eyeing me, and I know she wants me to go say hi and thank you to her friends, not actually enjoy myself with my friends."

I chuckle. "Bridesmaid for Hire is a business we invested in. Maggie Mitchell owns Magical Moments by Maggie, and she's an event planner. One of the branches of her business is offering bridesmaid services. For instance, Haisley's best friend found out before her wedding that she couldn't fly because she was pregnant, and Maggie filled in for her. They also help with planning, bachelorette parties, wedding day tasks, anything a bridesmaid might have to do, they're there for it."

Polly taps her chin. "So, I might be looking for someone to mentor Maple, possibly take over the responsibilities, or even guide her so she's not so overwhelmed. Since you two are the only ones in the wedding party, holding the responsibilities on your own can be difficult. So, would they do that?"

"They would," I say.

"Well, isn't that perfect?" She walks up to me and pats me on the chest. "I'll need an introduction because the wedding party consists of you and Maple, so this would be perfect to have help and take some of the stress off Maple's shoulders. So if you could orchestrate that intro, that would be great. Thank you, Hardy." And then she takes off.

I glance behind me and then back at Ken whose eyes are fixed on her backside. "Why does it feel like she's always controlled us?" I ask.

Ken sighs and smiles up at me. "I don't know, but she's had me by the balls since day one."

"Ken," she calls out. "Come here."

"And she beckons…" Ken says.

"And you follow."

"Always," he replies and then shakes my hand. "Stick around, man, I want to catch up some more, but let me make the rounds first."

"Not a problem," I say and then he jogs up to Polly where he places his hand on her lower back and kisses her cheek.

She smiles brightly up at him, and everyone around them nearly melts from the suffocating love in the room.

Fuck me, I want that.

I want to put my hand on a lower back, as odd as that sounds.

I want to look down at my girl and see her eyes sparkle, knowing I'm her man.

I don't want to be alone at a freaking engagement party, sipping on whiskey that's cooled by a fancy piece of ice.

I want someone I can whisper to about the radishes in the vegetable crudités which no one is going to eat because who really bites into a radish willingly?

No one.

I've finally shed the bitter weight of my father's demanding pressure from my shoulders. I feel comfortable with where I am professionally, and I'm ready to take that success and dedicate myself to someone.

And not just anyone, but possibly the girl I was once in love with.

Maple Baker.

The only question is how can I go about this without pissing off the bride?

And better yet, how can I possibly get close to Maple if her guard is already up?

There has to be a way. I just need to think of it.

CHAPTER TWO
HARDY

"HOW WAS THE ENGAGEMENT PARTY?" Hudson asks as I take a seat at the conference table where he's laid out a variety of baked goods, drinks, and an impressive fruit platter that is calling out to me.

"Good," I say as I sit then gesture to the display of food. "Don't you think this is a little much? We've been in business together for a few months now—I don't think we need to impress the Cane brothers."

"We did it for our first meeting here, so we need to keep doing it or else they're going to think we're cheap asses who were just trying to impress them the first go around. Understand hosting ethics."

"I don't think the term *hosting ethics* is a real thing."

"Look it up," Hudson says, nodding toward my phone.

"Why? Because you want to be embarrassed when I prove it's not real?"

"No, because I want to see the look on your face when you realize that I'm right about everything and maybe you should stop questioning me," he says.

I pick up my phone and pull up my search engine. "You are going to be so humiliated."

"You think I come up with this shit on my own? I'm following the rules of society."

I type in *hosting ethics* and press search. I scroll some of the first few links, not seeing anything until I stumble across a link that says "Miss

Manners' Rules on Hosting and Ethics." I lift a brow to my brother. "Is this what you're referring to?"

He leans in, his eyes narrowing in on the link. When he sits back, he adjusts his tie and says, "As a matter of fact, Miss Manners is a great source."

"You're an idiot," I say just as the door to the conference room opens and Jude, our new brother-in-law and business partner, walks in.

He always makes quite the entrance. The man is a fucking beast. And I say that with respect to myself and Hudson, because we're both tall, fit dudes, standing at six-foot-two with a decent amount of muscles packed onto our bones. Jude puts us to shame.

The man was built from glugging two dozen raw eggs every morning, lifting his house above his head as a blissful stretch, and pumping his veins with steel and pure, unfiltered black coffee.

Not to exaggerate, but he has a fist the size of my head, a chest that looks more like a parcel of land than bones and flesh, and biceps that make my legs quiver in jealousy and fear. Between you and me, I swear I've seen his muscles fire off even when he blinks.

The first day I met him, I remember saying to myself, *I hope he doesn't hurt Haisley, because there's no way in hell I'd be able to go head to head with the silent beast.*

Nope.

I'd have sent him a strongly worded and very displeased email instead.

Dear sir,

Don't you ever treat my sister like that again. You have disappointed me.

Good day,
Hardy Hopper

Thankfully, he's the nicest guy we've ever met, loyal to his core, and protective. He's perfect for Haisley.

"Morning," he says in his deep-timbre voice. Did you see the liquid in the glasses quiver? Yeah, his voice has the same impact as the stomp of a T-Rex. "Nice setup." He gestures to the food and takes a seat, the poor chair beneath him squeaking under his weight.

"See, Jude appreciates the food," Hudson says with a puff of his chest.

"I never said I didn't appreciate the food," I say as I reach for a muffin. "Just said that it was a bit much."

Hudson swats at my hand. "That's for our guests. Help yourself after they take their first pick."

"Christ," I say, shaking out my hand. "You'd think this is the first meeting with them. Why are you so jumpy?"

"I'm not jumpy."

I give my brother a once-over. "You sure are, and you have that look in your eyes, the concerned, uptight look."

"No, I don't," he says in frustration. "I'm fine. I just like to keep things professional."

I study him for a moment. "Did Dad contact you?"

"Why would you think that?" he asks as he attempts to casually lean back in his chair. But I can see right through him.

"Uh, from what I just said."

He folds his hands in front of him. "He might have sent me an email."

"What did he say?" I ask.

"Just another warning about the so-called lawsuit he'll be throwing at us. Nothing new, just that he sent it this morning, and since we're meeting with the Canes…well, I hate looking like a liability."

"We're not a liability," Jude says. "And don't let him tell you any other way. We spoke with our lawyer while making the move over, we did everything we were supposed to do, including offering four weeks' notice, which your father chose to ignore and fire you instead. He's threatened so he's threatening you."

See, Jude is the comforting barn in the room, huge *and* nice to have around.

Hudson nods. "Yeah, I know. Just don't want the Canes to regret partnering up with us."

"They won't," I say. "I mean, by the spread on the table alone, they're going to think we're a winning trio to be in business with."

Hudson smirks. "You're such a dickhead."

"Just putting it out there, if no one eats the fruit salad, I'm claiming it now," I say.

"Your sister actually asked for the fruit salad, since I brought it home last time," Jude says with a challenging brow.

Hudson smiles broadly. "Why don't you two arm wrestle for it?"

I drum my fingers on the table. "You know, I would, but I don't want to humiliate Jude like that, so I'm going to just let him take the fruit salad."

Hudson chuckles. "Yeah, okay, Hardy."

Jude fidgets with his suit jacket as he asks, "What did you do this past weekend?"

"My friends had an engagement party," I say. "Polly and Ken. I don't think you've met them, but I've known them since college."

"That's right," Hudson says. "So, did you see Maple at the engagement party?"

Of course he'd ask that, especially after I gave him shit for his breakfast spread.

Hudson has always thought I should be with Maple. When he found out that we broke up, he chastised me for an entire week about how I was a dumbass and shouldn't have let her go. And then, of course, periodically throughout the time we've been apart, he's told me to find a way to make up with her. To find her and tell her what an idiot I am, but unfortunately for his little matchmaking heart, our paths never crossed.

I don't blame his persistence though.

Everyone saw the connection we had.

When we met back in college, there was an instant magnetism between us. At the time, she was majoring in zoology and animal sciences, and as her passion was animal conservation, we spent many dates at the San Francisco Zoo. When she graduated, she got a job at the Denver Zoo where she was a zookeeper for the flamingos, her favorite animal. After a while, she was offered a field job in Peru to conduct research on the Chilean flamingos, observing their patterns to determine why they were endangered. And there was no way I could have followed her to Peru if I hadn't been able to follow her to Denver.

"Maple wasn't at the party," I say. "But, apparently, she's coming back to San Francisco for good."

"Who's Maple?" Jude asks.

"Hardy's ex-girlfriend who he let slip through his fingers," Hudson answers.

"The one that got away?" Jude asks.

"Exactly," Hudson says.

I turn to Jude. "We were going in different directions, so she was bound to get away. But now that she's coming back, I want to see where her head is at, maybe start talking again."

"Yeah?" Hudson asks with a smile. "I'd be surprised if you don't."

"The only problem is she wants nothing to do with me," I say.

"Who wants nothing to do with you?" JP Cane asks as he walks through the conference room door.

The second-oldest brother out of the three, JP is the most charismatic. He's been the face of Cane Enterprises for as long as I've known him but has also stepped into heading up the philanthropic arm of the company. He's charming, funny, and has an intense obsession with pigeons. Not sure where that stems from, but I know he's heavily involved in the "pigeon justice" community. Something about how humans domesticated them and then just pushed them aside, leaving the poor pigeons to fend for themselves…I don't know. He went on a rant about it once, and I couldn't honestly tell if he was being serious or not. Come to find out, he was.

We all stand from our chairs and greet JP with handshakes. When we take a seat, he repeats, "Who wants nothing to do with you?"

"Oh, we don't need to talk about that," I say.

"Breaker and Huxley aren't here yet, so we have time to kill," JP says. "And I've been up for hours thanks to the baby, so please, delight me in dating woes." He smirks and then picks up a muffin and takes a big bite out of it. "Shit, these are good."

From the corner of my eye, I catch the pride beaming from Hudson over the fact that JP took a muffin. He's going to rub that in my face later. Can't wait.

But back to me. Maybe discussing my dating woes will bring us closer, and if Hudson complains about me talking about it later, I'll just mention that.

"Well, my best friends are getting married, and Maple, my ex, will be there. She's the maid of honor and I'm the best man, and we're the only ones in the bridal party. I want to see if there's anything still between us, but the bride told me to back off because my ex wants nothing to do with me."

JP slowly nods as he takes another bite of his muffin. After chewing for a second, he says, "That's not going to stop you, is it?"

"I mean…should it?"

"Considering that we should listen to women more," Jude puts in, "I think maybe you should stay away."

"Facts," JP says. "But…what if she does still have feelings, but she's shielding herself so she doesn't get hurt? Let me ask you this: How did things end?"

"Amicably for the most part," I answer. "We both were going in differ-ent directions with our careers and knew it wouldn't work out. Granted,

I told her I would follow her, and it ended up that I couldn't. So I think there might be a hint of animosity there, but I can't be sure."

"There is," Hudson says.

"Animosity isn't a bad thing, disinterest is," JP says. "We can fix animosity, but we can't fix disinterest." He sets his muffin down on a napkin. "One more question. Does she mean something to you?"

I give his question some thought.

Our relationship was fun, easy, and we didn't get in many fights. We didn't have much in common superficially, but I didn't think that was a bad thing. She had her love of flamingos, and I had a love for the outdoors and the earth, which I've turned into farming. We understood each other and appreciated each other and when I was with her, I was happy. So was she.

I nod. "Yes, she does. And now that we're older, now that we've found ourselves, I wonder what we'd be like together again. I know that I still have feelings for her, remembering the good times we had… I don't know, it seems foolish not to explore if those feelings still exist, especially with her moving back here."

"Makes sense," JP says and then rubs his hands together. "Okay, I don't think you should make contact with her, because you don't want to make her or the bride mad." I feel a frown in my expression. "I think you can nod, say a friendly hello, but you have to keep your distance."

"The perfect way to get to know her again," I say sarcastically.

"Let the man finish," Hudson says, elbowing me.

JP nods at Hudson. "Thank you." He clears his throat and steeples his hands together. "You need some help on the inside."

I shake my head. "Polly, that's the bride, won't tell me anything, and her groom, my friend Ken, is completely clueless."

"Is there anyone else you might know that's involved in the wedding party? That will have access to Maple?"

"I don't think—" I pause, my mind swirling as the image of Everly pops into my head. Since she's spearheading Bridesmaid for Hire for Maggie, she could be the bridesmaid Polly requested. "Wait, there might be someone." I don't say who it is, because I know if I mention Everly, Hudson will immediately shoot the idea down and tell me to leave her out of it. He doesn't want personal needs mixing with business, but...fuck, Everly would be the perfect person to help me out. She's friendly, and we have a good rapport. I think she might be willing to help me with a little undercover action.

"Really?" JP asks with excitement.

"Really?" Hudson asks, seeming more skeptical. "Who?"

"Uh, another bridesmaid," I answer, not technically lying.

"I thought you said you and Maple were the only ones in the wedding party," Hudson says.

Fuck, he listens. Why do I always forget that?

"This girl is unofficial," I say.

"That's perfect then," JP says even though Hudson still looks skeptical. "See if she'd be willing to at least feel Maple out. Then, you can see if you should just drop the thought of getting back together with your ex, or possibly pursue it."

"Good idea," I say.

"I have them every once in a while," JP says with a smirk. "Now, I'm curious. Why did you two go in different directions? What does she do?"

"She's a zookeeper and studies at-risk ecosystems," I answer. "For flamingos."

JP slowly sits up, his eyes set intently on me. "Hold on a second. For... flamingos?"

"Yeah."

He presses his hand to the table. "You mean to tell me flamingos are at risk? And that she's out there, doing the hard work, trying to save them?"

Oh God...is this going to lead to pigeons?

"Uh, yeah," I answer.

His lips purse together as he slowly nods. "Where do I send a check? I'm all in. We need to save the flamingos."

Dear God…

To: *Hardy Hopper*
From: *Breaker Cane*
Subject: *Flamingos*

Hardy,

I like you, I really do, but next time I see you I might punch you, and I mean that in the nicest way. Ever since our meeting, JP has been talking nonstop about flamingos. To the point that in our group text he's sent, and I'm not exaggerating, twelve videos of flamingos. He's trying desperately to connect their lineage with pigeons.

Either way, he's now on a mission to save all feathered friends.

Please remember for the future, he carries a strong heart for saving animals, so for the love of God, do not mention any others!

Kind regards,
Breaker and Huxley

To: *Breaker Cane*
From: *Hardy Hopper*
Subject: *RE: Flamingos*

Breaker (and Huxley),

I send my deepest regrets. It was not my intention to spring this newfound love for exotic feathery friends on you. I'll be sure for the future not to bring up any animals of any sort. I would hate to see you be bothered by your brother and his incessant need to save the birds.

Sincerest apologies,
Hardy

To: Hardy Hopper
From: JP Cane
Subject: Help Save the Flamingos

Hardy,

JP Cane has set up a GoFundMe to help save the Chilean Flamingos in Peru. Please see the link below to offer your support. Don't forget to like and share on your social media.

Personal note from JP Cane:

Due to the disturbance in the Chilean Flamingos' natural habitat, thanks to egg-harvesting and human interference, these majestic creatures' population is decreasing at a rapid rate, and we have the chance to turn that around. By donating today, you can help these spirited birds live a simple, beautiful life in their natural habitat. Thank you.

JP Cane

CHAPTER THREE
EVERLY

"WHAT DID JUDE SAY?" I ask as I take a seat across from Maggie, my boss, at The Bean, our daily meeting place since our new office has been under construction.

"He said ten more days. Then everything should be done, and we'll be ready to move in."

"Really?" I ask as I blow on my coffee before taking a sip. "That soon?"

"Yup. I was just as surprised. He said he's been putting in some work himself, making sure all of the trim and touch-up painting is done to his standards."

I shiver from the thought of Jude walking through the office space, his construction manager shaking in his boots as Jude examines every last inch of the place. "I bet those standards are impossibly high."

"From the way he spoke, I'm assuming the same thing, but I'm glad we have him on our team."

"Me too." I set my mug down. "So, what's on the agenda today?"

"Well, we have a meeting with the florist today for the McCormick wedding. Right after, we head to Pier Heaven to go over table arrangements for the Barton wedding, and this morning we have a meeting with Hardy Hopper." I feel my body go stiff from the mention of Hardy. "And then we have some meal plans to look over, playlists to plan, and we need to finalize those ad copies and brochures."

"Busy day," I say as I clear my throat. "Uh, what's the meeting with Hardy Hopper?"

"He emailed me and says he has a client for us, wants to talk to us about it. A Bridesmaid for Hire client. Unfortunately, I have to take a phone call when he's here, so I was hoping that you could head up the conversation with him. Since this is your branch of the business, I thought that it would be okay?"

"Oh yeah, sure, no problem," I say as nerves trickle up the back of my neck. I wish I would have known sooner so I could feel more prepared.

I remember the first time I met him in person. It was after Maggie came home from the Hopper wedding. She was distraught and thought she was going to have to shut down her business thanks to Reginald Hopper and his menacing ways. But Hudson, Hardy, and Jude had other plans. They showed up to The Bean like knights in shining armor, ready to lift us up rather than tear us down.

They offered Maggie an opportunity—really an investment, their investment—and she jumped on it. Not only was she able to keep her thriving business, but also now her dreams of owning a storefront are about to come true. The storefront is going to offer us more space, a place to hold meetings, storage and so much more.

So yeah, the Hopper men aren't only easy on the eyes and brilliant businessmen, but they're dream makers as well.

"Perfect. Thank you." She marks something in her notebook, most likely checking off the task: Spoke to Everly about meeting with Hardy Hopper. I've given her some hints on organization and keeping track of all her tasks. She was pretty good, but since she hired me, she's phenomenal. "Okay, well, he's going to be here any minute, and I'm going to take my phone call in the booth over there if that's all right with you. When we're both done, we can head on over to the florist together?"

"That works," I say.

She smiles. "Great. Thanks, and let me know how the conversation goes. This could be our first Bridesmaid for Hire client." She crosses her fingers, and I hold mine up as well.

When she takes off toward the booth, I flip to a new sheet of paper and consider writing a header at the top: Hardy Hopper Meeting. But that seems a little much, especially since he would be able to see me take notes, which then makes me wonder, should I take notes at all?

Maybe not.

But...I always take notes.

Would he read the notes that I'm taking?

Would he question them?

What if there is only one thing that he says that is noteworthy, then what? He sees me write down one sentence and then nothing else, leaving me with an almost complete blank page?

Would he judge me for that?

Do I care if he judges me?

Of course I care.

I care a lot about what he thinks of me for many reasons, the main one being that he invested in Maggie and I don't want him thinking that she hired some one-sentence notetaker.

No, I should just commit everything to memory even if that goes against my nature.

No notes.

But...

Would he think I'm being irresponsible by not taking notes? You know those waiters or waitresses who take your order but don't write it down? And it's a long order, one with details, and all I can think is...are you going to remember? They always do, which is impressive in itself, but I do have my doubts—because I'm a notetaker.

So am I overthinking this?

Should I take the notes, or should I not take the notes?

"Hey, Everly."

My body stiffens from the sound of his deep voice, and my eyes shoot up just as Hardy leans down and presses a soft kiss to the side of my cheek before taking a seat.

Good.

Freaking.

Lord.

I don't miss the subtle brush of his beard over my sensitive skin.

Or the distinct scent of his cologne clinging around me.

Or the sheer masculine presence he has as he takes the seat next to mine, not across from me.

"How's it going?" he asks, looking so incredibly handsome in a blue and orange plaid long-sleeve shirt, puffy vest, and jeans. His hair is playfully messy, and his light-blue eyes pop against his sun-soaked skin and dark-brown hair. His carved jaw is coated in a thick beard, and his lips look so well moistened that I feel myself staring at them a touch longer than I probably should.

But it's not just his looks that has me feeling like I could lean into him and have the best hug ever. It's his effortless charm. His smile. His caring heart that he has for everyone around him. He knows the difference between right and wrong, he uplifts rather than crushes, and he is a pioneer for not only entrepreneurs sifting through the world of capitalism, but he is also a champion for women in business. I know this from the way he treats his sister and her independence from their family, and from the support he's offered Maggie.

He's the perfect package.

Everything about him.

Perfect.

I smile, trying to disguise my nerves from sitting this close to him. "Doing great. What about yourself?"

"Pretty good." He brings one of his legs up and crosses his ankle over his knee, casually leaning back in his chair just as a waitress brings him his cup of coffee. He offers her a breathtaking smile as he says, "Thank you very much."

The girl's cheeks flush—don't blame her—as she says, "You're welcome," and then takes off.

"So." He brings his attention back to me. "What are you drinking?"

I glance at my drink and then back up at him. "A caramel mocha. I try to distract my taste buds from the taste of coffee as much as I can."

"Chocolate and caramel is a good combination to go with." Ugh, he's so handsome, just look at those dimples trying to peek past his beard.

"What are you drinking?" I ask, feeling so weird because this is such a casual conversation that I would never imagine having with someone who owns a billion-dollar business with his brother. Well, is it a billion dollars? Maybe, who knows. I know they have a lot of investments, but who can be sure? He has a lot of money—let's just leave it at that.

"Been liking this almond milk vanilla latte lately. Pretty good."

"Oh, nice. I think that wouldn't be much of a disguise for my taste buds."

He shakes his head. "Definitely not. I think you would need a lot more than the hint of vanilla syrup and frothed up water-soaked almonds."

"Probably," I answer. "And are they even Hopper Almonds?"

"I glanced at the milk they're using…" He leans and whispers, "It's not a company we work with." He holds his fingers up to his lips in a hush-hush kind of way, which makes me chuckle.

"Drinking the enemy…how does that feel?"

"Not like a Hopper Almond, that's for damn sure." He sips his drink and then smacks his lips. "Yeah, you can tell the Hopper standard isn't in this secreted almond."

I try to hold back my smile but I can't, as I'm completely charmed by him. "And what would the Hopper standard be?"

"Well, high-quality filtration during the pulp removal process for one, and then of course, clearly, no one is smiling at these almonds and that's a key ingredient to a great-tasting almond, the smile."

"Oh, is that right?" I ask. "You smile at your almonds?"

"Not just me, all of the staff. From the beginning part of pruning, to removing the husks, to cracking open the shells, and safely cleaning the kernels, there are smiles all around, all day."

"I can see how that would produce a happy almond."

He sips his coffee again and then winces. "Yeah, you can taste it immediately. These competitors are all frowns."

I chuckle and pick up my mug. "Maybe you should try to speak to the manager, get them on your side."

"Perhaps..." He nods. "Perhaps I will."

God, he's cute.

And funny.

And easy to talk to.

Like I said, the man is perfect.

"So," he says, "shall we get down to business?"

"Of course, not that I want to stop you from educating me about your almonds, but Maggie told me you might be in need of our services."

He nods and grows serious. "Yes, my friends Polly and Ken are getting married and, well, their maid of honor is a bit overwhelmed and out of her comfort zone with the responsibilities. I know she wants to be able to do this for Polly, but she needs some hand-holding. I told them about Bridesmaid for Hire, and Polly was very interested. I told her that I'd feel you guys out and then set up an intro if it's a good fit."

"Well, first of all, thank you. We're just getting this portion of Magical Moments by Maggie up and running, so this means a lot to already have someone interested."

"Of course," he says. "Maggie did so much for Haisley that it's the least we can do."

"Well, actually, she wouldn't be heading up this side of the business, it would be me. I hope that's okay."

"I know that," he says and winks. "I took a gander at the business proposal. I know from what Maggie has said you can handle this effortlessly. She even told us that you're the backbone for the business."

I feel my cheeks blush. "Thank you," I reply. "I'm very lucky to have such a great boss."

"She's pretty awesome. Haisley also speaks very highly of you."

"Well, Haisley is a force. She's changing the business, and I love everything she's doing, so the compliment from her means a lot."

Lots of pleasantries, but that's how business is sometimes, talking each other up and building that trust in one another. Also, I'm not going to shy away from the compliments, especially from Hardy.

"She's a good sister to have." He smirks. "As for specifics, I think Polly would be looking for someone to almost be a mentor for her maid of honor, someone to help her navigate everything, to bounce ideas off of, and to help with any setup and planning that she might be responsible for."

"That's not a problem at all. That's what we're here for. We can assist in planning, managing the events so she can attend to the bride, and of course be there for any needs."

Hardy nods. "I think that would be perfect, exactly what she's looking for."

"Great," I say. "Well, if you think this could work, I would love to have a conversation with Polly."

"She'll hire you on the spot, guaranteed, especially if I give her my approval."

I press my hand to my chest. "That would mean a lot, Hardy."

"And hey, if it goes well, this might lead to more business. Both Polly's and Ken's families are very wealthy with a huge network of friends who would likely find your services very helpful. Could be a great jumping-off point."

"Wow, that's amazing. Thank you."

"Of course," he says. He lifts up his coffee, sips it, but keeps his eyes on me the entire time, as if he has something else he wants to say to me.

Cutting him to the chase, I ask, "Is that, uh, is that everything?"

He scratches his cheek and then stares down at his coffee. "Not exactly."

"Oh? There's something else you want to talk about?"

"Yes, but it's sort of awkward." He shifts uncomfortably, which I find endearing because normally this man is very sure of himself, confident, doesn't seem to have a worry at all. But from the tense set of his shoulders and the transition in his expression, I can tell there's something on his mind.

"That's okay," I reply. "I deal with a lot of awkward things on the daily. Being in the event planning industry, you wouldn't believe the number of weird things I have to take care of. So feel free to lay it on me."

"Okay," he says and then turns to face me. We're no more than two feet apart, so when those baby blue eyes settle on me, I remind myself not to get lost in them, to not openly sigh from just how mesmerizing they are, especially from the way they play off the stark contrast of his nearly black lashes.

Let me tell you, it's a challenge.

"So, I've been doing some thinking lately."

"Okay, what kind of thinking?" Jokingly, I add, "You don't want to join the wedding planning business, do you? Or better yet…be a bridesmaid for hire?"

He chuckles. "Imagine what that might look like, all decked out in tulle and lace, possibly a bow fastened in my hair."

"You very well might steal the show from the bride."

"Trust me, if I was in some sort of satin getup showing off my man-cleave, I would be stealing the show for sure."

I let out a cackle that is far too unattractive for my liking, but the imagery…

"You would like that, wouldn't you?" he asks. "Seeing me in something satin?"

I shake my head. "No, I think I'd prefer you in chiffon."

"Keep your fingers crossed, and it might just happen."

"Well, until that magical moment, what is this thinking you've been doing?"

He twists his mug on the table. "With Haisley getting married, Ken and Polly planning their wedding, and seeing how happy Brody and Maggie are, it has me thinking that I want the same thing."

His eyes meet mine, and I feel my stomach bottom out because…oh my God, is he…is he going to ask me out?

"You, uh…you want to marry someone?"

He chuckles and shakes his head. "No, I want to start dating."

Be cool, Everly.

Tread carefully. If he asks you out, don't joyously suck his face after giving a resounding yes.

Give it some deep thought and then nod.

Ponder the question, don't hop on his lap and bury his face in your cleavage as an acceptance.

"Dating, well, that is always fun," I reply, trying to stay calm.

This is my moment.

Sure, I've crushed on him for a few months now, even imagining what it would be like to hold his hand and walk down the pier—him looking down at me like I'm the only girl in the world and me looking up at him, knowing damn well he's the only guy in the world that gives me butterflies.

And perhaps I've scoured the internet for pictures of him, preferably with his shirt off, and I've come up short, but that hasn't deterred me, it's only spurred on my craving even more.

But given all of that, I need to not show my cards.

Keep the crush under control.

Let him ask you.

Then, cooly, with a possible hair flick, respond with *that would be cool...*

"In all honesty, I haven't done it in a long time." He pulls on the back of his neck in this cute, shy way.

It's okay, Hardy. I'll walk you through the process of dating. I'll hold your hand.

"It can be intimidating, but with the right person, I'm sure it'll be easier than you think," I say.

"Yeah, the right person matters," he says, his eyes matching up with mine. "Which brings me to my question."

"Yes, your question," I say leaning in just a touch. You know, show him I'm interested so he isn't too nervous.

Come here. Everly will take care of you, you hunk of a man.

"Well, I was hoping you could help me."

Remember how to date? Why yes, of course. I'd be more than happy to.

I heard sex on the first date is an absolute must in today's modern dating circuit.

"Of course, anything you need," I say.

"I'm glad you said that because, well, I hope I'm not too forward in asking this..."

As a matter of fact, Hardy, I've been waiting for you to ask, so please, by all means...ask away.

"But I was hoping you would be able to help me..."

Date you? Of course.

Remind you how to hold hands? I'm there for you.

Kiss those beautiful lips of yours? Don't mind if I do.

"Get to know my ex-girlfriend again."

"Of course, I would love to," I say with the biggest smile, only for my mind to register exactly what he said a beat too late.

Wait...

Did he?

Did I...

He said what?

"Really?" he asks.

Errr...

I nervously laugh. "Uh, yessss..." I drag out as my mind takes two large steps back to recount his exact wording.

Did he mention his ex-girlfriend? Is that what he said?

"Fuck, that's...that's amazing. Thank you, Everly." He leans back in his chair, looking positively relieved as I still try to understand what the hell is going on.

I take a sip of my coffee, trying to reset my brain before saying, "Your, uh, your ex-girlfriend?"

"Yes." He pushes his hand through his hair. "I failed to mention that she's Maple."

"Who's Maple?" I ask, feeling clueless.

"Maple," he says as if I'm supposed to know this. From my blank expression, he adds, "The maid of honor we were talking about."

Oh.

Dear.

God.

Maple is his ex-girlfriend?

The girl I'm supposed to mentor?

The girl I'll be spending a lot of time with for the foreseeable future as I show her how to be the perfect bridesmaid?

This can't be real.

Why would I say yes to this?

Oh, that's right, because you thought he was asking you out, you freaking nitwit.

"Oh, that Maple," I say awkwardly, following it up with a laugh and a dismissive wave of my hand. "She's your ex, sure, makes sense."

Does it though?

What are the odds?

Pretty high with my luck, apparently.

"Yes, we all met in college," he says. "Polly, Ken, me, and Maple. Maple and I dated for three years and then ended things when we found that we both were going in different directions for our careers. And now that her job has brought her back to San Francisco and we'll be spending some time together, I figured it would be a great chance to try to rekindle some things."

Yup, that sounds about right.

Why wouldn't he want to rekindle old feelings with someone he shared three years of his life with back in college? I'm sure he misses the good ol' days. I'm sure he has a lot of wonderful memories from that time in his life. I'm a year out of college, so I don't quite understand that kind of nostalgia. I would rather have my big toe slammed in a door than revisit a college relationship, but maybe that's just me.

"How, uh, nice…that you'll be in the same city as each other."

"First time in ten years."

"Ten years, huh?" I shake my head. "That would put you in your thirties, which means yeah, you're probably ready to settle down."

His smirk nearly makes me faint face-first into his lap. And what's really sad about all of this is I would gladly poke my eye out with his crotch.

Smell that desperation? It's deplorable.

"You say that as if being in my thirties is a bad thing."

"Nope, I like an older man," I say, but then catch myself. "I mean, not that I like you. I wasn't saying that in regard to you and me, more like… just in general. Men as a whole. Not you, because that would be weird, right? Eck, gross, not you and me. Never you and me. Forever and ever, never you and me. I meant just, like the olds, the silver foxes, the men with experience, but not you…never you."

He scratches his jaw with a smile. "Well, can't hear that enough."

"I wasn't trying to insult you, I just—"

"I'm kidding, Everly." He places his hand on my shoulder, probably to soothe the tension that has skyrocketed through my bones. But unfortunately for me, all his warm palm and long fingers do is make me stiffer in all areas…stiff and throbby.

Yes…throbby.

Because I have no self-control around him and even though he wants to rekindle a relationship with this Maple chick, who I'm sure is a beating heart of beauty and joy, I still feel like the old crone in the corner, clearing the cobwebs out from between her legs after a simple touch from the man with the devilish eyes and kind smile.

"Of course, right, you're joking. You're very funny." I wag my finger at him, hating myself more and more with every up and down flick.

He studies me for a moment. "Are you okay? Did I make you uncomfortable?"

"What? No, of course not. Did I make you uncomfortable?"

"No," he says. "But I feel like you're acting weird, and I hope it's not because of something I said. Or that I caught you off guard."

"Not at all. This is me being excited," I say for some stupid reason. "I love love, so if I can help out in any way, I'm your girl." I thumb toward my chest like a live action Little Orphan Annie. "So sign me up. You need help. I'm your girl."

"You sure?"

No.

Actually, remember that toe in the doorjamb thing? I would rather do double toes. Yeah, you read that right. Two toes being slammed by a door rather than suffer through getting Hardy back with his ex.

I couldn't think of anything I would rather do less.

"Positive," I answer with a smile. "Just, uh, just one question."

"What's that?" he asks.

"Well, since you're a seasoned man in his thirties who, though admittedly out of touch with the dating world, does seem to have a level of charisma, what would you require from me as an assistant?"

"That's one way to ask a simple question." He laughs but carries on. "Here's the thing. We ended things amicably, but there might be a hint of bitterness on her end. At least, from what Polly keeps saying."

"Oh?" I ask, intrigued as to how this perfect specimen of a man could elicit any sense of bitterness toward him.

"The thing is, she was studying zoology and animal sciences. Her main goal was to become a zookeeper for flamingos." Huh, did not see that coming. Not every day you run into someone who wants to take care of animals for their life journey. She sounds amazing already, which does not bode well for me. "And, well, she couldn't really follow me when it came to a job, so I had to follow her. I told her I would, but when my dad asked me to head up the agricultural side of Hopper Industries, I felt like it was an opportunity I couldn't pass up, especially since my relationship with my dad was already rocky at best. I didn't go to the school he wanted me to go to, and I was the one who gave him the most pushback about his business practices. I felt I could make an impact, so I had to go back on my word to Maple. We both decided to break up, even though she's the one who started the conversation. We hugged and went our separate ways. Though I reached out on occasion, she didn't do the same."

Uh, yeah, because Mr. Perfect wasn't going to be following her around like he promised. I think I'd be bitter too.

"I see, and she's said she doesn't want anything to do with you?"

"Polly told me she just wants to be left alone, but that doesn't mean she doesn't still have feelings. I would approach her myself, but Polly told me to stay away, and I want to respect that, but fuck...if there's something still there, something I could rekindle, I'd be open to doing that, especially since she's moving back." He lets out a deep sigh and sinks into his chair. "If Polly and Ken can break up but find love again, why can't Maple and I?"

Well, isn't that just the nail in the coffin of my unrealistic dreams?

Tacking on a smile because I can't believe I'm about to say this, I reply, "I guess only one way to find out, right?"

He grins brightly. "You're really down to help me out?"

"Of course, Hardy."

"Thank you, Everly. This means a lot to me."

"Hey, it's the least I can do."

He sits taller now and says, "Okay, let's go over your approach."

―――――――――

"You said yes?" my sister, Ember, screeches into the phone.

I set my purse down, hang my keys, and take off my heels before carefully putting them in my hall closet where I have all my shoes lined up perfectly.

"What the hell was I supposed to say?" I ask as I move into my quaint kitchen that's comprised of one countertop that shares space with the cooktop and sink. I pull out one of my premade dinners from the fridge, set it in the microwave, and heat it up.

"You were supposed to say 'this is an unprofessional ask and I'm uncomfortable helping you get back together with your ex because in fact I'm in love with you.'"

"I'm not in love with him," I say, irritated. I walk into my bathroom where I put the phone on speaker and set it on the counter as I undo the tight bun I put my hair in this morning. I shake out my long strands and let my scalp breathe. "And I...I answered before I knew what I was answering."

"What do you mean?" she asks.

I wet one of my reusable makeup removers and then start taking my makeup off. "I don't want to say."

"Uh, now you have to say."

"Really, I'm okay with keeping it to myself."

"That's not how this works—you call me, you tell me."

I work on removing my mascara, wondering why I called my nosey sister in the first place. "Fine, but don't judge me."

"Not making any promises."

Such a loving sister. "Okay...well, the way he phrased things, I was thinking that maybe he was going to ask me something else."

"And what was that something else?"

"I don't want to say," I reply as I hear the microwave beep, indicating my broccoli and beef is done warming up.

"Then how the hell am I supposed to help you if I don't know all the facts?"

"I wasn't looking for help from my big sister—I was looking for sympathy."

"It's as if you don't know me at all," Ember says as I lean down to the sink and splash water on my face before lathering my hands up with soap. "Do you really think I would sit here and listen to this story only to offer sympathy?"

"I hoped," I say in between splashes of water.

"You're wrong. I never just offer sympathy and I will never change, so stop trying to make me."

I chuckle as I dry off my face. "I'll never stop trying."

"You're wasting your time," she says. I lay out my skin care serums and start applying as she continues, "So tell me what you thought he was going to ask so I can make this all right in the world."

"I don't think there's a way you can make this right, but because I know you're not going to drop this, I was thinking that he was going to possibly ask me out."

There's silence for a moment and then, "Are you serious?"

"Yes, and don't make fun of me, I'm still sour about the whole interaction. But either way, I had it built up in my head that he was going to ask me out on a date, so when he asked me to help him get back together with his ex, I shouted a resounding yes before my mind could process what he was actually saying."

"Oh…my…God, Everly. That is soooooo embarrassing."

"I know! It's why I didn't want to say anything to you because I knew you would laugh."

"I'm not laughing."

My eyes roll even though she can't see me. "I can hear it in your voice, Ember."

"I might have quietly smiled to myself, but I don't take pleasure in your pain."

"Says the girl who laughed for ten minutes straight when I told you I accidentally farted in front of the best man at a wedding because he made me laugh."

"That's just comedy gold, but this is different. This was a special moment for you that was ruined."

I finish up with lotion on my face and then move to the kitchen where I take out my beef and broccoli and place it on the counter.

"It was not my special moment. It was a moment I wish I could forget."

"Did he know you were saying yes to something else?"

"I don't think so," I say, grabbing myself a cherry vanilla OLIPOP. "He asked me if something was wrong at one point while I was trying not to hyperventilate from my mistake, but I covered it up quickly. So no, I don't think he caught on."

"Thank God for that."

I take a seat at my small bistro table, then I cross one leg over the other and dig into my food. "I guess so, but that doesn't negate the fact that I still said yes to helping him out. Oh, and get this, Ember, his ex-girlfriend is a zookeeper for flamingos. Like…how adorable is that? Out of all the animals, she has to be the flamingo girl—they're so cute and cheery and pink."

"Ooo, yeah, that does trump event planner."

"I know!" I shout with broccoli in my mouth. "Not that I'm competition. He barely knows me, and he had a three-year relationship with this woman."

"Yes, but perhaps if she wasn't in the picture, there could have been a moment for you."

"Doubtful," I say as I scoop up some rice. "I'm bound to die alone."

"You're twenty-two, Everly. I'm pretty sure you have no right in claiming you're going to die alone, not until you're at least middle-aged with no prospects. Even then, there's still hope."

I set my fork down for a moment and stare at my wall. "Is it me, Ember? Am I the problem? Am I the reason I'm single?"

"No," she answers. "And why are you questioning this? I thought you were set on establishing your career before you started looking for love."

"I am," I say. "But there are nights like tonight, where I'm sitting in my studio apartment, eating a premade meal that I heated in the microwave and talking to my sister on the phone, and I think how lonely my life is. No offense to you."

"Some taken, but I forgive you."

"And you have Trevor, and that's amazing—I'm really happy for you, but that also makes me wonder if I'm missing out by not dating someone. And when Hardy started talking about wanting to find someone in his life, it just got me excited. Got me thinking. I don't want to be lonely, Ember."

"Are you?" she asks.

"A little," I answer. "And I know that to not feel that loneliness I'll fill it up with work, and I don't want to be that person. I don't want to be the woman who is solely identified by what she does. I want my job and the joy I put out in the world with planning these events to be a big part of me, but I don't want it to be all of me."

"So then start dating."

"How? I can't just pick a guy out at the grocery store and say *date me*. Plus I hear horror stories about online dating and the apps. Like a ton of ghosting."

She scoffs. "And there are also wonderful stories that come from going that route. It's a process, Everly. It's not going to happen overnight."

"I know, but—"

"And there are other ways as well. You can join a club, be a part of something bigger, like…a bowling league. Meet someone there."

"A bowling league?" I ask. "Ember, I've maybe bowled once in my life. No one wants me on their team."

"They might. And maybe there's a beginner one. Or maybe a bingo club."

"Bingo?" I nearly shout. "Ember, I'm not looking to date an eighty-year-old man."

"There might be young men there too. Maybe someone playing bingo with their granny. Now there's a man to consider, someone who cares so deeply for their grandma that they play bingo on Friday nights."

"I can guarantee you there are no young men hanging out at bingo halls."

"Well, then go to a bar," she offers. "You're in San Francisco, not some backwater small town."

"Ugh, those guys are always wanting to get laid, they don't want to meet someone for the real reasons, for developing a relationship. They're looking for a quick fuck and then they're out."

"I mean…is that a bad thing?" I can hear the humor in her voice.

"It is when I don't want that."

She huffs. "Fine, but those were good ideas."

"They were not."

"They would have been if you weren't so close-minded."

"Are you really going to tell me that going to a bingo hall to meet someone was a good idea? You're standing behind that?"

"You know, I don't have to take this kind of abuse. I'm a nice woman. I have things I could be doing right now, a husband I could be doing—"

"Okay, okay." I chuckle. "No need to get into the details. It'll just color me with jealousy."

"Fine, I'll spare you, but just so you know, I have options," she says. "I don't have to be on the phone with you."

"Well, I appreciate you taking time to talk to me, your measly little sister. You're a true hero."

"I like to think so," Ember says. "You know, there is one more option."

"What's that? Going to senior aquatics?" I joke.

"Well, going to the gym is an option, but that's not what I was going to say. We have a built-in matchmaker."

"Who?" I ask, confused.

"Trevor," she says.

"Trevor?" I ask flatly. "How on Earth is he a built-in matchmaker? I'm pretty sure he couldn't care less about my love life."

"Because we can ask him if there's anyone at his work that he knows is looking for a date. Would you be interested in a blind date?"

"I don't know," I say tepidly as my mind drifts to Hardy.

"Are you still caught up on the man?" Ember asks, knowing me all too well.

"I think so."

"Then you definitely need to date someone else, because if you're going to be helping him get back together with his ex, that leaves you in a tough spot."

"Ugh, you're right." I stab a piece of beef. There's no use thinking about someone else when they're clearly thinking about another person. "Okay, sure, yeah, set me up with someone."

"Ooo, yay. This is so exciting. Now…who should it be?"

"Just no creeps. Okay?"

"Promise."

CHAPTER FOUR
HARDY

"SO SHE DIDN'T THINK WHAT I was looking for was weird?" Polly asks as we take a seat at the coffee house where we are meeting Everly.

"No," I say. "Helping out brides and their bridal party is exactly what she does. They range from planning the entire wedding with Maggie, to helping with more intimate events like the bridal shower, to even smaller duties like assistance just on the day of with wrangling family members. They truly do it all at whatever capacity you want. And trust me when I say she's excited."

"Okay, because when I spoke to Maple about it, she was nervous, apprehensive, and embarrassed."

"Everly reassured me that this was normal. Not everyone is cut out to be a maid of honor. And that's okay. That's why they do what they do."

She eyes me suspiciously. "Why are you being so nice about this?"

"What do you mean?" I ask. "I'm always nice."

"You are, but you're being helpful, and I don't know how I feel about that. Ken's not even here." She studies me slowly, her eyes wandering. "You're hiding something."

"I'm not hiding anything," I say as I try to remain calm and collected.

"Yes, you are. There's a reason why you're doing this."

"Yes, that reason being that you're my friend."

She shakes her head. "No, that's not it." She pauses, wets her lips, and then her eyes widen. "Hardy Hopper, you're not trying to get in my good graces so I grant you access to Maple when she gets into town, are you?"

It's annoying how perceptive she is.

"No," I scoff. "Because first of all, I should already be in your good graces. We've been friends for a long time. Second of all, you said she didn't want me around, so I'm going to listen to you because I'm a good man like that."

Now she crosses her arms. "I don't believe a single word coming out of your mouth."

I chuckle and then level with her. "Listen, I'm not going to approach her, okay? But I'm also not going to be a dick to her when we're in the same room. But that said, I don't want you thinking I'm making a move when I do talk to her when we first see each other. I think it's fair for me to say a friendly hello, don't you think?"

"I do," she says. "But as long as it's a friendly hello and nothing else... like...like you stick your head up her shirt and whisper *hello, old friends*."

"When the fuck have I ever done that?"

She shrugs and chuckles. "I don't know, it was the first thing that came to mind."

"Christ, acquire a better image of me in your head."

She places her hand on the table. "Listen, I just don't need you scaring her away."

"I wouldn't do that. If anything, I'm just as happy that she's back in town as you are."

"Hey"—she points her finger at me—"none of that. There will be no happiness that she's back, understood? You will remain neutral."

I chuckle. "Whatever the bride wants, the bride gets."

"Good answer."

Just then, Everly walks through the door of the café. She glances around for a moment, but when she spots me, a beautiful smile passes over her face before she waves.

Yeah, I said beautiful.

It's no secret that Everly is a very attractive woman, especially dressed in a tight black skirt that reaches just above her knees, a black, tucked in button-up shirt, and heels. She's always put together, professional, and ready for business. Sometimes I wonder what she would look like if she took her hair down from that tight bun, if she wasn't so buttoned up but actually let loose. Because every time I've seen her, she looks like she's ready for any sort of professional experience to land on her lap. Not that it's a bad thing.

I stand as she approaches, and when she reaches me, I place my hand on her side and press a quick kiss to her cheek—like I greet almost everyone. When I pull away, I gesture toward Polly. "Everly, this is Polly. Polly, this is Everly..." I pause and wince. "Well, hell, Everly, I don't know your last name."

She chuckles and holds her hand out to Polly. "Everly Plum. It's very nice to meet you."

"Plum?" I ask. "As in Professor Plum?"

"Yes, a great-uncle of mine," she jokes before taking a seat. She also has a great sense of humor, something I was surprised to find out when I initially started talking to her. "I hope you weren't waiting too long. Finding parking around here can be a real nightmare."

"Tell me about it," Polly says. "Sometimes I wonder how Hardy can live in Nob Hill."

Everly looks up at me with those crystal green eyes, a color so soft and different that I don't think I've ever seen it on another person. "You live around here?"

"I have an apartment," I say. "I also have a place out by the farmland as well. I split time, but at the moment, it seems like I'm spending more time in the city."

"And you'll be spending even more time out here now that we're getting married in the next two months."

"Two months?" I say, feeling just as surprised as Everly looks, as her eyebrows shoot up.

Polly nods. "Yes, we had a bit of a change in plans. We were planning for a longer engagement, more like a year, but then Ken's sister's husband got orders to Germany, and they leave in a little over two months, so we're speeding up the timeline. I hope that's okay."

"Not a problem at all," Everly says, her face smoothing out as she opens up her notebook and starts taking notes. "We can work with that. I'm assuming you're going to want help with the bridal shower and bachelorette party?"

"Yes. My mom said she would take care of the parties, but I know Maple doesn't want that. She wants to be able to have a hand in planning. She just needs assistance." Polly pauses. "The thing about Maple is that party planning and social events have never been important to her, which is totally fine, but now that she's taken on the role of maid of honor, she's starting to panic that she won't be able to throw a good enough party for me. I told her it doesn't need to be elaborate, but I'm sure you can imagine her not agreeing to that. So I think having you here to mentor her will be a great help. Plus I think it would be nice for her to enjoy the event rather than having to work the whole time, if that makes sense."

"Completely," Everly says, her hand moving quickly over her paper, which I find fascinating. I don't think I've ever seen someone take notes as fast as her. "Are you going to be having a joint bridal shower, or will it just be the ladies?"

Polly looks over at me. "You know, it might be fun to have a joint one. Ken likes to be acknowledged, and I'm sure he'd love to be the belle of the ball at the party."

Everly chuckles. "We can do that. I can talk to Maple and see what she wants to do, if she wants a theme or not. Would you like Hardy included in the planning? Since he's the best man?"

I shoot Everly an appreciative look—she's already bringing me in to have moments with Maple. She's good.

"Um, that's okay, he's busy I'm sure," Polly dismisses me.

Smiling brightly, I say, "I don't mind helping. Might be fun to give some insight on the kind of things Ken might demand to honor him."

Polly's eyes narrow. "No, let's just leave this to Maple and Everly."

Not wanting to push her, I say, "Well, if you end up needing help, I'm here. I want to help out as much as I can. It's not every day your best friends from college get married."

"Wow, what a best man," Polly says in a sarcastic tone, probably understanding exactly why I want to help.

Ignoring the staring contest Polly and I are engaged in, Everly asks, "Would you also like joint bachelorette and bachelor parties?"

"Yes," Polly says. "We already spoke about that and would like to celebrate together, but not the night before the wedding—maybe we could do the weekend before. That way we're not all puffy and hungover the next day."

"Of course. I always suggest planning a night of debauchery a week before the wedding. That way, you can spend the night before the wedding with family at the rehearsal dinner."

"Love that idea," Polly says.

"Great." Everly makes a few notes, and I watch as her tongue peeks out while her hand moves rapidly over her paper. It's cute. "And I'm assuming, given the time crunch, the bachelor and bachelorette parties are going to be here in San Francisco instead of a destination party?"

"Yes, we don't want to make anyone go anywhere. I'm sure Ken will want to do some sort of throwback to college party since that's where we met, but Maple can clue you in on that."

"So can I," I say, raising my hand. "I can help out with those parties. I know all about the college days."

Everly glances up at me. "I can touch base with you and get Maple involved as well."

"That would be awesome," I say, knowing Everly is handling this balancing act so well already.

She makes a few more notes and then says, "And I have to ask, because my boss, Maggie, would be upset if I didn't, but do you need any help planning the wedding?"

"One of the reasons why I was looking for someone to help Maple is because the moms are busy planning, and I didn't want to add one more thing to their plate. That's where you come in. I think they have it handled on the wedding side, but if we need some help, would it be okay to reach out?"

"Of course," Everly says. "Maggie has a lot of connections and friends around town, so even if you need her to make a phone call, she'd love to help out. If anything, just to make an introduction for you."

"I really appreciate that. Thank you."

"Okay, I think that's all I have for you." Everly looks up. "And how can I get in touch with Maple?"

"She comes into town next week, but I'll give you her email. You can touch base that way for now, and then meet up when she gets in town. And I want you to know that she's shy and will probably feel embarrassed about this whole setup, so just be prepared for her to say sorry a lot."

"I'll be sure to make her feel at ease. This is completely normal. It's nice that you two care and have considered hiring help for her. This will be a fun experience and such a breeze for her that she doesn't need to worry about a thing."

"I really appreciate this," Polly says. "With Maple moving back to San Francisco, needing to find a place, and then us moving up the wedding, she's going to be very busy, so this will be such a weight off her shoulders."

"Glad I could be of assistance." Everly holds out a piece of paper to both of us. "Please write down your information for me. Name, phone number, and email, and if you can fill this out for Maple as well, I'd appreciate it."

Polly and I both fill out the form and hand it back to Everly who stuffs it away in her notebook.

"Great. I'll have Maggie reach out to you with the contract, and then we can get started on planning. Does that work for you?"

"Yes, that would be amazing," Polly says and then sighs in relief. "Thank you, Hardy, for introducing me to Everly. I think you and Hudson made a wise investment."

I glance at Everly. "I think we did too."

CHAPTER FIVE
EVERLY

To: Hardy Hopper
From: Everly Plum
Subject: The Meeting

Hey Hardy,

Wanted to reach out and see how everything went with the meeting. I didn't get to touch base with you after because I had another appointment, but wanted to make sure I covered everything you were looking for.

I believe with the parties being joint, it will be a lot easier to get you more involved with Maple. And if you have any ideas for Ken's portion of the bachelor party, let me know, as I'd be more than happy to go over them.

Thank you,
Everly

To: Everly Plum
From: Hardy Hopper
Subject: RE: The Meeting

Hey Professor,

I thought the meeting went great actually. Did you notice Polly's reluctance about getting me involved? She really doesn't want me to disturb Maple, so this is why you're key. Establishing some commonality with her, then getting to know her, then feeling out how she feels about me will be ideal. Then with that information, I'll know if I should pursue her.

I appreciate you doing this for me. I'm going to owe you big time. Do you like presents? I'm an excellent present giver.

Hardy

To: Hardy Hopper
From: Everly Plum
Subject: Professor?

Hardy,

Did you really call me professor? Is that because of your Professor Plum reference? Not sure how I feel about that. If you have a nickname for me, don't you think I should have a nickname for you?

Also, I like presents. And I don't think you're a better gift giver than I am. No one is. Sorry to burst your bubble.

Everly

To: Everly Plum
From: Hardy Hopper
Subject: RE: Professor?

Professor,

You are in fact right, the name comes from Professor Plum and, to be honest, I think it fits nicely. You came into that meeting like you owned that entire coffee house, like you could school anyone in the place, so to speak. Take no prisoners, right down to business. It was impressive. Also, I don't think we should call them nicknames, because what's really going on is you're going undercover for me, so I think we should consider them codenames.

And the gift giving thing…no way are you better. Ever gift anyone a boat before? Because I have.

10–4, over and out,
Hardy Har Har
(^^ My code name, do you like it?)

To: Hardy Hopper
From: Everly Plum
Subject: RE: Professor?

Umm…no.
No to Hardy Har Har.

That was terrible. Granted, it made me snort, but it's terrible. I'm not going to be in cahoots with someone who goes by Hardy Har Har. Do better.

And do you really think as a twenty-two-year-old, I've gifted someone a boat? Yeah, that didn't happen. But I don't have to flaunt my money to be a good gift giver—it's about the small things... Hardy Har Har. The thoughtful gifts. Maybe give that some thought.

Everly

To: Everly Plum
From: Hardy Hopper
Subject: Best Gift Giver

Oh, I know that it's the thought that counts and cash can't buy everything, but sometimes, when you need to buy a boat for someone, the cash does help.

And it hurts me that you didn't like Hardy Har Har. I thought it was clever, but I can't anger my partner in crime, so I guess I'll change it...to...Clod.

Clod Hopper.

Clodhopper.

Because, you know, Hardy HOPPER.

Now that's clever.

And before you ask, yes, I can be very clumsy. Just ask my ranch hand who got a poke in the ass with a pitchfork one time. *raises hand* Guilty.

Clod

To: Hardy Hopper
From Everly Plum
Subject: RE: Best Gift Giver

Clod is just as terrible as Hardy Har Har. I don't want to judge you, but you're not giving me much of a choice.

Also, how much of a poke with a pitchfork are we talking here? Did you draw blood? Did you pierce skin? Is there still a mark? Did he get you back? More details are needed.

And finally... I was wondering why you changed the subject of the email only to have a parcel dropped off at my table while I was sitting at The Bean, working. Don't get me started on how you even knew where I was, but I'm currently holding a purple game piece token that is very familiar. The kind of token you'd find in the game Clue. Did you happen to send me a Professor Plum game piece?

Everly

To: Everly Plum
From: Hardy Hopper
Subject: You're Welcome

I won't name my sources of how I know your whereabouts, but I figured there was a slim chance you would be there when the parcel was sent. Glad it worked out for me.

And yes, that is a Professor Plum token from Clue, but don't tell Hudson I took it from his game. I hope you hold this gift in high regard. Goes to show that I don't need money to be the best gift giver. Just a quick hand while stealing from my brother.

As for the pitchfork incident, I can't go into much detail, but I will say this. A trip to the hospital was involved, so I'll let your imagination do the rest.

And since you didn't like Clod, and you seem to be very picky, I'm going to let you choose my codename. That way there are no complaints and we can move forward with our espionage. Here are your options:

Colonel Mustard—no resemblance to the man or condiment, but if I could grow a mustache like him, I would.

Miss Scarlett—because just like her, I'm young, cunning, and very attractive. (And yes, thirties is still young, despite what you might think in your twenty-one years of age)

Henrietta Peacock—because if anything, peacocks are just as majestic as flamingos and I think I need to be one with the bird to complete this mission we're on. Don't you think?

Take your pick.

Hardy

———————

To: Hardy Hopper
From: Everly Plum
Subject: Henrietta

I think you know what I've chosen, not because you need to be one with the birds, but because I'm telling myself if you were a lady, you would be Henrietta Hopper, and nothing sounds better in my head than that.

So, you're welcome.

And as my first act as the professor, I sent an introduction email to Maple who will be referred to as Syrup from here on out. I told Syrup to take her time getting back to me so when I hear from her, I'll let you know. I want to get planning soon, but I don't want to be pushy.

Lastly, I think it might be best if we observe Syrup in her natural environment. I'd like to know what I'm dealing with and some insight from you would be best. If I'm not mistaken, she should be in town by now starting her new job. Care for a trip to the zoo?

The Prof

To: Everly Plum
From: Hardy Hopper
Subject: RE: Henrietta

And that is why your name is The Professor, because you're incredibly smart.

Yes, I think a zoo trip is needed. How does tomorrow work for you? Meet at the front around noon?

Come disguised, because we must wander undetected.

Over and out,
Henrietta

I shut my computer screen and stare out the window of the coffee shop, my mind whirling.

What on Earth did I just get myself into?

I'm headed to the zoo with the man I'm crushing on to get some intel on his ex-girlfriend so I can help him hook up with her?

While wearing a disguise?

And acting like I'm really happy and excited to be in this position?

I'll have to act like I want nothing more than for Hardy and Maple to be a match made in heaven where they ride off into the sunset, hand in hand, a charming rainbow arching over their heart-eyed heads.

Dear God, Everly, is this really where we are at?

Seems like it.

I let out a heavy, confused, and balled-up sigh.

The only question I have left to ask myself is…what the heck am I going to wear as a disguise?

CHAPTER SIX
HARDY

I PRESS MY FINGERS AGAINST the fake prosthetic nose that I glued to my face right before I came here, checking to make sure it's secure. I used the extra-strength glue, so it'll be a real bitch to take off later, and then I dabbled on some theater makeup to blend the nose into my skin. And I know you must be thinking, do you have experience in theater makeup, Hardy? The answer would be no, but I watched plenty of YouTube videos to make it look legit, and I spoke with the salesperson at the theater makeup store where I purchased the nose.

So, pretty sure I know what I'm doing.

Almost an expert after laying down this schnoz on my face.

And why the nose? Well, isn't it obvious? I had to do something that was going to make me look drastically different, and a fake nose, long wig, and fisherman's hat was the way to go. That's right, I purchased a wig as well, and man, does it make me look a lot like Jared Leto. And when I say a lot, I mean almost identical. The only difference? I probably have thirty pounds more of muscle than the man.

But when you add the crooked, slightly witchy nose, it takes away the appeal, which I think was smart. Otherwise, Maple would recognize me first. Thankfully she hasn't really seen me with this thicker beard either, so I think this getup will really keep me from view.

To top off the disguise, I strapped on a pair of old, paint-splattered sweatpants, a T-shirt that has a picture of a fish in a top hat, hanging on to a moon, and gathered my wig-hair into a ponytail. I considered adding a Cindy Crawford beauty mark but thought that would be stretching it.

Now if Maple recognizes me in this getup, well, then…she must have a distorted memory of me, that's for damn sure.

My phone buzzes in my hand with a text.

Everly: Where are you?
Hardy: Just outside the Wildlife Connection. Where are you?
Everly: Right out front.

I look up from my phone and catch a woman of Everly's height and body type, wearing a baseball hat, sunglasses, and a red dress with sneakers. From the long black hair sticking out the back of her baseball hat, I'm going to assume that's Everly.

"Hey," I call out, drawing her attention.

When she turns toward me, her mouth falls slightly ajar as she slowly lowers her sunglasses.

Her eyes carefully roam over my sweatpants, her brows contract when she takes in my shirt, and when her stare meets mine, she takes a step back.

Her nose scrunches up in the cutest way. "Henrietta?"

I chuckle and nod. "It's me."

She closes the space between us, her eyes on me the entire time. "Oh my God, what did you do to yourself?" she asks.

"I said to come in disguise, so I did." Because I want to give her the full effect, I spin for her while holding my arms out. "You like?"

She blinks a few times behind her sunglasses. "Are you…are you wearing a fake nose?"

"I am," I say, touching it. "What do you think?"

She studies me, a smile creeping over her face. "You look incredibly predatorial."

"What?" I laugh. "You think I look like a predator?"

"Oh yeah, a real creep, especially with the ponytail." She shivers. "Very...unbecoming."

"Unbecoming?" I ask with a scoff. "How could you possibly say that when I'm wearing a shirt like this?"

"It's a fish in a top hat clinging to the moon. Where did you even find something like that?"

"You know." I scratch the top of my fisherman's hat. "I was thinking about that this morning when I chose to wear it. I can't seem to place where such a shirt would have fallen into my wardrobe, but I kind of like it. Real breezy, real comfortable."

"It says *When You Fish Upon a Star*."

"I know." I smile. "Catchy, right?"

"It's not great."

I laugh. "Wasn't aware I would be participating in a fashion show today. And sorry, but I don't think you have room to speak—you look like one of those old lady mall walkers in a dress and sneakers," I counter.

"Was that supposed to be a burn?" she asks, a smirk dancing across her lips.

"It was. Did it not singe the way it was supposed to?"

She shakes her head and pushes her sunglasses up her nose. "Not so much."

"Well, I'll be sure to get you at some point."

"I look forward to it." She gives me one more once-over and shakes her head in disbelief. "Now, shall we get on with our spying?" She reaches into her purse and pulls out a set of binoculars. "I came prepared."

"Binoculars, nice. I like how you're thinking, Professor." I reach into my pocket and pull out two tickets. "I got our entry fees covered."

"Perfect." She nods toward the entrance. "Then let's go."

Together, looking like complete asshats, we walk up to the kiosk, and I hand over our tickets. A khaki-clad employee scans us in and hands us a map. Once inside, we step off to the side and Everly opens the map, giving it a good look. "Shall we go straight to the flamingos or should we ride the carousel first?"

"If you think I look like a predator, maybe we should stay away from the carousel."

She chuckles. "Very good point. So then, straight ahead to the flamingos?"

"Seems that way," I say.

"Now, are we going to creep around the flamingos, or are we going to walk up with confidence? What's the vibe we're going for?"

I stroke my beard and glance toward the center of the zoo. "I don't know, what do you think?"

"I think we need to own the disguises and almost live a second life. Really get into character, that way if she happens to look at us, you can feel confident in who you are."

"Smart," I say. "Okay, so who are we?"

"Think we can pass as brother and sister?" she asks.

I look her up and down and shake my head. "Not a chance in hell, not with this beak," I say, touching my nose. "I think we're going to have to go boyfriend and girlfriend."

"Are you trying to say I look like a person who'd date someone wearing a shirt that says *When You Fish Upon a Star*?"

I point to my chest. "Does it look like I'm the type of person who would date a mall walker?"

"It looks like your standards are low," she says with a smirk.

"That's neither here nor there. We have to face it—these are the cards we've been dealt. Maybe we should have coordinated outfits rather than surprising each other."

She laughs. "Well, it's a little too late for that now, don't you think?"

"Obviously. So unless you want me to walk into the gift shop and buy a new shirt, this is what you have going for you as your betrothed."

She winces. "I mean...maybe you could buy a new shirt..."

I narrow my eyes at her, which makes her laugh. "The fish in a top hat shirt is staying. It has character. Now, as my betrothed, I think you need to accept me for who I am and stop trying to change me or else we might have a break-up right in front of the flamingos."

"My God, we can't have that, we might shake the pink right out of them." She clutches her chest in a sarcastic horror.

"Exactly." I clear my throat. "Now, as for names, I think I would like to adopt the title Sir Phillip Minkle."

Her expression goes flat. "There is no way someone who is wearing a shirt like that has the title of sir."

"Uh, a guy wearing this shirt would one hundred percent have the title of sir. The fish is wearing a top hat, for fuck's sake. That screams high class. And, if I'm Sir Phillip, then I can use a British accent. Listen to this." I clear my throat and let out a deep breath. "Oy, look at them bloody birds."

After a brief pause, she says, "That is the worst British accent I've ever heard. No one says oy."

"Uhh, have you ever watched *Ted Lasso*? They say oy all the time."

"Well, if that's the case, I'm going to call myself Bindi Brown and use an Australian accent." She straightens up. "Ohhhrrr naurrrr, the pink buggarrs escaped. Fuck me dead."

"What?" I say on a laugh. "That...that was fucking terrible." I continue to chuckle.

"Ohhrr, get stuffed," she says continuing the worst Australian accent I ever heard. "Billabong and crocs on the barbie."

"Stop." I wipe at my eyes as tears form from laughter.

"Blimey, there are heaps of ankle-biters in this park, mate."

"Seriously. Fucking terrible."

"Ohhrr, rack off."

I chuckle some more. "You have to stop. You're going to make my nose fall off." I press against the prosthetic, hoping the glue is situated.

She lets out a wallop of a laugh as she grabs my arm to steady herself. Together, we laugh uncontrollably for a few seconds before we both calm down. Everly reaches into her purse and hands me a tissue so I can swipe at my tears.

"Maybe we just go by Phillip and Bindi," she says, once we're calm. "The couple from San Francisco that likes to observe the animals on weekdays to keep their relationship alive. We're into different mating techniques, thrive off getting our required steps for the day, and don't mind riding the carousel despite not being predators."

"Okay…but how do we feel about fish wearing top hats?"

She looks at my shirt and then back at me. "Clearly in favor."

"And what about the ankle-biters that are crawling around the park?" I lift a brow.

"If they come near us, we hiss."

I chuckle. "Is that hiss in unison?"

"Obviously." She tugs on her ponytail.

I nod. "I think that could work."

"Wonderful." She folds up the map. "Shall we?" She gestures toward the flamingos, which are tucked deeper into the zoo.

I hold my arm out to her, and she links hers through mine. "I think we shall, Bindi."

"Why, thank you, Phillip."

And then together, we head straight forward toward the flamingo enclosure, just past the carousel "ankle-biters" roaming all around us but not close enough to warrant a unified hiss.

Not much has changed since I was last here. Maybe a few signs. Plants and trees are bigger, but same pathways, same café, same…smell.

After a few moments of silence, she asks, "Have you been here before?"

"Yeah, Maple and I used to come all the time."

"Really?" she asks.

I look at her quickly as I feel something pop along my skin. "How's my nose?"

She looks up at me. "In place."

"Thanks, felt like it slid for a moment. And to answer your question, yes, back in college, Maple and I spent a lot of time looking over the flamingos. Being back here honestly brings up a lot of memories. There was this one time when we decided to share a coffee. Well, I didn't know she'd never really had a coffee before. It was her first ever and, Jesus, did she have quite the reaction."

"Oh? What happened?"

"She was hyper as shit, rattling off flamingo facts like she was an auctioneer."

Everly chuckles. "So you must know a lot about flamingos then."

"I mean, I know a good chunk of facts," I say as we close in on the habitat, which is a large pond in the middle of the zoo, encased by a wooden fence with plexiglass. Foliage, rocks, and trees decorate the enclosure, but it's open to the air, so if the birds wanted to, they could come right up to you. They don't though. The elegant creatures are standoffish at best. But I can remember standing right over there, next to the flamingo facts. Maple and I would spend so much time leaning on the fence while she talked about the flamingos. We would try to name them and remember them by their names, but never got it right. She would listen in on the zookeeper's speech, and I would delight in the tons of questions she would ask after.

"Care to share?" Everly asks. "Maybe I can act like I know something to get Syrup on my side."

"Ooo, smart," I say as we walk up to the fence. I glance around, looking for her, but come up short, probably best because my nerves are starting to play with me. We both lean on the wooden rail and take in the light pink, leggy birds, which are clustered together in serene groups across the pond. "Well, first things first, they do get their color from what they eat. Carrots, red peppers, dried shrimp. It's a real thing."

"You know, I always heard that but wasn't sure if it was true."

"It's true," I reply. "And their knees…those are actual carpal joints, so they can bend both ways."

"Really? Those knobby things?" she asks. "That's fascinating, Phillip."

I smirk. "And their necks, they have nineteen vertebrae. Where we only have seven."

"Which makes them incredibly majestic," she says.

"Correct, Bindi. Some say angels with pink wings."

Her lips quiver into a smile. "You know, Phillip, I have heard that."

"How could you not? I think it's on a shirt somewhere. A flamingo with a halo and a glint in their eye, with the saying *Angels with Pink Wings*."

"I bet it's nicer than a shirt featuring a fish with a top hat."

I lean in close to her ear and whisper-scold, "This shirt is a masterpiece and I beg you to find something better than."

"Literally any shirt, Phillip…any shirt."

"Clearly you have no taste."

"You might be right if you're my betrothed." Shocked, I turn to her, mouth ajar, which makes her laugh hard. "Now that's a burn, take notes."

"Wow, okay. Here I thought we were going to have a nice afternoon delight with the flamingos, but instead you come in here, guns blazing, ready to burn me every chance you get."

"It's best you know about me sooner rather than later." She bumps my shoulder with hers in a playful way.

"Well…noted."

We both chuckle and after a few seconds, I ask, "Have you ever fed flamingos before?"

"Uh no, have you?"

I nod. "Not sure if they do it anymore, but they used to have feeding sessions for the public. The zookeepers give you a cup full of water and dog food, you sit down, and the flamingos come up to you. It's pretty cool. They honk and make a mess of the water, a lot of fun."

"I would love that," she says as she looks around. "Now, how do you think we can figure out if they still allow people to feed them? Because I want to participate in something like that."

"Let me see the map," I say, holding out my hand.

Everly pulls it out of her purse and as she's handing it over to me, she chuckles. "God, you look so weird."

I smile at her and tug on my hat. "So, what you're saying is that I should wear this nose more often? Possibly grow my hair out?" I flip my ponytail. "Maybe buy you a fisherman's hat as well."

She laughs and shakes her head. "No to everything."

"Oh right, not a hat, but this shirt, you want me to buy you this shirt."

"Please...please don't."

I snatch the map from her. "So judgmental." I open it up and scan through the wording on the side, looking for any info on animal feedings, but I come up short. "Hmm, maybe there's a posting or sign around here." I scan the habitat, nervous that Maple might appear at any point to give a zookeeper talk, only to feel my skin go cold as I see someone off to the right, leaning against the rail and admiring the flamingos. "Holy shit," I say.

"What?" Everly looks up.

"Oh fuck."

"What?" Everly says, her panic rising with my reaction. "Do you see Maple?"

"No. That's...fuck, that's JP Cane."

"What?" she says. "Where?"

I lean in close to Everly, feeling like I'm on full display, and whisper, "Over there, off to the left. He's the one in the red shirt, leaning on the fence."

She looks over in that direction and then squints. "Ohhrrrr narrrr, are you sure?"

I chuckle at that fucking accent. "One hundred percent positive," I say. "Fuck, what if he recognizes me?"

"Hardy." Everly turns toward me. "I don't believe your own brother would recognize you right now."

"Are you sure?" I tug on my ponytail. "I thought I was disguised but now...now I feel very exposed."

"What are you talking about?" she asks. "I barely even recognized you. I feel like I'm at the zoo with the man from the pier who feeds the pigeons."

"Really?" I ask, my eyes shooting wide. "Fuck."

"What do you mean, fuck?"

I grip her shoulders, speaking in all seriousness. "JP would focus his attention on me if I look like I toss bread to the pigeons. He loves pigeons. He knows everything about them and if I look like a pigeon lover, fuck, he might want to start up a conversation. Ask me if he's seen me down by the pier. And if he recognizes me? How can I begin to explain what I'm doing? Shit, this was not a good idea. We should leave."

"Hold on a second," Everly says, stopping me from backing up. "You're telling me that you're more afraid to see JP Cane at the zoo than your ex-girlfriend?"

"She wouldn't recognize me—it's been ten years. But I saw JP the other day. He'd know me. He'd smell me."

"Ew, smell you?" she asks, a scrunch to her nose. "Do you think you give off some sort of recognizable pheromone?"

"I don't know...do I?" I ask, leaning in so she can smell me.

"No!" she says in an exasperated tone. "No one can pick up your scent."

Just then, a strong wind bursts through the air, kicking up my ponytail and blowing in JP's direction. His head lifts and he looks directly at me.

Holy fuck.

He can smell me.

I stand there, shocked, unable to move.

"He sees me," I say through a stiff, pursed mouth.

"What do you mean he sees you?" She turns to look but I stop her.

"No, don't look at him. He's looking at me. If you look at him, he'll know we're talking about him, and he can't know that we even recognize him."

"Then why aren't you looking away?"

"Because I think…I think he can smell me."

"Dear God, Hardy, he can't smell you."

"Phillip!" I whisper-shout. "Use my betrothed name, you fool."

That makes her laugh. "Sorry, Phillip, he can't smell you, no chance."

I glance in his direction and he stands taller, eyes on me. "Holy fuck, he knows me. He sees the resemblance. What the hell am I going to say to him? I'm supposed to be in business with this man. And he's going to see me on a weekday, dressed up as Phillip the Pigeon Man? How do I even explain that?"

"Technically, you're Sir Phillip Minkle, the betrothed, but if he comes up to you, tell him you're not who he thinks you are," Everly says as JP pushes off the fence.

"Oh fuck, oh fuck," I say, bowing my head. "He's walking over here. He's approaching. I repeat. He's approaching. Red alert. RED ALERT!"

"For the love of God," Everly says before tugging on my arm, pulling me away from the fence and spinning me right toward a bush.

Not expecting the change of position, I trip over my own feet, fall forward, and take a branch right to the face.

Well, not to the face, but to the prosthetic.

It's a quick jab.

A fencer with no defense, taking a saber right to the nose.

Touché. Horrified, because as I focus, I can see a branch attached to my face. I gently pull away but, instead of taking my glued prosthetic with me, my witch-nose tears off my face with a sticky pop and dangles from the branch, the false skin flapping in the breeze.

"Oh my God," Everly says, crouching down and covering her nose and mouth with her hand as she laughs.

"My nose," I whisper-shout. "I fucking lost my nose."

That only makes her laugh harder as she plucks it off the branch. A new piercing near the nostril.

"This is not funny," I say as I take it from her and we both straighten up. "What the hell am I supposed to do with—?"

"Do I know you?" a very recognizable voice says.

My spine seizes and my butt cheeks clench.

Dear.

Mother.

Of.

God.

With my back toward the man I didn't want to talk to, I look to Everly for help. Pleading with my wide eyes, begging for a life-saving moment.

He can't see me here, dressed like this, with a fake nose in my hand.

How the fuck do I even explain this?

I can't. It will get back to Hudson.

And I don't want to face the wrath of my brother. He can be very unkind when he's angry.

Thankfully, Everly's quick on her feet. She brings my hands up to my nose, with the prosthetic, and then says in her terrible Australian accent, "Ohhrrr narrr, he's got a bloody nose."

"Oh shit, really?" JP says. "Let me grab napkins." He takes off, and that's when I stare daggers at Everly.

"A bloody nose? How the hell am I supposed to produce blood when he comes back? And if you say you're going to punch me, I'm going to tell you right now, that's not an option."

She reaches into her purse and to my surprise, pulls out a few ketchup packets.

"Why the hell do you have those in your purse?"

"Don't ask questions," she says as she opens them. "Lower your hands."

I do as I'm told, and she squeezes the ketchup into my hand. "That's really thick blood."

"I'm not done." She takes out her water bottle now and squirts water into my hand, letting it thin out the ketchup. "Now put that up against your face. It'll be horrifying."

Knowing we don't have much time, I bring my hands and prosthetic nose up to my face just as JP comes back. "I've got the napkins," he says.

"Ohhrrr, what a noice bloke," Everly replies.

For the love of God, Everly.

Turning toward him, I keep my head down, but there is thinned ketchup spreading down my forearms, which of course scares the crap out of him.

"Oh fuck. Dude, you're…hemorrhaging."

Everly takes the napkins from him. "Nothing a little pressure won't take care of," she says, keeping in theme with her accent. "Here you go, Phillip."

I take the napkins and say in my British accent, "Thanks, mate."

"Yeah, of course," JP says. "Man, I swore I knew you, but I guess not. I'm sorry if I startled you."

"Totally fine," I reply, holding the napkins close to my nose.

But he doesn't leave—he keeps studying me. "You know, are you sure I don't know you?" I can feel actual sweat start to drip down my back. "You look so familiar." He snaps his finger and points at me. "Did I see you down at the pier the other day, feeding the pigeons?" *For the love of God.*

"Uhh…"

"He hates pigeons," Everly says, which of course causes JP to gasp.

"How could you hate pigeons? They bob their heads when they walk."

I just shrug, not wanting to lean on my poor accent to talk any more than I have to, which in turn causes JP to shake his head in disappointment. "Well, maybe read up on them, give yourself an education. We humans have done a lot to the pigeon population, and the fact that we just turn our back on them is disgraceful." He shakes his head and takes a step back just as he bumps into...*oh fuck*...

"Oh, I'm sorry about that," Maple says. "Didn't see you there."

Remember that sweat running down my back? It just doubled.

She...she hasn't changed.

Maple isn't one to dabble in social media, so I really haven't seen her in a long time, but I would recognize that face anywhere. Although this time, there seem to be deeper laugh lines around her eyes. Her face is more mature, not so rounded like in college. And her hair is shorter than what I remember, not cascading down her back in a low and tight pony-tail, but rather sitting higher on her head. But one thing for certain hasn't changed—she still has that sweet, innocent smile.

"Not a problem," JP says, before noticing her uniform. "Do you work here?"

"Yes, I do," Maple answers as she glances in our direction, but I turn my back. "With the flamingos in particular. Can I help you with anything?"

Please don't look at us. Please don't look at us.

"Great, I have questions about the flamingos I'd love answered."

"Not a problem at all," Maple answers, probably more than happy to help out a fellow flamingo enthusiast. "Follow me."

And then just like that, JP forgets about me and my bloody nose and takes off with Maple toward the center of the habitat's outer ring, far away from us. I duck behind the bush and exhale loudly. "Jesus...Christ."

Everly chuckles. "That was eventful."

"That was Maple," I say, causing Everly's eyes to widen.

"That girl talking to JP?"

"Yes," I reply. "That's her."

"Oh shit, let me see." She moves closer to the edge of the bush and leans over to get a better look.

"Don't let her see you."

"I won't."

I tug on her hand. "I'm serious, Everly, Maple can be very perceptive."

"Shhh, just sit there and hold your fake nose. I'm getting a good look." Everly's quiet for a moment as she scans the scene. "She's very pretty," she whispers. "It looks like she oils her hair, it's so sleek. Oh, look, she just made a whole group of people laugh. Maybe she told a flamingo joke. Oh Jesus, JP just slapped his knee he was laughing so hard. Not sure anyone has ever slapped their knee when I told a joke. Do you think it was funny?"

"I have no idea. I can't hear anything, as my ears are still ringing from the anxiety attack I nearly had."

She glances over her shoulder at me. "Dramatic much?"

"Everly, JP Cane almost figured me out."

"Yes, and if he had, you would have been taken away in handcuffs." She rolls her eyes and looks out at Maple again. "Okay, so she seems cool, relaxed, in her element. I think I can win her over with flamingos." She moves away from the bush and then nods her head toward the exit. "Ready to go?"

"Wait, that's it?" I ask.

"What else did you want to do?" she asks. "Go talk to her? Explore more of the zoo? Ride the carousel with your nose in your ketchup-soaked hand?"

"I don't know." I shrug. "I guess I just expected you'd to want to observe her more."

"I've seen what I need to see—plus I think I just saw a parent tell security about you, so, you know, the sooner we can leave, the better. Also, if you thought you were sweating being near JP and Maple, wait until they see you get carted out of here with a police escort."

And that gets me moving.

"Yup, maybe we should go."

"I think we should."

Together, with my hand over my nose, we head toward the exit, people looking after us, questions in their eyes.

When we near the exit, Everly chuckles.

"What's so funny?" I ask.

"Your skewered nose. I can't get the image of it dangling off the branch out of my head. Looked like a *shrimp on the barbie*," she finishes in her horrible accent.

I look over at her. "You're truly terrible."

She grips my arms and laughs wholeheartedly, which of course makes me laugh just as hard.

To: Hardy Hopper

From: JP Cane

Subject: There is still time…

Dear friend,

The flamingos still need your help. With every day that goes by, the habitat of the Chilean Flamingo is destroyed. With your simple donation of $5 or more, you can help save the flamingos and their natural environment. Help us save these majestic birds and the fragile ecosystem they live in.

Donate Here.

Thank you for being a friend of the flamingos.

JP Cane

CHAPTER SEVEN
EVERLY

"WHAT IS THAT IN YOUR hand?" Ember asks as she walks up to me, cutting through the crowd in the swanky restaurant.

My eyes snap up to hers. "Oh, nothing."

I attempt to slip the Professor Plum token into my purse, but Ember stops me and opens my fist, revealing the game piece.

Clearly confused, she looks up at me with a crease in her brow. "Why do you have a game piece in your hand?"

"Uh, long story," I say while I watch Trevor slip some money to the host, probably looking to get us a better table.

When Ember said she would hook me up with Trevor's friend from work, I told her I didn't think I could do a blind date, so she asked if I would go out with him if it was a foursome. That seemed less intimidating, so I said yes. But now that I'm here, I'm regretting that decision immensely.

I'm nervous.

I feel sweaty.

And I can't stop thinking about the one man I shouldn't be thinking about: Hardy Hopper.

At first, I was genuinely trying to catch him up on what was going on with Maple via email, but with every ding of my inbox, I fell into this easy rapport with him.

The joking, the teasing, the codenames. It was all so…addictive.

Then when he told me to meet him at the zoo in disguise, I was all in. Spending extra time with Hardy Hopper? Yes, please. I jumped on that opportunity so quickly, which only made this insatiable appetite I have for the man even worse.

Despite the skewering of the fake nose, the man pony, and the shirt, I can't stop thinking about our zoo trip, how it felt to be close to him. The way he makes me feel so comfortable, how he makes me laugh, the easygoing conversations. Ugh…he was charming, fun, and sweet, someone I could see myself dating. And now I'm carrying around a freaking Professor Plum token like a freaking lovesick teenager, wanting to hold it up to my cheek and make kissing noises because it reminds me of him.

Something is seriously wrong with me.

Ember studies me while folding her arms across her chest. "Why are your eyes shifting?"

"What are you talking about?" I ask, not daring to meet my sister's gaze. "They're not shifting."

"Then look at me."

"I am looking at you," I say, staring at her shoulder.

"Look me in the eyes, Everly."

God, she's annoying.

I bring my gaze to hers and under the glare of her pupils, I feel myself shrinking…and shrinking…

And shrinking.

Until… "Fine," I surrender. "The token was from Hardy. He had it delivered to me because he calls me Professor, because, you know… Professor Plum from Clue."

Her lips purse.

Her eyes search mine.

My metaphorical tail tucks between my legs because I know what's coming.

The lecture.

A lecture from my sister who never lets anything go.

On an irritated huff, Ember takes me by the arm and marches me over into a corner of the lobby, blocking me from our surroundings. Leaning in, she yell-whispers, "You're carrying around a token from him? Jesus, Everly, might as well be a candle from the way you worship this man."

"I don't worship him," I say, though I feel like there might be some validity to her statement. Which, if I think about it, means I'm pushing past pathetic to utterly humiliating. I don't think I've ever been this far gone over a man...ever.

"I can see it in your eyes—you were thinking about him just now, weren't you?" Ember says with an accusatory finger.

"No, I wasn't." I roll my eyes.

"Yes, you were."

"No, I wasn't," I reply defiantly.

"Then what were you thinking about?" She places her hands on her hips.

Uh...yeah, Everly, what were you thinking about?

"Uh...well...if you must know..." I pause, giving myself time to come up with something, anything, but my mind goes blank, so I say the first thing that rolls off my tongue. "I was thinking about pitchforks."

"Pitchforks," she deadpans.

"Yes," I answer. "Pitchforks."

"And why were you thinking about pitchforks?"

Nosey much? Sheesh.

"Because I heard a story about a ranch hand getting poked in the butt by one, so, yeah, I was thinking about that." She doesn't need to know said story was told to me by the charming offender in question.

She narrows her eyes. "And where would you hear such a story?"

This is why you should never have an older sister: because nothing gets by them, nothing. They're too smart, too inquisitive, and too much in your business.

"From…you know, the place that tells pitchfork stories."

"And what place is that?" she asks.

"Errr…" I look to the side and mumble, "TikTok."

"Ah, so if I went onto TikTok right now and looked up *pitchfork to the ass*, it would come up? Obviously, it would have to because how else would you have come across it if it wasn't a viral video?"

With every sentence she says, she gets increasingly annoying.

"Yes," I say with full confidence.

"Okay," she says as she brings her phone out of her purse and pulls up TikTok. As she types, she says, "Pitchfork to the butt." Her lips twist to the side as she searches, and searches, and when nothing comes up, she says, "Hmm, that's so weird, I don't see any videos that deal with a pitchfork poking the butt. Makes me think that you were lying and instead of thinking about pitchforks, you were actually thinking about something else, or better yet…*someone* else."

I roll my eyes and sarcastically laugh. "Oh, how little you know about me."

"Everly," she snaps, causing my innards to shrivel.

"Fine," I say. "I was thinking about Hardy, okay? We've been exchanging emails, and he's been so funny and sweet, and then he sent me this token—and I know what you're thinking, he's being nice because I'm helping him, and I'm sure that's the case, but it doesn't stop me from daydreaming and thinking about him and wondering what it would be like if he wasn't after his ex but instead interested in a woman like me."

Ember pinches the bridge of her nose as she takes a deep breath. "Everly, this is…this is embarrassing."

"I know," I groan. "I know, I don't need the reminder. I see how pathetic I am. I look in the mirror and I point at myself and I say, *pathetic. You are a pathetic woman.* But that doesn't stop me from thinking about him, about what could be." I lean in close and whisper, "I need help, Ember. I need you to slap me out of this." I tap my cheek. "Go ahead, slap me, right here. Give me a good knock back into reality." I tap my cheek again.

She stares at me with an unamused expression. "As tempting as that is, I'm not going to hit my sister, nor do I think that will work. What you need is a distraction, and we have the perfect one for you. One that will be here any second, so do you think you can forget about the freaking game token, push aside thoughts of an untouchable man, and focus on a person who is interested in meeting you?"

I let out a deep sigh. "You're right," I say. "You're very right. There is a man coming here tonight who will be the perfect distraction. Timothy, right?"

"Tomothy," Ember corrects.

"Tomothy?" I ask with a grimace. "Are you sure?"

"Yes, his name is Tomothy."

"Do people call him Tom?" I ask.

"No," Ember says emphatically. "God, do not call him Tom. He hates that. He goes by Tomothy."

"Are you sure? Because when you told me his name initially, I thought it was a typo in your text. But it's really Tomothy?"

"Yes, it's really Tomothy. I think it's a fun name."

"I think it's an old Victorian name for a kid with the plague," I whimper, and in my best Dickensian voice, I say, "Oh, little Tomothy, about to shrivel up from the Black Death."

"Everly," Ember scolds on a laugh. "It is not. This is a nice name, and he's a nice man, and you will enjoy his company—just watch. Your thoughts about Hardy will be completely washed away once Tomothy enters the chat. Guaranteed."

I'm going to murder my sister.

I hope she enjoys her last meal of chicken parm, breadsticks, and a side salad, because that's it for her.

She will not be seeing another day.

And do you know why?

One word: Tomothy.

I can't *believe* she set me up with this man.

First of all, he is easily seven feet tall. I know what you're thinking, not a bad thing. Could be worse. But he's so tall that the first thing I noticed wasn't his eyes, or his smile, no, it was his nostrils.

His very wide and very prominent nostrils—well-kept nostrils, though, which I have to give him credit for. Sure, this isn't a great example as to why my sister should be murdered, but there's something jarring about being greeted by a nostril and not a face.

And not that I have anything against tall men. I like tall men, but this man is so tall that I would need to stand on a chair to even consider a kiss goodnight. Which would never happen because I have acquired "the ick" where he's concerned and not because of his height or his nostrils.

I acquired the ick on multiple occasions.

First ick was when he checked his teeth in the reflection of his knife when we first sat down. He made a show of it, examining his pearly whites, moving his head back and forth to get all angles, and then swiping his rather thick tongue across the ivories, before setting his knife back down. Excuse yourself to the bathroom, sir, if you're that concerned.

Second ick was when he picked up his napkin and made a show of flapping it in the air and then tucking it into the top of his shirt. Could be endearing, some might say, but not when he made it a point to fluff his chest hair crawling out his collar and gently smooth it over the top part of his tucked-in napkin. No one wants chest hair on full display while biting into their breadstick.

Third ick—and this is a doozy—was when he started telling me about his cat, Hoodini, which at first was sort of charming, that was until he went into great detail about how he used to lick Hoodini when he was young. Got even more grossed out when he said he liked gnawing on Hoodini's paw because it reminded him of corn chips.

The only pussy he should be licking is…well…you know—hint, it's not a feline.

And I completely disassociated from the "date" when he discussed the complexities of female genitalia and how it wasn't fair for men to have to learn the ways around their pleasure. How women shouldn't have such convoluted parts because they're letting men down. How he thought this was a topic of conversation that would grant him a look at my "parts" I have no idea. If anything, I mentally slipped a chastity belt on and tossed the key into the Pacific Ocean.

And finally, I began contemplating my sister's murder when he told me that I had the same bone structure as a sickly praying mantis—this coming from the seven-foot-tall, lanky man. Compare me to a bug and we're done. Thank you, have a not-so-good day.

How on Earth did Ember believe this would be the type of man that would take my mind off Hardy Hopper? This only makes me want him even more.

"And this is what my finger looked like right when I broke it," Tomothy says as he flashes his phone toward me. Yup, we're onto the many injuries he's endured throughout his life. We went from a broken nose, to stitches in his chin, to a broken ankle, to a punctured hip, and now to a broken finger.

One glance and I'm gagging.

"Dear God, Tomothy," I say as I turn away from him. "That is disgusting."

"I know." He smiles down at the picture as if he just showed me an image of his most prized possession—which I can only assume would be his cat's corn chip paws. "It was quite gnarly. I can still hear the snap of my bone—"

"I need to go to the bathroom," I say as I rise quickly out of my chair. I toss my napkin on the table and turn toward Ember. "Care to join?"

"Not really," she says, shaking her head, probably knowing exactly why I want to go to the bathroom.

"Well, too bad," I say as I grab her arm and tug her out of her chair.

Silently, we work our way through the restaurant, toward the back, and right into the women's bathroom. When the door is shut, I turn toward her. "What the hell were you thinking? Tomothy? You think I should be dating Tomothy? The man with the incessant need to burp every time he takes a sip of his water? What the hell is up with that?"

"Yes, I found that a touch odd," Ember says while tapping her chin.

"A touch odd?" I whisper-shout. "Ember, he's vile."

"Now, now, he's not all that bad. He brought you flowers."

"That were half dead, and he told me he got them on a slashed price."

"Money conscious, that's not a bad thing," Ember says.

"When Trevor asked him how he was doing, Tomothy said, not bad, just upset he found a hole in his undies. He said *undies*, Ember."

"Some might find that endearing," she says with a shoulder shrug.

"And when I asked him what he did for fun, he said he liked to go to the piers wearing his female body inspector shirt."

Ember lightly winces. "I think that was a joke."

"No one laughed," I say through a clenched jaw. "Face it, he's disgusting, and this was a horrible decision. I will never trust you, ever again, when it comes to my love life."

She folds her arms over her chest. "I'll give you the fact that Tomothy is not the catch I thought he'd be, but he's better than pining after someone who's pining after another person."

"Listen, I'd rather be sad, pathetic, and alone clutching a Professor Plum game piece than ever see Tomothy ever again."

"That seems a bit harsh."

"It's the truth," I say just as there's a knock on the bathroom door.

Confused, we both turn around only for Tomothy to peek his head inside. "Ah, there you are. I'm experiencing some gas and wanted to see if you were too. Figured that was your reasoning for a quick departure to the toilets."

I turn to Ember and mouth "I hate him," before turning back toward Tomothy. "I'm not experiencing any gas, thanks for the inquiry though."

"Are you sure, because..."—he clutches his stomach—"things are happening down below."

Oh.

My.

God.

"As a matter of fact, yes," I say as I charge toward the door, moving him to the side. "I'm experiencing gastric distress and I need to go home."

Tomothy nods in understanding. "I get it. I only like to deposit in my own space as well, something we have in common." He smiles, and it takes everything in me not to lift his tie and stuff it up his very large but clean nostrils.

"And with that, I'm leaving," I say.

"Okay, sure, understand the rush," he says walking after me. "Shall I call you later to check in? See how it went?"

"I'd rather you not," I say.

"Then maybe we can plan for another date," he replies as we walk past a few tables in the dining area.

"I don't think that's in our future, Tomothy."

Not wanting to see Tomothy's reaction, I reach our table and grab my purse. When I look over at Trevor, he has a guilty look on his face, Ember standing directly behind him. I point at him and say, "You did this."

He nods. "I know."

"Do not do it again."

"Understood," he answers.

"Blaming Trevor for your intestinal bubbling?" Tomothy *tsks* at me. "You're the one who took the chance on the sausage, not him."

"Oh my God, Tomothy, no one asked you," I say, losing my cool.

He holds his hands up as if I've insulted him. "I don't think I appreciate your tone."

"Yeah, well, I didn't appreciate you telling me that you find the vagina too complex. How do you think you'd be able to pleasure me, Tomothy?"

"The women I'm with usually pleasure themselves," he says as if I'm stupid.

"And that's why you're single," I say, throwing my hands up in the air.

He folds his arms, his stature drawing attention from the diners around us. "And why are you single?"

"Because apparently I keep trying to date men with names like Tomothy who have impeccably manicured nostrils but like to lick their cats and gnaw on their paws."

Tomothy huffs. "You leave Hoodini out of this."

"Dear God in heaven." I roll my eyes and wave to Trevor. "Good night."

And with that, I take off, fleeing the restaurant and heading straight for my car. I need to find the nearest grocery store to buy a pint of ice cream I can drown myself in.

CHAPTER EIGHT
HARDY

To: Everly Plum
From: Hardy Hopper
Subject: Inquiring

Professor,

Just checking to see if you've heard anything from Syrup yet. I know it's only been a day since you reached out to her about this, but I'm eager to see if my ideas for the bachelor party will match up with her bachelorette ideas. Because I have some great ones. Here is my list already:

    Game: Beer Pong Tournament
    Drinks: Craft beers and Moscow mules
    Food: All kinds of dips
    Music: The best of Ed Sheeran
    What do you think? Killer party, right?
    Let me know what you think.

Henrietta

To: Hardy Hopper
From: Everly Plum
Subject: Re: Inquiring

Henrietta,

Are you trying to throw a frat party? Is that what's happening? And what kind of dips are we talking about here? Fancy dips? Canned dips? Crockpot dips? Dessert dips?

Usually when we throw a joint bachelor/bachelorette party, it's at a restaurant where we have tables to mingle at, an open bar, and a buffet. Were you thinking more along the lines of that? (I hope so.)

And no, I have not heard from her yet, but Polly was telling me that she's in the midst of moving so I'm sure she's busy packing and unpacking. I'll let you know when Syrup makes contact.

The Prof

To: Everly Plum
From: Hardy Hopper
Subject: All The Dips

Professor Plum,

I'm getting the distinct feeling that you're judging me and my idea. Would I be right with that assessment?

I will have you know that Ken and Polly might look like they're fancy, and their families might have money, but when it comes to a party, their number one idea of having a good time is a beer pong tournament and dips…and the sweet, melodic tones of Ed Sheeran. Just wait, I bet Syrup says the same thing.

Also, no offense, but your party sounds boring, like it's for adults or something…

Henrietta

To: Hardy Hopper
From: Everly Plum
Subject: RE: All The Dips

Henrietta,

Boring? You think my party would be boring? Ohhhh no. I throw one heck of a party. There's no way it would be boring. Your guests would be talking about the signature drink for years to come. The food would be so good, they'd go back for thirds. And the conversation would be so enthralling that it would take multiple clinks of a glass to quiet everyone down.

The speeches would marvel even the dullest person.

And at the end of the night, when everyone was going home, they'd praise the good time they had celebrating with friends.

I've been to all the parties I've thrown, and as an attendee, I give them a resounding hip hip hooray.

The Prof

To: Everly Plum
From: Hardy Hopper
Subject: RE: All The Dips

Professor,

You sure know how to paint a picture, but I guarantee Syrup will be in agreement. Your parties might have rave reviews, but you've never been to one of ours. It will blow your mind.

Just wait and see.

You might turn your nose up at the idea of a beer pong tournament, but I think after this party, you're going to change your mind.

And just so you know, I'm going to be gone for the next two days, headed out to the farm, but I'll be checking my email if you need anything. Also…don't be afraid to text if you need to. I won't bite.

Henrietta

To: Hardy Hopper
From: Everly Plum
Subject: Text?

Henrietta,

Texting? Do you really think we're at the level of texting? I don't know about that. I prefer the low pressure of an email. Gives me some time to think about a response rather than a quick quip in a text.

And going to the farm? What does that entail exactly? Inquiring minds want to know.

Are you going to poke anyone with a pitchfork again?

Throw some hay bales around? Wait…do you have hay bales on your farm?

Either way, please at least tell me you're going to wear overalls with your fisherman hat. Even if you don't, please don't ruin the image I have of that outfit on you in my head. Thanks.

The Prof

To: Everly Plum
From: Hardy Hopper
Subject: RE: Text?

Professor,

You know, you might be right. I don't think I'm ready for text messages either, do you know why? Because you're far too witty, I wouldn't be quick enough on the draw. So, I agree. We should strictly stay with emails unless an absolute emergency occurs.

And of course we have hay bales on the farm, what do you think we feed the almonds? See that response? I wouldn't have been able to come up with something so witty if this conversation was in text message form.

No to the pitchfork. I've been forbidden from using one now, so thank you for asking, not a sore subject at all.

Farm attire would consist of jeans and a T-shirt, sorry to disappoint. I've never worn overalls in my life.

*And what do I do on the farm? That's classified information—
but if my brother asks, tell him I'm working tirelessly—lifting soil,
fixing irrigation, and counting almonds. I'm definitely not just hanging out with the almond trees and staring up at the expansive sky.*

Nope. Work, work, work.

Henrietta

To: Hardy Hopper
From: Everly Plum
Subject: RE: Text?

Henrietta,

*If you're not feeding your almonds hay, then what the hell are
you doing over there?*

Also, why do you have pitchforks if you don't have hay?

And no overalls?

*Are you really a farmer? Or are you posing as one while you
actually do something else like…making origami swans in the
back of the barn.*

*And what are you doing with the paper swans? Do you sell
them? And at what price?*

*I have far too many questions. This is where text messaging
might have come in handy.*

The Prof

To: *Everly Plum*
From: *Hardy Hopper*
Subject: *Re: Text?*

Professor,

Like I said, all classified.

What I can tell you is that it's a no to the swans…though not to the origami. But you didn't hear that from me. Like I said, I'm putting in the sweat equity when I come up to the farm…

Oh, I have to go. My lemonade just arrived, and I have a tan to perfect before I return to the city. *Pops on sunglasses and stretches out on the lounger*

Let me know when Maple gets in contact.

Inquiring minds want to know.

Henrietta

CHAPTER NINE
EVERLY

To: *Everly Plum*
From: *Maple Baker*
Subject: *RE: Polly x Ken Wedding*

Hi Everly,

It's so nice to e-meet you. I'm sorry it took me a second to get back to you. I finally got settled into my apartment and was able to take a breath from the quick transition I had to make. I would love to meet up whenever you have availability. I have normal hours at the zoo. I kind of lucked out, and I don't work on the weekends either, so, pretty available.

   Let me know when and where works for you, and I'll be there. I really appreciate you doing this for me. It means a lot to give Polly the best experience ever.

Talk soon,
Maple

———

To: Everly Plum
From: Hardy Hopper
Subject: FWD: There is still time…

Want to gain some points with Syrup? Check this out, from JP
Cane. And because I care about your involvement in successfully
saving the animals, I added your email to the newsletter list…

Dear friend,

The flamingos still need your help. With every day that goes by
the habitat of the Chilean Flamingo is destroyed. With your
simple donation of $5 or more, you can help save the flamingos
and their natural environment. Help us save these majestic birds
and the fragile ecosystem they live in.
    Donate Here.
    Thank you for being a friend of the flamingos.

                                            JP Cane

The door to The Bean opens and my breath stills as I look up to see who it is.

Could it be her?

When a mother pushing a stroller comes into view, I bring my attention back to my iPad where I'm tapping away on an email.

God, I'm nervous.

Very nervous.

So nervous that I haven't touched my mocha since I sat down.

I know comparison is the greatest thief of joy, but this is it: I'm going to meet the girl Hardy is lusting after.

Maple Baker seemed very charming in her email. Then again, it was just an email, so she could be a raging bitch who disguises herself well through the screen of a computer.

Or she could be the sweetest, kindest human I ever met, which would be why Hardy wants to try something again with her.

Not to mention when I caught a glimpse of her at the zoo, I tried not to look too stunned, but oh my God, she was gorgeous. At least from what I could see. After all, there was a man without a nose next to me, covered in fake ketchup blood, which was incredibly distracting. This meeting will be more intimate, and I can tell the moment she says hello, jealousy is going to eclipse me. My dream of ever having anything with Hardy will be completely and utterly trashed. For some reason, a small part of me, a very small part of me, has hope that there's still a chance.

Maybe it's the emails that are giving me hope, or maybe it's the fact that I think I deserve so much better than a Tomothy. Either way, I'm still hanging on to a shred of hope, and I don't want that shred to be destroyed the minute she walks through the door.

The bell jingles with another visitor and my eyes shoot up, only for my heart to stutter in my chest as a beautiful blond walks through the door. Yup, that's her. Decked out in a pair of leggings and a crewneck sweatshirt that says *San Francisco Zoo*, she is so beautiful. Clear, smooth skin, full lips, bright blue eyes with long dark lashes…she is everything I am not when I look in the mirror.

She glances around for a moment and then when her eyes land on me, she offers me a large smile. Nalgene water bottle in hand, she walks up to my table.

"Please tell me you're Everly," she says on a wince. "Or else I just smiled like a fool at a complete stranger."

Ugh, she's even personable.

I chuckle, standing up as I hold my hand out. "I'm Everly. It's so nice to meet you, Maple."

She takes my hand in hers and shakes it. "It's so nice to meet you."

We both take a seat. "Do you want me to grab you a drink?" I ask her.

She shakes her head. "Coffee at this hour means I'll never get to sleep, plus I'm headed to the gym after this. I, uh, I joined the one around the corner from my apartment, and it seems very intimidating."

"Which one?" I ask.

"Bay City."

"Oh, I know which one you're talking about. I've been there a few times when I was meeting with a bride who was a personal trainer. It's a wonderful gym, but I know why you might feel intimidated. Lots of weight equipment, lots of men claiming their areas."

"Yes," she says demurely. "That was my fear when I joined, but I also really like using the weightlifting machines, and it's right around the corner from where I live, so hopefully I can make it work."

"I'm sure you will. Just put your headphones on and get to work."

She smiles, and it lights up her face beautifully. "That's the plan. Plus Polly thinks it'll be a great way to meet someone."

"Oh?" I ask. "Are you looking to date?"

"Not really, but you know how friends are when they're in love: They want you to be in love too."

"Oh, I know exactly what you mean," I say. "My boss, Maggie, has recently fallen in love and she's all about trying to hook me up with someone. Apparently, there's a brother of a groom from a wedding she just did who she wants me to meet."

"Is he your type?"

"No idea." I sigh. "But you know how friends are—they think they know what you want, when in reality they couldn't be more wrong." Or *sisters* for that matter…

Freaking Tomothy.

"I had that happen," Maple says as she brings her legs up and sits cross-legged on her chair. "A friend back in Denver tried to hook me up with her boyfriend's friend. Turned out this guy was obsessed with collecting napkins his dates used, and that tipped me over the edge."

"Oh my God." I cringe. "I just had a date like that the other night with a guy named Tomothy that my sister set up. It was so terrible." I lean in and whisper, "He said the vagina was too complicated for him."

"Oof, that's a big no."

We chuckle and it's such a sweet sound, the perfect little laugh that anyone could fall in love with. In all honesty, I can see why Hardy wants to try to get back together with Maple. She's so…easy to talk to and soft-spoken, but she also doesn't shy away from conversation. She seems like she'd be able to soothe the animals she works with using just her voice. Not to mention her smile, her laugh, her freaking gorgeous eyes…

Yup, I don't stand a chance.

Why on Earth would Hardy even look my way when he has someone like Maple right in front of him, especially given their history?

He wouldn't.

"Well, I guess we should probably talk about Polly and the wedding," Maple says.

"We should, yes," I reply as I flip open my notebook, ready to take notes.

"I first want to say," she starts, "that I'm embarrassed that I have to ask for help, but I'm not going to let my pride hold me back. I'm just not good at this, and since there are no other bridesmaids and the moms are busy planning the wedding, I feel much better that you offer this service."

"Of course," I say. "It's my absolute pleasure. I love doing this kind of stuff. I love weddings, and I want you and Polly to have the best time. I think sometimes, as we move through the process of a wedding, we forget that it isn't just about the bride and the groom—well, it mainly is—but it's also about those last moments you have with your friends before you're married, or those last moments with your family, and I think those moments should be cherished. Bridal showers and bachelorette parties offer us the opportunities to almost have that last hurrah before everything changes…if that makes sense."

"You know, I never looked at it that way," Maple says. "You're completely right."

"And that's why I'm here, to make sure you enjoy these planning weeks with Polly but also give her a beautiful party celebrating her and Ken."

Maple smiles. "I can see why Polly was excited about hiring you. You put me at ease right away."

"Just doing my job," I say with a wink. "Now, would you like to discuss the bridal shower?"

"I'd love to. I don't really have any ideas. If I was left to my own devices, I would probably have a flamingo-themed party and leave it at that."

I chuckle. "I'm not opposed to that idea, but I think flamingo themes can get cheesy very quickly. We could do classy flamingo. So we can pull colors from the bird like pinks and salmons, add in some tropical plants with monstera and palm leaves. Perhaps sprinkle in a touch of gold here and there. There's a curtain of bamboo we can rent. Let me pull up a picture." I tap away on my iPad and bring it up. Maple smiles at the picture. "We can rent a few of these at a cheaper cost and use them as the backdrop for central picture-taking locations, the food table, and gift area. We also have these beautiful woven wicker chairs that might be fun for the bride and groom to sit in—"

"Bride and groom?" Maple asks.

"Oh yes, did Polly not tell you? They want a joint party."

"Hmm, she didn't," Maple says, worrying her lip. "Does that mean the best man will be there?"

I catch the way she asks with a wince, as if she's afraid of my answer. Hell, I know exactly what's going on in her mind right now:

Please say no.

Please say no.

Unfortunately for Maple…

"Yes, he'll be there."

Her shoulders sag as she glances off to the right.

"Is that going to be okay?" I ask.

She bites her lip and then looks shyly at me. "This is going to be really awkward, and I'm sorry that I'm dragging you into this, but the best man and I used to date."

"Ah, I see," I say, my ears on full alert for anything she might say. "And from the look in your eyes, I'm going to assume things didn't end so well?"

"No, they did," she says. "I mean, I was kind of angry at the time, but I understood why we had to go our separate ways. That doesn't mean I was happy with it."

"I can understand that," I say. "Relationships can be very complicated, especially when there's a friend group involved."

"Yeah, this one was very complicated." Her eyes meet mine. "Have you met Hardy?"

Yes.

And I think he's perfect.

And wonderful.

And I'm so jealous that he wants you.

"I have," I say. "He was the one who introduced me to Polly. He and Hudson invested in Magical Moments by Maggie. That's one of the reasons we'll be able to meet at a storefront next time and not a coffee house."

"I see," Maple says. "I haven't really been in touch, and whenever Polly talks about him, I tell her to stop. I don't want to hear it. So I guess I'm out of the loop on what he's been doing on the business side."

I nod and consider telling her what he's done. How he's left his dad's company and started a new one with his brother, Jude, and the Cane brothers. How he's focused on helping, on what he loves best, rather than how he can make his father the next buck. But it doesn't feel like it's my business. That seems like something he needs to tell her, which will inevitably make her fall for him all over again, because how could she not?

Sigh.

"Well, perhaps you should catch up," I suggest, hating the thought.

She shakes her head. "Oh no, I don't want to be doing that. I just want to get through these wedding activities and then move on with my life." Her eyes meet mine again. "I hope that doesn't sound too cruel."

"Not at all," I say. "I can understand not wanting to be around someone you used to date, especially if it was serious. Was it?"

It lasted three years, Everly, of course it was serious.

"Um, I don't know," she says, which surprises me.

I half expected her to say that there was a ring involved but she never accepted. Going into this, I was thinking that to each other, they were the ones that got away. The timing was off, but the love was right.

But not knowing if it was serious, that's...that's new information.

"I know that might sound weird," she says. "But with Hardy, it was just...fun. You know? We had a conversation our senior year about our plans and what we were going to do about continuing our relationship, but before that conversation, we were just enjoying life. Studying, partying with our friends, it was simple...very simple before it got complicated."

"I see," I say. "I'm sorry if that was too much of a personal question—I just want to make sure I completely understand the situation."

"No, not too personal at all. I'm open to talking about it." She shrugs. "I just think I'm a different person now than I was then. What I might have thought was serious back then is probably not serious at all in the grand scheme of things."

"I totally get that. I've had some of those moments and I've seen them play out at events too. Sure, you want the event to be amazing, but when you look at the bigger picture, if the centerpieces were off, is that really going to dampen your outlook on life? Not really."

She chuckles. "I don't know, Polly's mom might think differently."

"Ooo, well, I'm glad I'm not a part of the wedding planning. I think working with you will be fun."

"I agree," Maple says with a smile. "I think this will be a great partnership."

Yes…it will. I look at the beautiful, smart woman across from me, the one I can't help but like, despite my jealousy. A great partnership indeed.

"I'm surprised you're talking to me," Ember says over the phone as I grab my dinner from the microwave and take a seat at my bistro table, alone once again. I'm surprised I'm talking to her as well after what she put me through, but desperate times call for desperate measures.

"The only reason I called is because I need some advice and I know you'll tell it to me straight."

"I pride myself on that," she quips.

"As long as you don't pride yourself on setting people up, that's all that matters."

"For the record," she says, an edge to her voice, "Trevor told me Tomothy was a cool dude, so I thought that was a sign of approval. After speaking with my husband, I've come to find that *cool dude* could mean a variety of things. I also learned to not ask him questions while he's playing Overcooked because he doesn't pay attention—he's too busy chopping and making sure he doesn't burn the rice."

"Uh, okay. Not sure what you're talking about there, but we're moving on because the last thing I want to do is talk about Tomothy."

"Don't blame you. On the way out of the restaurant, he spat a loogie and then examined it. Got on the ground and everything. The dude is not a winner."

"Disgusting," I say. "And moving on. I'm calling you because I'm in a bit of a predicament."

"Does this have to do with Hardy Hopper and your insane crush?"

"Sort of," I say, feeling my cheeks stain with embarrassment as I dip my fork into my pot roast. "I met Maple today, his ex."

"Really? What was she like?"

"Perfect," I say. "And I don't say that in a mean way. She just is. She's perfect. She has a very sweet disposition, soft-spoken voice, she's stunning, and she's so smart. She can hold a great conversation, is very humble, and seems like she's a great friend. She's the whole package."

"Are we upset about that?"

"I mean, does it suck? Yes, but also hard to hate someone who was really nice to talk to."

"That's annoying. If she was awful, this would have been easier."

"I don't know," I say before taking a bite of my pot roast. "I would have hated seeing Hardy go after someone who is awful or rude. That's not who I could see him with, but I could see him with Maple. I see why he wants to try to get back with her. It was obvious from the first five minutes I spent with her."

"Okay, so then what's the dilemma?"

"Well." I cross one leg over the other. "She was very adamant about not being around Hardy and not wanting to speak to him. She confessed that they were together and that they went their separate ways. She was a little upset about how it ended, but now she's a different person and she just doesn't want to go down that road again. She also said she wasn't sure how serious it was between them. So now I feel like I'm in this weird position because a part of me is like…yay! She wants nothing to do with him, let's get Hardy to move on and move on to me. But the other part is thinking did I just hear what I wanted to hear because I still want that chance with him?"

"Ahh, I see. Well, did she say anything about having feelings for him?"

"No, not really. She was very disinterested."

"So then, tell him that."

I nod even though she can't see me. "And after, should I ask him out?"

"Oh my God, Everly. No!"

"Why not?" I ask on a pout.

"Because the man is pining after another girl. Can we move past this, please? Do I need to set you up with another Tomothy?"

"No, for the love of God, please don't." I push my food around with my fork, taking in the emptiness of my apartment and how I wish there was someone else here with me, sharing these microwaved meals and enjoying the peace of the night. "I just think if she's not interested—"

"But you don't really know that after one conversation. I think you need to give it a chance, see how she reacts when she sees him after years apart—that could stir up feelings."

"Why are you on his side?" I ask.

"I'm not on his side. I'm trying to help you avoid heartache. I don't want you pining after a man who's interested in someone else. You're to do two jobs where Hardy and Maple are concerned. Fulfill your responsibilities as a bridesmaid for hire because, first and foremost, Maggie and the company will always come first. And then you're to be the middleman for Hardy until he can handle it himself. That's it. Nothing else. I love you, Everly, but that's all it could ever be, and you need to remember that."

I sigh sadly, knowing she has a point.

"I hate that you're right."

"I know. It sucks, but I think that's the best approach. And remember what I said, put yourself out there, try to date someone else. Get your mind off him."

"Yeah, sure," I say. "That's not what I wanted to hear."

"But it's what you needed to hear. He wants someone else. I hate to be harsh about it, but you…you don't want to be me, Everly. You saw what happened to me in college, when I was going after someone else who wasn't interested. It didn't end well for me, and I don't want you to get hurt. Trust me on this, please."

I think back to when Ember was in college. I was still in high school, but I remember her freshman year and the emotional torment she went through over a boy she thought was interested in her, but in fact was just using her to get close to her friend. It was a terrible situation that brought her back home. Luckily, she met Trevor after that, and he showed her what it truly meant to be loved, but it was a tough situation for her, so I get why she doesn't want me to go through something along the same lines.

"Okay," I say. "I'll push him aside and try to find someone else to focus my attention on."

"Thank you," she says softly. And then after a few seconds, she says, "Want to know more detail about Tomothy's loogie?"

"Good night," I say into the phone and then hang up.

CHAPTER TEN
HARDY

To: Hardy Hopper
From: Everly Plum
Subject: I Made Contact

Henrietta,

Contact has been made with Syrup. Out of respect to client confidentiality, I will try to keep this brief with few details but also offer you some information that will be helpful.

She is not excited about being in the same room as you.

She said things ended amicably, but she was slightly upset about it.

She said she had a lot of fun with you but wasn't sure how serious your relationship was.

Got the impression that she's been thinking about dating. Polly has been trying to set her up.

That's pretty much it. I didn't want to do too much digging out of fear of being too obvious, but yeah, seems like she's not very interested at the moment.

Not sure that's what you wanted to hear, but that's what I know so far.

The Prof

To: *Everly Plum*
From: *Hardy Hopper*
Subject: *RE: I Made Contact*

Professor,

*Huh…*scratches head**

She didn't think it was serious? If that's the case, why was she upset when it ended? Seems slightly contradictory. I will admit we didn't really talk about the future at all. The only time we did was when our senior year was coming to an end, and I told her I would follow her.

I think there's something she's not telling you or Polly that we need to get to the bottom of.

Think you're up for the task?

I don't think this mission is over, Professor, and I need you now more than ever.

Henrietta

P.S. Who is she thinking about dating? Did she happen to ask you to set her up with anyone?

To: *Hardy Hopper*
From: *Everly Plum*
Subject: *RE: I Made Contact*

Henrietta,

I will help as much as I can. I can't make any promises though. We will have to tread carefully because I don't want her to know I'm working for the enemy. I established a good rapport, and I don't want to lose that.

And no, she didn't ask me to set her up with anyone. Trust me, I'm having a hard enough time finding someone for myself, especially after the nightmare of a date I went on the other night.

Looks like it's going to be a tough road, Henrietta. Not sure of your chances.

The Prof

To: Everly Plum
From: Hardy Hopper
Subject: Never Give up

Professor,

I think there is one thing you need to know about me. I don't give up easily, meaning this new information is not going to deter me. I'm going to request a meeting to discuss the bridal shower, and I think you, Syrup, and I all need to be there. Let's get the initial awkwardness over and done with and work from there.

Can you schedule an appointment? I'm back in town tomorrow, and I want to offer up one of our properties for the shower venue. It's a storefront that is being used for all different kinds of events. The best part is that it has a spacious courtyard in the back. Kind of a diamond in the rough. Think we could meet there?

Also I'm going to need to hear more about your date. Details will be needed.

Henrietta

To: Hardy Hopper
From: Everly Plum
Subject: Here We Go…

Henrietta,

Syrup is going to be livid, but I think you're right. As it is my number one job to look out for the bride, I think we need to get the initial meeting over and done with in case there's any lashing out or kicking—never know how people might react.

I would hate to see you get kicked in the middle of the bridal shower. A comical crotch shot doesn't quite set the tone for romance in the air. I'll figure out when she's available and then shoot over a time.

And also…the details of my date will remain close to my chest. Nothing from that night needs to be repeated.

I'll be in touch.

The Prof

"Are you nervous, man?" Brody asks me as I check myself out in the reflection of the window one last time.

"Do I seem nervous?"

"You're really fidgety," he says, looking me up and down. "I don't think I've ever seen this side of you. I don't like it."

Brody is Maggie's man. When Haisley was getting married, he introduced us to Maggie, who then stepped in as a bridesmaid. Brody was also working for my dad at the time and, well, I won't get into the details, but let's just say Brody works for us now and he's quickly becoming one of our biggest assets. He has this innovative idea of turning old abandoned storefronts into pop-up stores and event spaces. Hudson and I jumped on it, and now he and I are standing in one of the spaces, taking in the potential that's surrounding us.

The idea is that the store is a blank space to rent, and the renter can use it for whatever they want. Business meetings, a temporary storefront, party venue—you name it, we offer it. And this is one of my favorite finds. We call it The Courtyard for obvious reasons. The front of the store is airy with white brick walls and large street-facing windows and some false walls to break up the space from being too loft-like. But as you move toward the back, it opens up into a decently sized courtyard with vines climbing up the brick walls and a painted cement floor that doesn't take away from the space, only adds to it. The courtyard has plenty of room for eight to ten round tables with chairs, and a space for a head table. I think it would be perfect for the bridal shower and if not that, then definitely the bachelor/bachelorette party.

"I'm a little nervous. Should I not be nervous?" I ask.

"I don't know." He shrugs. "You tell me."

"I don't know," I say. "I've never been in this situation before."

"Because you're so charming and wonderful that why would you ever be in an awkward situation with a girl, right?" Brody asks as he rocks on his heels.

I look him up and down. "You know, I don't like how comfortable you've become with me."

He lets out a roar of a laugh. "Because I'm not up your ass seeking your approval anymore? Sorry, I can go back to that if you'd like."

"I might." He chuckles some more and then grips his stomach on a wince. "You okay?" I ask him.

"Yeah, just been dealing with a stitch all day. Went a little hard on the running." He pats me on the back. "Everything with Maple will be fine. I'm sure when she sees you it won't be awkward at all, more like she's coming home."

"That might be stretching it," I say just as Everly walks through the front door.

Dressed in all black once again, with her hair slicked back into her signature tight bun, she chose a pair of dress pants and a blouse this time. Her heels click across the painted cement floor as she takes in the space.

"This looks amazing," she says as she walks up to us. I meet her halfway and greet her with a kiss on her cheek. When I pull away, I catch her brilliant green eyes studying me for a moment before she turns to Brody. "Hey, Brody."

He stays put and waves. "I'm not cultured enough to pull off the check kiss as a greeting."

Everly smirks. "I think that's a smart decision."

He taps his temple. "Not just a hat rack."

"Apparently. Maggie is a lucky lady."

"I'll be sure to tell her that, because after what happened this morning, I'm not sure she's considering herself very lucky at the moment."

"What did you do?" Everly deadpans.

"Well, did you know that her very expensive hair straightener is not supposed to be used to iron my clothes?"

"Oh my God, Brody," Everly says.

He holds his hands out in defense. "It was just the collar of my shirt. It was a quick zip of the iron, but she got angry and told me not to touch her things. I then asked her what qualified as her things because I planned on kissing her and if she considered her lips her things, then I wouldn't be able to kiss her, even though I consider her lips to be mine. Anyway, let's just say I had to chase her down the apartment hallway to get a kiss goodbye."

"How are you with someone?" I ask.

"Got me," Brody says, shrugging casually. "I marvel at my ability to have landed Maggie every day."

Turning away from him, I address Everly. "Is she coming?"

"She is," Everly says. "It took a lot of coaxing, but I convinced her that it would be easier to get the initial meeting out of the way before the actual bridal shower. She agreed, but do not come on too strong, Hardy."

"I won't," I say.

"And don't try to talk to her. Just...a simple nod of the head, maybe a curt hello. Don't try to ask her out."

"Come on," I say, my lips twisting to the side. "As if I would do that."

"You might," Everly says. "People do stupid things when they're nervous."

"I'm not nervous," I say.

"Yes, you are," Brody says, completely oblivious to me trying to play this situation cool. "We were just talking about how you're fidgety, and I've never seen you like this before. I think there's sweat on your forehead."

I swipe at my forehead with the back of my hand. "There's no sweat."

"I saw glistening," Brody says.

I turn toward him. "You know, I don't think I need you here after all. I can handle everything, so feel free to go home."

"Ooof, I'd rather not," Brody says. "I kind of want to watch this reunion play out. I'm invested now."

"Jesus," I mutter just as the door to the shop opens.

My eyes fly to the front where we all turn to watch Maple timidly walking in. Leaning in close to me, Brody whispers, "Be...cool."

"You be cool," I whisper back.

Everly shoots us a glare. "Both of you be cool." Then she heads down toward the front of the shop where she greets Maple.

When she comes out of the sunlight blasting through the front windows, I get a better look at her. Still in her khaki pants from the zoo and a green *San Francisco Zoo* polo, her hair is pulled back into a high ponytail and, like always, she's wearing minimal makeup.

She hasn't changed a bit.

When she walks closer, I keep my eyes on her, watching how she's obviously looking at everything but me. And when she and Everly reach us, an uncomfortable silence falls over the group.

Yup, this is awkward.

I know she doesn't want to talk to me.

Brody and Everly know.

Maple, I believe, wants to flee the minute she comes within five feet of me.

And now I wish there wasn't an audience for the initial greeting because I feel like all eyes are on us. Scratch that—I know all eyes are on us.

After a few seconds, Everly says, "Uh, Maple, you remember Hardy."

Jesus.

As if we didn't date for three years.

Of course she remembers me.

Finally, Maple's eyes meet mine, and I'm surprised to be greeted with a kind smile. "Yes, hello, Hardy."

Then more silence.

More tension.

More…unbearable awkwardness.

Doesn't help that from the corner of my eye I can see Brody grinning like an idiot as he looks between the two of us.

This is fucking stupid.

This should be easy; we're just making it harder than it should be.

I can greet her just like I greeted Everly.

I can keep it together and not say much, but this "practically strangers" act doesn't need to happen. I can greet her appropriately.

Trying to lessen this tension, I take a step forward to press a kiss to her cheek, but unfortunately for me, Brody takes a step forward at the same time to introduce himself, which knocks me off balance.

And listen, I'm not a slight guy. I have a good amount of muscle on my bones.

And Brody, well, he's about the same body size as me.

But to my horror, with one bump of his shoulder into mine, I lose my balance, tripping and falling forward...straight into Maple's unsuspecting chest.

A resounding thud fills the empty space as my face connects with her covered cleavage.

Yup, right into what some might call...her bosom.

Smack dab, right in the center.

And because she's much smaller than me, she can't withstand my weight, and together we topple over to the floor.

Her ample breasts cushion my face and break my fall.

My nose is shock-absorbed by her cleavage.

A ripple of bosom floats against my cheek as my mind screams "oh fuck!"

"Oh my God," Everly shouts once we're solidly on the floor.

From what I can feel—you know, since I can't see, given my face has been suctioned into her shirt—her legs are splayed out, her hands squirming beneath her while she attempts to free herself.

"Shit, fuck, I'm sorry," I say as I scramble to find my footing.

There's some shuffling around, some grunting, but when I finally gain control of the situation and pop up—off her breasts—I lift off the ground, humiliation crawling up my back as Maple scrambles to stand as well.

"Are you okay?" Everly asks, helping Maple straighten out her shirt.

"Fine," Maple says as she glances at me.

Her face is red.

Mine feels like lava.

And Brody is just standing there with a stupid fucking smile on his face.

Before he can say something moronic, I make the executive decision to skip the cheek kiss and lift my hand in a hello instead. "Uh…nice to, uh…nice to see you again," I say awkwardly as I brush off my hands, still feeling the impact of her shirt button on my forehead.

"Nice to see you," Maple says as if someone is forcing her.

Brody looks between us and then rocks on his heels. "And that is why I don't go for the cheek kiss."

God, I hate him right now.

"Maybe if you didn't bump into me," I say through the side of my mouth.

"I was trying to be polite and introduce myself. I didn't know that you shared the same body mass as a crisp fall leaf and you were going to blow right over." He grips my arm. "Don't you work out?"

"Yes, I work out," I say as I brush his hand off me.

"Huh, you know, it looks like it, but you took that hit like a grandma against a three-hundred-pound linesman. Maybe we should have your balance checked."

"My balance is fine," I say through clenched teeth.

"I don't know," Everly says, which causes my eyes to shoot to hers. "You did topple over pretty easily."

"Oh." Brody snaps his fingers. "Maybe he wanted to. You know, because of their history. Maybe he wanted to put his face on her breasts as a greeting." He says this as if Maple's not standing right in front of us!

"I did not want to do that," I say to clear the air. "I was trying to give you a kiss."

"What?" Maple asks, looking horrified.

"On the cheek!" I say quickly. "A kiss on the cheek. Not a kiss on the lips. Just on the cheek like I did with Everly when she came in. Like this," I say as I lean in toward Everly who isn't paying attention, so when I lean in to kiss her cheek, she moves her head, and my lips land on her nose instead.

"Oh God," she says, backing away and wiping her nose.

"Dude, what are you doing?" Brody asks, a wince on his face. I can't tell if he's disgusted with me or if he's still in pain.

"Fuck," I grumble as I stand tall again. "I meant to kiss your cheek."

Brody leans in. "You missed by a lot, man."

"I know I fucking did. I was just trying to show what I was trying to do," I say as my skin starts to prickle with embarrassment.

"Well, do you want to try on me? I'm the only one here you haven't assaulted yet," Brody says. "But I can't make any promises that I won't pucker up."

My nostrils flare as my eyes burn into his.

He nervously laughs. "Or we can just assume what a kiss on the cheek from you is like and try to move past this situation of you falling face first into your ex-girlfriend's bosom, followed by a nose peck to your event planner."

I catch Everly swiping at her nose again before she clears her throat. "How about we just move on and spare everyone the secondhand embarrassment."

"That would be great," Maple says, avoiding eye contact with me again.

"I mean, I'd appreciate the change in topic—I'm starting to sweat out of sheer horror for someone else," Brody says.

"I wasn't trying to kiss anyone," I say, just to clear the air one more time.

"You kind of were, dude," Brody whispers.

"Not like that," I growl. "It was purely friendly."

Everly clears her throat and looks me in the eyes. "We're moving on, so let's start by walking the property." Everly moves to the front and starts spouting off ideas on how to use the space while I follow behind with Brody.

Fuck, not a great start to this meeting. Nope, I'm coming off as the bumbling idiot who apparently has the balance of a ninety-year-old granny.

Breaking through my thoughts, Brody leans in close and whispers, "Everly told us both to be cool, and I don't think you're holding up your end of the bargain, man."

I glare at him. "Don't make me murder you before I leave."

"Hey, just trying to help," he replies in defense and then grips his side.

"It's not needed," I say between clenched teeth.

"What do you think, Hardy?" Everly asks.

I pause, feeling like a student that's been called on who wasn't paying attention.

"Uhhh…"

"He wasn't listening," Brody says. "Too busy sending silent murder threats in my direction."

What the fuck have I ever done to this guy?

Everly holds her composure, but her green eyes flash. "I was asking if you thought this space would work for a bar. Have it set up right at the front—people can drop off gifts and then grab a drink."

"Oh yeah, that works," I say as I stuff my hands in my pockets. "Is that, uh, is that cool with you, Maple?"

Her eyes meet mine again, and it feels odd…having her look at me after all these years.

It feels odd because there's something missing between us.

There's no spark.

No intrigue.

No lovesick eyes hoping and wishing for a rekindling.

And why is that?

Because of how things ended between us?

Or maybe because a great deal of time has passed, distance between us, which has dimmed the lights.

Either way, I don't plan on giving up anytime soon. If Polly and Ken can make their relationship work, then why the hell can't I make it work with Maple?

There's no reason.

I'm just going to have to put in the time, and I have no problem doing that.

"Whatever is best. I really have no opinion," Maple says.

"Well, I just want to make sure you like the setup," I reply.

"I have no idea about space, so really no opinion."

"Okay, but if you have an opinion, I want to hear it."

She nods. "No opinion."

"Are you sure, because—"

"She has no opinion, man," Brody says as he leans against a pole. "Christ." I shoot another glare over to him and all he has to say for himself is a simple shrug. "What? She doesn't."

Everly steps in before I can shoot off on Brody. "No opinion is great for me—means I can work around the room. Let me make a note." She jots something down on her notepad and then leads us toward the middle of the space. Maple's sticking close to her as Brody and I hang back.

"You're still not acting cool," Brody whispers as Everly points out the bathrooms to Maple and says something about having a basket in the women's room with toiletry supplies. "Your voice is all shaky and you're rambling."

"I don't need a fucking review from you," I say to him.

"Whoa, where's all the hostility coming from?" Brody asks.

"Uh, you're not helping the situation."

"What situation is that?"

"Uh, not making me look like a fool."

He winces. "Dude, there's only so much we can do. *You* need to stop acting like a fool, that would be job number one."

"I'm not. I'm just…I'm flustered."

"That much is obvious," he says with an eye roll.

"Can you at least try not to point shit out?" I say. "It's not helping."

"I think I'm helping just fine—"

"Hey, can you two pay attention?" Everly asks. "Why be here if you're not going to help?"

Brody points his finger at me. "We are, but he keeps second-guessing everything he's saying to Maple."

Oh my fucking God.

What did I just say? Is the man not listening?

"No, I'm not," I say. "I'm not second-guessing." I look at Maple. "I'm not."

"Then what were we just talking about?" Brody asks, actually looking confused.

Has he lost his mind?

"We were talking about how you should probably leave, since you offer zero value to this meeting," I say.

"I offer value. Look," Brody says pointing to the ceiling. "I helped paint that."

"How is that value?" I ask.

"Shows Maple that you know how to hire people who care about the work they do. Helps impress her. Aren't you impressed, Maple?"

Yup, I'm going to kill him. Actually murder one of our employees.

What the hell has gotten into him?

"Uh, sure," Maple says, looking so clearly uncomfortable that I can actually feel the sweat forming on my upper lip. It wasn't there before, but it sure as hell is there now.

"See, she's impressed." Brody elbows me. "Told you I was offering value. You're welcome."

"I think she's being polite."

Brody leans in and whispers, "Dude, telling her what she thinks? Not a great way to win her back."

Actual steam pours out of my ears as I stare down Brody with murder on my mind.

What the actual fuck?

The tension in the room grows so thick, so ghastly dense with humiliation, that I almost find it hard to breathe.

Thankfully, once again Everly steps up. "You know what, Brody, I think you should show Maple the loft space while I speak to Hardy by myself."

Ehhh, on the other hand…

"No, I don't think that's a great idea," I say, worried immediately that Brody is going to say something offhand to Maple. "Maybe we just go to the courtyard."

"It'll be fine, right, Brody? Because you're just going to talk about the loft and nothing else, right?" Everly urges him. Maple glances between all three of us, a question in her look. Fuck, what must be going through her head at the moment?

"I could talk about the loft for hours. Did you know I painted up there as well. I can show you my brush strokes," Brody says and then offers his arm to Maple to guide her up toward the loft. When she doesn't take it, he gestures toward the stairs instead. "Okay…right this way, milady." He pauses and then adds, "No, not milady. Milady is Maggie, and I doubt she'd like me calling anyone else that. Forget the whole *milady* thing. Right this way, Maple. Not milady, just to be clear, if you're anyone's lady, you're Hardy's lady." My eyes nearly pop out of my head, but before I can correct him, he corrects himself. "I mean, no, you're no one's lady, you're your own lady. No one owns you. Woman, yay!" He fist-pumps the air while I pinch the bridge of my nose.

He is unhinged, and I don't like him going up there with Maple because who the fuck knows what he's going to say.

But there is no stopping them as they walk up the stairs. When they're at the top, Everly pushes me toward the bathrooms so we're out of sight. "What the hell are you doing?" she whispers.

"What the hell am I doing?" I ask, pointing to my chest. "What the hell are you doing? You really think sending Brody up there with Maple is a good idea? He's a fucking loose cannon."

"I'm not concerned about Brody. I'm concerned about you. This is a train wreck, Hardy. I'm actually starting to sweat over here and I don't ever sweat."

"You're sweating?" I ask. "I'm fucking roasting with embarrassment. Brody won't shut up. He's making this worse. You need to send him away."

"He's not going to leave, he's too proud of his space."

"Then you go one way with him, and I'll go one way with Maple."

"Uh, not going to happen," she whispers. "She specifically told me not to leave her alone with you."

"Why? Is she afraid I'm going to bite?" I ask.

"No, probably afraid you might motorboat her again."

My face falls flat. "I did not motorboat her, I tripped and fell into her breasts."

"Ah, yes, isn't that what every man says when he finds himself nose deep in a pair of tits?"

Not…funny.

Crouching down and keeping my voice low, I say, "Do you really think as a way of greeting someone I haven't seen in years I would stick my head in their breasts?"

"I don't know, Hardy, you do seem to be a bit unhinged at the moment."

"I would never do that," I nearly shout but keep things contained. "I was going in for a kiss on the cheek, like I did with you. Brody tripped me and then *bam*, face to boob. That's not my fault. And it's also not my fault that you moved your face when I was trying to demonstrate what I was trying to do, thereby kissing you on the nose. That was unintended."

"It was a wet kiss."

My brows collide as I close the space between us, leaving our faces mere inches apart. "It was not."

"It took everything in me not to wipe it off. A fresh breeze from the AC still makes my nose light up."

"Not...funny, Everly."

"Uh, it's Professor to you, and I'm not trying to be funny, Henrietta. I'm telling you facts. That was a wet kiss."

"That was not a wet kiss." I puff my chest and then grip her cheek with my hand. "If you want to see a wet kiss, I'll show you a wet kiss," I say just as a throat is cleared off to the side.

Startled, I leap back, as if Everly is lava.

Unfortunately for me, my leap doesn't land me safely on the floor, oh no, because that would be too simple.

Nope. My startlement instead sends me backward, flat into the wall behind me...the very false wall behind me. You can only imagine, my weight is no match for it and before I know it, I'm tipping backward, the wall careening to the floor with me in a loud crash.

Drywall cracks around me, dust shoots up into the air, as I land on my back—and a shrill cry breaks out as Brody hurries to my side, Maple trailing in his wake.

"That wall took me an hour to paint and set up, and you just broke it," he yells, not bothering to check if anything on my body is wounded.

In case you were wondering, just my pride at this point.

Confused as to what just happened, I say, "Why wasn't the wall secured?"

"I hadn't had a chance yet. Why are you acting like Donkey Kong and tossing your man body into walls?" Brody asks.

"I didn't toss my man body into the wall. I was startled."

"Because we caught you almost kissing Everly?" he asks.

"Uh, no, I wasn't going to kiss her."

"We heard you say it, didn't we, Maple?" Brody continues.

Still on the floor, I glance up at Maple who nods. "I think you said you were going to show her a wet kiss."

Mother of fuck!

"I was not," I say, defending myself like a whiny child because honestly I'm exhausted at this point.

"Your hand was on her cheek," Brody says as he stands.

"Because I was frustrated," I say as I stand too. I dust off my clothes and glance around the room at the people incriminating me, who should be on my side.

"What could Everly ever do that frustrates you?" Brody asks.

I push my hand through my hair, hating every second of this goddamn meeting. This is not how I expected it to go, not even close. Brody and Everly are supposed to be friends, cohorts, aides in my mission to win back Maple, but for the love of God, they feel like sworn enemies—Brody more than anything.

"I'm not frustrated with Everly. I'm frustrated with you," I say to Brody.

"How does being frustrated with me make you want to kiss Everly?" He tosses his hands up in the air. "Color me confused."

I'm about to blow a gasket.

"He wasn't going to kiss me," Everly finally chimes in. "We were talking about how he accidentally kissed my nose, then I told him it was wet, and for some reason he thought it necessary to show me that it wasn't a wet kiss—and that's when you guys walked in. Now this all seems ridiculous. Can we perhaps act like a bunch of adults and move on with this conversation?"

"I'd like that," Maple says, relief in her voice.

"Great. Shall we move to the main space in the courtyard?"

"Yes," Maple answers, leading the way. She brushes by me, feeling even icier than she did before.

Fucking great.

"Okay, I'll send over the mockups for the decorations and then you can approve. I also have the party favors on my list, and food. I'll be in touch shortly," Everly says as Maple opens the front door to exit.

"Thank you, Everly. I really appreciate all of this. I'd be lost without you."

"Not a problem at all. That's what I'm here for. And like I said, day of, I'll guide you, but you'll be able to spend more time with Polly."

"That would be ideal. Thank you." And then to my surprise, Maple gives Everly a hug.

When they part, Maple waves at Brody and then looks at me. With a stiff smile, she gives me a nod and then takes off.

Everly shuts the door behind her and then spins around to face me. "That was a disaster."

"I fucking know." I turn to Brody, who is now leaning against one of the white brick walls, this one most definitely not false.

He breathes out a heavy sigh. "I feel like I blacked out. What happened?"

"What happened?" I shout. "Jesus Christ, Brody, you lost your god-damn mind."

"Did I? There was so much pressure to be cool that I felt like there were moments where I wasn't cool. Were there?"

I look at Everly whose jaw is slack just like mine, both of us in awe.

Let me recap for you…

Not only did Brody make little comments here and there about me being awkward around Maple, me trying to kiss Everly, and proceeded to bump into me every chance he got, but when we were back in the courtyard, he told Maple that during Haisley's wedding festivities he saw me with my shirt off in Bora-Bora and that the, and I quote, "old man still has it."

"You are not allowed to be anywhere near Maple ever again," I say. "You were a disaster, an absolute fucking disaster."

Brody dabs at his brow. "Ooof, I'm sweating. Why don't I feel so good? I feel all sweaty and pukey, and I have this pain right here that won't go away." He grips his side. "Did you bump into me in my side? It all feels so distant now that I can't recall."

"You bumped into me," I tell him.

"I almost passed out in the courtyard." He takes a deep breath. "Did you see me almost pass out?"

"No, I was too caught up with the way you explained to Maple how proportionate my nipples are to my pecs."

"I said that?" he asks and then chuckles. "I mean, could have been worse."

"What the hell is wrong with you?" I yell. "Christ, Brody. That was supposed to be an easy interaction, a quiet one, just getting used to being in the same room together, and you fucked it up."

"To be fair," Everly says, "you weren't as cool as you thought you were. You did press your face to her breasts within the first minute of her being here."

"Because of him," I say, gesturing to Brody, who now looks a little gray.

Everly must notice too because she says, "Uh, Brody, are you okay?"

Sweat drips down his forehead as he sinks lower to the ground. "Man...down," he says right before he passes out on the floor.

"Oh my God!" Everly shouts as we both crouch down and roll him to his side. I quickly check his pulse and notice how clammy he is.

"Still breathing, but pulse low," I say. "We need to take him to the hospital, now. There's one that's not that far away."

"We can take my car," Everly says.

"Help me lift him up," I say. Together, we slip his arms over our shoulders. I'm bearing most of the weight, and we race out of the shop, not even bothering to lock up, and head straight to Everly's car that's parked out front.

We set him in the back of the car, and I join him as Everly takes a seat on the driver's side. Within seconds, the car is on, and we're pulled out on the road. She presses a button on her steering wheel and says, "Call Maggie." The speakers in her car make a dialing sound and then it starts ringing. After the second ring, Maggie answers.

"Hey, how was the meeting? Did she love the venue?"

"Maggie, Brody passed out in the shop. We have him in the back of the car, and we're rushing him to the hospital."

"What? What do you mean he passed out?"

"He was acting really strange during the meeting, and I thought that maybe he was just nervous, but then he started sweating, complaining about pain, and then fell to the ground. He's still breathing, but he's clammy and currently unresponsive."

"Oh my God," Maggie shouts. "I'm…I'm in Almond Bay right now, at least two hours away if I don't run into traffic."

"Well, we can handle him for now, but I would get here as soon as you can. I'm not sure what's wrong, but it could be his appendix or something."

"Okay, oh my God, okay, I'm…I'm gathering my things now. Who is with you?"

"Hardy."

"Hey, Maggie, don't worry, we won't leave his side," I say.

"Okay, thank you," she says in a panic. "I'm getting on the road. Can one of you text me the details?"

"Yes. We'll keep you updated. Please drive safe."

"I will. Thank you."

With that, Everly hangs up and then weaves through traffic, clearly not caring if she's pulled over. It might actually help us if we could score a police escort.

I keep my arm on Brody, trying to prevent him from rolling around, but it feels impossible from the way Everly is driving. When she takes a quick turn, he comes to slightly, only to groan as his hand falls to his stomach. I'm worried he might puke. I've seen him puke before. I know he has a sensitive stomach, and the last thing I want is for him to throw up all over Everly's car—which she clearly keeps pristinely clean given there is not one speck of dirt on the floor.

"Do you have a bag?" I ask.

"Only a reusable one," she says.

"Hand it to me."

She reaches in her glove compartment and pulls out a reusable bag. When she hands it to me, I quickly unfold it and open it up just as Brody groans again. Yup, he's going to throw up.

"Buddy, if you can hear me, I have a bag right here by your mouth if you need to—"

A bump in the road causes his torso to lift off the seat, his eyes flash open and, before I can even think of an escape plan, his cheeks puff and he unleashes vomit right on my chest.

"Motherfucker," I shout as throw-up seeps into my shirt and clings to my skin.

Brody collapses back to the seat as Everly screams in horror.

"Oh my God, did he get it all over my car?" She rolls down the windows, the smell so putrid that I bring the bag to my mouth.

"No," I say, trying to take small breaths. "He got it on me."

I catch her glance over her shoulder for a moment, a look of horror crossing her features before she turns back to look at the road.

"Oh my God, that smells so bad."

"Yeah, try having it cling to your chest hair," I say as my stomach roils. "Fuck, I might puke."

"Don't. I can't have two pukes in my car."

"Trust me," I groan as I stick my head out the window. "It's not on your car. It's on me."

"Thank you," I say to the male nurse who gave me a set of scrubs to change into. "I really appreciate it."

"Not a problem," he says as I head back into the waiting room where Everly is sitting.

When she looks up and spots me, a small smile crosses her face. "Better?"

"Much." I take the seat next to her and slouch down.

The moment we brought Brody in, they put him onto a gurney and then took him into an exam room for testing. They knew right away that his appendix had burst, and they rushed him into surgery. We called Maggie, and she's currently stuck in traffic, which is clearly her worst-case scenario.

"Just got off the phone with Maggie again. She's about an hour away. Pretty sure she's defying all speed limits to get here."

"Yeah, I can imagine," I say as I rub my hand over my jaw. "Fuck, I did not see that coming."

"Me neither," Everly says.

"I thought he was just being a dick. Like he was trying to egg me on or something during that whole meeting. Come to find out, the man was fucking delirious."

"I mean, I guess it's better than thinking he was being a dick."

"True," I say. "We need to somehow let Maple know about this, because that was a disaster, Everly."

"It wasn't great," she says softly.

I sigh heavily. "She barely looked at me. She didn't even give me the time of day. When we broke up, we talked about our futures and mutually agreed on what to do. I don't understand why she's so hurt." I turn to Everly. "Did she tell you anything?"

"Not really," she answers. "Just that she wasn't really happy with how things ended."

I wrack my brain, trying to think of that time before we both went our separate ways. "I don't think I did anything that could have completely turned her off from me." I smooth my hand over my forehead. "But fuck, this seems like it's going to be much harder than I anticipated."

"Yeah," Everly says softly. "Are you sure this is the route you want to go?"

"She's the only girl I ever truly had a relationship with," I confess. "That has to mean something, right? Maybe...maybe it's just buried at the moment, and I need to find a way to dig it up."

"Maybe," she says. "Or maybe she moved on."

"Did she give you that impression?" I ask.

Everly looks me in the eyes for a moment. I can see that she's thinking, her teeth pulling on the corner of her lip. And then she looks away. "No, she didn't say anything like that."

"Okay, so maybe...maybe we just need to find out more about her. She can be very guarded."

"She seems to be." Everly crosses one leg over the other. "Maybe I'll invite her to help me make some decorations. Get to know her better that way."

"That's a good idea. And she would say yes to that because she wants to be helpful. Plus you can get some things done," I say. "Thanks, Everly, for helping me. I really appreciate it. I know you don't have to."

She smiles softly. "Well, maybe you can help me find a guy. Do you have any single friends?"

I chuckle. "I have a single brother, but he's the last person to date right now. He's really set on building up the business and proving to our father that we don't need him."

"And you're not?" she asks with a smirk.

"I am, but I'm not as psychotic about it as Hudson is. He's going to burn out quickly, I can feel it."

"I remember when Maggie was at that point with the business. I was trying to help as much as I could, but she wouldn't let me, and then when she burned out, I was there to pick up the pieces."

"Same thing will happen with Hudson," I say. "And I'll be there for him when he can't do it all by himself anymore. For now, I focus on what I can focus on, and that's the agriculture side of things."

"Do you like splitting time between here and the farm?" she asks.

"If I had it my way, I'd be out on the farm all the time, but I know that's not realistic. There are things here that need my attention, Hudson needs my help, and I want to be there for Haisley too. I know it's best that I split the time."

"Makes sense," she says.

I bump my foot against hers. "So you going to tell me about that date you went on?"

She groans. "I'll spare you."

"Please don't. We have time, and it'll keep my mind off what's going on with Brody. Maybe give me something to laugh about."

"Oh, you'll laugh," she says and then fully turns toward me. "So I've been wanting to get out in the dating world some more, which of course feels like a cesspool of disappointment, but I thought I'd give it a shot. My sister, Ember, told me she had the perfect date for me, a guy who works with her husband. His name's *Tomothy*."

"That should have been an immediate no." I chuckle.

"Oh, I know. I thought it was a typo. I thought his name was Timothy."

"Oh shit."

"Yeah, and let me tell you, if I could describe what a Tomothy would be, it would be this man. He was at least seven feet tall, monstrous. Impeccable nostrils, and I mention that because that's all I could really see when I looked up at him," she says while I laugh. "But he was the worst. The absolute worst, Hardy."

"Tell me how he was the worst."

"Well, when we first sat down, he picked up his knife and started checking his teeth in the reflection. Not terrible, but he lacked decorum. He also tucked his napkin into the collar of his shirt, which once again, not awful, but he was giving me the ick."

"Understandable." I rub my hand over my jaw, loving how intense Everly is getting with this conversation. The way she delivers and tells stories is hilarious. Always so into it, really captivating.

"Things got worse when he started talking about his cat and how he loved licking it because it was like he was the mama cat."

I grimace. "He fucking said that to you?"

She places her hand on my forearm. "With pride, Hardy. He said it with pride."

"Oh fuck, licking a cat? Okay, I can see why he wasn't the guy."

"That's not even the worst part," she says.

"Licking a cat isn't the worst part?" I ask incredulously.

She slowly shakes her head. "Oh no...I didn't mention how he also liked gnawing on his cat's paws, but we'll move past that for the thing that really tipped the scales for me. For some reason, he started discussing female genitalia and how it was so complex and not fair to men to have to learn how to pleasure a woman properly."

I feel my mouth fall open. "He didn't fucking say that."

Everly slowly nods again, as if sharing the year's biggest piece of gossip. "Yup, he did. Said he left it up to the woman to seek her own pleasure."

I slowly drag my hand over my forehead. "Jesus Christ. Talk about the perfect way to cock block yourself."

"All I could think about was him staring at a naked woman, confused about what to do with his fingers."

I let out a roar of a laugh, which is pretty inappropriate for a hospital waiting room. Thankfully, we're off in a corner, away from people, and no one even glances our way. "What a fucking moron. I bet if he actually spent time learning how to pleasure a woman, he wouldn't have to discuss gnawing his cat's paws, as he'd be in bed with someone."

"Probably, especially with someone who likes clean nostrils."

"You'd be hard pressed to find someone who doesn't like clean nostrils," I reply with a smile.

"I mean, I do." Everly points to herself.

"I do too," I say. "I even waxed my nostrils once. It was terrible, but that's how much I care about nostrils."

"A true sacrifice," she replies, patting my arm.

"Some might say heroic."

"Oh yeah, I think trophy-worthy for sure."

I smirk. "Well, I'm sorry that Tomothy didn't work out. What did you say to your sister after?"

"Oh, she was dead to me. I didn't talk to her for a few days."

"Silent treatment, effective technique. Did she feel the anger?" I ask.

"Oh yes, she did. And she apologized and blamed it on her husband."

"Smart lady," I say. "So that means you're still looking then."

"Yes, still looking."

"What's your type?" I ask.

She wets her lips and looks away. "Umm, someone who doesn't complain about the complexities of female genitalia."

I chuckle. Fuck, she's funny. "I think a fair requirement. What else?"

"Um." She twists her hands in her lap. "Someone who likes to laugh, joke, have fun. I feel like work can be very stressful at times, and it would be great to have someone that I could just relax with, forget about the stresses of the events we're planning. Someone to help me escape."

"I feel that," I say. "What else?"

"I'd like someone who isn't afraid to try new things. Food, adventure, perhaps a different show here and there. It would be cool if he liked cooking, because I hate it."

"You hate cooking?"

She shrugs. "I hate dinner."

"Why do you hate dinner?"

She shifts, looking slightly uncomfortable. "This is going to sound really pathetic."

"Bet it won't," I reply.

"Oh, it will. Trust me." She pauses for a moment and then looks me in the eyes. "I hate dinner because it's lonely. I grew up in a household where dinner is the time when you recount your day with your loved ones. You talk about the successes and the failures. You share stories and indulge in conversation. You know what I mean?"

"Not so much," I answer. "I mean, I get it. I get what you're saying, but growing up, we didn't have dinners like that. My parents weren't cold to us, but we also weren't always this cohesive family. A lot of nights, Dad was out with clients and partners or on business trips. Mom had her good days and bad, so it was kind of a free for all. Sometimes I'd eat with Hudson and Haisley, sometimes we'd eat alone in our rooms. Just depended. But then there were the rare nights where we'd all sit down at the table. Actually, I remember those nights. I remember the conversations." They were some of the best nights because we'd often end up teasing each other, actually relaxing. They were fun. Especially when the parents weren't home.

Why didn't we do that more often with each other?

"You know, I see why you miss that."

"I do," she says. "I hate going home to an empty apartment. I hate warming up a premade dinner and eating by myself at my table. Just feels so sad." She shrugs. "Would be nice to find someone to share that part of my life with."

"I get it," I say. "That's not pathetic at all, Everly. It's actually…sweet." She smiles softly.

"That's why I'm trying to see if I can rekindle things with Maple. I'm ready for more."

"I think we both are," Everly says.

"Then maybe I'll help you find someone as well," I reply.

She sighs. "Maybe."

What I don't get is *why* Everly is single. She's sweet, gorgeous, does not seem to have a mean bone in her body, and can definitely hold her own with the banter. And really, she's not asking for a lot. Companionship is something most people want. *So, I need to be hunting for a nice guy for her. Not a potato like Mr. Licks-his-cat's-paws.*

"He would have to be the right person though. I'm not going to try to set you up with some Tomothy. Fuck, no. It would need to be a...a... an Ezra."

"Ezra?" She chuckles. "What's an Ezra?"

"Well, he's not a Tomothy, that's for damn sure. But someone who would make you dinner when you got home—and not complain about the complexities of the female genitalia."

She chuckles. "Ahhh, I see. Now that would be refreshing. Do you happen to know any Ezras?"

I scratch my chin. "Not presently, but I'm going to do some digging for you."

Just then her phones rings, and she rushes to answer.

"Hey, Maggie. Nope, nothing yet. He's still in surgery. Okay, yeah. Drive safe, okay, and I'll be sure to let you know if we hear anything. Okay, bye."

She hangs up. "She's going to be an absolute mess when she arrives."

"Well, good thing we're here to help her out."

"Maggie, I love you so much," Brody says as he buries his head in her neck and holds her tightly.

The surgery was a success, thankfully. It was about an hour long, so when they finished, Maggie wasn't here yet, but because the anesthesia had to wear off, he wasn't awake. The doctor couldn't give us much information, but he did give us a thumbs up, which we relayed to Maggie.

When Maggie arrived, she was a bumbling mess like Everly assumed. The moment she saw us, she fell into Everly's arms, completely distraught, but when Brody woke up from surgery, we were allowed back to his room where he gave the doctor permission to talk about his surgery.

His appendix had burst, but there doesn't seem to be an infection. They'll be keeping him for the next 24–48 hours to observe him, and from what I can see, Maggie will be attached to his hip.

"I love you too," Maggie says, pressing a kiss to his forehead. "And next time you're in pain, please don't try to mask it as maybe something weird you ate or that you worked out too hard."

"I did run extra hard, and I thought I ate something weird." He shrugs, looking exhausted.

"I'm just glad you were delirious during our meeting and not an ass trying to make my life a living nightmare," I say.

Brody winks at me. "You're welcome."

"Well, I think we should him let him get some rest, and I'm sure Hardy wants to change into something else," Everly says.

"I can't believe you threw up on your boss," Maggie says and then pauses. "Although it feels fitting for you. He's seen you throw up twice, why not on him this time?"

Brody nods. "Very fitting. If I were to throw up on anyone, Hardy would be the one."

"Why me?" I ask.

"Because you're too pretty." Brody smiles and then rests his eyes, shutting them while he snuggles into Maggie. "Way too pretty. Beard and… eyes…pretty."

"And with that, I think we should leave," Everly says with mirth.

I don't know. I kind of like where he was going with the compliments.

After we offer Maggie and Brody a quick goodbye, Everly heads toward the hospital's exit. "Think I can catch a ride back to the venue where my car is parked?" I ask.

"Of course," she says. "Not a problem at all."

"Thanks. But first…would you like to go to dinner?"

CHAPTER ELEVEN
EVERLY

DID HARDY HOPPER JUST ASK me out to dinner?

This has been one of the craziest afternoons of my life. First, Hardy's reunion with Maple. What. A. Disaster. I've never seen a bumbling Hardy. So weird. I do not think Maple is into Hardy at all. And yet he still hopes. And then to end up in a hospital after driving like a madwoman to get here. Thank God Brody is okay, but again, what a weird afternoon.

Let's not forget that the man of my dreams, the modern-day Adonis himself, asked me to share a meal with him.

Um...yes!

"You know," he continues, "since we've been here for a few hours and I'm starving." His eyes plead with mine, as if I need convincing.

Ha, sir, I would eat dinner off your nose if you asked me. Fork and knife that meal right off the waxed nostril.

And I know what you're thinking...you're supposed to be moving on from the bearded beauty.

You're not supposed to be thinking about him in any other way than as the man you're trying to help reconnect with his ex.

But...

A meal with Hardy?

I have to live for this moment, if anything to help me through dates with men like Tomothy who prefer to talk about gastric distress.

"I would love to. My stomach has been growling this whole time."

"Then dinner it is," he says, and then to my surprise places his hand on my lower back as we make our way through the hospital.

Oh yes, just like that.

I revel in the feel of his warm palm against my clothes.

I cherish this walk.

From the antiseptic smell to the bad linoleum, I desperately commit it to memory, hating myself for feeling so strongly about this man when I really shouldn't. Ember is right—he's after someone else and I need to keep that on repeat in my head when he does things like ask me to dinner, or place his hand on my lower back, or tell me that I deserve way more than a Tomothy.

But mother of God, can I just soak this in for a second?

When we hit the parking lot and reach my car, I unlock it and open my driver side door only to quickly shut it, eyes watering at the stench. "Oh my God." I cover my nose and look up at Hardy in horror.

"Oh no," he says. "Did my body not soak up all of the puke?"

"Doesn't smell like it," I say.

Hardy pulls out his phone. "I'll take care of it."

"What are you doing?" I ask.

"Grabbing us an Uber." He lifts his eyes. "Pizza good for you?"

"Yeah, that works."

Hardy types away on his phone and when he's finished, he says, "Uber will be arriving in five minutes. We need to head to the front of the hospital." He nods toward it but continues to type away on his phone.

"What are you doing?" I ask again as we set off.

"Texting my buddy who owns a body shop. I'm going to have him grab your car and do a detailing."

Oh…okay, see? A true knight in shining armor.

"Oh, you don't have to do that," I say quickly.

"It's done," he says as we reach the front of the hospital. "Consider it a thank-you for everything you're doing for me."

"Hardy—"

"Or just a friendly gesture."

"Hardy," I start to say again.

"Or an 'I'm sorry.'"

My brow creases. "Sorry for what?"

"For not soaking up all the puke with my shirt." He winks.

"Don't be ridiculous." I toe the ground, feeling all shy and wooed by a man who is clearly not wooing me. "Maybe next time, though, puff your chest some more. Really give the throw-up a blank canvas."

"I'll keep that in mind."

My phone dings in my purse, so I grab it and see that there's a text from Maggie.

Maggie: Thank you so much for taking care of Brody. I can't imagine what I would have done if this had happened and he'd been alone at our place. I just keep thinking about how lucky I am that he was with you. You acted quickly and got him where he needed to be. I'm so thankful for you and for Hardy. Thank you.

I smile softly and text her back.

Everly: I'm glad we were able to help. Let me know if you need anything—I can drop it off.

Maggie: Thank you. Hattie was driving right behind me. She's going to my place to pick up some things and then coming here. But thank you. Can you just handle the joint email and cancel my meetings for tomorrow?

Everly: Of course. Let me know if there's anything else you need. Just take care of Brody for now and I got you.

Maggie: Thank you, Everly.

When I stick my phone back in my purse, Hardy asks, "Everything okay?"

"Yes. Maggie was just thanking us again. She mentioned how grateful she was that Brody was with us, and I keep thinking what would have happened if he got sick and he was alone? What would he have done?"

"Can't think about that kind of stuff." Hardy shakes his head. "Mainly because worrying about the what-ifs is never productive."

"You're right," I say.

He leans in closer. "And also because we're both people who live alone and thinking about that shit is scary."

For some reason that makes me laugh. "Yeah, makes me almost want to ask Tomothy if he's interested in date number two."

Hardy shakes his head. "Nothing should ever drive you into his arms again...ever. Burst appendix and all."

"When I say no one ever wants to share pizza with me, I'm not kidding," Hardy says as he picks up a piece from our shared pie. The Uber dropped us off at a hole-in-the wall Italian place downtown, and we may as well be in *Lady and the Tramp*, just minus the spaghetti. "They always say pineapple isn't supposed to be on pizza, but I don't agree."

"I've never had just pineapple, it's always accompanied by ham or pepperoni, but I'm not opposed to this. It's sweet, and the side of barbeque sauce is a nice surprise."

"Good, right?" Hardy asks, waggling his brows.

"I would say more along the lines of interesting."

"Hey, I'll take it," he says with a smile. "Maple never liked pineapple on pizza."

Which makes me a better fit for Hardy than she is, but we're not going to mention that or make this a competition because Maple is actually really sweet.

But just for my own personal record and satisfaction…ha, Maple, I can share a pizza with Hardy, and you can't.

Okay, pettiness is over.

"Shame," I say. "Because it's good. The dipping sauce I'm still adjusting to."

"Hang out with me some more and I'll win you over." He winks.

Boy, you have already won me over.

You won me over months ago.

After he swallows and takes a sip of his drink, he says, "So, tell me about your day."

"Pretty sure you know about my day," I say.

"Yeah, but you're not eating dinner alone tonight, so act like I don't know anything about what happened today."

Well…that makes my heart nearly beat out of my chest as I look into his perfectly blue eyes. With comments like that, he's making it next to impossible for me to even think about anyone else but him.

"Come on," he says. "Indulge me." He then clears his throat. "Hey, Everly. Nice to see you for the first time today. Tell me, how was your day? Any highs, any lows? Anything you want to share?"

I smirk and play along. "Hello, Hardy. It is great to see you for the first time today."

He leans in and whispers, "Well done."

"Thanks." I chuckle and then get back into character. "Wow, what a day. You'll never believe it."

"Sounds intriguing—tell me what happened."

"It started with a protein shake."

"Oh, we going back that far? Okay." He settles into his chair. "Tell me about this protein shake. What flavors are we talking about here?"

"Banana and peanut butter, my absolute favorite flavor."

"Killer combination, and what a way to start your day."

"Thank you. I thought so as well. I then went into a day full of annoy-ing admin work that no one likes but has to get done."

"Emails." He rolls his eyes. "Am I right?"

"You are so right." I chuckle. "But then I had this meeting that altered my entire day."

"Oh? Okay, lay it on me."

"Well, it started with the best man asking me to hook him up with the maid of honor."

"Hook him up?" Hardy asks. "Why can't he just ask her out himself?"

"Get this," I say loving every second of this. "They used to date back in college. Sounded like they were friends with benefits."

"Uh, is that what she said?" he asks, slightly wincing.

"No, but it's what I gathered from speaking with both of them. Apparently, they had some wild nights. Beer pong tournaments, Ed Sheeran playing in the background—the best man often cried when 'Perfect' came on. He also liked to sway in the corner by himself with just his beer bottle when the song played. I think the maid of honor, the ex, was jealous when he did that."

He quirks his lips to the side. "Are you sure he cried?"

"Positive. She showed me several pictures of him weeping. When I met up with him today, all I could think about was his ugly cry face and of course his sloppy kisses."

"Sloppy kisses, huh?" he asks, looking skeptical and hopefully picking up on the fact that I'm making up this entire thing.

"Yeah. She said sometimes it was like a tidal wave of slobber when they made out. And one of the reasons she dealt with a salivating man was because she had dry lips and found him to be a great way to moisturize them."

"That's...disturbing."

I let out a loud laugh and then shrug. "To each their own, right? Can't judge someone for wanting soft lips and finding a great way to keep them that way."

"I guess so."

"Anyway, I had to meet with both of them today, and if I could describe it in one word, I would say *awkward*."

"Awkward?" he asks with raised brows.

"Oh yeah. You should have seen the best man. An absolute disaster. He went to say hi to her and instead of offering a wave or a quick *hello* like a normal person, he face-planted into her breasts. Right then and there as a greeting."

"Are you sure he didn't trip? Or maybe someone bumped into him."

I take a sip of my drink and shake my head. "Nope. You could see it in his eyes the minute she walked up to him. He had his sights set on her breasts, and he wasn't going to have it any other way. Of course, he was like 'oh I tripped,' but we all knew what he was doing, greeting her nose to boob. Classless if you ask me."

He leans back in his chair, studying me, the corners of his lips tugging up. "But why would he greet her nose to boob? That doesn't make sense."

"Oh, it does to me. I found out he's part of this friend group that has a hard time understanding the intricacies of the female genitalia. Pretty sure he thought by going in nose to boob, he was getting her revved up for a lip-moistening make-out session."

He taps his fingers on the table. "This group, it doesn't happen to be headed up by someone by the name of Tomothy, does it?"

I wave my hand in dismissal. "Can't be sure. I tend to stay away from men with female complexes. Not worth my time. So yeah, after the motorboating attempt, we awkwardly shifted around the space. I tried to keep us on track and focused on the event, but he kept announcing how awkward he was feeling. Even at one point, he said his body was buzzing and then motioned to his...crotch."

Hardy's expression flattens, and I burst out in laughter.

"I don't think he did that."

"Oh, he did for sure. He said buzzing, and then with both hands pointed right at his weiner." I'm still laughing. "It took everything in me not to gag. It was so bad that I sent the MOH upstairs to check out a loft space, and that's when I told him he was blowing it and he needed to get his act together. You'll never believe what he did then."

Hardy folds his arms across his chest. "Let me guess, he tried to kiss you."

"Eck, gross, no, thank God. He swayed one way, then the other, and I was about to ask him what was wrong, but before I could, he passed out, fell right into my chest with a *thunk*. I couldn't hold his body weight, so we flew through a bathroom wall, erupted a pipe and, while I scrambled to get him off me, the place started to flood. The maid of honor came back downstairs and found him with his face pressed against my breasts. She was so insulted that she took off. I called the ambulance to help me with the passed-out man, turned off the water, and then rode in the ambulance with him where we found out that his appendix burst. So yeah, what a day."

He stares at me, a mix of humor and calculation crossing his features. "Yeah, that's quite the day."

"What about you?" I ask casually, picking up my piece of pizza.

"Not nearly as eventful. Just got some work done and then listened to a friend tell me the most insane lie I've ever heard."

"Ugh, people, always trying to gain attention by lying." I pat his hand. "Be happy you don't have to worry about that with me."

"I guess so." He chuckles and then leans back in his chair. "You know, Professor, it's shocking you're single."

"Oh?" I ask as I place the back of my hand under my chin. "After my story, do I seem like quite the catch?"

"You do," he says, sounding more serious than I expected.

Trying not to get caught up in it, I say, "Well, keep that in mind while you're trying to hook me up with someone that's not a Tomothy and more of an Ezra."

"I don't know...after that story, I might have to get you back."

"Vindictive behavior is very unbecoming, Hardy."

"I'll keep that in mind." He leans his forearms on the table. "Seriously, though, why are you single?"

"What do you mean?" I ask.

"I don't understand. You're clearly a good time, you're beautiful, you're so easy to talk to. To spend time with. You're hardworking, driven...well, that seems like a catch to me. If Hudson wasn't so caught up in his own world, I'd suggest he look this way, but I know that will only end up in disappointment. When his mind is set on something, he doesn't let it go. So...why are you single?"

I'm sorry. I'm still trying to catch my breath after he called me beautiful.

"Uh..." I say, inwardly squealing but trying to remain calm. "I don't know. Maybe I look for the wrong kind of guys."

Hardy being case in point.

"Well, I'm determined now to find someone worthy."

"Determined, huh?" I ask. "And all it took was a lie about you having sloppy kisses. Wow, I should have said that months ago."

He chuckles. "You can only learn from your mistakes, Everly, and move on from there."

"Noted."

Everly: I think I'm in love.

Ember: Dear God, Everly.

Everly: I know. I'm sorry. I really am, but let me just get this off my chest.

Ember: Fine...go...

Everly: He's everything. Oh my God. He's so funny and sweet and he understands my sense of humor, and even though he likes to dip his pineapple pizza in barbeque sauce, I can look past that because he has the best smile ever. And he got my car cleaned and it's never looked better.

Ember: What the hell happened in the last few days?

Everly: Love was blasted in the air, that's what happened.

Ember: You know, you were never this lovesick when we were young, but I think being in the wedding planning business has changed you. When have you ever fawned over a man like this? Seeing others in love is starting to make you insane.

Everly: Perhaps, but ughhhhhh, are we sure I can't sabotage the whole undercover bridesmaid thing, show him how perfect I am for him instead?

Ember: Everly…

Everly: I know…I know. Ugh, okay. I just had to get that off my chest. Everything is fine now. I'm moving on.

Ember: Good, now how do you plan on doing that?

Everly: Showing up at Hardy's office, naked, offering him my body.

Ember: EVERLY!

Everly: I'm kidding…partially.

Ember: Do I need to be concerned about you?

Everly: I want to say no…but maybe be on standby.

Ember: Good God.

CHAPTER TWELVE
EVERLY

"WOW, THERE IS NO WAY I can do that," Maple says as she looks at the cute yarn pom-pom centerpiece I made for the bridal shower.

"Trust me, it's so easy."

"I'm really not crafty at all," Maple says as she pulls her legs up on the couch in our new storefront. We still need to decorate and there are touch-ups that need to be made, but I asked Maggie if it was okay to meet Maple here to work on centerpieces and she approved. Thank God, because doing this in my tiny apartment would not have been ideal.

"You don't need to be crafty. The least crafty person can do this thanks to these." I pull out two different sized pom-pom makers, ridged plastic disks that will make this a breeze for her. "Think you can wrap yarn?"

"Yeah, I can do that," she says, looking hopeful.

"Then you can make pom-pom centerpieces. Look." I pull out one of the pom-poms from the bouquet. "We make the pom-pom, and then we just glue the stick to one end. We do this in all different lengths and sizes and then put them all together. All I need you to do is help me with the pom-poms and gluing the sticks, then I can do the arranging."

"That doesn't seem that hard," she says.

"I promise, it won't be hard at all." I then dump a bag of yarn between us, all different shades of pink and salmon. "Let's get to work."

I give her a quick tutorial on how to use the pom-pom maker and it takes her a second to get used to it, but once she figures it out, she smiles

to herself. I can see the pride in her eyes. And this is what I love, right here, helping someone do something for someone else. Not sure I ever thought this would be part of my career, but I enjoy being able to step in and be the essential behind-the-scenes person.

"I really like that we're making these instead of using real florals," Maple says. "Because you said you can save them and use them for another event, right?"

"Yup," I reply. "We have a large storage room in this building for this exact reason, so we can help supplement events with décor. It's a very eco- and budget-friendly model that is not only important to me and Maggie, but to the cooperative as well. The Cane brothers are big on sustainability."

"What's the cooperative?" she asks as she continues to circle yarn over the maker.

"Oh, that's the company that Hudson and Hardy started with the Cane brothers. Not sure how in the know you are, but Huxley, JP, and Breaker are the Canes, and they were direct competition with Reginald Hopper. Because things went sour between Hudson, Hardy, and their dad, they decided to join forces with the Canes. I won't get into details because that's not my place, but you can google the joint venture. It's been all over the business forums."

"Oh…interesting," Maple says. I watch her twist her lips for a second and a little piece of me—okay, a big piece of me—is hoping that doesn't intrigue her, but when she looks up at me I know that's not the case. "He seemed different the other day."

"Oh?" I ask. "How so?"

"Well, he just seemed nervous, fidgety, unlike himself. I've never seen him so unbalanced. In college, he was always very confident and sure of himself. Hardy from the other day was a far cry from college Hardy."

"Well, I'm sure there's a reason for that. Probably nervous to see you again. And then he went and slipped right into your chest—I'm sure that set him into a tailspin after."

Maple smiles. "I know that in the moment, I was just as startled as the rest of us, but it was kind of funny thinking about it later. Hardy from college would have dropped dead if he ever did anything that embarrassing."

"Really?" I ask, feeling slightly jealous that she knows a different side of Hardy.

"Yeah. He was definitely the cool guy back then, but now, it's as if he completely shed his confident exoskeleton and he's just...goofy."

"Maybe at times," I say. "But he still has that cool guy persona."

"Oh really?" she asks. "Do you guys know each other well?"

Oh shit.

"Uh, not really," I say. "Not as well as you know him. I've only seen how he's interacted with us since the joint venture, and he's always been so chill and professional. His behavior the other day surprised me."

She chuckles. "Yeah, to be honest, it was nice to see him act more down to earth."

"Oh yeah?" I ask, swallowing hard. "That's, uh...good. Maybe that means something."

"What do you mean?" she asks.

"Oh, you know, if you ever wanted to get back together, you'll feel confident that people change."

She shakes her head. "We won't be getting back together."

Ahh, what a shame.

"Why not?" I ask.

Her eyes meet mine. "I just think we're different people than we were back then, and I just don't think we're as compatible as we used to be."

Probably for the best, good luck with your future dating endeavors.

"People change sometimes for the better," I say for some stupid reason, as if I'm convincing her to date him.

"True." She shakes her head. "Honestly, I just want to get Polly married and focus on my work. The last thing I want to do right now is date someone."

Yes, focus on your work, Maple, probably smart.

"I can understand that," I say as I tie off one of the pom-poms and toss it into the center where we are starting a collection. "I was like that all last year, just focusing on work and getting settled. But now that I feel like I'm actually doing well, leading the charge on a new branch of business, the rest of my life feels disconnected."

"How so?" Maple asks, her kind eyes meeting mine as she pauses in her yarn wrapping. And I want to hate those kind eyes, I really do, but man, she makes it hard.

"I feel like I'm missing someone to share it with. I feel sad after I get home from work. There's no one to talk to, no one to hang out with, no one to share a meal with. It just feels lonely, and I don't want to feel lonely. And when I do feel lonely, I lean more into work, but I don't want to be that person. I don't want to wake up one day and think I missed so much because I was working all the time."

"But do you feel fulfilled with work?" she asks.

"I do," I answer, wondering how this became a therapy session for me, but those kind eyes are making me talk. "But I don't want it to define me, and that's okay if that's something you might want. I just…I'm surrounded by love daily. I see what a relationship can bring to someone's life, and I know that I shouldn't, but at times I feel jealous. I want that. I love watching couples walking down the street, holding hands. That's such a simple level of intimacy, a level that I haven't been able to truly experience myself. The men I dated in college were not really the coupling type, more in it for a good time. But that doesn't mean I don't long for that kind of intimacy. Kissing someone good night. Sharing a morning cup of coffee or a late-night glass of wine. Simple things. *Couple* things. I want that, you know?"

She slowly nods. "Yeah, I know what you mean. I was seeing this guy when I was in Peru. He was one of my co-researchers, and everything felt better when he was around."

Oh God, she was dating someone?

And why does that information make me feel like a CIA operative, like the enemy just revealed a big mystery that I've been waiting for.

"How did it end?" I ask. "I mean...if it did end."

"It ended. He was transferred to the San Diego Zoo." She shrugs. "We knew it was temporary. It's hard to get placed in the same zoo, especially when you study the same animal."

"Do you still talk to him?" I ask.

"Yes, we stay in touch, but that's all it is." She lets out a big huff. "But I understand the feeling of not wanting to be alone. Who knows," she continues, "maybe I'll think about talking to Hardy again."

Noooooooooo.

Go back to the Peru guy, he seemed...earthy.

"Oh yeah, cool," I say as I pull out a new color of pink yarn from my bag of yarn.

Stupid freaking Peru guy, why couldn't you study another animal? Huh?

"Do you like bowling?" she asks out of the blue.

I blink at her, confused by the subject change. "Uh, sure. I mean, I played it a couple of times, but I'm not very good at it."

"Well, I joined a bowling league to try to meet some more people. My friend Timothy at the zoo got me to join, and I know this might be a bold ask since we just barely met, but we're looking for another woman to round out the team. Think you might be interested?"

Timothy?

Or did she mean Tomothy?

Excuse me for being hugely concerned.

"Did you say Timothy or Tomothy?" I ask, needing some clarification.

She chuckles. "Timothy."

"Are you sure?" I press.

"Positive," she says with a strange expression, probably wondering why I'm so persistent.

"Okay, just making sure. I met a Tomothy that I would prefer never to see again." I secure my pom-pom and remove it from the maker before setting the ball to the side, pleased with how it came out. "Um, I'm not very good at bowling."

"Neither am I, but there are a lot of guys who play, and who knows, maybe you'll meet someone."

I consider it for a moment.

I do need to get out into real life more and not be so stuck in my event world.

If Maple decides she wants to get to know Hardy again, I know I'll have no hope with him. That's inevitable. So I need to move on.

Bowling with some strangers might be just what I need. And who knows, maybe I'll meet someone new and exciting. Someone who doesn't mind the complexities of the female genitalia.

One can only hope.

"You know, Maple, I think I will join you."

"Really?" she asks, looking very excited.

"Yeah, really. Could be fun and I'm into meeting new people."

"That's amazing. I'll tell Timothy. He'll be so excited."

"By chance," I say as I start making a new pom-pom, "is Timothy single?"

"He is," she smiles. "He's very much single."

"Is he...your type?"

She chuckles. "No, he's just a friend."

"Well then, I guess I should start thinking about my debut bowling outfit."

To: Hardy Hopper
From: Everly Plum
Subject: Pom-Poms

Henrietta,

I have some news. I spent some time with Maple today. We were making pom-pom décor for the bridal shower and we got to talking. She mentioned you and how…different you were the other day. Seemed like there's a possibility there for the two of you. I think you can move on to stage two.

You're welcome,
The Prof

To: Everly Plum
From: Hardy Hopper
Subject: RE: Pom-Poms

Wait…really?

After the other day, after my fumbling and bumbling?

After falling through a wall?

After falling into her breasts as a greeting…

You think she's interested?

How the fuck does that happen?

You know what? Don't answer that, I'm just going to accept what you said and ask how do you propose we move to stage two? Me being able to actually talk to her outside of the events. I feel like there needs to be a smooth transition.

About these pom-poms, are you still making them? Maybe it's something I can help with.

A grateful Henrietta

To: *Hardy Hopper*
From: *Everly Plum*
Subject: *RE: Pom-Poms*

It had something to do with you being less cool…her words, not mine. Although I might have agreed with her.

I don't know, maybe she liked the idea of you being a goof, but either way, she seemed open. Well, more open than before.

We do still have to make some pom-poms as well as a few other décor items, so you can come help as well if you want. I'm finalizing details with Maple, but it will probably be after work today. Hopefully you can make that happen. I'll let you know what time once I hear from her.

Until then, think of more ways to embarrass yourself. She seemed to like that.

Maybe you can bend over and your pants split right down the crack. Or I can loosen the screws on one of the chairs in the storefront so when you take a seat you land flat on your ass. Maybe you accidentally glue a pom-pom to your hand…or your head…or your elbow.

Perhaps you could think you're cutting the string for the pom-poms but accidentally cut your shirt instead.

Let me know. I'd be more than happy to help you embarrass yourself.

The Prof

To: Everly Plum
From: Hardy Hopper
Subject: Splitting my pants

I don't know why I'm gravitating toward ripped pants, but there's something about it that screams a must-do. Maybe in a Harry Styles kind of way. Did you see that clip that went viral of him splitting his pants during his tour? Right up the front. I think a frontal rip is better than a back rip. Back rip makes me think there's a bit too much cake in the trunks, whereas a frontal rip is all about what's happening in the crotchal—yes, I made up that word—region.

What do you think? Should I pre-tear my pants in an inconspicuous way and then lunge to grab something, only to split the crotch wide open?

Feels like a winning situation all around.

Henrietta

To: Hardy Hopper
From: Everly Plum
Subject: RE: Splitting my pants

You know, I wouldn't have pegged you as someone who wants to have a crotch split in public, but here we are, discussing your best options for letting the breeze in through the front door.

I have to ask, what's the state of your underwear?

Before we start ripping pants open, I think we need to account for what your underwear looks like right now. Especially if a full *frontal is involved, we have to be certain that the underwear is up to standards.*

The Prof

To: *Everly Plum*
From: *Hardy Hopper*
Subject: *Best Undies IN TOWN!*

Plum...I'm surprised you even have to ask the state of my underwear.

I'm a clean man.

I wash in all crevices, a daily deep clean.

Clothes are always laundered with care, folded, and gently used.

There are no holes, no frail hems, no...stains.

My underwear is the most impeccable underwear you will ever come across. So please...please don't ever question if my underwear is ready to flap in the breeze, because it is. It's more than ready. It's prepared to be strung up on a flagpole and waved around like a flag because of how perfect it is.

Some might say my underwear can double as a napkin.

A placemat.

A pillowcase.

A washcloth.

People have said they wish I would give away my underwear because of how amazing it is. So, yes, my underwear is more than ready. No need to converse about the fabric that clings to my crotch every day.

No underwear will ever be better than this underwear.

Henrietta

To: Hardy Hopper
From: Everly Plum
Subject: Dear...God...

You know, Henrietta, a simple "yes, my underwear is good" would have been just fine.

Now I have the image of your underwear being used as a place mat ingrained in my head.

Not happy.

The Prof

To: Everly Plum
From: JP Cane
Subject: Dear Friend

Dear Friend,

Did you know that the people of ancient Rome used to eat flamingo tongue as a delicacy? Think about that for a moment... tongue from innocent flamingos. It's so horrific.

Thankfully, we're not living in ancient Rome and the threat of flamingo tongue ending up on plates is no longer a concern, but do you know what is a concern? The fragile habitats these beautiful birds live in.

Please join me in helping save their habitats from destruction.
Donate Here.
From the bottom of my heart, thank you.

JP Cane

———————

Everly: I'm sitting in my car, about to walk into a bowling alley for a bowling league that I agreed to take part in…as an actual bowling league member. I think this is the start of me losing my mind.

Ember: Losing your mind? I think this is a great idea! Look at you getting out there. Are you going with anyone?

Everly: Maple…yes, that Maple, the one that Hardy wants to date.

Ember: Ehhh, that's a little weird.

Everly: I'm trying not to think about it. She said there's a guy here, Timothy—that was not a typo: Timothy, not Tomothy—who might be a good match for me. So I'm giving this dating thing the old college try.

Ember: Interesting. I guess anything is better than a second date with Tomothy.

Everly: Literally anything.

Ember: Are you nervous?

Everly: Of course I'm nervous. I've never bowled for competition in my life, the last man I met spoke about licking his cat, and my hands are clammy no matter how many times I rub them on my pants.

Ember: Ahh, young love.

Everly: Young love? Love is not even in the picture at this point. I'm just trying to make sure I don't make a fool of myself.

Ember: Ooo, good luck with that. Remember the time we took you to Trevor's work party and you were talking to a guy and tried to drink your soda but didn't have your lips lined up with the hole, resulting in you pouring orange soda all over your face?

Everly: How is this helping?

Ember: It's not but the memory made me laugh.

Everly: Glad I could entertain, but I'm going to have to go because I see Maple. Wish me luck.

Ember: Good luck! Text me later. I want to know all about Timothy.

I'm sure she does.

I stick my phone and keys in my purse and climb out of my car. "Hey, Maple," I call out as she's about to grab the door to the bowling alley. She glances over her shoulder and when she spots me, a relieved smile crosses her expression.

"You came," she says as I close the space between us, and then to my surprise she gives me a hug.

"Did you think I wasn't going to show up?" I ask.

"I was slightly worried that you might not, but I'm glad you did because I didn't want to do this alone."

"Have no fear—I'm here and I'm ready to grab a drink, so when I suck at bowling, I can blame the booze."

She chuckles. "Very smart idea."

"Stick with me, Maple, I have all the smart ideas."

Together we walk into the incredibly crowded and boisterous bowling alley. This is not what I was anticipating. I thought maybe a few people milling about, fellow comrades talking about their latest night out, maybe a roll of a ball here and there. But this...wow. We're talking full lanes, people in matching shirts and wrist guards analyzing bowling balls while polishing them with rags. Pints of beer crowd around plates of nachos and pizza, and the interesting scent of food mixed with stale feet floats through the air, despite the newer, renovated bowling alley.

It's loud.

It's overpopulated.

And there isn't a chance in hell I'd stay if Maple wasn't here with me.

"Uh, wow, this is intimidating," I say while taking in the scene.

Maple steps closer. "Yeah, incredibly intimidating—what were we thinking?"

"We must have had a wild hair in us because my introvert is trying to crawl out of my skin at the moment," I say.

"Yeah, this is more intense than I expected," Maple replies.

"Maple," a man says, walking up to her.

Tall with blond hair, he has the body of a swimmer, broad shoulders and a narrow waist, and perched on his nose is a pair of dark-rimmed glasses. Well, he's a nice man to look at.

"Timothy," Maple says with a smile. "Thank God. I don't think I would've been able to find you in this crowd."

"It's why I headed toward the front. We're over on lane twelve. I grabbed your shoes already—thanks for sending me the sizes in advance. And I'm about to run to the bar, so what can I get you to drink?"

"Well, first of all, this is Everly," Maple says.

"Oh shit, I'm sorry," Timothy says. "Where are my manners?" He holds his hand out to me, and I take it. "Everly, it's really nice to meet you. Thank you for joining the team. We needed at least two girls, so you two being here allows us to play."

"Not a problem. It's always fun to do new things," I say awkwardly because Timothy is an attractive man. A very attractive man. And apparently, I've lost all ability to function as a normal human.

He smiles kindly. "Well, can I get you anything to drink? We have two pizzas already and some buffalo wings. But I'm loading up on beer."

"Could I get a seltzer?" Maple asks.

"Same," I say.

"Alcoholic?" he asks, brows raised.

"Yes," Maple and I say at the same time, making Timothy laugh.

"On it, ladies. Head down to lane twelve, the guys are waiting for you."

"Thanks," Maple says and then Timothy takes off.

I turn to her and whisper, "Okay, he's hot."

She laughs. "Timothy is one of the most highly sought-after zookeepers at the zoo, at least that's what has been told to me. He doesn't want to date anyone in the same profession though. Hence why we work so well together as new friends."

"Good to know. What animal does he take care of?"

"The rhinos."

"That's so cool," I say.

"If you ask him about his line of work, he won't stop talking about them, so prepare yourself."

"Noted," I say as we head toward lane twelve.

We weave through people, past rows and rows of untouched bowling bars, and to the very end of the bowling alley where lane twelve is situated. And just like Timothy said, there are two pizzas on the high-top table, along with beers and buffalo wings.

Two guys are sitting on the bench and chatting as we walk up.

"Hey," Maple says, raising her hand in greeting. "I'm Maple and this is Everly."

"Hey, I'm Mario," one of the guys says as he stands. Dark hair, dark features, with some dark chest hair peeking through the V-neck of his shirt.

"And I'm Sven," the lighter-haired man says. "Great to meet you."

We smile and then of course stand there awkwardly. Finally, I ask, "How do you know Timothy?"

"Went to school with him," Mario says. "And before you ask, no, I'm not a zookeeper. I work in finance. I brought my other friend as well—he's in the bathroom."

"And Timothy used to date my sister," Sven says. "She's married to someone else now, and I told her I wasn't giving up my friendship, so… here I am."

That makes me chuckle. "At least you're honest about it."

"I was devastated when they broke up," Sven says. "Worst mistake of her life and now she's married to a guy who is just…okay. He sure as hell can't tell me tales about rhinos, that's for damn sure."

"Maple? Everly?" A familiar voice pulls our attention to the right where Hardy comes into view.

Uh…

What is he doing here?

"Hardy?" Maple says.

He steps into our area and sticks his hands in his pockets. "Are you two playing with us tonight?"

"Us?" I ask, blinking a few times.

"Yeah," Hardy says.

Maple and I exchange glances and then look back at the men.

"Uh, do you know each other?" Mario asks the obvious.

"We do," Hardy says. "I used to date Maple back in college, and Everly works under the cooperative. She's also helping with Polly and Ken's wedding."

"Oh wow, small world," Mario says.

Incredibly small.

So small that it almost feels like someone is messing with us.

Because what are the actual odds?

"This isn't going to be a problem, is it?" Sven asks, looking nervous.

"Timothy was really looking forward to being able to put a team together. He'll be so disappointed if you guys walk out."

I look over at Maple again who is shyly glancing at Hardy.

Uh, will this be a problem?

Yes.

Yes, this will be a problem.

This will be a big problem for me.

The last thing I want to do is watch Hardy and Maple rekindle their relationship right in front of me. It's one thing to help make that connection, but it's another thing to witness it unfold.

I'm hoping Maple feels just uncomfortable enough to back out.

Fingers crossed.

"Well," she says as she twists her hands in front of her. Go ahead, tell them this would be awkward, so we're just going to go grab a drink at the bar and hang out there. "I don't want to disappoint Timothy." *Uh, no, Maple. That's not the correct answer.* "So I guess we can stay. Unless you want to leave, Everly?"

All eyes fall on me.

Sven's pleading eyes to not disappoint Timothy.

Mario's interested eyes that keep scanning me up and down—not a fan of that.

Maple's unsure eyes, begging me to stay.

And of course Hardy's eyes, imploring me to grant him this opportunity to be closer to Maple.

Damn it.

Damn all of them.

Damn every single one of them and the bowling balls they picked out.

I hope they all throw gutter balls the entire night.

"Oh, no," I answer, as chill as can be. "I'm ready to bowl."

The group releases a collective sigh, pizza boxes are opened, and smiles are met all around.

Great. Can't wait to see where this evening takes me.

CHAPTER THIRTEEN
HARDY

WHAT ARE THE FUCKING CHANCES of Maple and Everly showing up to be the two girls we needed on our team?

Slim. Very fucking slim.

Not sure how the universe planned it this way, but I'll take it.

I was just planning on doing some bowling tonight, enjoying some company with the guys, eating some pizza…but now…now there's an opportunity presented to me, and I'm going to snatch it up.

"Did everyone meet each other?" Timothy says as he approaches with a tray full of more drinks.

"We did," Sven says. "The girls actually know Hardy."

Timothy glances over at me. "Really?"

Sven leans in with a smile in his voice. "Hardy and Maple used to date."

"Wait, seriously?" Timothy asks.

"Back in college," I say. "Now we're in a wedding together—our friends from college are getting married, and Everly is helping with the planning."

"Wow." Timothy smirks. "Shit, I had no idea. Is, uh…is everyone good?"

"We're good," Maple says as she places her hand on Timothy's shoulder.

Don't like that.

Keep your hands to yourself, Maple…or on me.

"Perfect," Timothy says. "If anyone needs to go to the bathroom, maybe go now because once we start, the league likes to keep the games moving."

"I should go," Maple says. "Do you need to go, Everly?"

"I'm good," she says.

"Okay." Maple looks around. "Where are the bathrooms?"

"I'll show you," Timothy says, guiding her away from us.

Once they're at a good enough distance, I turn to talk to Everly, but she's right next to me before I can even look for her. "Henrietta," she whispers while Sven and Mario are testing the balls they picked. "I'm sweating."

I chuckle. Okay, not what I was expecting her to say. "Why?"

"Uh, because you're here."

"Do I make you nervous, Plum?"

Her brow creases. "No, but this is unexpected. This is outside of our plan. We were looking for a slow transition, not a full-on foray into hanging out."

"Says the girl hanging out with my ex. When did you become friends?"

"Very quickly," she says with her chin held high. "She's pretty cool and promised a good time—and possibly the chance to meet some people. Also I'm doing this for you, to talk you up if I get a chance." She looks me up and down. "When have you ever thought about bowling? You don't seem like the bowling type."

"And you do?" I ask on a laugh. "I think this is the first time I'm ever seeing you in leggings. I didn't even know that you owned them."

"Of course I own leggings. My God, Hardy."

I chuckle. "Sorry, but all I ever see you in are professional clothes with your hair tied back in a bun."

She grips the low bun that rests at the nape of her neck. "It's an easy hairdo."

"There's nothing wrong with it," I say. "But if anyone is going to bowl between the two of us, it's me."

"Billionaires don't bowl."

"Yes, they do," I counter. "They just usually bowl in their own bowling alleys in their homes."

Her lips twist to the side, causing me to laugh. "Either way, how do you want to handle this? Are you going to talk to her? I think you should at least say something like…wow, what a great night."

"Wow, what a great night?" I deadpan. "That's the kind of conversation you want me to have with Maple? That's awkward as shit."

"Uh, yeah, and at least it's better than falling into her cleavage as a greeting."

My expression flattens as I stare down at her.

She smirks. "And remember she liked the awkward. She liked the goof. She thought it was endearing, so to warm her up we need another nose-to-boob situation without actually doing nose to boob."

"You want me to be awkward?"

"Don't you think that's the best strategy? I've done some immense work on my end, building you up and trying to integrate you back in her life. She likes the awkward, so let's give her the awkward."

I scratch the side of my cheek. "You're right."

"I know I'm right, now, how is your underwear?" she asks. "Because bowling would be the perfect time to split your pants."

I roll my eyes dramatically. "I told you, underwear is always good, but these are nice pants—I don't want to split them."

She glances down at my pants and then back up at me. "What makes them nice? They seem average at best."

"They're not average. Easily above-average pants."

"How so?" She steps back and studies them. "They're jeans. They look okay."

"Okay?" I ask, feeling my jaw go slack in shock. "They're more than okay. They're my best jeans."

"Best jeans? That's a bit of a stretch because I just don't see it. If I were you, I'd be ready and willing to rip the crotch on those."

"I'm not ripping the crotch of these jeans," I say. "Think of something else."

"Something else to embarrass you?"

"I mean, if that's the route you think we need to take?"

She taps her chin. "How do you feel about a fake fart? I'm good at making fart sounds with my mouth. Listen to this…pfffft."

"Uh…no."

"Shame," she sighs. "Okay, what about losing your balance and smashing your head into the wall. She seems to like it when you put your head into things."

I glance at the wall and then back at her. "No."

"That was a good one, but okay. Uh, you babbled a lot last time, so maybe you can do the same thing this time. Ooo, or drop the bowling ball on your toe. Hilarious and awkward."

"And painful," I say.

She waves her hand in dismissal. "Oh, who really cares about pain?"

I point to my chest. "I do. I care about pain."

"Seems like you should care less."

"You're slowly starting to lose the title of The Prof."

"And you're rapidly gaining the title 'Henrietta with all the pain complaints,'" she counters with a hand on her hip.

"I don't like how quick-witted you are," I reply.

"And it's a shame you're so terrible at banter." She lifts her chin.

"I'm not terrible, I'm just—" I start just as Timothy walks past me, Maple following him. He brings her to the balls where he shows her the different sized holes and weights.

I feel a jolt of jealousy and lean in close to Everly. "Are they a thing?"

Everly looks over at Timothy and Maple before shaking her head. "Just friends. He doesn't want to date people in the same field as him. Apparently, Maple was thinking I could get to know him."

That causes my brows to raise. "Oh really?"

"Stop that," she says with a swat to my arm.

"Stop what?" I ask with a smile.

"Do not take this as an opportunity to embarrass me. You're the one who fumbles, and I'm the one with class."

"I usually don't fumble," I say. "I'm usually chill and easygoing. I have no problem talking to people, so don't compare me to the likes of Brody."

She gasps and holds her hand to her heart. "Don't you dare speak so terribly of the ill. He's fresh out of the hospital."

"And doing fine," I say with an eye roll.

"Still, it's terrible to pick on the less fortunate."

I chuckle as Timothy says, "So, have either of you bowled before?"

Maple joins us as well, which causes me to break out in a sweat. Fuck, maybe Everly is right, maybe I am the awkward one. I attempt to keep my eyes off Maple but rather focus on the people actually talking in the group—I'm sure it would creep her out if I stood there, heavy breathing while staring at her.

Be cool, man.

Be cool.

"Not regularly," Everly answers. "But I've chucked a few balls before." Why did she say it like that? "But can't say much for this guy. He was just squealing about how he can't remember the last time he wasn't plummeting balls into the gutter."

Squealing? Come on, Everly.

Timothy glances my way. "I thought Mario said you were decent."

"He was being kind," Everly says. "You know how men can be, pumping each other up, but I'll tell it like it is. We need to remind him where to roll the ball...toward the pins, right, Hardy?"

I feel my nostrils flare. "Yes, toward the pins."

"Maple, on the other hand," Everly continues. "I think we might have a ringer—we shall see."

"I don't know," Timothy says with a smile. "She was confused about the different balls."

"It's called a fake-out, so you're surprised when she does well, or not surprised when she sucks," Everly says while tapping her temple. "She's a smart one."

"She is," I add for good measure but get zero response from Maple.

"Well, help yourself to some pizza. I think we're going to get started very soon."

"Thanks," Everly says and then grabs a plate. "I wonder if they have pineapple."

"You like pineapple on your pizza?" Maple asks.

"Love it," Everly says as she lifts one of the lids, revealing pepperoni.

Shyly, Maple looks up at me. "Do you still like pineapple on your pizza?"

"Can't get enough of it," I answer. "Do you still hate it?"

"It's not great," Maple answers.

"Looks like just pepperoni and cheese," Everly says as she places a piece of pepperoni on her plate and cheese on mine. "Figured you would go for the cheese," Everly says. "Didn't you mention in the questionnaire I had you fill out as the best man that you can't handle spicy foods? Didn't want to give you pepperoni and risk the toots."

Uhh…what?

Everly, what the fuck?

Maple glances between us, looking confused. "Are you guys friends?"

"No," Everly says, shaking her head. "Just exchanged some emails, and as someone who needs to help plan things, it's good to know who I'm working with. He said he didn't want a lot of spicy food at the parties because it gives him the toots. But you'd know that, right, Maple?"

"Um, I can't recall." Maple looks up at me. "Did you toot a lot after eating spicy foods?"

I look between the two of them, loathing Everly in this moment. I get what she's trying to do, but couldn't we have gone with something other than flatulence?

"You know, I think it's something that I've developed recently," I answer, feeling that wave of sweat start to trickle down my back.

"That's what happens when you get older," Everly says before taking a bite of her pizza.

"Yeah, but I think it's something I'm working on with my doctor, so hopefully it's solved soon," I say.

"Fingers crossed," Everly says, holding up her fingers. And when Maple isn't looking, she winks at me.

I know I want to get to know Maple again, but so far her impression of me is that I like to greet people by motorboating them, I stumble, fumble, and bumble my way through every conversation, and apparently I toot when I eat spicy foods.

I can see the attraction already.

She must be frothing at the mouth, ready to date me again.

———

"It has to be beginner's luck," Everly says after her second strike in a row.

Yeah, in a fucking row.

I glance up at the scores and sigh at how terrible I'm doing. I know we prepped Timothy for me to be pretty good, but I think we can assume that was a lie. I'm terrible, but I didn't think I'd be so terrible that I'd be thirty points behind the next person…the next person being Maple.

Jesus Christ, man. Keep it out of the gutter at least for one go-around.

Everly takes a seat next to me, looking loose and free. She's been chatting it up with Timothy every so often, making him laugh. Maple has been sitting next to me as if we're complete strangers. Stiffly.

Occasionally, Everly will turn toward us to engage, but for the most part, it's been me and Maple staring down the pins in front of us, not saying a goddamn word.

She wanted awkward? Well, I'm handing it out in droves right now. I still have no clue how this is happening. Sure, it's been ten years since we've seen each other, but we used to talk all the time. Easily. *Didn't we?* I mean, we spent so much time together when we weren't studying, or out with our friends…surely, we used to talk. She hasn't even asked me anything about myself. Hudson was her biggest fan, and yet she hasn't even mentioned him. Or Haisley. Nothing. No interest in my life. *But have I asked her about hers?*

Mario picks up his ball and gets into position. While he's preparing to run his turn, I decide to take a chance and talk to Maple because something has got to give. I can't do this silence anymore.

"So, this is fun, huh?" I ask.

Not quite a great opener, but it's something.

"Uh…sure," Maple says.

Great.

I clasp my hands in front of me as my lips press tightly against my teeth. "Bowling…huh? Crazy."

I feel her eyes on me, but I don't dare turn to look at her, because I know what she must be thinking…what the hell happened to Hardy?

Because bowling, huh? is not really the kind of conversation I used to have.

"Yeah, bowling," she replies.

I clear my throat, trying to gain any semblance of intelligent conversation. "Balls hitting pins, who knew?"

"Probably the guy who invented bowling," she replies.

I nervously laugh but it comes out more as a donkey bray than a laugh. A solid hee-haw, which draws her attention toward me again. I keep my eyes straight ahead, because I can't possibly look her in the eye when I'm holding this kind of conversation. "Wonder if the inventor was any good."

"Not sure," she replies. "But you're not doing very well."

I smooth my hands over my thighs, exhibiting what is probably a deathly shade of red on my cheeks.

"Yes, well, in the years we haven't spoken to each other, I unfortunately haven't been working on my bowling game."

"No?" she asks. "What have you been working on?"

Okay...okay. She's talking, changing the subject, throwing me a freaking bone.

This is perfect.

Now it's time to shake off the stink and show her the kind of man I've become over the last few years.

"Educating myself about almonds, working on sustainable farming, perfecting my chocolate lava cake recipe."

"Chocolate lava cake?" she asks, a pinch to her brow. "You bake?"

No.

I don't.

I don't know why I said that last part.

I felt like I needed three things to dazzle her with and the chocolate cake thing just came flying out.

"Well, only chocolate lava cake," I answer.

"And how is the recipe?"

I lift my beer to my lips and answer, "Not great."

That makes her chuckle, which puts some ease in my chest because fuck, she's been cold as ice every time we're near each other.

And that's not how it used to be.

We were so free with each other.

Conversation was easy.

Our time spent together was relaxed, simple.

It seems like she's changed...or maybe I've changed. Who knows.

"Sounds like you might need a new recipe," she says.

"Yeah, possibly. Maybe I'll send a note to Martha Stewart, ask her if she has any tips."

"You're up, Maple," Timothy says.

Oh. Thank God.

Gives me a second to regroup.

Maple stands and moves toward the balls where she picks up the pink one she's been using all night. She studies the pins and then sheepishly walks up to the alley, brings her hand back, and shoots the ball forward. She doesn't move; she just watches the ball race down toward the pins and when they collide, she turns and walks back to the ball return.

She doesn't cheer.

She doesn't look at her group.

She just waits.

And I think...I think my assessment about her is right.

Sure, I've changed since college—we all do. If you haven't, you're not growing as a human. But Maple has changed in a different way. She's more withdrawn, isolated. Makes me wonder, did Peru change her?

Polly had made it seem like Maple was reluctant about coming back, but she doesn't want to be here at all. Maybe she wishes she was still in Peru. I would have no idea. It feels like something I should ask, but not something right now, in the middle of the bowling league where we are sitting dead last. Seems like too deep of a conversation.

Since I'm after Maple, I stand as she picks up her ball to shoot for a spare. Not sure what pin is standing up, but she has one on the left she has to knock down.

"Think you'll keep the ball straight this time?" Everly asks as she looks up at me from where she's sitting. One of her legs is crossed over the other and she's sporting a playful smirk.

"Why the hell would I want to break my gutter ball streak?" I ask. "Fuck no, I'm going to pitch it into the gutter twice this go-round."

"I like your tenacity," she replies.

"If I'm going to do something, I'm going to do it right," I say with conviction, which only makes her smile even wider.

"You know, it would help us if you didn't throw a gutter ball," Timothy says. "I heard that there might be eliminations in the league."

"What?" I ask. "How is that possible? Isn't this for fun?" I look around the bowling alley, taking in all the participants in matching shirts. Some people have their own balls, their own shoes…their own wrist guards. Some are doing the fancy ball curving technique that I pretended to do one time—and nearly broke my wrist in half. Maybe this is more serious than I thought it was.

Timothy scratches his head. "You know, I might have signed up for the wrong league."

"Which means…you need a strike," Everly says as she stands and walks over to the ball return with me after Maple earns a spare. "I think it's the ball you're using." She pokes at the blue ball I've been failing with all night. "It might be too heavy for you."

"It's definitely not too heavy for me," I say.

She steps in close and whispers, "It's okay if you're not throwing the same ball as the other guys. There's no shame in throwing a lighter ball."

"It's not too heavy," I repeat.

"Why don't you just try something lighter, maybe something lighter on your gentle wrist."

I hold up my arm and show her my wrist. "There is nothing gentle about this. This is a man's wrist."

"Yes, of course," she says in a mocking tone. "Very manly, Hardy. But your score doesn't match the girth of your manly wrist, so maybe we try something different. We can't screw this up for Tomothy."

"*Timothy*," I correct her.

Her eyes widen as her hand covers her mouth. "Oh shit, you're right. Oh my God, have I called him Tomothy?"

"I don't know," I say. "Have you?"

She winces. "I really hope not." She recalls her conversation, her lip worrying to the side. "Did I?"

I chuckle. "How the fuck should I know, I've been on lonely island with Maple talking about the inventor of bowling and my terrible chocolate lava cake recipe." I lean in close and whisper, "Spoiler, I've never made one in my life."

"Then why the hell are you talking about it?" she asks.

"Hell if I know, Plum! Things are going sour over there. Like the ship is sinking and there are no life vests in sight. It's really uncomfortable."

"For heaven's sake, you dated for years. You can't tell me there's nothing to talk about. Maybe an old memory. Like...oh hey, Maple, remember the time I got my hand stuck in the cookie jar?"

"What am I? Twelve?"

"I don't know, Henrietta. You tell me. You're the one bowling with a current score of fifty."

My eyes narrow, and a small smile appears at her lips.

"Uh, can we move this along," Timothy shouts.

Everly picks up the pink ball and hands it to me. "Trust me, this is the cure to your gutter ball streak. Try it."

"It feels like a feather," I say.

"Which is great for the gentle wrist." She winks and takes a step back, leaning against the wall and shooing me forward with her gesturing hand.

Rolling my eyes, I don't bother to argue with her as I take the pink ball and stick my fingers in the tiny holes. Feeling like an absolute fool, I get into position, visualize the pins in front of me, and then take three steps forward as I bring the ball behind me. And all together, I swing my arm forward and shoot the ball toward the pins.

Right toward the...

Nope.

My fingers get stuck in the holes of the ball and instead of sending the ball down the oiled-up alley, I shoot it up into the air...straight into the low ceiling above me.

"Oh fuck," I cry right before plaster rains all over our lane.

Everly covers her head.

I skitter back in fear.

And what feels like the entire bowling alley turns our way as the ball falls out of the ceiling and to my luck...straight into the gutter.

Silence falls over our group as we pathetically watch the pink ball very slowly, and very dramatically, make its way down the gutter toward the pins.

Plaster in my hair, my nostrils flared, I turn toward Everly who has both hands over her mouth, eyes wide, mirth in her expression.

"Are you happy?" I ask her, arms wide.

Her shoulders shake.

A chuckle falls out of her mouth, and then she crumples to the floor in a fit of laughter.

Yup...she's happy.

To: Everly Plum
From: Hardy Hopper
Subject: $157.89

Professor,

Do you see that number in the subject line? That's how much I owe the bowling alley for the replacement ceiling tile and labor to fix it.

Is it a drop in the bucket compared to what's in my bank account? Of course.

Is it a tidal wave of cost to my ego...yes, I shall never recover from this.

Not to mention being eliminated from the league after one night...because of my poor performance. It's a tough pill to swallow, and I'm afraid I'll never show my face in public again.

Not to mention after the chocolate lava cake convo with Maple, that's where we left things. I don't think she wanted to be seen with the man who crashed a bowling ball in the ceiling.

WHAT IS HAPPENING TO ME?

Henrietta

———————

To: Hardy Hopper
From: Everly Plum
Subject: RE: $157.89

In all honestly, I'm typing this email through teary eyes as I'm still laughing about the bowling ball smashing into the ceiling.

I don't think I've stopped laughing.

Anytime I think about it, I buckle over and my eyes water.

Easily one of the top moments of my life. So if anything, we might have been kicked out of the league and you have to pay an invoice for damage, but my God, you've brought me a tremendous amount of joy.

If it makes you feel any better, I think I did call Timothy "Tomothy" once, and every time I think about it, sweat erupts on the back of my neck.

Maybe we both should just duck our heads and never show our faces in public again.

The Prof

P.S. You still good for finishing up the bridal shower décor on Thursday?

To: Everly Plum
From: Hardy Hopper
Subject: RE: $157.89

I'm going to be straightforward with you—calling someone Tomothy instead of Timothy doesn't even come close to rocketing a bowling ball up to the moon and then back down to Earth where it settled in the gutter once again.

Not comparable.

You may show your face in public.

I, on the other hand, am going to bury my head in a bag of almonds.

And yes, still on for Thursday. See you there, Plum.

Henrietta

To: Hardy Hopper
From: JP Cane
Subject: Be an ally

Dear friend,

Now is the time to be an ally for the flamingos. Now more than ever they need you. We appreciate your donation, but to truly be an advocate, we need you to be the voice as well. Help us spread

*the word that a simple donation of $5 can help our research-
ers provide a safe and healthy environment for these majestic
creatures.*

*Join us this Saturday as we spread the word through social
media about the loss of habitats and the nearing of endangerment for the flamingos.*

Side with the pink!

*Squawk.
JP Cane*

"Why are we doing this?" I mutter to Hudson as he presses the elevator
button that leads up to our father's office.

"Because he called, and even though we don't answer to him anymore, we still need to save face with the man. He's our father, after
all."

"Well aware he's our father, but there is nothing productive that will
come from this meeting."

"Maybe not," Hudson says, "but I think we at least owe it to Haisley
to go."

And there's the one thing that will make me do anything: the mention
of my sister's name.

After her wedding, things went downhill for our family. Hudson and
I stepped out, not putting up with our dad's manipulative ways. We took
Haisley with us and teamed up with his competition. It's been a smart
plan, although stressful, given our dad's very vocal disapproval. But we've
watched how he runs his business for a while now, stepping on the toes
of those who are smaller than him so he can gain an inch. Hudson and I

would rather lift up the smaller businesses and invest in them than try to steal their ideas and create cheap knockoffs.

We want the best minds working for us…working with us.

We have the almond company leading the way with profits with a meeting with Maggie's friend, Hattie, who lives in Almond Bay and who sells the best almond extract on the west coast.

Maggie just opened her storefront for Magical Moments by Maggie, and her schedule is becoming increasingly busy to the point that she's starting interviews for another employee.

Brody and Jude are working on five multiuse event spaces like the one we're using for the bridal shower, while our small marketing team is starting to create materials that will change the course of pop-up shops and meeting spaces in the Bay Area.

And Haisley is working on two more themed vacation rentals, one in San Francisco and one in Almond Bay.

We're all connected, and Hudson is leading the charge.

We're already successful. There's no reason to be at our father's beck and call anymore. But I understand needing to play the game even though I don't like it.

The elevator dings and opens up to our father's office floor. The dark paneled wood walls, gold fixtures, and black tiled floors feel stuffy now rather than what my father intended—an intimidating symbol of wealth and power. In all honesty, the façade of it all just feels ridiculous. To me, with wealth comes responsibility, the duty to help others around you, to promote and support them. My father treats wealth as if everyone around him should bow before him, beg him for eye contact, only to offer it to no one. A disgusting outlook on business.

We're stronger in a group, stronger when working together. Stronger when endorsing rather than tearing down—a motto my dad would never adopt.

His assistant sits at her desk, her phone perched at her ear as we make our way toward our dad's office.

Instead of bypassing her, something our father would do, we stop at her desk where she tells us that our dad is expecting us and to let ourselves in.

We offer her a nod and with Hudson leading the way, we push through the heavy door of my father's office. He's sitting on the couch, smoking a cigar, with one leg crossed over the other.

Even though he watches us walk through the door, he doesn't bother to move, doesn't even flinch. Instead, a billowing puff of white smoke leaks out of the corner of his mouth and right into the air, clouding his face and filling the room with a familiar sickly-sweet scent. "Take a seat, boys."

Immediately, the hairs on the back of my neck stand at attention. Something doesn't feel right.

Something screams revenge.

Pushing past the uneasiness, Hudson and I both take seats across from him and match his casual stance as we lean into our seats and wait for him to lead the conversation. He's the one who called us into this meeting, after all.

Unsurprisingly, he goes for intimidation. He taps his cigar on his ash tray and then takes another puff.

Oldest trick in the book.

Too bad for him, we've learned all his tactics throughout the years.

Just get on with it, Dad.

After a few more seconds of silence, he clears his throat. "How is this pithy co-op you've created?"

Going with petty today, sounds about right for him.

"Interested in investing?" Hudson asks. "Because unfortunately, we have all the investment we need at the moment."

I catch the flare of my father's nostrils and mentally fist-bump Hudson, knowing that slight comment cut Dad.

"I don't tend to invest in projects that I don't believe will succeed."

Jesus, what a moron.

I make a note to never be so full of myself that I can't see a good idea when it's sitting right in front of me. Arrogance can be the death of a good businessman, and right now, it has a chokehold on my dad.

"We're not here to prove our worth to you, Dad," Hudson says, ignoring my dad's insult. "If you brought us into your office to degrade us, then we have no reason to stay. If you want to be a man and speak to us in the way we deserve, then please, tell us why we're here."

Thank God Hudson is leading the charge because I don't think I would be as well-mannered as him when speaking to our father.

Dad's lips twist to the side, and he sets his cigar down on the ashtray, letting it burn in place. When he straightens up and looks us in the eyes, he says, "I'm suing you."

Yup.

Saw that coming.

It's something Hudson and I mentally prepared each other for, knowing damn well our dad would not go down without a fight. It's the kind of man he is. Luckily for us, we not only have an amazing law firm working for us, but so do the Cane brothers. They're unmatched for what my father surely has planned.

"Thought you would say something like that," Hudson says as he reaches into his jacket pocket. The man is fully prepared. He tosses a business card on the coffee table between us. "There's the contact information for our lawyers. Feel free to send your baseless, frivolous lawsuit their way." Hudson taps my shoulder. "Let's go."

We stand just as our father does as well, rage behind those aging eyes of his. "You realize you have broken this family," he says, taking a different tactic. "Your mother is beside herself. She won't get out of bed. She's so distraught over losing her children."

"Really?" I say, stepping in. "Because every time I call her, she's either busy or doesn't answer. Seems to me if she was so broken, she'd pick up the phone."

Dad's eyes narrow. "She's so disgusted with you she can't even stomach the mention of your name."

"And whose fault is that?" Hudson asks.

"Yours," Dad says. "I never would have done something like this to my father. Abandon him and the empire he built."

"We're not going through this again," Hudson says. "We've talked to you about our reasoning. From your impending lawsuit, the reasoning for parting ways with you is just." Hudson shakes his head and gestures for me to leave, but for some reason, I stay put as I look my father in the eyes.

"You are disappointing," I say to him. "This business, this need to succeed? It's overshadowed what's really important in life, and that's the relationships you build and the people around you who you love."

"And you haven't done the same thing?" he asks. "I distinctively remember you making a decision out of college that made you choose business over relationships."

"What are you talking about?" I ask, clearly not as composed as Hudson.

"Maple," Dad says, letting the sound of the *p* pop off his lips. "You had the chance to be with her, to go to Denver with her, but you chose business over her."

"I chose family," I say, my defenses rising.

He shakes his head. "You chose guaranteed success. Don't try to fool me. You were lost in college. Everyone around you had a good head on their shoulders and a path for where they wanted to take their future. You were the one struggling. You were the one looking for a purpose. An opportunity was presented to you, a chance to succeed, something you hadn't had a taste of yet, and you took it instead of following your girl. You broke her heart for your own self-satisfaction."

"That's not...that's not how that went down," I say, even though... fuck, it sort of feels like that's how it happened. *Is that why she cut off all contact and didn't seem to want anything to do with me?*

"Let's go," Hudson says, his hand on my shoulder now, pushing me toward the exit.

"Believe what you want," Dad says, "but you've made decisions just like I have. The apple doesn't fall far from the tree, Hardy, as much as you wish to believe it does."

We're out the door before I can respond. With his mouth close to my ear, Hudson whispers, "Say nothing."

So in silence, we make our way past Dad's assistant and press the button to the elevator. It dings immediately, and we get in. When we turn around to watch the doors close, Dad is standing outside his office, a smile on his face.

And the sight of him, so pleased with himself, feels like a knife twisting in my gut. *This* is how it's always been with him. For as long as I can remember. His deliberate attempt to grate on my nerves, getting under my skin, trying to tear me down while lifting Hudson up. Luckily for me, Hudson has a good head on his shoulders and has never let our dad drive a wedge between us, even though he's tried many, many times.

Hudson is smarter.

Hudson is more clever.

Hudson is top of his class.

Hudson knows what he wants with his life…what the hell do you plan on doing?

With every comment, every backhanded insult, Dad tried his damnedest to make it a competition between me and Hudson, but we didn't let him. Hudson led the charge, always lifting me up, always being there for me, always making sure I'm part of the conversation, not the one taking the orders.

And even now, with the pressure of the new business, Hudson includes me. He helps me find my best assets of what I can offer and highlights those assets, letting me take the lead.

The doors to the elevator close, and Hudson turns to me. "Don't," he says. "Don't let him play fucking mind games with you."

I lean against the elevator wall. "I know." I let out a deep breath, even though his words ring true—well, somewhat true.

"Do you? Because I can see the wheels in your head turning," Hudson says. "Don't spiral on me, Hardy. This is what he wanted—he wanted to get in your head."

I push my hand through my hair. "Hard not to let him when..." I look up at Hudson. "Fuck, there's truth to what he said."

"There's no truth in it," Hudson says. "You knew you wanted to be a part of the family business. We spoke about it back when you were a senior. I talked to you about helping out, about Dad's impossible standards and his wayward business practices. We had the conversation of what would happen if we joined forces, if we could help make a change. Do you remember that conversation?"

I nod. "I do."

"That was the reason you stayed here in San Francisco. That was the reason you didn't follow Maple. You didn't choose success over her—you chose a relationship with your father, with your brother. You wanted to make a difference."

"Yeah, look how well that went," I say on a huff.

"I think we both know we can't change him if he doesn't want to change. We tried, Hardy. We attempted to reform him, to make him better, but as time went on, we realized he was stuck in his ways. Was the effort worth it? Yes, because we gave it a shot. We know we tried."

"And now what?" I ask. "I hurt someone else for nothing."

"But did you?" he asks. "Is Maple hurting?"

"She can barely talk to me," I say.

"Because of how you ended things? You're assuming you hurt her, but maybe you had nothing in common in the first place, and maybe... maybe she's realizing it."

The elevator doors open, and Hudson leads the way, me following close behind him, my mind reeling.

We had things in common.

We did…

Right?

CHAPTER FOURTEEN
EVERLY

Maple: I'm so sorry, Everly, but I can't make it tonight. I feel sick about it. I know the shower is in two days and I should be there, finishing all the decorations, but without getting into any details, we're having a flamingo emergency.

I READ MAPLE'S TEXT AND then look up at all of the decorations I've laid out on the table. It's not a problem—I can easily take care of everything.

Everly: Don't even worry about it. That's why I'm here, to help.

Maple: I feel terrible.

Everly: Don't. I promise, everything will be okay. I believe Hardy might even show up. Haven't heard from him though since I texted. Either way, I can get it done. No worries. I'll see you on Saturday.

Maple: Okay. Thank you so much, Everly.

Everly: Of course.

I set my phone down and kick off my heels only to slip on my slippers that I keep here in the office when I don't want to be click-clacking around. Maggie is gone for the day, prepping for a wedding this weekend and a rehearsal dinner tomorrow after a half day full of interviews and not finding anyone that she's interested in hiring.

I appreciate her being very particular on who she plans to bring on board. She wants someone who has experience, someone who can add to our team where we might not be as strong, and someone who we can get along well with. So far, she's coming up short.

But like she said, she'd rather work harder right now in order to get it right.

Focusing on the pom-poms that need to be finished, I take a seat in one of the chairs along our large conference table, just as the front door to the store opens. I glance over my shoulder to see Hardy walk in.

His hair is disheveled in that way he seems to perfectly wear all the time, but instead of his classic jeans and T-shirt, he's wearing a navy-blue suit and a white button-up shirt. The expensive-looking fabric clings to every contour of his frame, leading me to believe that it was specifically tailored to his body.

Dear God.

He's so handsome.

"Hey," he says as he walks up to me. "Sorry I'm late." And then, just like every other time he's greeted me, he leans down and presses a kiss to my cheek.

And like every other time, my skin tingles as his beard rubs against it and his cologne lingers in the air between us.

"Not late," I say as I try to act as cool as I can, despite the way he just spiked my internal temperature. "I was just getting started."

He unbuttons his suit jacket and removes it, showing off his impeccable chest, thanks to the way his button-up shirt pulls against it. Pecs flat and thick, lats like boulders, and a tapered waist that leads to a cinched belt. "Where's Maple?" he asks, rolling up his shirt sleeves.

"She texted and said she can't make it. Flamingo emergency. I told her I'd take care of everything." I meet his eyes. "If you want to take off too, I can handle everything. I know you were probably here to get close with Maple."

His brow creases. "I'm not about to leave you to do this by yourself. I'm here to help too, so put me to work."

"Are you sure?" I ask, studying him. There's something disconcerting about him right now. A pinch of annoyance in his brow, an air of irritation. The normal jovial man is absent and in his place is someone working through something in their head. "Hopefully this is not too bold, but you seem to be in a different frame of mind. Maybe not in the mood to make pom-pom arrangements."

He takes a seat and leans back in the chair before pushing his hand through his hair. "I need to do something to take my mind off the bullshit I went through today." His eyes meet mine. "So let's do this."

I knew something was off. I could tell the minute he walked into the building. Given the way he's dressed and the edgy tone in his voice, a part of me wonders if it has anything to do with his dad.

But I'm not going to ask, because first I don't think it's my place, and second I don't want to put him in a worse mood than he already is.

So instead, I'm going to try to alter his night, bring him joy and get his mind off things.

"Okay, I can teach you the complexities of building the perfect pom-pom bouquet, but I must warn you: If we're going to do this, then we're going to do it right." I pick up my phone and I pull up Door Dash. "How do you feel about Philly cheesesteaks?"

His brows raise in interest. "I feel fondly about them."

"Perfect. I'm starving for some dinner so I'm going to order us some."

"I can grab it if you want," he says.

I hold up my hand. "Consider it a peace offering after I gave you the bowling ball that you sent to the moon."

That brings a smile to his face. "So you're accepting partial blame?"

"I'm accepting the fact that maybe your wrist wasn't as gentle as I assumed." I smile at him and then type away on my phone. "What would you like to drink?"

"Water is fine," he says.

"And any chips?"

He scratches his cheek. "You know, I'm not opposed to sea salt and vinegar."

"Really?" I ask, tearing my eyes from my phone to look at him.

"Oh shit, please don't tell me you're one of those people who can't stand sea salt and vinegar."

"I'm not," I say as I lean forward, hand on the table. "I'm a lover of the SSV."

"Are you really?" he asks while I slowly nod, which makes him laugh. "Well, fuck, Plum. Look at us having the same good taste."

"Some might say great taste," I reply before finishing up the order. When I'm done, I open up my Spotify app and say, "Okay, next task, mood music."

"Mood music?" he asks as he crosses his arms. "What kind of mood music are you talking about?"

"Pom-pom making music," I say and scan through my playlist. "Hmm, what are your thoughts on Missy Elliot?"

"Love her," he answers. "Perhaps possibly distracting because I might be tempted to stand on this table and pelvic thrust my way through 'Get Your Freak On.'"

"Although that's something I'd love to witness, good point. Far too catchy to be making delicate pom-pom bouquets." I scan some more. "How do you feel about some show tunes?"

"Uh, the only show tune I probably know is 'Greased Lightning' and I don't think we want to play that on repeat."

"That would be a no," I reply. "Okay...are we in the mood for Christmas music?"

"Have you lost your mind?"

"Just checking you haven't," I say. "You passed the test. Good job." I flip through more playlists and then land on one that I'm truly curious about. "What about Whitney Houston?"

"You mean the greatest voice to ever grace the planet?"

"Pardon me?" I ask, blinking a few times. "Did you just make that bold statement?"

"Do you not agree?" he asks, unfolding his arms.

"Uh, I vehemently agree. I just wasn't expecting you to say such a thing. To make such a claim."

"Well, believe it, Plum. Whitney was God's gift to our ears."

"I guess we found our playlist then," I say as I connect to the store's Bluetooth speakers. "Get ready to go on a journey of incomparable timbre and vibrato."

"Don't need to prepare me, I know exactly what kind of journey we're about to embark on."

The first few notes of "I Wanna Dance With Somebody" plays through the speakers, not too loud where we can still hear each other, but the perfect volume to fill the silence.

"And there she is," Hardy whispers with a sigh.

"One of my favorite songs," I say. "When I was in second grade, I danced to this in a talent show with a boy named Trent. It was considered a real banger routine."

"Was it now?" he asks. "Care to show me some moves?"

"I don't think we're there yet in our working relationship."

"Oh, we're there," he says leaning forward. He nods at me. "Go ahead, show me one move."

I ponder it for a second, but then think *who the hell cares*? It's not like anything can get more embarrassing than him shooting a bowling ball into the roof. He's set the standard, and I'm not sure I'll ever be able to reach that.

"Okay, one move, but after this display of choreographed perfection, we need to get to work on these pom-poms."

A handsome smile passes over his lips. "Deal."

I stand from my chair and move toward a more open space.

His eyes fall to my slippers and then back up to my face. "I like the footwear."

"You try wearing heels on concrete all day, unbelievably uncomfortable." I clear my throat and then get in position, with my hands above my head. "Are you ready?"

"I've never been more ready in my life." He faces me and folds his arms over his large chest, his gaze intent on me.

"Five, six, seven, eight," I say right before I sweep one arm down and back up, then the other arm. Then I twirl and salsa my leg forward, then the other, twirl, and then jazz hands.

The smile that remains on Hardy's face is easily the most attractive sight I've ever seen. I'm pretty sure I'd happily perform my dance all night if it means that smile stays.

He claps his hands, chuckling. "Wow, those are some moves."

I take a seat and nonchalantly say, "Told you, choreographed perfection."

"Emmy-worthy."

"I know," I say with a smirk, which causes him to laugh. "Now, you owe me some pom-poms."

"A deal is a deal." He looks over the supplies on the table. "What the hell do you want me to do with this?" He lifts up the pom-pom maker, and it flops around in his hand.

"That's the pom-pom maker. You take yarn, weave it around, cut, and then tie. It forms the pom-pom that we will glue on a stick for the centerpieces. I also need some for the garland. I have a whole bin full and was going to string them together with this." I hold up a very large sewing needle.

"Jesus," he says. "That looks like it came from a medieval torture chamber."

"If you're not a good helper, then you're going to experience the kind of torture it could provide." I playfully jab it in his direction, and he lifts his hands in defense.

"Hell, I don't want that. I'll be good, I promise, Mistress Plum."

I let out a laugh. "Such a good subservient."

With a smirk gracing his lips, he says, "Maybe I can string the pom-poms. That seems like an easy job that I can't fuck up. Making them scares me."

"It's easy to make them, but if you're more comfortable stringing, you can do that too."

"Thanks," he says as I hand him the needle. "Christ, look at this thing! It could have come in handy today."

"Oh? Looking to jab people?"

"One person in particular."

"Yeah?" I ask as I set up the bin of completed pom-poms in front of him. I also help him string the needle before he gets started. "Want to talk about it?"

"Not really," he answers as I show him how to string the first pom-pom, jabbing the needle and pulling the string through. "But fuck, I feel like if I don't get it off my chest, I'm going to be miserable company."

"You've been pretty enjoyable so far," I say.

His eyes flash to mine. "It's the Whitney Houston that's masking my shit attitude."

"She did wonders with her voice—I think we both know that."

"True," he says and then sighs. He sticks the needle through a pom-pom and asks, "I assume this conversation will stay between us? I wouldn't want it getting to Maple or anything."

"I wouldn't tell her anything personal, Hardy. I know we joke around, and I've been helping you with making a new connection to her, but I don't want you thinking I'm telling her your deepest, darkest secrets."

"I know you wouldn't. I just want to make sure." He trusts me. There's something so satisfying about that, earning another human's trust. It's almost as if we're becoming friends.

Hell, I know we are, and I like it. I might not be able to have him as mine, but friends…I can take that.

"I get it," I say. "And feel free to not even talk about your shit day today. Instead, we can talk about Whitney Houston and how 'The Star-Spangled Banner' should never be sung by anyone else but her."

"I bought the single." He winces.

"The one that was released on CD and all the proceeds went to the funds set up for firefighters and police officers affected by 9/11?" I ask.

"That very one."

I pat my chest. "I got it too."

"Really?" He shakes his head. "I've never met another person who bought that."

"Clearly you're not hanging out with the right people," I say.

"Clearly." He threads another pom-pom on the string while I start making more. "Well, it looks like I'm hanging out with the right person now."

"You are." If only he saw that connection as something worth pursuing. But what keeps surprising me is how comfortable I feel with this man. I should feel intimidated. He's a very wealthy man and has serious street cred. And yet, he's so down-to-earth. I've never felt so comfortable with someone so quickly, which makes it even harder to realize that his heart is determined on being with another woman. But I refuse to focus on that right now. He seemed stressed earlier, so it's my aim to help him get out of that slump. "You should congratulate yourself on making the smart decision to start spending time with me, Henrietta."

"Maybe I will with a beer later."

"Ooo, are you a beer drinker? Need to crack open a cold one after a long hard day?"

"Not really," he says. "I mean, I drink, but it's not like a routine for me when I get home from work."

"What is your routine?" I ask.

"Are we getting personal?" he asks with a raised brow.

"We are. We shared our love for Whitney, you've told me extensively about your impeccable underwear, the next step is obviously sharing with each other our bedtime routines. So, do you sleep with a stuffie? Yes or no?"

He smirks. "No."

"Oh yeah, me neither. Eck, gross. Who does that?"

He sits taller, pausing his stringing. "Everly Plum, do you still sleep with a stuffie?"

"No," I say even though I know for a fact there's a well-loved stuffed worm named Mr. Pooty Pie on my bed at the moment.

"You do," he says, finding way too much joy in this. "You sleep with a stuffie."

"You say that as if that's a bad thing. Remember, I'm, like, ten years younger than you. I'm still fresh from the crib."

"The fuck you are," he says, making me laugh. "You're a grown-ass woman with a stuffie."

Holding my chin high, I say, "So what? Do you look down upon those who find comfort in polyester stuffed animals?"

"No." He shakes his head.

"Because it seems like you're judging, and for a man who bowled below an eighty with one bowling ball blasting through the ceiling, I don't think you have any room to judge."

"How long are you going to hold that over my head?"

"As long as I can." I wink.

"Oddly, I find that fair."

"I'm glad that you do," I say.

"How about this," he says as he levels with me. "I'll tell you my after-work routine if you tell me who you're cuddling into at night."

"With no judgment," I add.

"With no judgment," he agrees.

"Fine, but you have to promise you won't tell your sister. I still want her to think I'm a consummate professional, someone she can trust in partnering up with in business and not some overgrown toddler who still snuggles into a stuffie at night."

A smirk tugs on the corner of his lips. "Promise."

"Okay, deal, but you go first," I say.

He nods. "Well, depends on where I am. If I'm out at the farm, I usually don't get back to the house until late because I really like walking up and down the rows of almond trees. It's soothing to me. So when I do get back to the house, it's a quick dinner and show for me before I'm down for the night."

"Seems pretty basic."

"That's my life, basic as it comes. And when I'm here in the city, I leave the office as soon as I can, sometimes I take emails home with me, but try to avoid it. I hit up the gym in my building, and depending on my mood, I'll either walk to one of the nearby restaurants in my neighborhood, or I'll order something. Then finish the night with a show and then bed."

"Huh, I half expected you to tell me you were going to some rich man's smoking club after work where you gab about your day."

"Do you really think I would be here making garlands if I was part of a smoking club?"

"True," I say. "A smoking club member would be far more into himself, and despite the clean shave around your beard and your masculine scent, I'd say you're not really that into yourself."

"If I weren't part of the corporate world, I'd look a lot different."

"How so?" I ask.

"Well, I'd have longer hair. Maybe a longer beard. I wouldn't be wearing this constricting suit, that's for damn sure. I'd live in a beanie, flannel, and jeans. Perhaps carry around an axe just for the hell of it. I'd have dirt grooves in my hands from being outside all the damn time, and I'd have the worst farmer's tan, a tan so bad that when I took off my shirt, people would think I'm still wearing one."

I chuckle. "Wow, quite the image." And yes, I would put my hand up to see that gorgeous sight. *You can take that shirt off right now if you like, Hardy Hopper. I would not complain at all. Farmer's tan or not.*

"And I wouldn't have to answer time-sucking emails or attend boring business meetings."

"Would you consider this a boring business meeting, or responding to my emails as a time suck?"

"Actually, this meetup is a bright spot in my day, and I look forward to your emails, even if they can be somewhat emasculating."

"They are not emasculating," I say on a huff. "They speak the truth. If you find that emasculating, that's your fault. I shall not cater to you because you're too weak to hear the truth."

"Damn, don't you need to scream out a war cry after such a statement?"

"I can if you want," I say.

He shakes his head, his expression full of mirth. "For the record, I'm never too weak to hear anything you have to tell me."

"Is that so?" I ask. "Well, in that case—"

He holds up his hand to stop me. "Just not when I'm down from a rough day."

I smirk. "Noted."

He finishes up his garland, and I take it from him to tie it off before starting a new string for him. When he raises a brow, I say, "Did you think you were just making one and getting a free meal out of it? No way, sir. You're here to work."

With that, he starts stringing pom-poms again.

"Okay, so are you going to tell me about your stuffie?" he asks.

"If you must know," I say, clearing my throat, "he's a stuffed worm that I've had since I was three. He is the only love of my life, and I can't imagine a day when I put him in a box or offer him up to someone else. He has feelings, and I intend to honor them."

Hardy lets out a boisterous laugh. "So you have that whole *Toy Story* complex then?"

"How can you watch that movie and not assume all of your childhood toys have feelings?" Whispering, I add, "It's gotten to the point, Hardy, where I believe that the plate I eat on at night is so relieved that I picked it to fulfill its plate duties, that if I put it back in the cupboard in exchange for a bowl, it will cry."

"Dear God," he whispers.

"I know. It's a problem. So yes, Mr. Pooty Pie still has a central location on my bed."

"Hold on a second," he says, pausing his stringing. "You named your stuffed worm Mr. Pooty Pie?"

"Yes," I reply. "Do you have a problem with that?"

"Not a problem, just wondering where the name came from?"

"A child's brain, Hardy, where else?"

He chuckles. "You got me there."

———————

"So," Hardy says as he unravels his sandwich from the wrapper, "tell me about your day."

"What?" I ask, confused.

"You told me that you hate dinner time because you always eat alone. Well, I'm here eating with you and you're not alone, so tell me about your day."

Well, doesn't that just kick me in the freaking heart.

The man is not only attractive and funny, but thoughtful and considerate. The fact that he remembered that conversation just goes to show how amazing he is.

"Oh, uh…well, it was fine. Nothing too exciting happened. Lots of admin work today. Oh, I don't know if I told you this, but one of the best men that I'm working with, he has a crush on the maid of honor. They used to date, and I've been attempting to help him find love with her again. It's been a slow process because he likes to chuck bowling balls up into ceilings, which I think scares her. Not sure she was into the whole Hulk show he put on."

Hardy's lips twist to the side, not amused. "Uh-huh, well, maybe things are going slow because you're not doing your best work."

"It's hard to create magic when your beans are sour," I say.

"What the hell does that mean?" he laughs.

"You know, *Jack and the Beanstalk*, magic beans, he could make things happen because the beans were prime time, cream of the crop. It's difficult to create that magic when the best man I'm dealing with isn't showing up as the most enchanting human she's ever seen."

"Hey, I asked about your day. I'd say that's pretty enchanting," he counters.

"I'd say that's the bare minimum requirement for men."

He chuckles. "Very true." He picks up a salt and vinegar chip and chomps on it. "In all seriousness, do you really think I'm not bringing the magic?"

"No, I think you are," I say. "Only teasing you. I think it will take time for her to adjust to everything around her and seeing you again. Give it a second."

"I will," he says and then nods at my sandwich. "How is it?"

"Divine," I say before taking a large bite and making a show of it, shoving a good portion in my mouth. He looks surprised for a second, and then determination sets in his features and he opens his mouth and takes an even bigger bite from his sandwich.

Together, mouths full of Philly cheesesteak, we chew and stare at each other.

It takes all of three seconds before I snort, sending a chunk of meat across the table and right in front of his laid-out wrapper.

I grip my hand over my mouth, both horrified and entertained, while he chuckles. But with his mouth full, it sounds more like a gurgling than anything.

And from there, it's a fit of laughter.

To the point that both of us grab the to-go bags from our meals and spit our partially chewed sandwiches inside.

"Fuck," he roars before he laughs some more.

I join him, gripping my stomach as tears form in my eyes.

"You're disgusting," he gasps.

"Me?" I croak. "What about you?"

"You're the one snorting meat out of your nose."

I hold my finger up in contention. "That did not come out of my nose. That came out of my mouth while I snorted out of my nose. It was a double whammy of exhalation."

"That's a fucking term?"

"It is and trademarked by me, so don't you dare try to use it."

"Show me the paperwork," he says while jabbing his finger onto the table. "Show me the paperwork, and I won't use it."

I hold up my palm to him. "See, double whammy exhalation, trademarked by Professor Plum, so good luck debating that in court."

His lips turn up as he studies me. "You're right, you have me in a chokehold. No way can I beat that ironclad paperwork."

I shrug and pick my sandwich back up. "Don't mess with me, Henrietta. I know what the hell I'm doing."

I'm about to take a bite of my sandwich when he says, "Can you pick up the snorted, double whammy exhalation meat? Rather not stare at it while I finish my sandwich."

"Oh right, sure."

"How does this look?" Hardy asks as he moves his centerpiece toward me.

Oh dear.

It's an opaque fluted vase which Hardy has stuffed full with pom-poms glued on sticks, each stem the same height, offering no color differentiation or texture. I believe a toddler could have done a better job.

"Not bad," I lie.

"Really?" he asks, full of hope.

"No, it's terrible."

His joy immediately vanishes. "Why must you pump me up only to push me down?"

"Builds character," I answer before moving over to his side of the table. "Okay, remember what I said about having different variations and textures?"

"I recall something of the sort," he answers.

"And what do you have in your vase right now?"

"All pom-poms of the same color," he replies.

"Yes, that's correct, good job, Hardy." He gives me a look, clearly not appreciating my condescending tone. I sheepishly smile. "Well, although it's a great selection of the same size and color pom-poms, why don't we pull some of these out..." I pull out almost all of the pom-pom sticks, leaving just two. "And then we pick a few others in different colors and textures. Like, mix the small with the big and then use some of these twig balls and bamboo sticks as fillers." I pick up a few and arrange them in the vase, showing him just what I mean. When I'm done, I turn the vase toward him. "What do you think?"

He studies it for a moment. "I think I should go back to stringing the pom-poms."

I chuckle. "You were very good at that."

"I was, and I thought that maybe I could expand my decorating résumé with centerpieces, but from that demonstration, we all know being a rookie in the end zone is not where I need to be."

"Smart choice, but I want you to know I'll be here to nurture you with knowledge if you ever do decide to go back into the end zone—until then, stick with the garland."

"Great idea," he says while he picks up the giant needle again and starts threading pom-poms onto the string. "Is this what you do for every event?"

"Depends," I say. "We have a great deal of supplies in our stockroom from other events that we'll reuse. For instance some of the table runners and backdrops we are using for the bridal shower have come from other events. We will reuse all of these pom-poms and vases. We also have a big warehouse in the back where we keep everything that we need, of course organized all neat and tidy."

"I wouldn't expect anything less," he says, picking up a pink pom-pom and stringing it. "What got you into events?"

"Do you want the lame answer or the real answer?" I ask as I stick some bamboo stalks into the vase for some final fillers.

"There are two answers? Well, you have to know I'm going to say both."

I wouldn't have wanted it any other way.

"Well, the lame answer, and I mean the answer probably everyone would expect, would be. . .I love being able to help people have a memorable day. That is not a lie—it's the truth. There is nothing that gives me greater joy than seeing how my help has brought someone else happiness. That being said, I think it's a generic answer."

"Very much so," he says. "What's the real answer?"

"I was obsessed with the movie *The Wedding Planner* with Jennifer Lopez and Matthew McConaughey. After watching it, I told myself that's what I wanted to do with my life. It took place in San Francisco, it featured the neat and tidy life that I love, and she got to plan weddings. Just seemed like the perfect journey for me."

"You know. . .I've seen it a time or two."

"Really?" I ask, surprised.

"Yes. Haisley loved it as well. She made me watch it a few times with her." He finishes with his current string, so I help prepare a new one. "Now, my question is have you ever fallen in love with the groom?"

"Never," I answer.

But I've fallen in lust with the best man…

"Think you ever would?" he asks.

"No," I say. "I believe too much in love to mess around with something like that."

"Yeah, you don't seem like that kind of girl," he says.

"No? What kind of girl do I seem like?"

"Putting me on the spot, Plum? Okay." He shifts in his chair and looks me up and down. "Well, for one, you're the type of girl one doesn't mess with, meaning you have your shit together. You're organized and knowl-edgeable. Pretty sure if someone was trying to tell you that you were wrong about something when you were right, you'd let them hear it."

"True."

"But past the tough exterior, as in, you know, how to stick up for your-self, you're very kind, you want to make people happy. You don't break the rules, you follow them to a T, but you also know how to have a good time. You enjoy joking around, being playful, and not being serious all the time." He wets his lips. "How did I do?"

"Pretty spot on, Henrietta. I'm impressed."

"Thank you." He takes a mini bow. "I can be observant."

"I've noticed. It's a good quality in a man. Maple is lucky, because I've seen quite a few men who just don't pay attention. Who are more consumed by their video games or the world around them to notice what their partner likes or needs."

"You speaking from experience?"

I slowly nod. "Yes. Haven't really found any true catches out there in the world who have blown me away with their personalities. Especially in college, lots of duds."

"You will," he says. "You're a catch, Plum. You'll find the right person."

I feel my cheeks heat up from the compliment. If only he would see that I could be the perfect catch for him.

"Who knows, maybe Timothy and I will hit it off."

"Timothy or Tomothy?" Hardy asks with a smirk.

"Timothy," I answer with a straight face. "As far as I'm concerned, Tomothy is dead to me."

"Poor guy didn't even have a chance at disappointing you with his lack of knowledge about the female genitalia."

"Oh no, he disappointed me day one, so no need to give him another chance." I start on my last vase, sad that I'm almost done, but also glad because it's getting late, and I don't want to be doing this anymore, even though I'm having a good time with Hardy.

A great time actually.

I'm grateful Maple had to cancel. And not only because of my massive crush and how awkward it would have been if she'd been here, but I've really enjoyed spending time with him, just real time, with nothing between us.

"So, Timothy, huh?" he asks.

I shrug. "He was cute. He was fun to talk to. Could be an enjoyable date. Perhaps I'll ask Maple for his number. Makes me nervous though—I haven't been on a date in a really long time."

"Same," he says. "Not sure how it even works anymore."

"I think there's food involved."

"And conversation." He pauses and looks between us. "I guess like tonight."

I bring my hand to my chest playfully. "Why, Hardy Hopper, are you saying we were on a date tonight?"

"I'd feel bad for you if we were. Not sure I was much of a gentleman."

"Now, now," I say. "You didn't leave the table when the meat flew out of my mouth."

"True." He points at me. "Very true. Rather chivalrous, if you ask me.

And when the food was dropped off at the door, I was the one who got it and brought it to the table."

"Such a valiant act," I say. "See, any woman's dream date."

He puffs his chest. "Damn right."

Chuckling, I finish up the final vase and then take a seat as he uses up the last of the pom-poms. "So, are you feeling better than when you arrived?" I ask.

"I am," he says. "Much better. Thank you, Everly."

I shrug. "Just here to serve."

When he's done putting the last pom-pom on the string, he hands it over to me so I can tie it. "Do you have a close relationship with your parents?" he asks.

I can see where this is going so I tread lightly. "Pretty close," I say.

He nods. "What's that like?"

"Umm…" I stand and start collecting our trash from the night. "I guess kind of like having siblings, but older. Especially at this age. Sure, they offer their parental support, but they seem more like people I can go to when I need someone to talk to. Not so much parenting, more like friendship now."

He pushes up from the able, picking up some garbage as well and bringing it over to the trash can. "I've never been close with my dad. I've tried and we've had some good moments, but I think those good moments have been filtered out by a lot of bad moments."

Not wanting to overstep, but also wanting to help him shake this funk he's in, I say, "Was today about your dad?"

He nods and then pushes his hand through his hair. "He's a dick, Everly. I try to give him the benefit of the doubt, I really do, but then he goes and says shit that presses my buttons, things that he knows will get under my skin, and that's exactly what he did today."

"I'm sorry," I say. "You deserve better than to be taunted by your father. That's not fair."

"It isn't." He leans on the table. "I wish it was different. I think about it all the time, how I might have turned out if maybe he'd been more nurturing and less competitive."

"Well, if it's any consolation, I think you've turned out pretty great, Hardy." I walk up to him and press my hand to his arm. "You're nothing like him. From what I know about your father and what I know about you, I'd say that the apple has fallen very fall from the tree."

He stiffens and looks at me, a crease in his brow.

Uh, not the reaction I would have expected from him.

"Did I…did I say something wrong?" I ask in a worried tone.

"No, it's just…well, fuck." He threads his fingers through his hair. "My dad used the same phrase with me today, but with a completely opposite intent. He told me that I was exactly like him, pushing aside what's important in favor of success."

My brow furrows. "That's not you at all," I say. "If anything, you're the complete opposite. Trust me, your dad would not have stayed all night to help me with decorations. He wouldn't have offered to chat with me about random things. He definitely wouldn't be a fan of Whitney Houston."

He chuckles. "No, no, he wouldn't."

"You are not like him, Hardy, and I think the more you try to tell yourself that over and over, the better off you'll be. I know it's probably hard to shake off whatever he said to you today, but just remember, you're a good guy who cares about others. If you weren't, you wouldn't have a business with your brother that has helped many people already."

"Yeah." He moves his hand over his beard. "Think it's just going to take some time to get that through my head."

"Then it takes time," I say. "And that's okay. Greatness doesn't happen overnight." Trying to lighten the mood, I say, "Do you think I just woke up like this? All perfect and amazing and creating well-structured centerpieces that are functional and whimsical at the same time? No, I had to work at it."

He chuckles and then to my surprise, he wraps his arm around me and pulls me into a hug.

Yes. Please.

Now if only this meant so much more. If only it was the start of something romantic.

If only…

But I think at this point we all know where I stand with him, fully in the friend zone. But it doesn't stop me from taking full advantage of the embrace. So I loop my arms around his torso, tell myself not to bury my head in his chest, and instead just casually hug him back. "Thank you, Everly. I really appreciate it. I appreciate you. I appreciate tonight. It was just what I needed."

"Of course," I say as he lets go of me far too soon.

He lets out a deep sigh. "Want me to help you move these vases somewhere?"

"Oh, no, that's okay. I'm going to move them over to the venue with Maggie tomorrow, so let's just leave them here."

"Not a problem. Do you need help tomorrow?"

"Nope, but we'll need you to help the day after, an hour before the party."

"You know I'm there," he says as he grabs his suit jacket and slips his arms through the holes. "Think I should wear pink to go along with the theme?"

"I'd prefer you wear a pink suit with a pink flamingo hat. I think that will have the biggest impact on the party."

"Don't joke, because you know I will."

"I dare you," I say as we head toward the front of the store.

"Oh…it's on. Just you wait, Plum. I'm going to be quite the vision in pink."

"For some reason, I totally believe it."

CHAPTER FIFTEEN
HARDY

"YOU DID NOT WEAR THAT suit," Everly says as I walk into the venue wearing a flamingo-pink suit that took me all day yesterday to find.

Did I work much? No.

Did I scour San Francisco for a pink suit that would fit me? Of course I did.

And I'll be honest, I never really thought an ankle pant would look good on me, but here I am, looking stylish as fuck. Very well might change up the suit pants to these. I have nice fucking ankles.

I spin in place and then flash open the sides of my jacket like Michael Jackson. "I did, and I look amazing."

Everly laughs and nods. "You do."

"Glad you can admit it," I say as I take in the venue space that has been completely transformed. Once a blank space with white walls, it's now decked out in rented plants ranging in size, pom-pom garlands, and bamboo backdrops. To the right just as you walk in is a white bar with two kissing flamingos on top of the counter and a placard listing drinks propped up against it, one being a signature cocktail for the bride and groom.

The courtyard in the back has been transformed with a combination of couches, chairs, high-tops, and tables, all mixed in together to create a more lounge feel than a banquet. Pinned along the courtyard's brick walls are the endless number of string pom-poms I worked on the night before, way more than what I was able to finish, paper fans in a range of khaki colors, and more rented plants.

The venue looks nothing like it did the other day and everything like a jungle that came to life overnight. The only thing missing is actual real flamingos.

Consider me impressed. Very, very impressed.

"Wow, Plum. You did all of this?"

"With help, of course," she says, her hands clutched in front of her as she takes in her brilliant work.

I glance at her. "You're not even breaking a sweat."

"Well, I worked on it this morning and then changed after. Can't be hauling around centerpieces in a dress."

"Well, it looks amazing in here," I say. "I thought you were going to need my help."

"I know, but then I took charge, and once I got going I just wanted to finish. I do have some things in the back, like favors that need to be put together, but that shouldn't take too long."

"Show me the way," I say.

"Maple is already back there helping," Everly says as a caution.

"She is?" I ask. "Did she help you decorate?"

"No," Everly says with a shake of her head. "She just got here, and I put her to work." She leans in close, the smell of her sweet perfume floating between us. "In case you were worried that you looked like a slouch arriving after her."

"I wasn't thinking slouch, more like dick in the pink suit."

"And here I thought you liked your suit."

"I do," I say as we head toward the back. "But not when it seems like I show up late and everyone else is putting in the work."

"Good thing you showed up right on time then," Everly says as we cross over into the courtyard.

I pause at the doorway and take in the decorated space. It's incredible.

The brick walls are covered in vines that extend all the way up the sides of the buildings, giving the space the appearance that we're in the middle of the jungle. The white couches and tabletops brighten up the darker space while the garland, pom-poms, and table runners add to the theme but don't overtake it either. It's truly an impressive combination of a themed party while working within the elements provided.

"This looks phenomenal," I say to Everly. "I mean, truly incredible."

"Thank you," she says, a light blush creeping up on her cheeks. "I'm very happy with how it turned out."

"So am I," Maple says from where she's seated at a table, stuffing some bags. "I'm so grateful for you."

"Just doing my job," Everly says and then brings her hands together. "I'm going to check on the catering and make sure the bar is set and ready to go. Maple, think you can show Hardy what to do with the favors?"

"Of course," Maple says.

Everly presses her hand to my shoulder, winks, and then walks away.

She can decorate *and* set up small moments with the girl I'm trying to get back together with. She can create a warm and stylish event. She shows empathy when it's needed, levity too. She can do it all—and without breaking a sweat. She's unmatched. *Is there anything she cannot do?* I head over to the table where Maple is working and just as I'm about to take a seat, she says, "Never thought I'd see the day when Hardy Hopper is wearing an all-pink suit."

"I'm full of surprises, Maple." I chuckle and glance over the materials on the table and pick up one of the personalized cookies. It's a cutout of a flamingo and written on the body is *Polly and Ken*, with a heart between their names. Cute. "Think you'll be able to eat this flamingo cookie without guilt?"

"I don't know," Maple answers. "It looks delicious, but eating a flamingo goes against everything I believe in."

"I understand the dilemma. But this flamingo doesn't have feathers or a beating heart, so..."

"True," she says, glancing my way with a smile. A very familiar, warm smile. Feels like comfort. Like going back home after a long semester.

I clear my throat. "So what are we doing?"

"We're sticking a cookie and a thank-you note that talks about the importance of flamingos into each of these bags and then tying them up. Think you can handle it?"

"I think so," I say. I pick up a bag and stuff a cookie in it, along with a thank-you note, and then tie it at the top. "How's that?"

She examines my work. "Looks good to me."

"Perfect," I say as I reach for another. "So, you missed a fun time the other night, full of pom-pom garlands and centerpieces."

"I know. I felt bad about that," she says, sounding a lot more like herself than our last few interactions. "But it seems like you guys did a good job."

"Yeah, Everly's great. She knew exactly when to pull me from making the centerpieces and put me back on garland duty."

"You're telling me you couldn't handle the arrangements?" she asks.

"Not so much," I say.

"Surprising," she says with a touch of mirth.

Okay, this is progress.

This is way better than the bowling alley.

Sure, I'll admit that I wasn't at my best that night and conversation wasn't flowing, but this is a step up for sure.

As we continue to work, I ask, "How are the flamingos?"

She glances my way. "They're good. I think they're still getting used to me, so it's been a little different. When I was in Peru, we weren't interacting with the flamingos, we were observing, so it's like a change of mindset for me. I tend to find myself just watching them at times and have to be reminded that I'm a caretaker, not an observer."

"I can see the challenge in that. Have you bonded with any of the flamingos?"

"Not like in Denver. But I'm sure it will take some time. The other zookeepers are pretty good friends, so fitting into an already established friend group is hard as well. Not to mention I'm not super outgoing, so… it's just been an adjustment."

"I would say you're pretty likeable, Maple."

"Thanks," she says and softly smiles. "It's just…different."

"I'm guessing you're missing Peru."

"Think about it every day," she says on a wistful sigh.

"Why did you have to leave?"

"The research grant was up, which meant it was time to leave. We all had to look for new jobs and, well, there was an opening here and I decided to apply. Thought it would be nice to be close to Polly again. Which it has been, but I'm going from living in a permanent tent for two years to a real apartment with running water and, well, it's just a change." She lowers her head. "I miss a simpler life."

"It was simple there?"

"Very," she says. "You didn't have all of the distractions that you have now. It's you and nature and the people and animals around you—that's it. You get to watch the stars dance across the sky every night. Fall asleep to the sounds of the wild, wake up to crisp morning air rather than the honking and yelling of people trying to make it through their morning commute." She shrugs. "I just miss the silence and peace."

"Yeah, that makes sense," I say. "Would you ever do it again?"

"In a heartbeat," she says. "But from what I've heard, there haven't been any research projects coming up for my field any time soon. I've come to terms with the fact that I'm going to have to adjust my mindset."

"Are you okay with that?" I ask.

"I'm going to have to be."

"Yes, right over there, that would be great," Everly says as she moves into the courtyard. She glances over at us. "How are you guys doing? Good?"

"Good," I answer.

"Perfect." She winks and then takes off.

I watch her depart for maybe a few seconds longer than I should because Maple says, "So, anything going on there?"

"Anything going on where?" I ask her.

"With you and Everly?"

"What?" I ask, shocked. "No." *Uh, hello, can't you see that I'm trying to rekindle something between you and me?*

"Just seems like you're close."

"I mean, we've been working together, but that's about it. She's just a good friend."

A friend who's trying to help me get back together with you, Maple. Jesus Christ.

"Okay, because Timothy was asking," she says. "I think he likes her and was thinking about asking her out, but he was nervous."

"Nervous about asking Everly out?" I say. "She's chill—he shouldn't be nervous at all."

"I think the whole dating thing makes him nervous."

"Oh, I can see that." I think about it for a second and then the most brilliant idea comes to mind. *Oh Hardy, you clever fucking man.* I try to hold back my smile to avoid revealing how proud I am of myself. "What if we all went out as friends? Like a hang out?"

"What?" she asks, looking confused.

"Well, instead of Timothy and Everly going on a date alone, you and I could go with them too and offer them some cushioning so they don't feel like they're on a real date. We could pass it off as a hang out. Like when we were bowling, but this time it's just the four of us, and when they're comfortable, the next date could be just them."

"Oh." She thinks about it for a second while she continues to put cookies in bags. "Maybe."

"Would you be uncomfortable?" I ask, wanting to gauge where her head is at. "You know, since we used to date?"

Her eyes flash to mine. "I mean, not really." She lets out a deep breath. "Maybe two weeks ago I would have completely turned down the idea because I didn't want to see you, but yeah, maybe it could work."

"Why didn't you want to see me?" I ask. It's such a heavy question, I doubt she'll answer right before the bridal shower.

But to my surprise, she says, "Come on, Hardy. It wasn't like things were completely amicable between us."

"I thought they were," I say as shame fills me, "but I could see that wasn't the case after talking with Polly."

She shrugs. "I just assumed things were going to be different when we left college. I was just...surprised by the way things turned out, that's all. You said you'd follow me to Denver, then all of a sudden you changed your mind, no real explanation given."

"Yeah, I know." I bite down on my lip. "It had nothing to do with you and everything to do with my dad."

"I know you think that helps your case, but to me, it just seems like I wasn't important enough."

"That wasn't the case, Maple," I say quietly. "I thought...hell, I thought we understood each other, that you saw I was trying to make my dad see me. You knew things were always so volatile. He...well, he promised me a good future with Hopper Industries, so I took it. I know that's not a good reason, and I had every intention of keeping in touch with you, but you stopped talking to me."

"Because I didn't think I was worth your time," she says.

"You were, Maple." I push my hand through my hair. "I was just... fuck, I was trying to take advantage of an opportunity." *To either change my dad or to maybe change me.* "Hindsight is twenty-twenty. I know that was a waste of time now."

"Why was it a waste of time?" she asks, the tension easing up between us.

"Because he hasn't changed a bit. He's the same scheming asshole he's always been, and no matter how much I want to believe he could be a different person, I'm just delusional. Some people will never change, and he's one of them."

She slowly nods. "Well, maybe it was for the best, because if we were still together, I'm not sure I would have gone to Peru, and that's an experience I don't think I could have lived without."

"Yeah, maybe it was for the best," I say and look her in the eyes. "I'm glad you had such a great experience in Peru. Maybe if we do that group hang with Timothy and Everly, you can tell me more about it."

"Yeah, maybe," she says offering me a smile, which makes me relax.

Good. See? Baby steps. That's all this is…baby steps.

"You've been talking to her," Polly says when she comes up to me, a signature cocktail in hand, looking beautiful in a white lace dress. Ken is across the room, talking to some family members, also dressed in all white, which makes me chuckle. If the bride can wear white, so can the groom.

"Kind of hard not to talk to the maid of honor when you're throwing a joint bridal shower," I say to her.

"But you've been talking to her a lot."

"I wouldn't say a lot," I counter.

"More than I wanted you to talk to her," Polly says.

"I'm assuming you still have a problem with me talking to her?"

"I don't want you to hurt her," Polly whispers.

"I wouldn't," I say.

"Are you sure? Because she seems to think that maybe something is going on between you and Everly."

What the hell?

"No," I say. "She asked me that as well. Nothing is going on between us. We're just friends. I told Maple that today. Why would I try to pursue someone if I was talking to another woman?"

"Ah-ha," Polly says. "I knew it, you *are* pursuing Maple."

I roll my eyes. "Come on, Polly. Do you really think I can stand here and watch my ex come back into my life and not be interested?"

"Yes, it's called self-control."

"Let me ask you this," I say. "How come you can have a second chance with Ken, but I can't have a second chance with Maple? We were there when you and Ken broke up. It wasn't pretty. So why am I the one put on blast?"

"Because Maple is different," Polly says. "If she had the opportunity, she never would have come back here. She would have stayed in Peru. Don't make her regret coming back."

"So you're acting selfishly then?" I ask, not really wanting to start a fight with her at her bridal shower, but she's also the one who brought it up.

"I am," she says with no shame. "And if I thought your intentions were pure, then maybe I wouldn't be so tough on you."

"What makes you think my intentions aren't pure?"

She gives me the look that says "Come on."

"When have you ever been serious about a relationship?" she asks.

"Pretty sure dating Maple for three years was serious," I say.

"After that, Hardy. She was your one and only relationship. And even then, you guys never really spoke about forever like Ken and I did. You were having fun. She was looking for commitment from you, and you weren't giving it to her."

"I did," I say. "For those three years, I was hers and only hers."

She sighs. "I mean…like commitment to the future. I don't think…I don't think you loved her the way you thought you did."

"You don't know that," I say.

She takes my hand and gives it a gentle squeeze. "I saw the way you would look at her, the way you look at her now, and there's something missing, Hardy. The spark. The excitement. It's not there. I think you like the idea of Maple, the connection you had, but I'm not sure that connection was strong enough. I don't think that connection gave you what you really wanted. You didn't feel it deep within you. It was all surface."

Was it?

I didn't think it was surface level. I had a connection with Maple—I didn't make that up in my head.

Then why didn't you follow her? I have so many words swimming in my mind. My dad's verbal vomit accusing me of being just like him—loving work over family and commitments. But then I consider Everly's comments. She thinks I'm nothing like my dad, and I'm coming to realize that Everly knows me quite well.

But then Maple's words come to mind.

Because I didn't think I was worth your time. They stunned me. Is that how she perceived me at the end of our relationship, or all the way through?

There's something missing, Hardy. The spark. The excitement. It's not there. I think you like the idea of Maple, the connection you had, but I'm not sure that connection was strong enough. I don't think that connection gave you what you really wanted. You didn't feel it deep within you. It was all surface.

If that's true, then it makes sense why I was content to let her go. And that is staggering. I just don't know if I can believe that yet.

Polly stands on her toes and leans in to press a kiss to my cheek.

"Thank you for today," she says, releasing my hand. "I know how much you did to make this happen, and I'm really appreciative of it. Of you."

Smiling softly despite the question she just put in my mind, I say, "You know I would do anything for you guys."

"We know, and we love you."

With that, she moves through the crowd and walks up to Ken. He places his arm around her and brings her in for a kiss. I watch them, the ease in their movements, the love they clearly share for each other, the comfortable companionship.

Is Polly right? Was it never that deep between me and Maple?

Were we ever at a level of love that Ken and Polly share?

I thought we were.

But now...now she has me doubting myself.

"Hey," I hear Everly say as she steps up to me. "Are you really planning a foursome date with Maple?"

I glance over at her, those pretty green eyes peering up at me. "I offered it," I say. "I thought that maybe you wouldn't mind since you mentioned wanting to get to know Timothy more. Maple says he wants to get to know you but is nervous and, well, I just thought it would be a great way for everyone to hang out—but then we could go off into our respective couples. I thought it was pretty genius, something the professor would have come up with."

"You don't think that's going to be awkward?" She twists her hands together.

"Why would it be awkward?" I ask. "If anything, we can help warm each other up. I can bring up Whitney Houston, and you can tell Timothy how much you love her."

That brings a smile to her face. "Do you think he'd be impressed or startled by my insane knowledge of Whitney Houston's life?"

"Obviously impressed," I say.

"I think you're right." Her shoulder lines up with mine as we stare out at the party. The signature cocktails are an absolute hit—the beer stocked up has barely been touched. Guests are milling about, compostable plates in hand full of mini egg rolls, shrimp cocktail, and vegetable crudités, while Ken and Polly are surrounded by laughter as light music mixes in the background, setting a romantic mood. "I could regale him with facts about *The Bodyguard* and how Kevin Costner held off production for a year so Whitney could finish her concert tour."

"Kevin knew she was the only one who could play that role," I add.

Everly grips my arm. "The movie wouldn't have been the same without her."

"It wouldn't have," I continue. "And when David Foster told Kevin Costner that the slow start of 'I Will Always Love You' would never play on the radio, Kevin said he didn't care—he wanted that version of the song."

"And look what happened," Everly says. "Number one song for fourteen weeks straight. Eat that, David. Even Dolly Parton said she forgot about licensing use of the song, and when she heard Whitney's version for the first time on the radio, she said no one would ever sing it better."

"Because Dolly knows best," I say. "Did you know she took the money she made from the royalties of 'I Will Always Love You' and built a school with it? She calls it the school Whitney built."

"I didn't know that," Everly replies. "God, I love Dolly so much."

"How could you not?" I ask. "Although I saw this meme about her the other day that said *I love Dolly so much and she's a gift to this world, but why couldn't she have sung about working 11–3 instead?*"

Everly lets out a laugh, the sound so sweet. "I mean, I bet if Dolly sang about it, we would have complied as a society."

"Easily." I smile down at her, wondering why the hell I can't have such an easy conversation like this with Maple? More of that doubt starts creeping in, doubt I wasn't ready to face today.

Everly lets out a sigh. "Well, if you think the foursome will help you and Maple, I'm up for it, but can it be a dinner? Nothing active like bowling or mini golf or…painting a picture while drinking wine."

"I heard paint and sip is a lot of fun," I say.

"I don't need to get drunk to know I'm terrible at painting—I can tell you right here, right now, that a paint brush should never be in my hand."

"That surprises me," I say. "Given your creative nature, I'd think you could paint."

She shakes her head. "Terrible at it."

"Well then, a simple dinner it is. I know a few places that are pretty casual and offer a vibe that could work for a foursome."

"Is that the official term we're riding with?" she asks.

"I think so, unless you want something more complicated."

"Please, entertain me with a more complicated term."

Smirking, I say, "Hmm, we could call it 'the foundation of double dating trickery created and brought to you by Professor Plum and Henrietta Hopper.'"

"Ooo, now that has a nice ring to it. Especially enjoyed the usage of 'trickery.'"

"We can make bracelets for the occasion," I say. "You know, like those friendship bracelets that are lyrics to a song, but with just the beginning letter to each word. Ours could be…" I think about it for a second. "Uh… TF…ODDT…what else did I say?"

She chuckles. "Maybe we just call it the foursome."

"Might be best," I say. "I can still make commemorative bracelets."

"You make a few pom-pom garlands and now you're a master at stringing all the things."

I place my hand on my chest. "You've unlocked something inside of me that I don't think I can stuff away. A man must string."

She laughs. "Well, I look forward to my bracelet. Okay, I'm going to get back to work. Go mingle, have fun. Maybe eat a few of those meatballs because my God, if you don't, I might eat them all."

"In that case…" I move away from her and straight to the meatballs. When I glance over my shoulder at her, she's smiling brightly and shaking her head at me.

See, everyone…just friends.

———

"Now that everyone is gone, I can give you my present," I say to Polly and Ken who are sitting in their special wicker chairs, looking exhausted from the day's events.

The shower went off without a hitch and it's all because of Everly. She was running around everywhere, taking charge, making sure Polly, the moms, and Maple could enjoy themselves rather than worrying about the food, the drinks, or the guests.

"You didn't have to get us anything," Polly says as I hand them a card from the inside of my suit jacket. "The pink suit was a present in and of itself."

"It's true," Ken says. "I don't think I'll ever see you in anything else but that suit. If our moms would allow it, I'd demand you wear that at the wedding as well."

I tug on my suit coat. "You know, I think I look pretty damn good in pink. And these pants, aren't they nice?" I show off my legs to my friends.

"I never noticed your legs before," Ken says. "But those pants highlight them in a way that's undeniable. You have great stems, man."

"Never skip leg day," I say with a wink.

"My God, you two," Polly says as she pops open the envelope. She takes out the card, opens it up and then pauses. Her eyes lift to mine, her brows rising in question. "Hardy, what is this?"

I stick my hands in my pockets. "It's your gift—combo wedding and bridal shower. Figured you would want it now so you could plan."

"What is it?" Ken asks, leaning over. When he sees what it is, he starts to shake his head. "No fucking way. Dude." He takes the piece of paper and stares down at it. "How the hell did you remember this?"

"I remember a lot of things," I say.

"We can't accept this," Polly says.

"The hell we can't," Ken says as he stands and pulls me into a hug, causing me to laugh. "This is amazing, dude, thank you."

Polly stands as well and gives me a hug. "This is too generous."

"It's not...not for you two," I say.

Ken stares down at the paper and then over at Polly. "Finally going to make that trip to the elusive St. Hopper in Bora-Bora. And our own bungalow over the water for two weeks." Ken shakes his head. "I won't want to leave."

"Is your dad okay with this?" Polly asks. "I know you've been on rocky terms with him."

"He doesn't know," I say. "This voucher is under your names, and if you don't get the five-star, VIP experience, then you let me know, because I'm friends with management. They're expecting you."

"This is...this is really amazing," Ken says. "Thanks, man."

"Of course," I say and then bring my hands together. "Okay, I'm going to head out. Do you guys need help with anything else? I think the family handled the gifts."

"We're good."

"Oh good," Everly says as she walks up to us from the front of the store where she was talking to the bartender. "I was hoping you hadn't taken off yet. I was talking with the caterer. All leftover food has been packed up and put in your car, so enjoy."

"Thank you," Polly says. "This was...this was amazing. And I loved the flamingo theme. It felt just like something Maple would do."

"Just followed her direction," Everly says as Maple walks up too. She was helping with the presents and clean-up, even though Everly told her not to worry about it.

"Is there anything else that needs to be done?" Maple asks.

"Nope, I think we're all set," Everly says. "I hope you guys had a wonderful time. Now we have the bach parties to plan."

"Right, I need to email you about that," I say to Everly.

"Ooo, can't wait. Can't imagine what you might wear to that."

I tug on my suit. "Maybe I'll go another round in this suit. It went so well."

"Wearing the same outfit twice in a row?" Polly jokes. "Tacky, Hardy."

"If you think your bach party is going to be anything but tacky, then you need to put other people in charge, right, Maple?"

"What the heck are you planning?" Maple says, looking up at me.

"You got your flamingos, so now it's my time to shine." I put my arm around Everly and squeeze her close. "We're going to deliver the best party you've ever seen…best."

Polly and Ken look between us, eyebrows raised, before Polly clears her throat. "Something to look forward to then." And then she offers me a smile.

The kind of smile that tells me there's something going on in that head of hers, but nothing she's going to share.

> *To: Everly Plum*
> *From: Hardy Hopper*
> *Subject: The Ultimate Party*
>
> *Professor,*
>
> *A few things.*
>
> *For one, great job at the bridal shower—I'm really impressed with you. I know your help really allowed Maple and Polly to have a great time together. Same with me and Ken, so thank you, in case I didn't say it already.*
>
> *Two, I spoke with Maple, who spoke with NOT Tomothy, and they said they're available this Wednesday for dinner. You good with that? I can make reservations at The Beard.*
>
> *Three, the bach party—are you ready to go back to college? I know we've talked about it before, but we need to confirm all the details, including the Ed Sheeran playlist, how many beer pong tables we need, and the dips. Because remember, we need all of the dips.*
>
> *Henrietta*

To: Hardy Hopper
From: Everly Plum
Subject: RE: The Ultimate Party

Henrietta,

I'm so glad you enjoyed the bridal shower. It was my first event that I headed up all by myself under Maggie's company, and I would be lying to you if I said I didn't cry when I got home. Your words mean a lot to me, so thank you.

Wednesday works. I'm oddly nervous. NOT Tomothy is a nice guy, so I shouldn't be this nervous, but I am. I really hope it's not awkward. I tend to say stupid things when it's awkward. You might have to keep me in check.

I have already been looking into different venues that will offer us the space we need for beer pong, the alcohol, and the music. There's a great place near the pier that just opened up their roof top. Have you heard of Sailor Ninety-Nine? Pretty chill space, offers beer pong tournaments, but also will close off for private parties. It's right in the heart of San Francisco and has transportation options for everyone, so there will be no drinking and driving. There are also local hotels if people are coming from out of town as well. Link below. Let me know what you think. The second option I've been thinking about is testing Haisley's Clueless-themed rental. Part of us joining forces with the Bridesmaid for Hire branch is that we team up with her rentals and throw bachelorette weekends there. Might be a great trial if you're cool with that, and you can find that link below too.

The Prof

To: Everly Plum
From: Hardy Hopper
Subject: Uhh…excuse me?

You cried? Why did you cry? I don't like that you cried. Next time if you're crying, call me—you have my phone number.

Wednesday will be fun. I won't let you make it awkward.

Sailor Ninety-Nine sounds great. How do you do that? Find an amazing space in seconds? Will they let us bring dips? And can we control the music? Also, put the tab on me, as I've got this one covered. I know Maple will want to help out, but put her in charge of something else, like a few dips. I'll take care of venue and drinks and any other food.

As for the second option, I'm all for trying this out because I know it would be great for Haisley as well. The Clueless rental is classically charming with its nineties nostalgia, something I know Polly would love. Plus the backyard is huge. I'm all for this, but if Haisley doesn't have the availability or isn't ready, Sailor Ninety-Nine would be great.

Henrietta

To: Hardy Hopper
From: Everly Plum
Subject: RE: Uhh…excuse me?

I wasn't crying because I was sad. I was crying because I was overwhelmed. I sent pictures to Maggie of the event, and she told me how proud of me she was and, well, it all just came crashing down. It was a good day.

Maybe we should have a code word for me if I start to say something stupid to NOT Tomothy. Maybe something like... platypus or... mandarin orange. Possibly Boogie Boogie. Let me know.

And yes, we can bring our own food. I'll let Maple know about the dips. She already sent me some dip recipes that she and Polly used to make. She's excited about the theme and is pulling a bunch of pictures from college of you and all your friends. I have a plan for pinning them on strings around the venue. So if you have any pictures, let's incorporate those. I'll be sure to speak with Haisley about our options, and I'll speak with Sailor Ninety-Nine as well and let you know which one works best.

*I would never say this to your face, but I will type it out... I'm kind of excited about the party. *winces**

The Prof

To: Everly Plum
From: Hardy Hopper
Subject: RE: Uhh...excuse me?

I knew it! I knew I was going to win you over with this idea. It was the dip recipes, right? The best one Maple has is her buffalo chicken dip. Fucking magic.

Maybe I should talk to Maggie, see if she needs someone coming in with brilliant dip ideas. Think she'll hire me? I know she's seeking out a new employee. Maybe that person has been right under her nose this whole time…

To: Hardy Hopper
From: JP Cane
Subject: The Rockhopper needs you.

Dear friend,

Recently in my mission to help save the Chilean Flamingo, I stumbled upon a story about a penguin. Not just any penguin, but the Southern Rockhopper Penguin, a troubled bird on the verge of death due to an oil spill off the coast of Chile. Volunteers spent nearly an hour trying to clean the oil out of the bird's feathers. Thanks to the efforts of the volunteers that day, Rocky was saved.

Now nearing endangerment, these waddling fellas are in need of your support as they suffer the loss of their species from overfishing, climate change, and pollution from oil spills. But you can be the difference by donating today.

Donate Here.

Help save these adorable munchkins and be the change in their lives.

JP Cane

CHAPTER SIXTEEN
EVERLY

"WAIT, WHAT ARE YOU DOING?" Ember asks over my speaker phone as I fix my makeup for the date.

"You heard me, Ember," I say, feeling exhausted from the day.

"You're going on a double date with Hardy and Mabel?"

"*Maple*, and yes, but I'm going because they're setting me up with Timothy. Maple is friends with him, you know, the guy from bowling, and I guess he was nervous so we're doing this foursome thing. Plus it helps out Hardy."

"And you're okay with that?" she asks.

"I have to be," I say as I blot some powder over my T-zone. "He's set on her, Ember. And shouldn't you be happy I'm moving on?"

"I am happy that you're looking toward someone else to date. I think that's great, but I'd rather you not do it with the guy you're crushing on."

"Well, this is the option at the moment. I'm sure the second date won't be a foursome. I think it's just to warm everyone up, you know?"

"I get it. And you think there's going to be a second date?"

I pick up my curling iron and start curling the ends of my hair, feeling off-kilter with my hair down. Can't remember the last time my hair wasn't in a bun or a ponytail. But I figured might as well get dolled up and act like this is a real date.

"When we spoke at bowling, he seemed real cool, easy to chat with, which confuses me. I don't understand why he's nervous to go on a solo date with me."

"Maybe he's comfortable in social settings at first but one-on-ones make him nervous."

"Perhaps," I say. I blow out a low breath. "God, Ember, I hate dating. I just wish I had someone in my life without the process of finding them."

"But isn't that where the fun comes in? Testing different people to see if they're the one for you?"

"No," I answer. "I just want someone, that's all, no testing. I just want the universe to place the man I'm supposed to be with right in front of me without any of the work."

"Do you really think that would be fair to the rest of us who have gone through terrible date after terrible date?" Ember asks.

"Uh, after the date with Tomothy, I think I deserve the universe to place a man right in front of me."

"Tomothy was not that bad."

"Ember," I say in a stern tone, which makes her laugh.

"I didn't tell you this, because I thought that maybe you were still too raw after our joint date, but when Trevor got back to work, Tomothy couldn't stop talking about a date he went on and how he was too good for her."

"Stop," I say, pausing my hair curling. "He did not say that."

"He did."

"Did Trevor put him in his place?"

"Trevor is a quiet one, you know that, but he did send an email to the company gossip who spread the word."

I chuckle. "Ah, classic Trevor. And did word get around?"

"Quickly," Ember says.

"Freaking Tomothy. That man will haunt me forever. Did I tell you I had a dream the other night and he was in it? I came home and he was sitting at my table, gnawing on his cat's paws."

"Oh my God." Ember busts out in laughter. "That's disgusting."

"I know, I can still hear the sound of the gnawing."

"I might throw up. Stop talking about it."

I chuckle and finish up my hair. "Okay, I need to go, I don't want to be late."

"What are you wearing?"

I glance down at myself and say, "High-waisted jeans, red off-the-shoulder crop top, red lips."

"Ooo, that sounds good. You look great in red."

"Thank you," I say. "I feel a little awkward because my hair is down, and normally I'm either in professional clothes or loungewear, so this is slightly uncomfortable."

"It's only a few hours—suck it up."

I chuckle. "Such a loving sister."

"I know. Have fun and remember, you're on the date with Timothy... *not* Hardy."

"Oh my God, Ember. I know!"

She laughs. "Love you."

"Love you."

———

This is the problem with being someone who needs to be early to every occasion, not on time, but early, because now that I'm here, I'm waiting in the restaurant's entryway for everyone, hoping and praying Timothy doesn't show up first because I can already tell I'll be awkward.

I need a good buffer. Hardy or Maple will do. Any kind of buffer.

Just someone.

I lean against the wall of the entryway, scanning the restaurant and taking in the atmosphere. It's pretty chill here, fun, boisterous. Not pretentious, which is key. I think we'll have a good time, especially since there's a large bar in the middle of the space. I considered sitting at the bar while waiting, but didn't want to look like I needed a drink to relax, even though a drink right about now would be ideal.

The door opens to the restaurant, and I glance over to spot Hardy walking through.

Thank God.

He's wearing classic jeans and T-shirt—the way his shirt clings to his chest looks amazing, and his jeans are rolled up over his ankles just enough to show off his brown boots. He has the whole sexy lumberjack look down.

He looks to the right where I am yet his gaze skims over me, continuing to look around.

Did he not see me? It's not that dark in here.

I lift off the wall. "Hardy."

He turns to the right again and when his eyes land on me, his expression morphs into surprise. "Oh shit," he says. "I didn't recognize you, Everly."

He walks up to me, places his hand on my waist, and leans in to press a kiss to my cheek. When he pulls away, his eyes fall to mine. "Hell, you look good, Professor."

My cheeks flame from both the compliment and the feel of his lips on my cheek. *Stop, Everly. He wants another woman. Stop enjoying his cheek kisses so much.* They mean nothing. He gives them to everyone.

"Thank you," I say as I catch him giving me another once-over, which only increases the temperature in my body. That's the last thing I need right before Timothy gets here. No one likes a sweaty mess on a foursome date.

"I don't think I've ever seen you with your hair down," he says as he tugs on a curl, his eyes still focused on me. "I like it."

"It feels weird having it down," I say.

"Well, it looks really good."

When our eyes meet, he smiles sweetly, and fuck me, I wish this was just me and him. I wish this date was between us and only us. I wish he wasn't interested in Maple but interested in me. I wish Timothy wasn't even in the picture.

I wish he'd put his arm around my waist and guide me through the restaurant, so *we* would spend the evening talking, laughing, and casually touching each other. Then, when the time was right, he'd lean in, lift my chin with two of his fingers, and kiss me, but this time, it would be on my lips.

Ugh, maybe Ember was right—maybe this was not a good idea.

"Oh, here they are," Hardy says, nodding toward the entrance where Timothy opens the door for Maple. He leans in close. "Be cool, Plum."

Sure…right, be cool. *And just how am I meant to be cool when the man next to me smells so divine?*

Maple walks up to us, her hands clasped together while Timothy follows closely behind. "Hey," she says to the both of us.

Jealousy rips through me as Hardy leans in and places a kiss on her cheek in a greeting—this time not falling into her chest. And then he shakes Timothy's hand. "Good seeing you, man. Surprised you want to have dinner with me given how I ruined your bowling league dreams."

Timothy chuckles. "I blame myself for not reading the rules. I didn't know we were going to be eliminated right away. I was talking to a friend about it, and he said they do that to weed out the people who aren't serious."

"They probably knew we weren't serious the minute Hardy tossed a bowling ball in the ceiling," I say.

Hardy gives me a look that makes me chuckle.

"Yeah, that didn't cast the team in a good light. We made a lasting impression but not a good one," Timothy says before turning to me. "Hey, Everly. You look nice."

"Thank you," I say. "So do you."

He does. He's a very handsome guy. Lankier than Hardy, but that's okay—I've never really dated anyone with the kind of muscle Hardy has. I like Timothy's glasses and the scruff on his jaw. He has kind eyes and a great smile. He's the guy that makes you pause for a moment when you're in the grocery store because he catches your attention.

"Thanks," he says, and then we all stand there, awkward and silent.

Timothy smiles at me.

I smile at him.

Maple smiles at everyone.

Hardy smiles at Maple.

I shift.

Timothy sticks his hands in his pockets.

Maple clutches her purse.

Hardy rocks on his heels.

God, this was a really bad idea.

"Uh, well, should we let the hostess know we're all here?" I ask.

"Yeah, great idea," Hardy says and then leads the way.

He speaks to the hostess, charming as always, and she brings us to the back of the restaurant, seating us in a four-person booth. Hardy steps to the side so I climb in on the right, expecting Maple to sit next to me but when Hardy slips in instead, I'm completely surprised. Timothy sits across from me and Maple sits across from Hardy. The hostess sets down our menus and tells us that our server will be with us shortly.

Hardy's broad shoulders take up most of the room in the booth, which means our arms are pressed together. He shifts and then places his arm behind me along the bench.

"That better?" he asks.

I'd prefer your hand on my thigh.

"Uh, yeah, sure, whatever you're comfortable with," I say.

"Kind of small booths, don't you think?" he asks.

"Yeah, a bit tight, but if you need to plaster me against the wall, feel free."

He turns toward me, brows raised. "Plaster you against the wall, Plum?"

I think about it for a second and then say, "Uh, not like that."

"Like what?" he asks, smirking.

"Like the perverted way you're thinking."

"I wouldn't say that's perverted. I'd consider that passion."

"Tomothy would consider it an inconvenience to him."

Hardy lets his head fall back as he laughs. "You're right. He's too good for such a thing."

"Far too above a plaster to the wall," I joke.

"That guy…I feel bad for whoever he ends up with." Hardy shakes his head and stares down at his menu.

"Do you know what my sister told me before I came here?"

"What?" he asks.

"She said that he was walking around my brother-in-law's office, boasting about the date he went on and how he was too good for me."

"The fuck he did," Hardy says, setting his menu down. "He fucking said that?"

"Yeah. Luckily, my brother-in-law told the office gossip the truth and it spread like wildfire."

"Good. Man, that guy, the audacity."

"I know. And I had a dream about him the other night."

"Why the fuck would you do that?" Hardy asks, making me chuckle.

I turn toward him. "Trust me, I didn't want to dream about him, but he had a cameo. He was in my apartment when I came home, sitting at my table, gnawing on his cat's paws."

"Oh fuck." Hardy shivers. "That's called a nightmare."

"I know. It was traumatizing. When I woke up, I was nervous that I'd turn to the side and find him there, at my table."

"If that happened, I'm pretty sure I would have heard your scream all the way in my apartment."

"Easily," I say with a smile. I pick up my menu and then look up at Timothy and Maple, who are staring at the both of us. "Oh, sorry about that," I say. "Just some guy I went on a horrible date with."

"Is that why you called me Tomothy while bowling?" Timothy asked.

Hardy snorts next to me, and I elbow him.

When eyes fall on him, he apologizes. "Sorry, but she was terrified that she'd called you Tomothy and, well, I'm so happy to hear the confirmation."

"I'm sorry," I say, feeling my face go red from embarrassment. "Clearly, you are nothing like Tomothy. I was just…I was nervous and I think worried and—"

"Everly, it's fine." Timothy smiles. "I thought it was funny."

If he met Tomothy, he probably wouldn't think it was that funny.

"Glad you have a sense of humor," I say. "Because I was horrified."

"Timothy should be horrified that you called him Tomothy," Hardy says. "No one wants to be compared to that man." That's exactly what I just thought.

"Have you met him?" Maple asks Hardy.

Hardy shakes his head. "No, just heard horror stories about him."

"Stories we don't need to get into at the moment," I say.

"Hmm, funny," Hardy says turning back to his menu.

"What's funny?" I ask.

"Well, you can talk to Maple about my flatulence, but I can't talk to Timothy about Tomothy, the cat foot gnawer."

"Ah, I see," I say. "Reason being because I'm trying to make a good impression with someone I'm just meeting, whereas Maple already knows your flaws."

"How is that fair?" he asks.

"It's not." I smile at him.

His expression morphs into mirth before he turns back to his menu. We all take a few minutes to figure out what we're going to get and when the waitress stops by our table, we order drinks and our food at the same time.

Hardy went with the burger and a craft beer. Timothy ordered a veggie burger—found out he's a vegetarian—and a lager. Maple—also a vegetarian—went with a salad and a water while I ordered a soup bowl and an alcoholic lime seltzer.

"Soup bowl sounds good," Hardy says. "Maybe I should have gone for that."

"You can have some of mine if you let me eat some of your fries."

"Ooo, I don't know about that, Plum. I'm a real fry fiend."

I shrug. "Your loss, because I know you're going to crave my soup the minute it's placed in front of me."

He scratches the side of his beard. "You're right, I probably will. One sniff will push me over the edge. Fine, but you are limited on how many fries you can have."

"And how many would that be?" I ask him.

"Five."

"Five?" I nearly shout. "And how much access do you have to my soup?"

"Unlimited."

"Uh, no deal. Five fries for unlimited access to my soup, how is that fair?"

"I never said I was going to be fair."

"I'd reconsider your offer, because right now, there's no way I'd share my soup with you."

"We'll see when the food gets out here."

I fold my arms. "Yes, we'll see."

Hardy turns to Maple and Timothy who are quiet on their side of the booth. "You guys going to fight over Maple's salad?"

Timothy glances at Maple and then shakes his head. "It has walnuts in it, not a fan."

"Really?" I ask. "Is it that way with all nuts or just walnuts?"

"A lot of nuts," Timothy says.

"Hear that?" I elbow Hardy. "He probably doesn't like your nuts."

"But everyone likes my nuts."

I look at Timothy. "Millions of people have had his nuts in their mouths."

Timothy's nose scrunches up in confusion, causing me to laugh. "Hopper Almonds. Those are his nuts."

"Oh," Timothy says with a slow nod. "I thought you were talking about his testicles."

I nearly snort over the technical term. I would have just said balls.

"I don't know him that well," I say. "So not a nuts fan, huh, Timothy? Even candied nuts?"

Timothy shrugs while Hardy says, "Have you had the candied nuts down by the pier?"

I turn toward him, gripping his arm. "Oh my God, by the carousel?"

"Yes," he says, his eyes widening.

"My absolute favorite. Whenever I'm down there, I always stop by and get two bags. I limit it to two or else I'll make myself sick."

Hardy holds up his hand. "I get five."

"Five?" I cry. "Do you eat them all in one sitting?"

"Two per sitting, and I save the last to savor."

"Two per sitting, my God, that would be a dream. I'd get so sick though."

"Work yourself up to it," he says. "I can help. Next time we have to do décor, I'll bring some and we can binge. Maybe you can snort one out of your nose like you did with the meat."

I poke his arm. "I told you that didn't come out of my nose. It was the double whammy exhalation."

"Ah, right, how could I forget?"

I turn to Timothy. "I promise I don't snort meat out of my nose."

"Quite the party trick if you did," he says. "Maybe something to work on."

"I'd rather not be known as the girl who snorts meat out of her nose."

"I don't know," Hardy says. "It has its charms."

"These are so good," I say, grabbing another of Hardy's fries. "The seasoning is spectacular. And the crispness is unmatched."

He dips a piece of bread into my soup. "The crust on this bread is fucking incredible. Do they make this in-house? They have to if it's this fresh."

"I think I saw on the menu that they make all breads in house, including your burger bun."

"That would explain why it's so good." He pops his piece of dipped bread in his mouth and groans. "So good." He then turns to Maple. "How's the salad? Are the walnuts making it?"

She pushes the lettuce around on her plate. "I think the walnuts are the best part."

"Are they roasted?" I ask as I lift my drink up to my lips to wash down the fries.

"I think so because they seem to have a smokey flavor."

"Delicious," I say. "What about your veggie burger?" I ask Timothy, who opted for a side salad rather than fries—big mistake, but I'm not going to point that out. He must see it from the way these fries are seasoned. So good.

"Burger is decent," he says. "The patty is pretty basic, but the sauce elevates it."

"Sauce can make or break a meal," I say. "How long have you been a vegetarian?"

"Since high school," he says. "So over ten years."

"Wow, that's incredible. You too, Maple?" I ask.

"No," she answers. "More recently, from when I was living in Peru. It wasn't very easy to cook up meat, or food for that matter, so I just sort of stopped eating it and I've kept it going."

"Makes sense," I say and then the table goes quiet, everyone picking up their food to eat.

Timothy has been pretty reserved this whole time, not saying much unless I ask him a question, then he starts talking. Hard to have a conversation with someone if they're not going to join in. Couldn't imagine what this date would be like if Hardy wasn't here.

"So, Timothy," I say while scooping up my soup with my spoon. "How are the rhinos?"

"Critically endangered," he says before going back to his burger and taking a large bite.

Okay then...

———

"I never would have guessed that you're a big chocolate fan," I say to Hardy, who's taking slow bites of the chocolate cake he ordered. It's chocolate on chocolate and covered in peanuts.

"Oh, I'm a huge fan. Can't get enough of it."

I slice off a piece of his cake that he ordered for the table since it's so big, like nearly half the cake, four layers of ooey gooey goodness. Unfortunately, Timothy and Maple don't want any. We even offered the inside of the cake to Timothy so he didn't have to deal with the nuts, but it's a no go.

All the more for us is what I say.

"Me too. I think chocolate has to be the best flavor. Out of the original three—vanilla, strawberry, and chocolate—chocolate takes it by a landslide."

"There really isn't much competition," Hardy says. "Vanilla is so bland, and strawberry is more like a kid's flavor. Chocolate has a robust taste that complements pretty much everything. Strawberry, not so much. Vanilla, well, it just takes on the flavor of anything that it's paired with. Chocolate can complement and stand on its own."

"Sounds like you need to be the face of chocolate," I say.

"I would proudly do that."

"Ooo, you could wear your pink suit while boasting about the deliciousness that is chocolate, throw people off, make them think you're about to praise strawberry, but then bam, chocolate."

"I like the way you think, Plum," he says. "Maybe even wear a shirt under the suit that says *chocolate lover* and when I go to surprise everyone, I tear open the suit jacket and reveal my shirt."

"Slightly tacky, but entertaining. I approve."

With a smile, he digs his fork into the cake and asks Maple and Timothy who are just sitting there, staring at us, "You sure you don't want any? It's really good."

"Positive," Maple says. "I was actually thinking about taking off. I have a bit of a headache from a long day in the sun, and I want to rest my head."

"Oh no," I say. "I'm sorry. I hate work headaches; they're the worst."

"They really are," Maple says. "Um, just tell me what I owe for the bill—"

"It's on me," Hardy says. "The whole meal. I really enjoyed the company tonight."

"Me too," I say. "I've had a lot of fun."

Maple softly smiles. "It was nice." She slings her purse over her shoulder as she stands. "Thanks for dinner." She waves and takes off. *Weird. That headache must really be bugging her.*

"I, uh, I think I might head out too," Timothy says.

"Oh no, really?" I ask. "Do you have a headache too?"

"Early morning," he says.

"Well, let me walk you out," I say. I shove at Hardy. "Move, you ogre."

"Ogre?" he says on a laugh. "I'm anything but an ogre." He moves out of the booth, and then I shuffle out as well, leaving my stuff behind.

I look Hardy in the eyes. "There'd better be cake when I return."

"Can't make any promises."

I roll my eyes and then follow Timothy to the front of the restaurant. He doesn't exit though, sparing me from the chilly night air.

"Well, I hope you had fun," I say to him. "Maybe a good meal?"

"It was a good meal," he says, putting his hands in his pockets and not looking me in the eye.

"Is there something wrong?"

When he looks up and our eyes meet, he says, "You like him."

"Huh?"

"Hardy," he says. "You like him."

"What?" I say, as my lower back starts to sweat. "No, I don't."

"Come on, Everly," he says. "Don't lie to me. If you're worried I'm going to say something to Maple, don't. I think she witnessed the same thing I did at dinner."

"What did you witness?" I ask.

"That there's a connection between you two. I saw it at bowling, though I wasn't sure if it was just because you're friends, but tonight… it was evident."

I shake my head. "There's nothing going on there."

"Maybe not," he says. "But there probably should be, and I'm not mad about it, Everly. I'm really not. I think it might be in your best interest to pursue something with him."

"There's nothing there," I say.

"There is," he replies. "And I think you're too blind to see it at the moment."

I shake my head again. "Trust me, Timothy. There's nothing going on…on his side." I look away, feeling the weight of that sentence heavy on my shoulders.

"I think you're wrong," he says. "I saw the way he was looking at you tonight, the ease he has around you. There's something there." He tilts my chin up, looking me in the eyes. "You just need to find a way to pull it out of him."

I bite on my bottom lip, guilt consuming me. "I…I don't want to like him, Timothy."

"But you do."

"I'm trying not to," I say.

"And how's that going for you?" he asks.

"Clearly not well." I twist my hands together. "Was I that obvious?"

"It was pretty clear that we were on a date with the wrong people."

"I'm sorry," I say. "I…I didn't mean to exclude you."

"I know," he says. "And at one point, it was kind of comical, watching you two go back and forth, especially when you were fighting about dessert and if you should get the giant cake or two small desserts to share. It was really fucking obvious then that you two should be together."

"I thought everyone would eat the giant cake. You proved me wrong."

He chuckles and then sighs. "You know, Everly, I think under other circumstances, we could have had some fun together, but I know when to step down."

"I…I wish I wasn't feeling this way."

"It's okay," he says. "But now you can go for it."

I shake my head. "No, I can't. He's all in with his feelings for Maple. I don't…I don't want to try to be with someone who likes someone else." The minute my words fall out of my mouth, I realize that's exactly what was happening with Timothy.

He realizes it too because he kindly smiles and then takes a step forward.

"Can I give you a hug?"

"Yes," I say before he wraps his arms around me and squeezes me tight.

"You'll never know until you try," he says into my ear. "I think there's something there, but you just need to make him see it." When he pulls away, he places his hands on my shoulders. "It was really nice meeting you, Everly. If you ever get over your feelings for Hardy or things just don't work out, give me a call." The corners of his mouth tilt up.

"I will," I say. "And I'm sorry, Timothy."

"Don't be." He looks past me toward the table. "Now go make that guy fall for you." He winks and then takes off, leaving me feeling so many things.

Sad.

Embarrassed.

Excited.

Nervous.

How did this dinner seem to become a date between me and Hardy with two onlookers?

Is that what Maple saw as well? Will she be angry with me? Did I do that?

"It was really fucking obvious then that you two should be together."

Did I commandeer Hardy's attention the whole night? Is that why Maple left early...*and abruptly?*

Oh God, I hope not.

If I had my phone, I'd text her, but it's with Hardy.

Feeling incredibly insecure and weird and...ugh, this is exactly what Ember told me not to do and there I was, having the best time with the wrong person.

Sighing, I head back into the dining area where Hardy is now sitting on the other side of the booth. His fork is poised at the cake, ready to dive in as I take a seat.

"I'll have you know that I didn't take one bite while you were gone."

I barely smile as I lean back in my seat.

"Did he kiss you?" he asks with a waggle of his brows.

I meet his eyes. "No, he told me that it wasn't going to work out between us."

Hardy sets his fork down. "Wait, seriously?"

"Yeah. It's fine. Not sure there was much of a connection there."

"There could have been if he talked more. He was silent most of the night." Hardy shakes his head. "What a fucking idiot. He had the opportunity to get to know an amazing woman and ruined it. His loss."

I pick up my fork and pierce a piece of cake. "I might drown my sorrows in this chocolate."

"Mind if I join you?" he asks as he takes a piece as well. "Pretty sure Maple was just here to help you. She barely spoke to me as well, and I think the headache thing was a cop out." He lets out a deep breath. "I think I just need to be open and honest with her."

"What do you mean?" I ask.

"I mean, just ask her out, tell her I want to see her again...date."

My stomach twists into knots. I knew I was right. Timothy can assume all he wants about how Hardy feels, but at the end of the day, it's Maple he wants. There's history there, familiarity. I can see how Timothy would think otherwise though. Hardy is a nice guy. He's outgoing and...God, he's nothing like his father. But Hardy isn't interested in me, he's just... he's friendly.

"Do you think that's a mistake?" he asks.

I glance up at him and peer into those blue eyes, eyes I wish I could wake up to in the morning. Eyes that I wish I could stare into without a hint of worry that he might see right through my gaze. Eyes that I wish would light up when I walked into the room.

But they don't.

They light up for Maple.

"No," I say, slicing another piece of cake with my fork. "I think if you want something, you have to ask for it. Maybe no more of this beating around the bush stuff. There's only so much I can do on my end. Just go for it." *She's a lucky woman.* I'm just a lovesick girl.

"You're right," he says. "Fuck, you're so right."

I am. *Hardy only sees me as a friend. As a partner in his quest for Maple.* I just want to cry.

"Polly won't yell at me now that she's seen us at the bridal shower. Maple seems to be able to talk around me. We even had a discussion about our past. I think I just need to put it all out there. Maybe...hell, maybe I'll visit her at work and wait for her to get off. We could walk around the zoo, she can show me around, be in her element when I ask her."

Yup, that would probably do it.

I slowly nod. "Great idea, Hardy. She'll for sure say yes."

"You think so?" he asks.

Our eyes meet. "I know so."

"Well, thanks for dinner," I say as we head out of the restaurant.

"You're welcome," he says.

"So, I guess I'll get going."

His brow creases.

"Get going? You're not going to walk off some of this cake with me?"

"What do you mean?" I ask.

"We nearly shared an entire half of a cake." He pats his abdomen. "If I go home now, I'll just lie in bed and grip my stomach, wondering why I made such bad choices. You can't let me do that—you need to help me understand eating that cake was a good thing, so we need to walk."

"Walk where?" I ask.

"Haven't you ever enjoyed some window shopping, Plum?" He nods toward the bay where all the touristy shops are. "Come on, let's go wander."

My brain is telling me this is a bad idea. Very bad idea.

I should leave the man to wallow in his terrible cake-eating choices.

But my heart...my heart wants this. My heart wants more time with him. My heart wants to pretend that in some far-off land, this could be about me and him.

Deciding to make a bad decision, I say, "Where do you want to go?"

He smirks. "Follow me."

Together, we head down the hill, toward Fisherman's Wharf and bustling Jefferson Street. "Have you ever been down here?" he asks.

"Yeah, here and there, more toward the pier for the nuts," I say. "But I've never really gone into any stores. I guess I'm not one to buy souvenirs of the place where I live."

"Why not?" he asks.

I shrug. "I don't really know."

"So you're telling me you don't have a San Francisco shirt?"

"Do you?" I counter.

He pauses and then turns to me, a look of surprise in his expression. He scratches the side of his head. "I don't think I do have one."

"Oh my God, and here you're giving me grief."

"You know, I think we need to right this wrong. I think we need to purchase San Francisco shirts today."

"Obviously that's what needs to happen," I agree. "And dare I say… possibly matching?"

"Clearly they have to be matching," he replies. "What are we, barbarians?"

"I know I'm not."

"And I sure as hell am not. You saw me back there with that cake… no cake left behind."

"It was an impressive takedown of a confectionary treat."

"Thank you." He curtly bows like a doofus. "When you were not kissing Timothy, I took a selfie of me and the cake."

"You did not."

He brings his phone out of his pocket and flashes the front screen.

"You made it your wallpaper?" I ask.

"It was a good fucking cake. If you need to know one thing about me, Plum, it's that I like the sweet stuff even when I try to tell people I don't."

I stare at the picture of him and the cake and chuckle to myself. "That picture is ridiculous."

"It's a memory I never want to forget." He places his phone back in his pocket and says, "Okay, let's go find shirts."

Together, we cross the street and head toward Fisherman's Wharf. A trolly passes by, tinging its bell while tourists stop to take pictures near Umbrella Alley. The skies are clear, the sun setting, and even though there's a chill in the air, I feel warm as I walk next to Hardy. His arm occasionally bumps against mine, and it takes everything in me not to take his hand, link our fingers together, lean into him and his touch.

This is not a date, Everly.

This is a friendly hang out.

Do not do anything stupid.

"Are you an In-N-Out fan?" he asks as the fast-food joint appears up ahead. Unlike the typical free-standing location, this one is tucked into an already existing building. It looks more like an old-timey movie theater rather than one of the flagship restaurants.

"I am," I say. "Big fan. What about you?"

"I think it would be very un-Californian to not be a fan."

"Agreed," I answer. "It's all about the Double-Double animal style."

"Easily the only thing you can order from there. Do you ever dip the fries in the leftover sauce that drips from the burger?" he asks as he points at a souvenir shop up ahead with a large sign stating T-shirts are sold there.

"My favorite way to eat the fries," I say. "And you know what, I get really irritated when people say they can't stand the In-N-Out fries."

"Me too," he says. "Fuck, sorry they're made fresh and don't have carcinogens inside of them."

I pause on our way toward a souvenir shop. "Do other fries have carcinogens?"

He chuckles. "Probably not, but that was the first thing that came to mind."

"I believe if you like In-N-Out fries then you have a refined palate, one that can enjoy the good taste of a potato."

"Agreed, and if you prepare them properly, then you're in for a solid meal. There are salt packets offered by the ketchup for a reason. You lightly dust them with some salt, dip them in the burger sauce, and then munch, munch, munch."

"Clearly, munching all day every day," I say.

"I love to munch," he replies with a wink, and I feel my cheeks go red. "Glad we're on the same page though. Not sure I could have matching San Francisco shirts with someone who doesn't like In-N-Out."

"It would be an immediate no for me," I reply.

"Hardy?"

We both look straight ahead where Breaker Cane, the youngest of the Cane brothers, is standing outside of a souvenir shop, holding some bags in hand.

"Breaker," Hardy says as he walks up to him. They shake hands, and then he turns to me. "You know Everly, right?"

"Briefly met before walking into a meeting," Breaker says. "How are you, Everly?"

"I'm great. How are you doing?"

"Good," he says. "Out shopping with the wife. We were down at the wharf with JP and Kelsey for dinner. Then JP wanted to go sit on the pier with the pigeons—and I'm not dealing with that bullshit—so we decided to do some shopping. Found some new games to play while we're in town for the week."

"Where's Lia?" Hardy asks.

Breaker nods toward the store. "Inside—apparently she found something she wants to get me as a gift, so she has sent me outside."

"Ooo, I wonder what it could be," I say.

"Probably a wooden puzzle game. There were a bunch in there. My guess is she's going to learn how to play it first, then give it to me and show me how amazing she is at it."

"That's my kind of girl," I say.

Breaker winks. "Mine too." He looks up at Hardy. "So…what are you two doing?"

"Going to find San Francisco T-shirts. We realized neither of us has one, and now we're here to right a wrong." Hardy pats his stomach. "Also looking to walk off some cake."

"What kind of cake?" Breaker asks.

"Uh, have you ever been to The Beard? They have a chocolate-on-chocolate cake covered in peanuts, and it's fucking huge. We got that."

"I feel like I've heard of it before, but I've never tried it," Breaker says.

"Highly recommend," Hardy replies.

"Good to know—maybe we'll stop by tonight and grab one to go."

"I think that might be one of the best ideas you've ever had," Hardy says. "Well, we're going to head down toward the wharf."

"Careful," Breaker says. "You might run into a sobbing JP, who is trying to be one with the pigeons. I already got a text from Kelsey, wishing we didn't leave them alone. Now she has to try to drag JP away on her own." Breaker shrugs. "I was not getting into it with him. Didn't have the strength."

"I knew he loved pigeons…and flamingos now, but I didn't know he was into pigeons that much," I say.

"Obsessed," Breaker says. "I've never seen a sane man lose his mind over something so…stupid before. And sure, pigeons need love too, but to cry because they're, in his words, 'walking all cute with their heads bobbing,' that's just absurd."

I chuckle because the thought of this billionaire, known for his savvy business briefings and unique ideas, crumbling at the sight of a pigeon is just too much for me.

"And then his newfound love for flamingos." Breaker leans in. "Are you getting the emails too?"

Hardy slowly nods. "I've donated twice now. I feel obligated. Just got one for penguins. The picture of the penguin covered in oil...fuck, it got me."

"You've donated twice?" Breaker shakes his head. "Dude, you can't let him take over your life like that."

"Are you talking about JP?" a beautiful woman asks as she comes up to Breaker and loops her arm through his.

The smile that breaks out across his face makes me feel so jealous because having someone in your life love you that much is what dreams are made of.

If only.

Breaker wraps his arm around who I'm going to assume is Lia and presses a kiss to her cheek. When he pulls away, he says, "We're talking about JP."

"Figured he'd be the topic of conversation. I told you if we went to dinner with them down here, he was going to talk about pigeons nonstop."

"I know," Breaker groans. "He was adamant about the restaurant location and now I know why." Turning to us, Breaker says, "Sorry, this is my wife, Lia. Lia, this is Hardy Hopper—not sure you two have met yet— and this is Everly Plum. She works with Maggie under Magical Moments by Maggie."

"Oh, how nice to meet you," Lia says with a bright smile. "I'm so excited that you guys have teamed up with the Canes. I've enjoyed visiting San Francisco more since you've created the co-op."

"Oh, do you not live here?" I ask, clearly not in the know. Maybe I should do my research.

She shakes her head. "No, we live in Los Angeles, but since the Hoppers and Canes have merged, we've been spending a little bit more time up here."

"Do you ever go down to Los Angeles?" I ask Hardy.

"Not often," he says. "Maybe once or twice. Mainly JP comes up here to talk with us. Surprised you're here, Breaker."

"Yeah, JP wanted to talk about another building he thinks we can turn into low-income housing, and I came up to look at it, see if it was feasible. I think your brother was talking about having a meetup this week while I'm here."

"That would be great," Hardy says. "Well, I don't want to keep you guys. Enjoy the rest of your evening."

"You too," Breaker says. "And if you happen to hear wailing down on the pier, you know who it is."

"We won't even go near him—we'll give him some privacy," Hardy says, making me chuckle.

"If he wanted privacy, he wouldn't be sobbing in public." Breaker offers us a smile and a wave. "Have a good evening."

"You too," Hardy says and then they take off.

"He's really nice," I say. "And Lia seems very sweet."

"She is. They're actually college friends."

"Oh, really?" I ask as we walk into a souvenir shop full of kitschy shirts, hats, and mugs. You name it, they have it.

"Yeah, they bonded over Scrabble and were friends for a really long time, although they never dated in college. Breaker was telling me that it wasn't until Lia was engaged to someone else that he realized he was in love with her all these years."

Why does this feel like my current situation?

"Wow," I say as we move around the shop. "I'm assuming she didn't marry the other guy."

Hardy shakes his head. "No, the other guy was completely wrong for her, and Breaker pointed it out. He told me the best thing he ever did was open his eyes to see that their friendship was so much more." We walk toward a table of shirts that seems promising. "I feel like that's what I want for Maple, you know? Open her eyes, let her see me for the man I am now, not the man I was back then."

God, just the mention of her name makes me feel ill. Not because I don't like her—because I do, I think Maple is amazing—but because I'm jealous.

I'm so freaking jealous of her.

Because I see you for the man you are today, Hardy.

I'm right here.

Waiting.

Hoping.

Wishing you would give me a chance. Even look my way.

Open your eyes...

"What's so wrong with the guy you were back then?" I ask.

He picks up a navy-blue shirt with a simple font scrolled across the front that reads *San Francisco.* "I wasn't sure of myself in college. Wasn't quite in tune with what I wanted, what I wanted to accomplish. I have a set idea now, and I have a passion—two things that she had in college."

"Just because you were unsure of who you wanted to be and what you wanted to do in college doesn't mean you were any less worthy than who you are now," I say as he folds the blue shirt back up and puts it on the table. "A lot of people don't figure out what they want until they're older."

"You had it figured out," he says.

"I'm different. I was set in my ways from an early age, and frankly, I'm very lucky I was able to interview with Maggie and she took a chance on me, because my industry is very hard to break into. If it weren't for Maggie, I'd probably be working a corporate job that has very little in common with what I really want to do. And I sure as hell wouldn't be heading up fun and innovative projects like Bridesmaid for Hire."

He picks up a green shirt and examines the front. "Nonetheless, you had it figured out and I wonder if that bothered Maple. That my life was always undecided."

"I don't see how that could bother her," I say while he holds a T-shirt up to his chest, checking out the size. This design is better, with a vintage inspired font. "I like that one."

"Enough to wear it?" he asks.

"Easily," I say.

"What's your size?"

"Um, I would probably want it bigger, so…a large."

He plucks a large for me and an extra large for himself. "I think we need hats too." He moves over toward the baseball caps, and I follow him.

Bringing him back to our conversation, I say, "I don't think you should put down the guy you were back in college, Hardy. Clearly, he has shaped you into the man you are today, and that man is wonderful."

He looks over his shoulder at me with a raised brow, curious. "You think I'm wonderful?"

I roll my eyes and move past him. "You know, I told myself not to offer you any compliments because I knew you were going to make a big deal about it. I was right."

"Of course I'm going to make a big deal about it," Hardy says. "The professor said I'm wonderful. I think my job here is done."

"What job?" I ask.

"Convincing you that I'm the most amazing man to walk the earth."

I knew that months ago.

"And why would you need to convince me of that?" I ask while I pick up a baseball hat and place it on my head.

He tugs on the bill. "So you can speak highly of me to Maple instead of telling her that spicy food gives me gas."

My smile barely reaches my cheeks. *Of course, this always comes back to Maple.* Every single time this comes back to Maple.

"This one works." He picks up the same hat and places it on his head. "You know, we could be twins."

I look up at him, his tall stature eclipsing me easily. "Twins?" I ask, not wanting to be twins with the guy I adore. "Pretty sure we're far from being twins."

"Not according to Danny DeVito and Arnold Schwarzenegger."

"Are you really referencing a movie from the 1800s?"

"1800s?" he says on a gasp. "Try the eighties."

"Ooof, sorry, I was born in the two thousands."

His mouth falls open and he stares at me blankly, his expression making me laugh. "No, that's not fucking right."

I nod. "It is. Sorry your old man brain can't comprehend."

"I don't have an old man brain, you have...you are...fuck...two thousands?"

I chuckle. "Yup."

He lifts up his hat and pushes his hand through his hair. "Fuck, when you put it like that, I feel like the older brother whose parents had an accidental pregnancy later on in life."

"Oh God, don't refer to yourself as my brother," I say before I can stop myself.

"Why not?" he asks.

Because that would mean I have a crush on my brother and that's frowned upon in our society.

Because I've had naughty thoughts about you.

Because this whole time, I wish you were kissing me like Breaker did with Lia.

Those aren't brotherly things.

"Uh, because I think sharing a cake like we did tonight is sacred...not something you do with your sibling," I say, wincing internally. It's not a good excuse, but I needed to say something.

"You know," he says, "that was a sacred moment tonight, wasn't it?"

"It was," I say, grateful that he's going along with the idiotic narrative I've created.

"One might say the kind of sacred moment you celebrate with matching hats and shirts."

"I could not agree more." I hold up my hat on my head. "I think this is the winner."

He taps his chin. "You know, I think it is, the only question now is… do we get matching mugs too?"

I glance over at the kitschy display of San Francisco mugs. "I think it's necessary."

"Agreed."

He smirks and then pulls me over to the mugs. I steal glances of him, committing this small moment to memory. I might not be able to have him, but I do have these moments, and these are the ones I'll hold close to my heart.

CHAPTER SEVENTEEN
HARDY

To: Everly Plum
From: Hardy Hopper
Subject: Almond Bay

Professor,

So I'm up in Almond Bay today, talking with the Rowley sisters, Aubree and Hattie, about a partnership. Have you ever been up here? They sell almond extract and these amazing cherry almond cookies...I grabbed a dozen to bring back to San Francisco because, Jesus fuck, they're good. I'm going to have some sent to your office when I get back.

Also, Aubree and her husband, Wyatt, showed me around the farm...a potato farm. They take the potatoes and make vodka, then they take the vodka and infuse it with almonds to make almond extract. The entire process was fascinating. You probably know all of this through Maggie, but I got to see it firsthand, and it was pretty fucking cool.

And I know you didn't ask for this trivial update, but I thought it was interesting. Not to mention, I wanted to tell you that I'm available any time this week, pending my return tomorrow, to go over any bach party stuff, since that's coming up next week.

I can't comprehend how quickly this wedding is coming together. I got fitted for my suit the other day with Ken and he was practically bouncing off the walls he's so thrilled—and might I add, very excited for the dips.

Anyway, expect cookies soon and I'd enjoy a full review. Thanks.

Henrietta

To: *Hardy Hopper*
From: *Everly Plum*
Subject: *RE: Almond Bay*

Henrietta,

Almond Bay is so cute. I love it there. And The Almond Store is the sweetest place. I bought some almond extract and I've hoarded it, using it for only the best of recipes. And the cookies, I can already tell you, are a fifty out of ten. They are my absolute favorite. If I knew you were going up there, I would have asked you to buy more so I could freeze them and save them for a special night...alone...in my apartment.

But I'll look forward to the ones that you send to the office. I'll be sure not to share with Maggie. She visits Hattie enough that I deserve to have some of my own.

By the way, have you heard from Brody? He came into the office the other day announcing he's made a full recovery. He then joked around about being a disaster when he was delirious before his appendix burst. He's had a few disasters, and he couldn't tell which moment was worse. It was a competition between the appendix and passing out in Bora Bora when he thought a snake had bitten him. He told me the story and I voted for the fake snake bite.

He couldn't control the appendix, but the fake snake bite— that was all on him.

Do you agree?

Eager to hear your response.

The Prof

P.S. Not much to do with the bach party. Everything is pretty much set up, and I'm just waiting on Haisley. I think it's going to be a go with the house. Working with catering right now on dips and drinks. Also working on that playlist. Wasn't planning on many decorations, but rather using the rental's Clueless-inspired theme to lead the way. Let me know if you want anything else.

To: Everly Plum
From: Hardy Hopper
Subject: RE: Almond Bay

Professor,

Back in San Francisco, and if it weren't for a stack of meetings on my schedule, I would have dropped off the cookies myself, but unfortunately wearing a suit and acting like a grownup has prevented a personal delivery.

For a moment, I considered showing up to the meetings in my pink suit but thought better of it. It didn't prevent me from

*teasing Hudson about wearing it, which in turn made him beg
me to have some semblance of professionalism. Can you tell who
the uptight one is?*

*As for Brody, yes, we've heard from him. I talked to him on
the phone and I'm really glad he's doing better. He said Maggie
was getting really clingy because of how scared she was. Said she
was more scared about the appendix than the snake bite.*

*Which brings me to your question…easily the snake bite
outweighs the appendix bursting. But there were some other
things that happened on that Bora Bora trip that could have
been equally embarrassing. I saw him throw up in the sand, and
I've seen his bare ass on the beach after Maggie pantsed him. I
watched him almost get his penis speared, and I've also seen him
shake his ass in a tiny Speedo on a rocking boat. I would classify
that entire trip as a loss for him, a never-ending disaster that will
forever live rent free in my mind.*

*And if there's nothing else for the bach party, then I'm good.
As long as we're set with the dips. Remember…the dips are
important. I will live and die on these dips!*

Henrietta

P.S. I drank my coffee from our special mug this morning.

———————

"Thanks so much," Hudson says as we finish up our last meeting of the
day. "Appreciate your time."

"Of course," Peggy says. She's from a marketing firm we might consider hiring. The chances are slim but possible.

She exits the conference room, and when the door clicks shut behind
her, Hudson exhales and leans back in his chair.

"What did you think?" he asks.

I lean back too and loosen the knot of my tie. "I think I'm not cut out for this corporate stuff. Why can't I be like Jude and be more hands-on? Be in the thick of construction or, I don't know...making sandwiches for people."

"What?" he asks, dumbfounded. "Hardy, I need someone in these meetings with me. I need someone helping me make decisions, and since you're my brother and partner, you need to be here."

"What if I gave you the go-ahead to make any decision you want," I say...*joking*.

"Only to have you bitch about it later? Not a fucking chance."

Damn it, he knows me too well.

"What if I promised not to bitch?" I ask.

"I know you—that promise would not hold."

I push my hand through my hair. "You're right."

I might hate these meetings, but I do have an opinion, and I want to do this right. Maybe I can convince Hudson that instead of suits and stuffy meetings, we can opt for jeans and interviews while playing ping-pong. That way, everyone wins.

Hudson turns his chair. "So...Breaker said something interesting to me while you were in Almond Bay."

"Oh?" I ask. "Was it about JP crying on the pier over pigeons?"

He shakes his head. "No, it was about you."

"What about me? That I was charming and charismatic, and he wishes I was the one he was meeting with instead of you?"

Hudson's expression flattens. "No, that's not what he said."

"Shame, I bet that's what he was thinking while you droned on about numbers and figures."

Ignoring me, Hudson continues, "Said he saw you by the wharf with your girlfriend, Everly."

"Oh shit." I chuckle. "He thought Everly was my girlfriend?"

"He did."

"Did you correct him?" I ask.

"I did, told him she was helping with a wedding you're part of."

"Okay, good."

"Is, uh…is anything going on there?" he says, an interested look in his eyes.

"With Everly?" I ask and then shake my head. "No, man, she's a good friend." I scratch the side of my face. "More of a friend than I was expecting, actually. She's been helping me find a way to get back together with Maple. We were actually on a foursome date the night Breaker ran into us. Everly was supposed to be with a guy named Timothy, but he checked out early. His loss, because Everly is pretty chill." I considered telling Hudson he should go out with her, but I know he'd say no. Also…I think Hudson might be too uptight for Everly. She needs someone fun and exciting.

Not some stodgy stick-in-the-mud like my brother.

And not Timothy, now that I think of it. He said Everly looked "nice" that night. *Nice.* A comfortable pair of jeans is nice. Everly looked stunningly beautiful, not…nice.

Not to mention he barely spoke to her. Barely interacted with her. She asked him about his beloved rhinos and he literally said two words. *Idiot. He's a fool for not wanting to date Everly.* She's becoming one of my best friends. A person I email about random things. Someone I think about every day, wondering how she's doing. She's a real catch, and Timothy is an absolute moron for not recognizing that.

"How did Maple feel about you hanging out with Everly after?"

"She had a headache and left early. Not a great showing for me. I was actually talking to Everly about it, and she said I should just tell Maple how I feel and stop trying to beat around the bush with my feelings. So that's where I'm headed after this. I'm going to change quickly and then go to the zoo."

"Does she know you're coming?" he asks.

"She does." I loosen my tie even more. "I'm actually pretty nervous about it."

"You think she's going to turn you down?"

"Not sure," I say. "I've been getting mixed signals from her, and I'm unsure where she stands. We had a pretty short conversation about our past when we were at the bridal shower, and that made me think we might have a chance, but the foursome date was weird. She was quiet, Timothy was quiet, and they both left early. I don't know. I don't want to sit around and guess anymore. I want to just talk to her about it and see where she stands."

"And where do you stand?" he asks. "Do you really think she's the one?" *The one...*

"I don't know." I shrug. "But I would hate if I didn't at least try. We had a good relationship in college." Despite what Polly said, I'm sure I wouldn't be feeling this...desperate to rekindle the relationship if it had just been surface-level. Maple wouldn't have felt as if she'd meant nothing to me when we broke up if it hadn't been great in the first place. She's here. I'm here. And as Everly said, why not try? "Might as well give it a shot, since she's back in San Francisco." I nod. Yep, that's what I want.

"And you want to be in a relationship?" Hudson asks, almost looking confused.

"I do," I say. "I see what Polly and Ken have. I see what Haisley and Jude have. It would be nice to not be so alone. Don't you feel lonely?"

"No," he says just as there's a knock at the door. "Come in," he calls out.

The door tentatively opens, and Hudson's new assistant and Jude's little sister, Sloane, pops her head into the room. "Um, hi, is this an okay time?"

"Yeah," Hudson says as he sits taller and adjusts the sleeves of his jacket. Sloane, although nervous most of the time when she has to speak to us, was a solid hire. Well-organized, acts like a bodyguard despite her curvier stature, and keeps us both on track with our schedule. I wasn't too sure about hiring Jude's sister, but she is fresh out of college and given the job market, she really needed something reliable. Hudson said he would take a chance on her, and Jude promised she would not let him down.

So far, he was right.

She nervously moves farther into the conference room. "Hudson, you have a phone call from Huxley Cane. Seemed like he wanted to discuss something important."

"Sure," Hudson says, standing and buttoning his suit jacket. "Be right there. Thanks, Sloane."

She offers him a soft smile, her eyes connecting with his for a moment before she curtsies and leaves.

I stand with Hudson. "Uh, when did she start curtsying?"

Hudson rolls his eyes. "That wasn't a curtsy."

"It looked like it," I say. "Her body dipped and then she left. Don't tell me you're making the poor girl curtsy to you. That's something our father would do."

"Oh, fuck off—you know I wouldn't do that."

"I don't know, all this power might be going to your head." I'm so ready to get the hell out of this suit.

"You calling me Dad?" he asks with a raised brow.

"Not even a little." I grip his shoulder. "By the way, have you heard anything from him?"

"Not yet," Hudson says. "But this is typical. He's trying to make us nervous. He's all about intimidation in real life and in business. He likes to make people sweat. If there even is a lawsuit, he's going to take his fucking time sending it over."

"Yeah." I run my hand over my beard. "You're probably right about that."

"I know I am," he says and moves toward the door. He nods at me. "Good luck at the zoo. Let me know how it goes."

"I will," I say. "And pretty sure after the other night, I'm going to need all the luck I can get."

Hardy: Testing…testing…Professor, are you there?

Everly: Hold on…are you texting me?

Hardy: I am. Is that not the proper protocol when looking to chat?

Everly: We communicate through emails.

Hardy: Would you prefer I send you an email right now instead?

Everly: I don't know, you've caught me off guard.

Hardy: I can send the email. Just say the word.

Everly: No, no, if anything, I'm flexible. Let me just take a deep breath and prepare myself for instant access to the *wonderful* Hardy Hopper.

Hardy: Man, I should text you more often if you're going to toss out compliments like candy.

Everly: Sorry, autocorrect, "wonderful" was actually supposed to be "incredibly annoying, slightly needy, and pathetically attached to his undercover bridesmaid."

Hardy: Jesus, that's quite the autocorrect.

Everly: Crazy how evolved technology is, huh?

Hardy: Just insanity.

Everly: So…how can I help you?

Hardy: What makes you think I need help? Maybe I was tapping into your phone just to say hi.

Everly: Were you?

Hardy: Technically no, there was a question.

Everly: And that question would be…

Hardy: Uh, by chance, would you have any more of those cherry almond cookies left?

Everly: You're kidding, right?

Hardy: Wish I was.

Everly: Hardy, even if I did have some cookies left, do you really think I'd share with you?

Hardy: I shared my chocolate cake with you, and technically I'm the one who bought the cookies, plus you're a nice human so, yeah, I thought you'd share.

Everly: When it comes to the cookies, I'm not nice. I'm greedy, and you don't want to be around me because I bite.

Hardy: I don't mind some biting. *wiggles brows*

Everly: Hardy Hopper, don't you dare wiggle your brows at me.

Hardy: Would you prefer that I *waggle* them?

Everly: I don't want any eyebrow movement from you. None. Keep your eyebrows to yourself.

Hardy: You know, I'm finding you to be…how do I put this in a nice way? Rude in text messages.

Everly: Rude? You're calling me rude? When you come into my phone, demand I give you my cookies, tell me you will bite me if I don't, and then wiggle-waggle your eyebrows as if that's supposed to make it all better. Oh no, sir, not going to freaking happen.

Hardy: Huh, also you lie a lot.

Everly: It's called exaggerating for comedic effect, honestly, Hardy. Must I teach you everything?

Hardy: You know, I can't recall all the things you've taught me. Care to regale me with the list?

Everly: Some people have to work. We can't all flounce around in pink suits while shopping for souvenirs. I'm busy.

Hardy: Oh, pardon me. I wasn't aware I was cutting into your pom-pom making time.

Everly: Wow, Hardy…just wow.

Hardy: LOL. So I'm going to take that as a no on the cookies?

Everly: How did you ever guess?

Hardy: Wild suspicion. Okay, well, I'm at the zoo and about to go see Maple. Wish me luck.

Everly: Good luck. Don't trip and spear your nose with a branch.

Hardy: Thanks…that's helpful.

Everly: Always here for you.

I lean on the rail that overlooks the flamingo exhibit. Bushy trees surround the exhibit while a green pond rests in the middle. And at the center of it all are the Chilean flamingos that Maple loves so dearly. I know exactly why. They're a very funny species with their long necks, stick-like legs, and thick beaks. Their colors range from salmon to rose to light pink, and the honking sounds they make are comical as they strut around the water, pecking with their bills and splashing around while looking for food.

Can't imagine what it must have been like observing them in Peru. Considering the hustle and bustle around me—the tour groups and families with screaming children—I can see why Maple is having a hard time adjusting.

While I wait, I glance over to the left where I spot the bush Everly and I hid behind when JP found us. Smiling to myself, I think back to the look on Everly's face when my nose came off, and then her quick thinking with the ketchup packets.

Christ, she's great.

Smart and funny, quick-witted. She just…gets me.

Who would have thought?

This morning when I drank out of the mug which we both got, I thought about how after we purchased them, we tried on nearly every pair of sunglasses in the next shop we visited, including the ones that were in the shape of animal faces. I chuckled, remembering the way she quacked like a duck and flapped her imaginary wings.

Not sure I've had that much fun with a person in a while.

And despite eating that giant piece of cake, I dragged her all the way down to the wharf where we bought some candied nuts for the road and tried to find a crying JP to at least observe him in his natural pigeon-loving state. Kelsey must have been able to drag him away before we got there. Shame, because I was looking forward to taking a video.

Before I walked into the zoo, I was feeling apprehensive, clammy, and ready to bolt, which was why I texted Everly. I knew just hearing from her would calm me down. And I was right, it did.

She seems to have that effect on me. One of the many reasons why I like her so much.

"Hey," a voice says, drawing my attention. When I glance over my shoulder, I catch Maple walking up to me. She has a backpack strapped to her back, and she's removed her nametag from her shirt, probably attempting to show people she's off duty.

"Hey," I say as I lean in and press a kiss to her cheek. She looks exhausted. "How was your day?"

"Pretty good," she says. "One of our flamingos had a baby that just hatched, so I got to hang out with him all day."

"That sounds like fun," I say.

"It was." She looks up at me. "So…why did you want to meet me here?"

Getting right down to business, okay.

"Thought we could hang out. You could show me around, and we could talk."

"How about we just talk?" she says and then nods to the right. "Let's go to the Leaping Lemur Café."

Just talk, that's never good.

"Sure," I say, following her.

We enter the café, and being all business, she walks over to the drinks, grabbing a water in an aluminum bottle, and I do the same. When she walks up to the cash register, she starts to pull out her wallet, but I stop her and pay for the drinks myself.

"Thank you," she says and then finds a table off in the corner. We both take a seat and she uncaps her drink, takes a sip, and then meets my eyes. "Why are you here, Hardy?"

Jesus. Okay, so she's really getting down to business.

"Do you want the small talk or the 'get to the point' conversation?"

"Get to the point," she says.

Okay. Can't say I remember Maple being this. . . direct in college.

Like the night at the bowling alley, she seems detached, disinterested. I had hoped to reminisce for a moment, but it seems she has other plans.

"To the point, that I can do." I clear my throat. "Well, here goes. When I heard that you were coming back to San Francisco, I wanted to get to know you again, see if there was still a connection between us. I wanted to ask you out on a date. Polly clearly wasn't happy with that idea because she didn't want me to scare you away, so I tried to take it slow, ease my way back into your life. Maybe it hasn't been as smooth as I would have wished, but here I am, trying to ask you out."

She tilts her head to the side, confusion in her brow. "You want to ask me out?"

"Yes," I say on a laugh. "Has it not been obvious?"

"Uh, not even a little," she says. "Especially after the other night."

"What do you mean?" I ask.

"The dinner at The Beard."

Oh, that.

"I mean, I thought maybe Timothy was a touch quiet if that's what you're talking about, but I don't see how—"

"*Hardy,*" she says, as if I'm not saying something I should be saying.

"What?" I ask.

"Are you being serious right now?"

"Uh. . .I'm being as serious as I can be."

"So you're trying to tell me that you'd rather date me than the person you should obviously be dating?"

"What the hell are you talking about?" I ask.

"Everly," she says simply.

"What about Everly?" I ask.

"It's obvious that you two have something."

"We're friends," I say, but she shakes her head.

"You're more than friends."

"Uh, no, we're not," I say. "We've only ever been friends."

"Maybe physically you've only ever been friends, but there's so much more to your friendship. It was obvious the other night, and I'd already glimpsed little signs here and there."

I shake my head. "No, you're wrong. We're just friends."

"Timothy said the same thing," she continues. "That's why he didn't stay long—because he saw exactly what I saw."

I shift uncomfortably. "Sure, maybe we talked a bit more that night and joked around, but it's because you two weren't really talking at all," I say.

"Because you didn't give us much of a chance," she replies. "And please don't think that I'm mad at you or anything like that, because I'm not. I'm actually happy for you."

"Happy for me, for what?"

"For finding someone you so easily meld with."

"Maple, listen—"

She places her hand on mine. "Let me ask you this. Why did you want to get to know me again in the first place, in all honesty? Was it because you've truly missed me all of these years, or was it because...I don't know, you saw what Polly and Ken have and you thought you might go for the same thing?"

"I..." I pause because I know what the right answer is—the answer every person would want to hear. They were missed.

But did I miss her?

Did I miss Maple?

After she left for Peru, did I pine for her?

No, Hardy. You got on with your life and focused on work.

Does that mean that I've imagined a close, deep relationship that was, in reality, only surface level? *Was I that blind?*

"If it takes you a second, I think we know the answer," she says.

"Maple—"

She squeezes my arm. "It's okay, Hardy. You don't need to apologize, you don't need to say anything to appease my feelings. Tell me the truth. Why did you want to start things back up with me?"

I pull on the back of my neck, an uneasiness trickling down my spine. "I was ready for something more in my life and you were back in town."

"I was convenient."

"Fuck, Maple, when you say it like that, it makes me sound like an ass. You weren't convenient. I wanted to see if something was still there between us."

"Do you think there is?" she asks, looking genuinely curious.

I study her for a moment, those kind eyes, that familiar smile. We had fun together. There's…familiarity. We have friends and history. But what about lust?

Love?

Do we laugh together about the weirdest and most random things?

Is she the first person I think of when I need some human interaction? And am I the first person she thinks of?

Do we buy each other cookies…matching mugs…matching shirts?

What about the deep-rooted connection Polly was talking about?

I think it could be there, if we were to try hard, if we were to dig it up and bring our lives back to college where we were…

What were we?

Boyfriend and girlfriend?

But that was just a title.

We were together.

We were in love, right?

Three years of dating has to account for something, right?

Anything?

But fuck, why does it feel off? Why do *we* feel off? And is that why I haven't sensed any attraction from Maple? I know when a woman is interested in me, but Maple hasn't shown...*any* interest.

For a moment, I considered the idea that maybe it would take her time to warm up, but by now she should be warm, warm enough to feel something.

But I don't...fuck, I'm not sure I feel anything.

Looking away, I shake my head. "I don't think so."

"Because you have feelings for someone else," she says.

"No," I answer. "I don't have feelings for Everly."

"You don't?" she asks. "That's really surprising, because in the three years we dated, I don't think you and I ever had the sort of connection that you have with Everly. It's different between you two. The inside jokes, the teasing, the laughing. The way you were so comfortable around her, as if you've known her forever. How you shared food, how you were intent on listening to every little thing she had to say. You two are more than just friends."

"But we aren't," I say as Everly's beautiful face comes to the forefront of my mind.

Those green eyes that seem to glisten when she looks up at me.

That cheeky grin when she attempts to put me in my place.

That long, dark hair, curled at the ends, swishing over her back as we walked down Jefferson Street...

"And I'm sorry to say this, but I'm not the only one who thinks this. Timothy backed off, because he didn't want to get in the way of you two. Also...I saw the way you looked at her, Hardy. You might not realize it, but when your eyes meet, both of you light up."

I lean back in my chair, my mind whirling.

Her eyes light up when she sees me?

I've never fucking noticed.

I look off to the side. "I've never thought about her that way."

"Maybe you should," Maple says. "Answer me this. Were you disappointed when we left? Sad that your 'date' with me had ended? Did you guys stay longer or head straight home?"

Well, fuck. When she asks that question…

"We, uh…we finished the cake and then we took a stroll down toward the wharf." Her eyes widen, and I know exactly what she's thinking.

"Hardy, you never go down there."

"I know," I say, feeling a wave of stress and anxiety rip through me all at once. "But I wanted to walk off the cake, and then we were talking about souvenirs, and we ended up getting matching shirts, hats, and mugs…" I sit taller in my chair and look Maple in the eyes. Her knowing eyes. Her amused eyes.

"Hardy…" she says. "Come on."

I grip my hair, distraught, anxiety ridden, heart pumping, mind about to explode.

"Holy shit," I whisper, causing Maple to laugh. "Fuck, do I…do I like Everly?"

Maple chuckles some more and sips her drink. "You do."

"But…I wasn't. I was trying…fuck." I grip my hair tighter, my mind replaying how she looked the other night with her hair down, how I felt this tingling sensation push through me when I leaned in to kiss her cheek.

How I liked that we sat next to each other in the booth and how she let me drape my arm behind her.

How she laughed endlessly throughout the night, her gaze fixated on mine when we shared a joke together.

Not to mention when I see that I have an email from her, I genuinely get excited. I love hearing from her, seeing what kind of quick wit she's going to use, or what kind of bizarre question she might ask. They brighten my day.

I think of the night I went to her office to help with décor for the bridal shower. I was in such a shit mood, pissed at my dad, and not wanting to interact with anyone. But Everly made everything better that night.

She seems to always make things better.

Holy.

Shit.

Do I...fuck, do I like Everly?

"Hardy?" My eyes connect with Maple's, and I can feel myself start to spiral. She must see it too because she gently places her hand on mine. "I can see that you're thinking over every interaction you've ever had with her."

"I...I never thought of her that way."

"And now you are."

"I'm just...fuck, I feel all sorts of confused."

"It looks like it." She softly pats my hand again. "Probably not what you want to hear, but I do think it's kind of funny that you had no idea when it was so obvious. Even at the bridal shower, I had my suspicions, but I was just playing along with whatever you guys wanted."

"Yeah," I reply distantly, my mind still reeling.

I think about Everly a lot.

When I was in Almond Bay and in The Almond Store, I thought about getting her one of the mugs from the store, but opted for cookies instead, knowing she would like them better.

This morning, when I was drinking out of my mug, I thought about how pretty she looked that night, dressed in red, her eyes shining.

On the way to the zoo, I was hoping she emailed me, but when no message from her was to be found in my inbox, I felt the need to text, anything to just hear from her...

"Jesus Christ," I say, my feelings hitting me harder than I ever could have imagined. I drag my hand over my face and stare down at the table. "Fuck, Maple, do you think it was obvious to her?"

"I'm not sure," Maple says. "It seemed like you guys were in your own little world. I wouldn't be able to say. And would that be a bad thing?"

"Yes," I say. "I don't...fuck, I don't want to make her uncomfortable."

"From the way you two interact, I doubt she's even the slightest bit uncomfortable around you."

I bite down on the corner of my lip. "Do you think she feels the same way?"

Maple shrugs. "I could see it, then again, Everly is also pretty guarded. I guess there's only one way to find out, huh?"

"And what way is that?" I ask.

"Uh...ask her out."

I start shaking my head. "No way."

"Why not? You can't say you're not ready, because you were here to ask me out."

"You're different."

"How am I different?" she asks.

"Come on, Maple. I know you, we've done this before—"

"I'm familiar," she says.

"I mean...for lack of a better word, yes."

"There's nothing wrong with that," she says. "I'm not offended in any way if that's what you're thinking. Yes, it was easy between us. We were together for three years and we almost became complacent in our relationship, but when it was tested, there wasn't much substance to keep us moving forward. And we've both changed since then—do you really think we'd be able to build a better foundation, especially since we are so vastly different?"

"I guess not," I say.

"But with Everly, there's already a foundation of friendship. You clearly like hanging out with her. You like talking with her. Do you find her attractive?"

"I mean…she's beautiful," I say.

Maple smirks. "She's very beautiful." She caps her water and adds, "All the things you need for a relationship are there, so what's the hesitation?"

"I don't want to lose her as a friend. I've sort of become pretty close with her over the last few weeks. Hell, I think I talk to her more than to anyone else."

"And that doesn't tell you something?" Maple shakes her head and then stands. "You're a smart man, Hardy. I know you're going to figure this out. But you're the one who has to come to the conclusion of what you want—no one else."

I stand as well, feeling unsettled.

I tug on my neck. "So I'm guessing me asking you out is a no?" I smile to let her know I'm joking.

She pats my chest. "That would be a big no, but thank you for thinking of me."

I sigh. "I'm sorry, Maple."

"Don't be sorry—"

"No, I'm sorry for the past, how things ended. I need you to know it wasn't you, and it had everything to do with my dad…with me."

"I know," she says quietly. "It wasn't meant to be, and I'm seeing that. But I will say this. If we'd stayed together, I doubt I would have gone to Peru, and that was an experience I would have been so disappointed to have missed. So it all worked out in the long run. Maybe you needed me coming back to San Francisco to make you realize you're ready to commit. If Everly is that person, then I truly hope it works out. From what I saw the other night, you two could very well be perfect for each other." She winks and then takes off, leaving me in the Leaping Lemur Café with so many questions.

So many thoughts.

And all of them are focused on one person…Everly.

CHAPTER EIGHTEEN
EVERLY

"I AM SO BEYOND IMPRESSED," Haisley says as she takes in the storefront. "This is incredible."

"Thank you," Maggie says. "Jude did such an amazing job on the renovation, and we are so grateful for him."

Haisley smiles at the mention of her husband's name. "He's pretty amazing, isn't he?"

God, look at the adoration in her expression. To love someone that much, I wonder what that's like.

"He is," Maggie says. "We're grateful for him and your brothers. They have truly helped elevate the business."

"You elevated it," Haisley says. "They were just there holding the ladder for you." She winks and then turns toward me. "So, are we good for the bach party?"

I nod. "Yes, we're all set. I stopped by the place earlier today and ran through details with the rental company. They were able to set up the clear cover for the pool, which they said we could easily offer as a rental anytime a party might need it. I've cleared noise ordinances, so as long as everything is wrapped up by eleven—since it's a weekend—we should be good. Catering is all set, and I was able to speak to them about future engagements. I told them if this goes well then we'll consider a partnership with them. They also said they provide private chefs for weekends, so that could be part of the Bridesmaid for

Hire package we offer. And the space truly is special, Haisley—I'm so excited."

She smiles brightly. "Thank you. And yes, I'd love to team up with a caterer, but this trial run is exactly what we need. Working out all the kinks with Hardy's friend is the perfect way to do it. I'm glad you thought of this."

"Me too. And once we nail down the details, figure out what worked and what didn't work, then moving forward we can talk packages and other options. Then we can move onto promotions and opening it up to the public, possibly lease the new house…"

"Such a good idea," Haisley says. "And the new house will be done in a month or so, at least that's what Jude told me last night. He really wanted to make sure your storefront and some of the pop-up shops were complete first before bringing his entire crew into my house. But now that we are going to be all hands on deck, we should be ready soon."

"And what's the theme of this new one?" Maggie asks. "You haven't revealed it yet."

Haisley smiles. "Well, I was going back and forth for a bit but settled on what I think will probably be the best and most sought-after theme… Barbie."

I gasp and grip her hand. "Oh my God, Haisley."

She smiles brightly. "I know. I'm really excited about this one. Picking out all of the décor and furnishings has been a lot of fun."

"My mind is going a mile a minute," I say. "Think of all the fun bachelorette party weekends we can throw. I'm thinking some sort of life-size Barbie box girls can stand in and take pictures in the backyard, white sunglasses, Barbie shoes divided by color in jars, maybe a try-on closet, and pool parties with giant flamingo blowups."

Haisley's eyes light up. "Oh my gosh, yes. And pink towels with their names."

"So cute. Ugh, I love it. It will be perfect. I can't wait to see the space."

"You will be the first to see it when it's done, and then we can start putting together packages."

"Deal," I say.

We turn to Maggie who is smiling brightly. "This makes my planning heart so happy."

"Mine too," Haisley says and then glances at the time on her phone. "Okay, I have to bolt, Jude is waiting for me. Thanks for the meeting, ladies, and Everly, if you need anything for the party, let me know."

"I will. Thanks," I say and then we hug before she takes off. Both Maggie and I move back to the conference table and sit back down. "What time is it?" I ask.

"Almost time for our next meeting."

"Is it weird that I'm nervous?" I ask Maggie.

She shakes her head. "No, because I'm nervous too."

"Why are you nervous? You're the one who hired this girl."

"I know." Maggie chuckles. "But that doesn't mean I can't be nervous. I was nervous when I hired you. I wanted to look put-together, like I knew what I was doing."

"Well, for the record, on my first day you were very well put-together. I was so intimidated that I went back to my place that night and brainstormed all the ways I could be organized for you and how I could help you improve your process."

"Ah, so some intimidation is what created the amazing system we have now?"

"Yup," I say.

She smirks. "Well, then, guess I should lay down the hammer with this new girl, right?"

"I mean, equal parts intimidation and sweet would be best," I say. "So make sure she knows that when you ask for a list of all the catering companies in the area that make fresh, soft pretzels, you get it by the end of the day—but then afterward, you will take her to go try one."

"Yes." Maggie slowly nods her head. "The perfect combination."

"Exactly. Now, what's her name again? Because I think I've blacked out."

Maggie laughs. "Her name is Scarlett Marshal. She went to school at Brentwood University in Chicago, is older than the both of us, but I think she has way more experience, which gives her the upper hand. She's been working in events within the sports field for a few years and moved here with her husband because he was traded."

"Traded?" I chuckle. "You make it sound like he's a playing card."

"I mean, he probably is on some sort of card. Her husband is Hutton Marshal."

I feel my brow crease in question. "Why is that name familiar?"

"Because all of San Francisco was roaring in happiness when he was traded to the San Francisco Fog Horns as their new starting wide receiver."

"Wait." I grip Maggie's arm. "Are you saying our new employee's husband is a professional football player...meaning...?"

"Meaning we're opening up the possibilities of growing even more, with the chance to expand with the team and their charitable events."

"Holy shit, Maggie."

"I know." She gives me a giddy smile. "It was one of the reasons I hired her—she comes from that event sector, has great contacts, and is already forging a relationship with the new team. She's also very smart and has a great personality."

And this is why Maggie is an amazing businesswoman, because she doesn't just look at what she needs in the present, but she also looks at what is needed in the future. With the Hoppers' support, using us for various events within the company, and this new hire bringing in a whole other side of commercial, charitable, and sporting events, Maggie could expand the company into one of the biggest in the Bay area if she does it right.

"Well, I'm excited to meet her. And also, this is totally unprofessional, but...have you seen Hutton Marshal?"

Maggie glances over my shoulder at the front door and then leans in. "The man is made of steel, and I've never stared at a man drinking milk the way I stared at that picture he did for that Got Milk campaign."

"Yes," I nearly yell. "The milk picture. Oh my God, so good."

"And don't tell Brody that," she says sternly. "He'll get a complex, especially since he hasn't been able to work out lately. He's very sensitive about his figure at the moment."

I roll my eyes. "The man is built."

"I know, that's what I keep telling him, but he's still fragile. This morning he told me he's only eating carrots for the next two days to get lean again."

"And how long did that last?" I ask, knowing Brody well enough now.

"He sent me a picture of him eating a donut about an hour ago."

I chuckle. "That's what I thought."

"Oh, she's here. Be cool," Maggie says just as the front door to the office opens and in walks a woman in a matching pantsuit—just not the politician-style pantsuit you're probably thinking. This was tailored for her. Long, flowy pants with a short, cropped suit top. She's wearing three-inch heels, and the red of her lipstick is so sharp that I find myself staring at it longer than I probably should.

She's put-together.

She's stylish.

And she's everything I strive to be.

"Scarlett," Maggie says as she walks up to her. "I'm so excited you're here."

Scarlett flashes straight white teeth in a beautiful smile as she walks up to us and holds her hand out. "Maggie, nice seeing you again." She turns to me. "You must be Everly. It's such a pleasure to meet you."

"You as well," I say. "Maggie has been telling me amazing things about you."

"Oh, please." Scarlett waves her hand in dismissal. "If anything,

Maggie was singing your praises during my interview. The Bridesmaid for Hire branch is probably one of the most intuitive and unique programs I've ever read up on. Genius. I foresee it being copied all around the country."

"The goal is to make sure it isn't, that *we* can provide the bridesmaids across the country," I say.

"Very smart," Scarlett says.

"Well, come, sit down," Maggie says. "I thought we could start this with a company meeting and talk about goals and expectations. Does that work?"

"Of course," she says. "Can I just use the bathroom quickly? I'm trying to get my water in for the day and it's running right through me."

Maggie chuckles. "Of course, down the hall and to the left."

"Thanks," she says, her heels clicking down the hallway.

"I'm going to check on her desk one more time, make sure it's set," Maggie says.

I nod and pull up my phone so I can check my email.

I scan through it, seeing a few interest forms for the soft launch of the Bridesmaid for Hire program, a few here in San Francisco. We want to test out our services, make sure we are viable, and then once we establish ourselves, we plan on branching out farther, eventually operating across the country, like I told Scarlett. Might be slow, but we want to do it right.

I scroll past them shamelessly because that's not what I want to read, not when I see an email from Hardy.

I've become so accustomed to opening my email and looking for his name, so when I don't see it, I can't help but feel a pang of sadness. His emails have fed my addiction in a way they shouldn't. But today? Today, though his name is right there, in my inbox, my joy is muted. I'm not as keen to open this email, as it might be the one reporting his success with Maple.

The email that confirms I will officially need to back away from Hardy.

I click on the email and read it.

> *To: Everly Plum*
> *From: Hardy Hopper*
> *Subject: Checking In*
>
> *Hey Everly,*

I pause from reading.

Everly?

When has he ever called me Everly in an email? Maybe at the beginning, but I'm always Professor.

That's odd. Maybe he was in a rush.

I continue reading.

> *With the party in two days, just wanted to make sure everything was set and if you needed help with anything. Give me a shout if you do.*
>
> *Hardy*

Hardy?

He's signing it...Hardy?

That's odd.

So not like him.

Actually, very unlike him.

The back of my neck feels prickly as the last few days run through my head. Did I do something wrong? Did I do anything to upset him? Have I said something out of turn?

I don't think so.

I mean...I haven't reported back about Maple, but he was just going to go for it. Maybe…oh God, what if things didn't work out with her? Maybe he's in a bad mood because of that.

Needing reassurance that I didn't do anything wrong, I write him back.

To: Hardy Hopper
From: Everly Plum
Subject: RE: Checking In

Henrietta (are you still Henrietta? Just checking.)

Everything is good on my end. Talked with Haisley today, and we're all set. Spoke with Maple, and she's good to go. Nothing else needs to be done.

Is everything okay over there? Little confused by the email. Wanting to make sure you're okay.

The Prof

I press send and set my phone down just as Maggie and Scarlett join me at the table.

"Okay, everyone ready?" Maggie says. "Let's begin."

———

To: Hardy Hopper
From: Everly Plum
Subject: Hey…

Hey Henrietta…Hardy, whoever you are,

Still haven't heard back and just wanting to make sure all is

okay with you. Let me know if you need anything or have any
questions.

Thanks,
The Prof (Everly)

To: Everly Plum
From: JP Cane
Subject: Thank you for your donation but...

Dear friend,

We appreciate your support in our endeavor to help the Southern
Rockhopper Penguins, but there's still so much more that needs
to be done. Please be the voice that we need to spread the word
about these beautiful creatures.

We would be forever grateful if you could share your story
about your connection with the penguins and encourage others
to step up like you have.

The Rockhoppers are counting on you.

Sincerely,
JP Cane

Everly: Hey Hardy, you there? I sent you a few emails and didn't hear back, so I wanted to check in with you and make sure everything was okay. Also, I got another email from JP asking for donations. I caved, now I'm on an email-a-day basis with him. How bad would it be if I block his email?

Everly: From your lack of response, I'm going to guess pretty bad.

Everly: Okay, not blocking him, but just checking in…did you block me?

Sitting at my desk, I stare down at my phone as I slowly nod my head as reality hits me.

Yup, I think he blocked me.

It's the only explanation.

That or he's been abducted.

Or his fingers were chopped off.

Gasp!

What if he lost his fingers in a farming accident?

What if the guy who took the pitchfork to the butt was out for revenge and got Hardy's fingers stuck in some sort of almond machine and Hardy lost all his fingers?

He could be laid up in a hospital bed right now.

Or…

More likely, he could be busy with Maple because I did my undercover work so well, and now they're back together, and the last thing he wants to do is talk to me because he's wrapped up in a wonderful second chance romance.

He's too busy walking through the zoo with her.

He's too busy taking her to The Beard and sharing a chocolate cake with her.

He's too busy buying matching shirts…

Oh God, cue the tears.

Would *they* get matching shirts? I mean, why wouldn't they? There would be no reason for them not to. They're a couple; therefore, they would have matching shirts.

I worry my bottom lip as anxiety rolls through me.

This is what was supposed to happen.

He was supposed to get back together with Maple—I guess I just didn't expect to be completely dropped from his life, though. I thought that we were at least friends.

I stand from my desk and pick up my water glass. I walk toward the kitchen, my slippers shuffling across the concrete as I go to fill up my glass with more water.

Maggie just got a shipment of vases for an upcoming wedding that we're storing for the florist since they're out of room. The boxes line the hallway for now until we can move them into storage. If I wasn't wearing a pencil skirt, I would move them right now, get out some of this nervous energy, but with my luck, one squat to pick up a box will tear the skirt wide open.

When I reach the kitchen, I fill up my water before leaning against the wall and staring out toward the storefront's main lobby.

This is what you signed up for, Everly. To help Hardy get back together with Maple.

You knew this was coming. There was no way Maple wouldn't fall for the man all over again.

And yet it feels like my heart is slowly...painfully being ripped out of my chest with every breath I take.

Dramatic? Maybe, but I just...God, I liked him and there was a slim part of me that thought...maybe, just maybe there was more for us.

Looks like I was wrong.

I take a sip of my water and sigh.

God, what I wouldn't give for his ghosting to be due to a farm-related accident.

I've never wished for someone to lose their fingers before, but here I am.

And all I can say is I'm not proud of it.

CHAPTER NINETEEN
HARDY

SHE WOULD LIKE THIS SHIRT.

Actually, she'd probably love it.

A crab posing in a beret with a paintbrush and the name *Leonardo da Pinci* under him.

She'd think it was funny, clever, and stupid all at the same time.

She'd love this store. I could see her strolling down the boardwalk-style sidewalk of Almond Bay, a small coastal town in Northern California, admiring the Victorian buildings, pastel colors, and adorable flower boxes. That's what she would call them, *adorable*.

I could see her spotting the souvenir shop and with a humorous glint in her eye asking me if I wanted to go in. I, of course, am always up for an adventure with her and would jump on the opportunity.

We'd walk into The Almond Outpost and the first thing she would say is how she likes the wide plank floors. I'd agree with her. Then she'd ohh and ahh over the shirt selection up front, the generic Almond Bay shirts, but then she'd gasp when we head toward the back, because she'd see the outpouring of bad puns stitched and inked onto various items of clothing.

She'd rifle through them, holding them up to her chest, like...like this one...

A horse dressed up as Obi Wan with the slogan *May the Horse Be With you* under it. Almond Bay Equine Rescue.

Or this one, two croissants holding hands with a heart above their heads and the text *You're the one I croissant.*

I actually think she might like that one best since she's a romantic.

Actually, I know she would like it best. She'd chuckle, but she'd also get those heart eyes she seems to get when something makes her really happy. They glisten and twinkle...

Fuck.

I drag my hand over my face. Mother of God, what is wrong with me?

I think we all know what's wrong with me.

I've recently stumbled upon the realization that the girl who's been becoming my best friend is actually the girl I should have been pursuing this entire time.

I've probably been pining over her and never realized it.

Maybe all those emails—all those interactions—was me slowly falling for her and not having a goddamn clue.

Moron!

If my life was a book, readers would be shaking their pages, yelling "Wake up, idiot! She's right under your nose."

I probably would have still ignored all the anger from the peanut gallery because that's how big of a moron I am.

Sighing, I thumb through T-shirt sizes and stop when I reach the larges.

She likes a large shirt.

She likes them big because she wears them with leggings or spandex shorts. I know this because we had a long conversation about it. And she also doesn't like white shirts on her, she says it's too stark of a contrast against her complexion. She prefers darker colors, and I think she's right to an extent. Darker colors look nice on her and make her eye color pop, but fuck, when she wears red...

In my humble opinion, red is her color.

This shirt is red. Should I get it for her? If this was a few days ago, I probably wouldn't have even given it a second thought. I would have purchased it for her and then surprised her at work. I would have said it was from a friend to a friend. She would have thanked me with a hug, I would have inhaled her sweet perfume and thought *wow, she smells good*, but never done anything about it!

Jesus Christ.

Like I said, moron.

"Can I help you with anything?" a store clerk asks as she comes up to me.

"Oh, I'm good," I say with a wave, not really wanting to gab.

"Isn't that a great shirt?" It seems like the store clerk has other ideas.

"Yeah. Like the pun. I also like that the croissants resemble Danny and Sandy from *Grease*."

The clerk laughs. "That was my favorite part. Never saw a croissant with sideburns before."

"Yeah, clever," I say, the humor in my voice barely audible.

"Well, I have more sizes in the back if you are looking for something else, just give me a shout."

"Thanks," I say.

And then, thankfully, she walks back to her counter, leaving me alone with the shirt.

Should I get it?

Why would I?

It's not like I've spoken to her in the last few days. It's not like I've answered her emails or even thought about texting her back. And why, you might ask? Because I'm having a hard time processing, that's why.

Because I'm worried that I have these strong feelings for a girl who has put me wholeheartedly in the friend zone.

Because I like her so much as a friend...and more, but worried that if I actually make the move, I'm scared she'll say no.

I'm afraid of losing what we have.

Although, because of my negligence, what we have is slowly starting to fade anyway.

"Hardy?"

Christ, can't a guy hem and haw over a shirt in peace?

I turn around and find Brody standing behind me.

"Brody?" I ask. "What are you doing here?"

"I'm here with Maggie—we're visiting Hattie." While I'm in town for business, Hattie and Maggie are best friends. Hattie is the owner of The Almond Store, one of the Rowley sisters I'm meeting with. I've been working with both of them on a contract to resell Hopper almonds as well as use them for their almond extract. We've also been working on a possible partnership, taking their almond extract nationwide and in stores. "Hattie didn't mention meeting up with you."

"Maybe she likes to keep her business to herself," I say as I set the shirt down, but of course Brody notices it.

"*You're the one I croissant*?" he asks while looking up at me. "Getting a little present for Maple?"

"Not so much," I say.

"Uh-oh, why does that sound like things haven't worked out the way you were hoping? Was it the way you fell into her breasts when you greeted her?"

I pinch the bridge of my nose, and I walk past him. "Not in the mood, dude."

"Hey," he says, pulling on my arm. "What's going on?"

"Nothing," I say. "I'm going to head back to the inn."

"Hold on," he replies. "I have to grab some socks because I'm an idiot and forgot to pack any. Hattie and Maggie are hanging out tonight—want to grab a burger with me? We can talk. Serious talk. No jokes."

I look him in the eyes, a *no* on the tip of my tongue, but before I can change my mind, I nod.

"So, we've talked about sports, the weather, and cherry almond cookies," Brody says as he picks up a fry from his plate. "We've also touched upon a new pair of shoes you're considering purchasing as well as what cologne I'm wearing. Now that we've gotten all pleasantries out of the way, care to tell me what's going on with you and Maple? Or do you want to discuss the difference between one button undone on a dress shirt or two?"

"Fascinating topic," I say. "Would love to dive deep into that. You know, I've always thought two was kind of douchey but—"

"*Hardy*," Brody says in a stern tone, which is shocking given this guy is barely ever serious.

I sigh and wipe my mouth with my napkin before putting it on the table.

"Whatever I say, you can tell Maggie, but she can't tell Everly, okay? I mean that, man. I can't have this getting back to her."

"Everly?" he asks. "Did something happen with Everly?"

"Dude, just promise me."

He nods. "Okay, yeah, I promise, it won't get back to her."

"And I can trust you, right? The appendix has been removed, so we shouldn't have any more embarrassing truth moments from you, right? You're going to be able to hold back?"

"Since I've had the appendix removed, I've actually been more polished, reserved. I think the appendix was the thing that was causing mayhem in my life."

I eye him suspiciously because I don't think anyone would believe that.

"You can trust me, dude," he reassures me, and call me crazy, but from the serious tone in his voice, I think I believe him.

So I go for it.

"Maple turned me down. Wasn't interested in starting things up again. I don't want to get into detail about the reasons, but what it comes down to is that our connection wasn't as strong as I assumed it was back in college."

"That sucks. I'm sorry, man."

I press my lips together and stare at the fry scraps on my plate. "She pointed something out to me, though, that I'm still trying to process."

"Is this about Everly?" he asks.

I slowly nod. "Yeah, Maple brought it to my attention that I have feelings for Everly." Brody's eyes widen but I continue, "And the more she talked about it, the more I realized that she was absolutely right."

"Holy shit," he says. "That's a bit of a twist."

"Yeah, tell me about it." I sigh. "I mean, fuck, man. Maple is so goddamn right. All I can think about is Everly. I look forward to seeing her, hearing from her, talking to her. Those shirts I was looking at in the store—I was thinking about which one she would fucking like, what size and color she would prefer. I could picture her in the croissant shirt, I could see her bright smile, loving it so much. I feel like I know this woman, down to my very core, and that freaks me the fuck out."

"Why does that freak you out?" he asks. "That should only spur you on to want so much more with her. It sounds like you might have found your person, so I would lean into that. That's what I did with Maggie."

"You and Maggie are different," I say.

"How so?" he asks. "I was crushing on her when I first met her but never made a move because she's my best friend's sister. I had a momentary lapse in judgment when I made out with her at her brother's wedding but put an end to it. I didn't think I had a chance to be with her, but when we broke that barrier in Bora Bora, everything changed, and I fell hard. I was all in. How is this different?"

"You weren't friends before. You hated each other."

"Ehh, there's a very thin line between love and hate," he says. "But I get what you're saying—you're afraid to lose her as a friend."

"Exactly, it feels so weird to say because it's been such a short time since we've been hanging out and talking, but I really rely on her. She's my go-to person right now. And if I make a move, I'm going to lose all of that."

"True," he says. "But she might feel the same way and you might have a whole lot to gain."

"At what risk, though?"

He shrugs. "That's something you're going to have to figure out on your own."

"How did it go?" Hudson asks as he takes a seat at the conference table across from me.

"Good," I answer as I adjust my suit jacket. I fucking hate these things. You would think since we now own our own company that we could relax on the dress code, but Hudson likes to maintain a sense of professionalism. I want to know who came up with the rules that wearing a suit screams professionalism. Shouldn't it be about how you carry yourself and not about what you wear?

"Care to elaborate?" he asks as he leans back in his chair and crosses one leg over the other. "Did you set up the account with Hattie and Aubree?"

I nod. "I did, and we spoke about the possibility of expanding their almond extract into a nationwide brand. They're on board with the idea, which means we need to start looking into cost of production. I told them we want to keep the recipe and leave the process to them, that we just want to back them and also partner with them so they use our almonds."

"That's great," Hudson says with a smile.

"What's the smile for?" I ask.

"Just interesting that we've branched off from our dad and now we have our hands in all sorts of businesses. Almond extract wasn't on my list, but I can see the potential, especially given the numbers they turned in. With some financial backing, they can really take off, more than they already have."

"Yeah, it should be great," I say, my voice flat. And, of course, Hudson notices the lack of enthusiasm.

"What's going on with you? I thought you'd be excited about this. You love your almonds."

"I do," I say. "Just...some personal things going on."

"Does this have to do with Dad?" he asks. "Because we still haven't heard anything. Don't let him intimidate you with the frivolous threat of a lawsuit. He has nothing on us, and you bought the almond branch outright from him. He had no problem letting it go. And now that we're capitalizing on it, that doesn't mean we need to be worried."

I get the feeling he wouldn't be overly pleased about my feelings for Everly, and there is no way in hell I want to talk to him about them until I actually figure out what I plan on doing.

Therefore, I go with his line of thought and leave it at that. "Yeah, his loss, right?"

"His loss," Hudson reiterates. "Now, I have to talk to you about your schedule. I know being in the office isn't your favorite thing, but I need you here more. We're taking on more projects and it's more streamlined if you're here to go over them. I'm starting to get overwhelmed, and you know the farm is doing fine on its own. They don't need you there once a week."

I grit my teeth because this is the last thing I wanted to hear right now. Sure, I know I need to be in the office more. I need to be there for Hudson, and I don't mind these new projects—they're invigorating, especially when you get to see them grow into what you planned—but fuck, the farm is my safe place.

Where I like to go to think.

Hang out.

Just breathe.

I stopped by on the way home from Almond Bay and walked through the almond trees, thinking about Everly and how much I'd like to show her the farm. How fun it would be to walk her through the ins and outs of how we took a few acres and made it into so much more. Something that's so much bigger now. I want her to be proud of me, as odd as that sounds.

"From the disgruntled look on your face, I can see that you don't agree."

"It's not that I don't agree, it's that I just like it better there."

"I understand," he says. "Truly, I get it. You were never made for the office, but I need you here now. I'm not saying you're going to be here forever, but I need you in the city while we still have things processing and we're still growing. I need you talking in person to the people we're hiring. Once we find the proper flow, then you can start working remotely, but for now, I'd prefer you only go to the farm once every two weeks, maybe even three."

"Christ," I mutter as I pinch my brow.

"Hardy—"

"I know," I say as I look my brother in the eye. "I get it. And I don't want you irritated with me. I'll be here."

"I don't want you irritated with me either," he says. "I know what your passion is, Hardy. I know it was hard for you to find, but once you found it, you created something that has provided a huge income stream to our company. The almonds are the reason why we're able to invest in other things. I want to get you back to them, but it's just going to take time."

"I know," I say softly, wishing he wasn't making so much sense.

CHAPTER TWENTY
EVERLY

I STARE AT MY PHONE, wondering why there hasn't been a response from Hardy. Not yesterday and not today. The party is tomorrow, and now I'm starting to worry that I truly did something wrong, something to upset him. If this is what it feels like with no contact for two days, then how am I going to deal with him being so immersed in Maple that he doesn't speak to me again? *I thought we might be able to maintain some semblance of friendship, no matter how much it hurt me. Foolish, Everly. Foolish.* I don't like these weird vibes.

Such weird vibes that I find myself standing outside Hardy's office building, wondering if I've lost my mind.

And maybe I have.

But I've also felt sick.

So freaking sick over all of this that I need to just…as he put it, check in.

Before I can lose my nerve, I push through the front doors of the office building, only to run straight into the man I came to see.

"Everly," he says, startled. "What are you doing here?"

It takes me a second, but when my eyes focus on him, I immediately notice his dark blue suit, which is perfectly tailored to his broad shoulders and tapered waist. And despite how good he looks, I know just how uncomfortable he is.

But the suit is not what's pulling my attention—it's the confusion in his expression and the hard set in his shoulders. He seems angry.

Angry at me?

I have no idea. But that's all it takes for me to lose all the confidence I gained to come here.

So I do the only thing I know to do. I lie.

"Uh, something is wrong," I stammer.

"What?" he asks as he pulls me to the side.

You, you're what's wrong.

You're acting weird.

You're not talking to me like you normally do.

And I don't know how to deal with it. It's either confront you or cry.

"Uh, the dips," I say. "Something is wrong with the dips."

"What do you mean?" His brows pull together.

"The, uh…the caterer can't accommodate all of them," I say, even though that's not true.

"They can't?"

"They can't," I say with a shake of my head. "And I thought that coming down here to tell you would be the best way to break the news that I was going to, uh…spend the evening making some dips for the party. So have no fear," I say with a fist pump. "Everly is here."

Oh God, why did I say that?

That is humiliating.

But to my good fortune, a small—and I mean minuscule—smile tugs on his lips. "You came here to tell me the caterer's not able to make all the dips and that you're going to make them yourself?"

"Yup." I nod. "I was, uh, I was going to email you, but you see I didn't get a response from my earlier emails or texts and, well, out of fear of you not receiving the information, I thought I should just tell you in person. I hope that's okay."

"Yeah, that's fine." He studies me for a second, his gaze nearly making me melt. "Well, do you need help?"

"Help with what?" I ask.

"Making the dips."

"Oh, the dips." I wave him off. "No, I'm good. Was going to head off to the grocery store, buy the ingredients and start putting everything together, so no worries. Just wanted to inform you of what's happening, so anyway, yeah, that's what's going on." I smile awkwardly. "*Anywho.*" I thumb toward the door. "Going to hit up the grocery store now, so have a good night and see you tomorrow. Okay, see ya. Bye."

I rush out the last few words and then turn on my heel and head for the door.

Humiliating.

This was absolutely humiliating.

What the hell was I thinking?

Coming here and trying to see if he was okay. Of course he's okay; he's a grown man, so if he wants to call me by my real name in an email, he has the right to do so. If he wants to ignore my emails and texts, also, he has the right to do that too.

No need to check in on him. That's what stalkers do.

Stalkers do this.

They check on people after not hearing from them for one day.

That's what I am, a stalker.

A stupid freaking stalker.

God, I'm disgusted with myself.

I make it outside of the building and head toward the parking garage, where I left my car for a cool twenty bucks because I'm a frivolous stalker apparently.

Tucking my purse against me, I brave the windy day, duck my head, and continue toward the garage. Then I feel a tug on my arm.

I nearly scream bloody murder—until Hardy's face comes into view.

"Christ," he says as the wind whips around us. "I was calling your name."

"Oh, I'm sorry," I say. "I couldn't hear you."

Yup, couldn't hear you over my own self-hatred.

"I said I can help," he replies.

I wave him off again. "Not necessary. You go home, pop open a beer, enjoy a show or a game, and then go to sleep knowing the dips are taken care of and everything is on the up and up for the party. Okay?" I pat his shoulder. "Have a good night." I start to turn away, but he grabs my arm again, stopping me.

"Everly, I can help."

"Yup, heard you loud and clear, and I appreciate your insistence, but as I said, totally under control, shouldn't have even bothered you with this dip emergency. But I need you to know it's all handled and the dips shall prevail." I raise my fist to the sky, hating myself.

He studies me.

Truly studies me.

Those blue eyes are searching, trying to find something—I'm not sure what, possibly the lie that's making my feet sweat—but I will go to my deathbed holding this lie close to my chest.

No set of crystal blues is going to unleash the truth from me.

"Okay," he finally says.

"Okay?" I ask, surprised that he's giving up.

He nods. "Yup. Okay."

"Well, then…okay." I smile. "So, uh, have a good night."

"You too," he replies, so I nervously turn away from him and head toward the parking garage again, but as I take a few steps forward, I realize I'm not alone.

I glance over my shoulder to see him following right behind me.

"What are you doing?" I ask.

"Going to my car."

"Oh, right, because you drive. You're a grown-up and you drive, so why wouldn't you go to your car? Silly me." I bonk my forehead with my palm.

Yeah, keep it up, Everly, you're not humiliating yourself in the slightest.

I walk into the parking garage, Hardy still following behind, and I head up to the second floor. When I hear him climb the stairs with me, I say, "Oh, second floor as well?"

"Yup," he replies.

"Cool, yeah. This is...this is like one of those moments where you say goodbye, not realizing you're going in the same direction, so you have to awkwardly walk next to each other."

He doesn't respond so I just zip my lips and move forward. When I see my car over in the distance, I point at it. "Thar she blows." His brow raises, and I nervously laugh. "Not sure why I put it like that, in an old-timey sailor voice, maybe I have the Fog Horns on my mind. Are you a, uh, a fan of football? Do you like the old rough and tackle?"

I wince because...*rough and tackle*? Where the hell did that come from? Someone who should be committed, that's where.

"I like the Fog Horns," he says.

"Oh cool, yeah, well...Ooooooooooo, uhhhhhhhhh," I say in the classic Fog Horn chant. Of course, that makes him pause in his path to his car.

"Did you just make a foghorn noise?"

I did, and now I want to stick my head under the hood of my car and slam it down a few times.

"Yes." I swallow. "Was that, uh, was that not the impression you were looking for?" I'm sweating. I'm actually sweating so terribly that my shoes are about to fall off. It's like a slip and slide inside the soles. "If not, I have other impressions, uh...like a crow." I clear my throat. "Ca-caw. Ca-caw." *What the fuck are you doing, Everly?* "Real lifelike, right?"

I swear if I put a quarter between his brows right now, he'd be able to hold it there. "Yeah, really lifelike."

"Thanks." I curtsy because, why not? I have no control over my body anymore, might as well treat him like the goddamn King of England. "Well, I shall be on my way," I say in a British accent. "Pip

pip, cheerio, and off I go." I salute him, duck my head, and walk straight up to my car.

I'm so humiliated. So embarrassed. So beyond infuriated with myself that I unlock the door and shuffle inside where I press my head to the steering wheel and mutter, "You are a fucking moron. Pip pip? Who the fuck says pip pip?"

"I liked it."

"Ahhhhhhhhhhh!" I scream at the top of my lungs as I see movement in my passenger seat.

Locked into pure survival mode, I raise my hand, flatten it, and jab the invader's throat with a quick whip to the jugular.

A gust of air flies from his mouth as a low groan fills the small space.

Got him!

Satisfied, I allow myself to confront my attacker, and that's when I realize it's Hardy.

"Oh my God," I yell. "Oh God, I didn't know. When did you…oh, God, can you breathe?"

He coughs, he sputters, and he takes a few deep breaths.

Dear God, I broke his esophagus. Karate-chopped right through his ligaments and muscles.

I rest my hand on his shoulder as he gasps for air.

Do I perform CPR?

Do I call 911?

Do I check for a dent?

After what feels like minutes, he finally turns to me, hand on this throat, and says in a very squeaky voice, "What the hell…did you…do?"

I lift up my hand and flatten it like a plate. "I, uh, I knife-handed your throat. Did you…did you not like that?"

"What the fuck do you think?"

My lip curls into my teeth out of nerves as I say, "I don't think you liked it."

"Correct," he says, still gasping for air.

"I'm sorry. I didn't mean to, but you startled me, and it was pure self-defense. I could have grabbed my stun gun. Do you want me to test that on you? See which would have been worse?"

"Does it look like I want you to do that?"

"Not so much," I answer and then grab my water bottle from my purse. "Would you like something to drink?" Maybe we can test for holes.

He shakes his head and then leans back in his seat. He takes a few deep breaths, and when he seems collected, he says, "Just drive."

"Drive?" I ask, very confused.

"Yes, drive."

"Drive where?" And then it hits me. "Oh God, the hospital?"

"No," he says before I can panic. "To the store."

"The store? For ice? Medicine?"

He pinches his nose. "For the dip ingredients, Everly."

"Oh, yes, for the dip—" I pause. "Hold on, are you coming with me?"

"Yes," he says, exasperated.

"But…why?"

"Because I'm not going to make you do it alone."

"You're not making me do anything," I say. "I told you I could handle it. So, no need to help. Now can I drop you off at your car? Possibly take you to Urgent Care?"

He exhales loudly and then turns as much as he can in his seat to look me in the eyes. "I'm not going to battle over this with you, Everly. I said I'm helping, so take me to the goddamn grocery store before I lose my shit."

Yikes!

Okay.

So…clearly not in the best of moods. Not sure why. I mean, the knife-hand probably didn't help, but he started off in a bad mood. I just pushed him deeper into the darkness. Does this mean he and Maple didn't get together? *Is he angry at me because my advice was wrong?* After all, I did suggest he had the green light to go ahead with her. *Shit.*

He's giving off the vibe that he doesn't want to talk about it, so I'm not going to push. Which means…we're going to the grocery store.

I wasn't intending to actually make any dips tonight, so I need to come up with a plan and quick.

"Sorry about that," I say as I walk back up to Hardy, who's standing in the middle of the cracker aisle with our cart. He has placed come Club crackers in the cart along with some Triscuits. Not sure what he has planned for those, but we're not going to need them. "That was the caterer," I say.

"Oh?" he asks.

"Yup, the manager actually. He called to apologize about the miscommunication—they're actually going to make all of the dips, so… looks like we don't need to worry about any of that." I slap my hands together as if dusting them off. "Easy peasy."

Gripping the cart handle, he stares at me. "So…we don't have to make dips?"

"Doesn't look like it. What a relief, huh? I don't think I even have enough room in my fridge for all those dips. I would have had to bring all the groceries to the office and make them there and, I'll be honest, I think there might be a ghost in that building because I don't like being there at night by myself. So, yeah, close call. No ghost encounters tonight." I smile up at him, but he doesn't return the gesture.

Instead, he pulls on the back of his neck and turns away.

Okay, I thought he'd be relieved, but if anything, he just looks more miffed. *God, he must wish I never came to his office this afternoon.* And now he's stuck with me until I drop him back at his car.

"But, you know, if you want to make some dips, we can totally do that too. Just warning you, if things are a little off at the office, I told you about the possible ghost."

Instead of answering, he picks up the boxes of crackers and puts them back on the shelf, then he directs the cart down the aisle and makes a left.

Uhh…

I chase after him, following him through the grocery store until we reach the frozen foods section.

He moves right in front of the pints of ice cream and opens the door.

"Oh, in the mood for some ice cream? Don't blame you—I love a good pint for dinner every once in a while."

He grabs a coffee-flavored ice cream and sets it in the cart. Then he gestures to me. "Pick what you want."

"Oh, that's okay—"

"Grab a pint, Everly," he says in a tone I really haven't heard him use before.

What the hell has happened to the fun, easygoing Hardy?

I feel like I barely know this man.

Same body, same face, but the attitude, all grumpy and growly? Someone's replaced him with another person, and I need to find out who did this.

Not wanting to test the waters, I reach into the freezer and grab a pint of cookies and cream, always an easy go-to flavor that satisfies any mood.

He takes the pint from me and puts it in the cart as well, then he moves down to the end of the aisle where the syrups and toppings are. He picks up chocolate syrup, a vat of sprinkles, and some cherries. Then he walks us over to the dairy section and snags a can of whipped cream. The paper goods section is next, where he grabs a small pack of wooden spoons.

"Need anything else?" he asks, looking at me.

"Uh…a drink?" I ask, very confused as to what he's doing.

"Right," he says.

He moves the cart toward the front where the coolers are next to the registers. "Take your pick," he says as he moves in to grab a Coke Zero. I lean in next to him and grab the same thing. We both place them in the cart and then he walks over to self-checkout.

Quietly, he checks us out. I don't even bother to try paying because I know he'll probably growl at me to put my wallet away.

Instead, I grab a paper bag and pack up our groceries while he finishes paying. Once we're back in the car and I'm behind the wheel, I look over at him and ask, "Where to?"

"Nowhere," he says as he opens the bag and hands me my ice cream.

"Oh, are we eating here?"

"Yup," he says.

Then in silence, he opens everything, lays it out along the center console, and then hands me a spoon.

"Eat some ice cream. You need to make room for the toppings."

Unsure what the hell is going on, I do as he says and take a few mouthfuls of ice cream off the top of the pint. And once there's a big enough divot, I drizzle some chocolate into the pint, along with some sprinkles, whipped cream, and cherries.

Then in silence…we eat.

Both staring out the front window, looking out toward the nearly empty parking lot. What I wouldn't give to understand what's going on in his head. What his reasoning is behind the ice cream. Why he's acting so strange.

After a few minutes of silence, I can't take it anymore, so I ask, "How's your throat?"

"Fine," he answers curtly.

"The ice cream helping it?"

"Yeah."

"Good, I'm glad," I say as I tip my head against my head rest.

That's that. A simple yeah. Nothing more.

We continue to eat our ice cream, occasionally adding on sprinkles, cherries, whipped cream, and chocolate syrup.

It's a comfortable silence despite the questions rolling around in my head. The largest being *what happened with Maple?* But I am too chicken to ask that.

After another few minutes, I realize I can go about this one of two ways: I can either ask him what's going on and why he's acting weird, or I can try to get him out of the apparent mood he's in like I did when we were making pom-poms.

Knowing the latter will be better for his sanity I say, "I could eat a whole jar of maraschino cherries if no one was looking."

He exhales. "Same."

"I think I would be incredibly sick from all the sugary syrup goodness, but I wouldn't regret it. I would think about doing it the next day."

"I wouldn't wait until the next day," he says. "I'd just grab another one."

"Makes sense," I say, both of us staring out the windshield, not bothering to look at each other. "You did claim to eat two bags of candied nuts in one sitting, why not two jars of cherries?"

"You shaming me?" he asks.

"Nope. Merely impressed over here. If I had the stomach for it, I'd be doing the same thing. Maybe it's a good thing I don't have the stomach for it though. I would find myself in a pile of cronuts."

He leans his head to the side to look at me. "You like cronuts?"

"Obsessed," I say. "If you say you don't like them, I'm going to need you to vacate my car. Thank you."

"I love them," he says softly.

"Are you a fan of all flavors or is there one in particular you love?" I ask as I scoop up more ice cream.

"I'm afraid to say."

Thank God he's talking. It might be a mundane conversation, but it's better than him growling at me.

"Why?" I ask.

"Because what if it's the same as you?"

"Oh, the horror," I deadpan. "That would be the worst thing that could ever happen."

He lightly chuckles. "We have too much in common."

"I know, terrible thing, isn't it?"

I feel his mood start to lighten up, his shoulders relaxing, and for the first time since I ran into him in his office building, he actually looks me in the eyes. "Would be terrible," he says. "Means I'd have to get another matching shirt with you."

Gah, those eyes. They slay me.

If only there was a smirk, I would melt right here in my car.

"Another matching shirt? Yuck. You're going to make me throw up just thinking about it," I say. "Gross. Disgusting. You know what, don't tell me your favorite cronut flavor because if we have to get another set of matching shirts, I might just dunk my head into the bay to scream out my disgust."

He chuckles. "Can't have you screaming into the bay—you might scare the sea animals."

"One hundred percent I would scare them. You've never heard me scream. And under water, the whales would think an octopus got its tentacle stuck under a rock."

"Ooo," he winces. "Terrible sound."

"Tell me about it. So glad we're saving all the whales from having to listen to that."

"Real saviors over here," he says.

The joking tone, the easygoing nature…it fills me with relief, because whatever was bothering him felt like a heavy weight on my shoulders. Being this close, it almost felt like it was difficult to breathe, to focus, to concentrate on any sort of conversation.

But now, it's like the air is flowing again, the ease is rolling, our friendship feels reinstated.

"But off the record, in case you needed to know, my favorite is the matcha Oreo," I say.

I glance over at him and catch him shaking his head.

"What?" I ask.

"The fucking whales are going to hear it."

A smile plays on my lips. "No. Nope...no. Don't even say it. I'm going to be mad if you do. Because at this point, it's like, get your own opinion, Hardy. Stop copying me."

"Who's to say I'm copying you?" he asks.

"Uh, I said it first, therefore if you say the same thing, that would be *you* copying *me*."

"I have my own opinions."

"Uh-huh, okay, so then Mr. I Have My Own Opinions, what is your favorite cronut flavor?"

"Matcha Oreo," he says.

"Oh my God." I dramatically roll my eyes. "There you go, copying me."

"Nope." He shakes his head. "Do you know how I know I'm not the one copying you?"

"Oh, this should be good—please, enlighten me."

He smirks. "Because I'm older than you, by so many years that you couldn't even pay for a cronut by yourself a few years ago—therefore I win."

Expression flat, I turn to him. "You're kidding, right?"

"Nope."

"First of all, I appreciate you acknowledging the many years between us, it's about damn time. Second of all, I could buy a cronut by myself several years ago because I've been working since I was thirteen and I've been saving since then as well. So, yeah, I would have been able to buy one. And thirdly, my generation is more open to things like cronuts, whereas yours tends to be stuck in the mud when it comes to trying new things."

"Uh...not fucking true. I grew up in the age of technology. The reason you have a phone with apps on it is because of me."

"Oh, so you invented the first iPhone?" I slowly clap. "My God, I didn't know I had a technological marvel in my car."

"You do," he says, chin held high. "If it wasn't for my generation accepting technology and allowing social media into our lives, you wouldn't even know what a cronut was because you never would have seen it go viral. So I believe a thank-you is in order." He leans his ear in toward me. "I'm waiting."

"That's the most absurd argument I have ever heard."

"Absurd or correct?"

"Absurd," I say on a laugh.

"Well, we can agree to disagree."

"I guess so." Feeling full, I cap my ice cream and set it to the side. I turn in my seat and face him. His head leans to the side to look at me as well. His usually blue eyes seem almost grey under the light of the parking lot. Wanting to still keep the mood light, I ask, "Have you recruited a beer pong partner for tomorrow?"

"Not yet," he says. "Figured I'd pick from the group. I need to assess who's available first, maybe make them try out for me before I make a final decision."

"Tryouts, huh? You must be good if you're going to hold tryouts for a partner."

"I'm very good," he says and then flashes me his wrist. "This has won me many a tournament."

"What has? Your cockiness?" I smirk.

"That," he says. "And the strength of my wrist and the flick of my fingers. All you have to do is tell me which cup, and it's in."

I shake my head. "God, it's going to be so great seeing you eat those words tomorrow night."

"No fucking way. I'm the king of beer pong."

"I love the confidence, Hardy. I think it will serve you well."

"Do you think someone else is going to beat me?" he asks.

"I've heard Polly and Ken have been practicing."

He shifts in his seat. "Have they? They said that to you?"

"They did. They seemed pretty serious about it."

"Shit," he mutters under his breath and then looks out the window. "They can't win."

"It's their party. Might not be a bad thing if they win."

Hardy shakes his head. "No, they can't." And then to my surprise, he opens the car door and is out in a matter of seconds.

Confused, I scramble to follow him, taking my almost empty pint of ice cream with me.

"Where are you going?" I call out.

"You'll see," he says, heading right back into the store.

"You know, when I was thinking about what I was going to do tonight, this wasn't it," I say as I stand four feet away from my open car trunk that's lined with aluminum party cups half filled with water.

"Never should have brought it up," he says as he holds a ping-pong ball in hand. He lifts his arm, and with a slight flick of his wrist he tosses the ball toward the trunk, and lands it in a cup—the eighth one in a row. He's one away from completing the pyramid.

"When you make this next one, are you going to be satisfied that the old man still has it?" I ask.

He glances in my direction, completely unamused. "No, when I'm done, you're up next."

"What do you mean I'm up next?" I ask. "I'm not playing tomorrow."

"The hell you're not. You're an honorary bridesmaid, which means you need to play. Also, I'm not running the risk of you ending up as my partner without any training."

He turns away from me and sinks the last ball.

"Training? Do you really think you can train me in a grocery store parking lot?"

"I can. Now come here." He tugs on my hand and places me in front of him. Then he grabs some of the floating balls and brings them over to me. He's shed his suit jacket, rolled up his sleeves—and completely lost his mind.

He hands me a ball. "Let me see you shoot without any proper training first."

"Really?" I ask.

"Yes, really. I'm being serious, Everly, so if you can match my seriousness, I'd appreciate it."

"Oh, I'm sorry," I say, and I arrange my face into a scowl. "Is this better?"

His nostrils flare, but then he says, "Much."

"Okay." I shake out my arms, stare at the cups, and then lift my arm. "Here we go." I cock back my wrist and shoot the ball. "Alakazoo!"

The ball pings off the top of the trunk door and then right back at us.

Hardy scoops it up like a professional, and then with a deadpan expression, he asks, "What the fuck was that?"

"Uh, I tossed the ball."

"No, what was the *alakazoo*?"

"Oh, that was my added flair. Pretty nice, huh?"

"It was horrible."

Hands on my hips, I turn toward him. "Uh, pardon me, there was nothing horrible about that. Actually, it was quite charming."

"Says who?" he asks.

"Me. And it's a lot better than all your heavy breathing."

"I was not heavy breathing," he counters.

"Uh, does this sound like heavy breathing to you?" I ask right before I slouch and breathe forcefully out of my mouth.

"Jesus Christ, exaggerate much?"

"No, actually. That was one of the most accurate things I've ever portrayed."

To my surprise, he grips both of my arms and forces me to look him in the eyes. "Everly, this is serious. I need you to focus."

"Why is this so serious?" I ask.

"Because," he says. "This dates back to our college days, when competition was high and the last person to win a beer pong tournament was me. It was our send-off game, never to play each other again, but now that we're back...I can't lose the title."

"Oh..." I say. "So this is like opening up a closed case."

"Exactly," he says. "Ken and Polly think they're coming for the win, but we can't have that."

"And what makes you think we'll end up being partners?" I ask. "Because that's a lot of pressure I don't think I'm comfortable with."

"Trust me," he says, turning his head around. "I think it's going to happen."

"Okay, well. That terrifies me, but if there's a slim chance that might happen, maybe you can show me a tip or two."

"I'll show you everything," he says and then stands behind me, his chest to my back.

Immediately, I'm filled with warmth at the press of his body against mine.

My mind wants to escape to a moment where this is not Hardy teaching me how to properly throw a ping-pong ball, but where he's swooping in behind me because he likes me and he wants to be close. Where maybe he'd turn me around, wrap his arm around my waist, and ask me to dance under the dim lights of the grocery store parking lot.

Unfortunately, that's not the case.

He drags his hand down my arm, sending a chill all the way up my spine as the pads of his fingers trace over my skin until they reach my hand. Then he gently wraps his fingers around my wrist and raises my hand up.

Softly, he asks, "Are you listening, Everly?"

To every freaking thing...

"Yup," I say casually, even though nothing about this feels casual.

"Okay, first, I want you to grip the ball with your middle finger, index finger, and thumb. Gives you more control rather than using just two fingers."

"Okay," I say as I grip the ball appropriately.

"Next, you have to decide if you're going to go for a quick shot, like this." He releases my hand, picks up a ball and then shoots it off, like a fastball straight into a cup, very impressive. "Or with an arch." He takes another ball and floats it into a cup. Oddly, it's a bit of a turn-on seeing such accuracy. Ridiculous, I know, but it's kind of hot. "Let's see what you're better at."

"Probably neither," I say.

"Remember, it's all about the wrist."

"Okay." I prop my arm up and stare down the cups. "So just… shoot it?"

"Yup," he answers, still standing behind me.

"Okay." I let out a deep breath, and then on my mental count of three, I toss the ball like a fastball straight to the front cup—and it bounces back at us, hitting the ground first.

Hardy scoops the ball up. "Not bad, better than I expected actually."

"Really?" I ask. "I didn't make it in the cup."

"Yes, but you hit the cup. I assumed you were going to end up with the ball in your ear after the whole *alakazoo* incident. See how you shot better without the flair?"

"Flair made it more interesting, but I can see your point. Also I would like to point out that yelling *alakazoo* could be distracting to the other team, possibly crippling."

"Unless magic is spouting from your finger when you say *alakazoo*, I can't fathom how it could be crippling."

"Well, clearly you've never been attacked by the giggles."

He leans over so I can see his eyes. "Do you have giggles that come out of your finger?"

I chuckle. "No. When drunk, if you find something funny, you can easily get lost in the laughs and that's what *alakazoo* has the potential to do. If Polly and Ken get attacked by the giggles, they won't be able to toss the ball properly, which will result in you securing your precious win. So, you know, something to think about." I shrug.

He stares at me for a few seconds and then moves back around me. "Let's just focus on getting the ball in the cup for now, and then you can add flair if you need to later."

"I think that's a fair compromise." I shake my arm out again and then lift it up to shoot. "So you want me to do an arch this time?"

"Yes," he says. "See if that fits you better."

"Okay, and launching in three, two—"

"We don't need a countdown," he says.

"One," I finish, shooting the ball over the open trunk door. It bounces off the back windshield and onto the ground, pinging around.

Hardy grabs the ball and then looks me in the eyes. "I think the arch is out."

"Yeah, seems so." I smirk, which causes him to smile.

"Let's stick with the straight shot and see if you can get some in that way."

"You got it, King," I say as he hands me the ball with a raised brow. "That's what you prefer I call you, right? You did claim the title earlier so I'm assuming that's how you'd like me to refer to you."

"Hardy is fine," he says.

"What about Henrietta?" I ask. "Or are you over that?"

He looks down at the ground. "Yeah, I meant to talk to you about that."

Uh-oh, back to the mood shift.

"Oh? What did you, uh…what did you want to talk about?" I ask.

He pulls on his neck and looks me in the eyes. "That's all over and done with."

"The nicknames?" I ask.

"No, I mean…yes, but no."

"Okay, that's confusing."

"You can call me whatever you want, but the whole Maple thing... well, I'm relieving you of your duties."

Oh...

So I was right...and they're going to date. *Why is he here with me? Is this like a soft letdown? Did he see...or even worse, did Maple tell him that she suspected I like him?* And I thought I'd embarrassed myself earlier. This is far worse. This time here is like a...pity party for Everly. *Oh. God.*

My stomach twists in knots as I attempt a smile. "Oh wow, why didn't you tell me earlier?" I say as I swallow down my emotions. "That's awesome. Are you guys officially dating now?"

"Dating?" he asks. "Uh, no."

"Oh, but you said I was relieved of my duties," I say.

"Yeah, because she's not interested," he mutters.

She's not interested?

In Hardy?

How?

He's so...God, he's everything.

"Oh," I finally say. "I'm...I'm sorry, Hardy."

He shrugs. "No biggie. Thanks for the help though. I appreciate it."

Is that why he pulled away on the email? Because it wasn't fun and games anymore now that he got the answer to his pursuit?

Probably.

Does that mean...does that mean all the fun is over?

The emails are done?

No more hanging out?

If so, then that puts a whole damper on this evening—this could be the last time we do anything just the two of us. Now that we don't have Maple in common, what's going to bring us together?

"Oh sure." I twist my lips to the side. "Are you sure there isn't anything else that I can do to help?" I ask.

He shakes his head. "No. It's a done deal."

"Okay." My eyes meet his. "Are you okay?"

"Yeah," he says, exhaling. "Not sure rekindling something from the past was a great idea, especially since we've both changed so much, so I get it. We're good."

I stand there awkwardly, not sure what to say.

I mean…my heart knows what to say.

Well, if you're not going to go out with her, care to give me a try? I might not take care of flamingos and I might not have this cute, sunny disposition, but I do like matcha Oreo cronuts so I have that going for me.

"Anyway, do you want to give the tossing another try?" he asks, clearly antsy to change the subject.

"Yeah, of course," I say.

But this time, instead of standing behind me like before, he stands to the side and feeds me balls, one right after the other while I shoot them at the cups, missing every time because my head's not in it.

After a few more misses, I turn to him, defeated. "I don't think you should have me as a partner—this is terrible."

"It's not great," he says while staring at the ball-less cups.

"It's not."

"Maybe you're tired," he suggests.

"Or maybe I just suck," I say.

"Could be the case, but it's also dark and chilly out here, so you're probably not in your element."

"Possibly," I say. "Maybe we call it quits because the more I miss, the more my confidence is disintegrating."

"Understandable," he says. We pour out the water from the cups into the planter bushes a few spots down, and then place the stacked cups in my trunk along with the ping-pong balls.

Once I've turned the car on, I ask, "Shall I take you back to pick up your car?"

"Yeah, that would be good," he says.

I pull out of the parking lot and head down the road toward the parking garage. This has been a weird night, full of ups and downs, leaving me feeling like I don't quite know where I stand with him. And as I draw closer to the parking garage I feel this sick sense of panic.

Panic over not seeing him as often. Not communicating like we were. Not bonding as much. I hate to admit it, but even though I was attempting to help him hook up with someone else, I still enjoyed the moments I had with him. I still savored the moments I spent staring into his eyes—and knowing that he doesn't need me anymore makes me extremely sad.

Tomorrow very well might be one of the last times we hang out, and I don't know how I feel about that.

Actually, I do. I feel sick.

When I arrive at the garage, he tells me not to pull in so I don't have to pay again. I park on the side of the road instead.

"Thanks for the ride," he says.

"Of course. Sorry about the confusion with the dips. At least we can rest easy tonight."

"We can." After a few seconds of silence, he grips the handle to the door. "Well, I guess I'll be going."

That panic skyrockets inside of me and before I can stop myself, I say, "I don't want to stop talking."

He glances at me.

"Huh?"

Oh God, Everly, you're such an idiot.

I twist my hands together, trying to find the right words. "I'm sorry if this is out of line, but I just…I've enjoyed our chats and whatnot, and I don't know, I guess I'll feel sad when they end." I shrug, trying to look casual. "I like our emails."

He slowly smiles. "I enjoy them too, Everly."

"Cool, so maybe we can be pen pals or something. Like once a week."

That makes him laugh.

"You want to be my pen pal?"

"I mean…I've never met someone else who likes the matcha Oreo cronuts like me, while also taking credit for the invention of social media. Seems like someone I should keep talking to, you know?"

"How could you not keep in touch with someone like that?"

"Exactly, you see the dilemma."

"I do." He smiles softly. "Don't worry…Plum, I'll keep in touch." And then with that, he's out the door and closing it behind him.

Why does it feel like he's not going to keep to his word?

CHAPTER TWENTY-ONE
HARDY

"SO...WHAT DO YOU THINK?" MAPLE says, coming up next to me at the party as people mill about, grabbing drinks and food and mingling with Polly and Ken.

I have to hand it to Everly, she really knows how to throw a party... and Haisley knows how to build a themed house. Boa garlands are strewn from patio pole to patio pole. Couches are strategically placed throughout the space with black and yellow plaid pillows. Along the back wall of the patio, there are picture frames of all different sizes hanging with pictures of Ken and Polly throughout their relationship. Black and yellow plaid table clothes drape over tables, displaying mini cupcakes, each decorated with a fondant medallion and the words "As If" written across in icing.

"I think everything looks pretty good. People are happy."

"I meant what do you think about Everly...seems like you can't take your eyes off her." Maple bumps my shoulder.

"Not true," I say as my eyes fall on the girl in question. She's over by the bar, talking to the catering manager.

Today, she came to the party with her hair down, which has quickly become my kryptonite. I feel weak when it's loose around her shoulders, like I might do something stupid. I feel this need to touch it, run my fingers through it, wrap my fist around it.

And instead of wearing one of her pencil skirts or pantsuits, she's in a pair of brown high-waisted pants and a black long-sleeved shirt that has cutouts along her torso, showing off her skin. The moment I saw her, I knew I needed to keep my distance. She came up to me at one point, and I awkwardly waved, but then said I needed to check on the dips—which was stupid, because it was the third time I'd checked on them to avoid her.

And why am I avoiding her?

Because Maple has gotten in my head.

Everly is no longer my cool friend.

No, she's a girl who isn't just cool but fucking perfect. She's immensely attractive, so goddamn funny, and she seems to have a chokehold on me that I wasn't expecting and because of that, I can't seem to find an easy way to interact with her.

You like her, Hardy.

And…I do.

It's a battle I'm fighting within myself.

And I don't know why I'm fighting the battle. The smart man would be like, *yup, you like her, you fucking idiot, go after her.*

But what if she doesn't like me back? Hell, she said she wanted to be *pen pals.*

Fucking pen pals.

What the hell am I supposed to do with that?

And have I been awkward around her?

One hundred percent.

I've avoided her. I've not answered her emails, her texts. I've tried to distance myself out of self-preservation, but all it's done is make things worse.

Like last night. The look of defeat in her eyes when I was trying to be professional around her nearly split me in half. Sharing ice cream with her, chatting, showing her how to shoot a ping-pong ball, all highs.

Highs that I thought about before I went to bed and when I woke up this morning.

I thought about her all goddamn day. I've completely chickened out and have avoided her at all costs tonight. Because now I think she's gotten the hint and has stayed away as the party has started to unfold.

"You are such a liar," Maple says. "What's going on in that head of yours?"

"I don't know," I say with a defeated sigh. "Fuck, Maple. It's like I'm nervous or something. I don't get nervous around women. I don't start to sweat and act all weird and fidgety, but with her I do."

"Because you care what she thinks."

"I care what you think," I say. "And I wasn't out of my mind approaching you."

"Maybe because it wasn't a high risk," Maple says. "If I said no, if I turned you down, would you really be broken up about it? And before you answer that, I can answer it for you. It's a no. But now you've gotten to know Everly, you've grown an attachment to her, and if she rejects you, well, that's a rejection I'm not sure you can stomach."

How fucking accurate is that?

Because she's right. A rejection from Everly would send me spinning because I don't want to be just friends. I sure as fuck don't want to be pen pals. The stakes really are higher, and it's the reason I find myself on one end of the backyard and Everly on the other.

"I'm right, aren't I?" she asks.

I scrub my hand over my face. "Fuck, this is all your fault."

"My fault?" She chuckles. "How is this my fault?"

"Because…your return got me thinking that I wanted a relationship, and I thought it would be easy with you—though we both know it wasn't—and now you're telling me I have feelings for someone else, which I do, and now I'm a sweaty, nervous, fidgety mess."

"And that makes me so happy."

"My pain is causing you happiness?" I ask her.

She smirks. "It is. I like seeing you like this. And I say this without jealousy or anger, but I don't think you ever acted this way around me...ever. Which means the connection between you two is much stronger."

I fully turn toward Maple. "Do you know what she said to me last night?"

"She loves you?" Maple clasps her hands together in hope.

"Uh, no. If she said that, do you think I'd be a nervous wreck, talking to my ex in the corner right now?"

"I guess not." Maple chuckles. "What did she say?"

"She told me that she wants to be *pen pals*."

Maple lets out a snort and covers up her nose. "No, she didn't."

"Yeah, she did. Fucking pen pals, Maple. What am I supposed to do with that?"

Maple shrugs. "Buy stationery?"

"Maple," I groan. "I'm being serious. I think...fuck, I think I'm in the friend zone with her."

Maple shakes her head. "There is no way you're in the friend zone. I saw the way she looked at you the other night."

"Like I was her best friend, possibly big brother?"

Another snort.

"No...like she liked you."

I shake my head. "You've been in Peru for far too long. There is no way she was looking at me like that."

"Only one way to find out," Maple says and then to my horror, calls out, "Everly!" Everly glances in our direction. Maple waves her over. "Come here."

"What the hell are you doing?" I ask through clenched teeth.

"Nothing embarrassing," she replies, and from the glint in her eye, I can tell that her consumption of alcohol has already spurred her on to cause trouble.

"I don't trust you," I say.

"Whatever you do, try not to fall into her breasts as a greeting."

"You're not funny," I say quickly before Everly steps in front of us.

"Everything okay?" she asks.

"Everything is great," Maple says. "We actually wanted to thank you for all the hard work you put into the party. We couldn't have done it without you."

"Oh, of course, it's my pleasure," she says, glancing at me very quickly but then returning her gaze to Maple.

"And now that everything is running smoothly, maybe you can have some fun," Maple says.

"Oh, no, that's okay. I'm just here to put out fires."

Maple dismissively waves her hand. "Please, there are no fires to be put out. At least have some dips and a drink. Hardy was just telling me how he'd love to show you his favorite dips."

Dear God, does that sound lame.

"You were?" Everly asks, suspicion on her face.

"Oh, yeah. Really want to show you the dips," I say. "You know, since they're my pride and joy."

"I thought the Ed Sheeran playlist was your pride and joy." She cocks her head to the side, and it's so fucking cute.

Jesus, what has happened to me?

"That too," I say. "I have two pride and joys, sort of like children, you know? Equally proud of both."

"Are you comparing your dips and playlist to children?"

"Yes," I say as I rock on my heels. "Something wrong with that?"

"I guess not," she says. "Anyway, don't worry about me, you guys have fun." She smiles and starts to turn around when Maple shouts.

"He was trying to be nice," she calls.

Err, what?

Where the hell is she going with this?

And please don't let it be embarrassing.

Everly's brow creases, and she turns back around to us. "What?"

"Hardy," Maple says. "He was trying to be nice. He actually really wants you to taste my dips—the ones he asked me, and not the caterers, to make special—because he thinks they're off. He told me because I'm a vegetarian now and can't taste-test the end product, I didn't make them properly. I think they look fine, but anyway, he was trying to casually get another opinion without bringing attention to my possible shortcomings."

What the hell is Maple doing?

Have the roles been reversed?

Is Maple the bridesmaid undercover now? Because if she is, she is not doing a good job.

How many drinks has she had?

"Oh…well, I think everyone seems to enjoy the dips," Everly says. "I haven't heard anything different."

"Can you just go check with him?" Maple says, pushing me toward Everly, not making this obvious at all.

"Sure, if you would like me to, I can," Everly says.

"Thank you. I really appreciate it." Maple clasps her hands together in front of her, creating prayer hands as a thank-you.

Together, Everly and I head over to the buffet of dips, some made by the caterer, and three made by Maple.

"Everything seems fine," Everly says, taking the investigation seriously. If only she knew. "What makes you think they're not good?" she asks as she picks up a plate.

"Uh, just seemed off," I answer.

"Okay, well, let's see. I've never had buffalo chicken dip before, but we can see what's going on here." She takes a Club cracker and dips it into the buffalo chicken, scooping out a chunk. She moves over to the dill chip dip, which is basically sour cream, dill, and some weird chipped beef Maple found. And then the last is a seven-layer taco dip that is my favorite. Once her plate is full, she glances at me. "Aren't you trying these too?"

"Right." I fill up my plate as well, and then together, we step off to the side, finding an open high-top.

"You had these dips in college?" she asks.

"Yeah, they were the three classic ones at every party," I say.

"Seems fancy, especially this dill one."

"Well, we were fancy back then," I reply.

"Oh…so fancy. You guys were partying with your pinkies up," she teases.

"We were. The fanciest college kids you probably ever met."

She smirks and then takes a bite of the buffalo dip. I do as well and it's fucking good. Brings back a wave of memories.

She chews for a moment and then swallows. "I don't know what you're talking about," she says. "That's good."

"You know, I think you're right. Maybe I got a weird bite at first."

Her eyes narrow. "Hardy?"

"Hmm?" I ask.

"If I take a bite of the rest of these, are they going to taste just as good and you're going to agree?"

"Probably," I say, attempting not to wince.

"Uh-huh. Care to explain to me why Maple is lying about the dips?"

"You know, I can't really be sure. I think living among the flamingos has made her a little kooky."

Everly sets her plate down. "This has nothing to do with the fact that you've ignored me since you've arrived?"

"What? Ignored you?" I nervously laugh. "Who said I was ignoring you?"

"Hardy, you haven't even muttered a word to me. And I get it, okay? You don't want me to be your partner for beer pong." She touches my arm, and fuck me I want her to move it up and to my chest so I can pull her in even closer. "It's okay. I'm not offended. I know I didn't do a good job last night, and if I were you, I'd be avoiding me as well. So let me put you out of your misery and tell you I won't be participating today."

Christ, that couldn't be further from the truth.

"Everly, you—"

"There he is," Polly says as she walks up to us. "Maple said you're partnering up with Everly to try to take me and Ken down. Is that true?"

Uhhh...

"Oh, no," Everly says with a shake of her head. I watch as her soft hair floats across her face. "He's not partnering up with me."

"He's not?" Polly asks. "Then are you not playing?" she asks. "Everyone else is partnered up."

"Maple is?" Everly asks.

"Yes, she's with Jerry." I glance over at Maple who is standing next to one of our old college friends, chatting it up. How long has she been planning this out?

"So are you really going to chicken out and not play us?" Polly asks. She thumbs behind her to Ken who is stretching his wrist. "He's been practicing, dusting off the rust. He's ready to, in his words, 'take you down, all the way downtown.'"

A snort pops out of Everly before she covers her mouth.

"Tell him his trash talk is shit," I say.

"I already did. Let's just say I'm not marrying him for that reason. He's lucky I didn't break the engagement off after that comment." Polly tugs on my hand. "Seriously, come play. You didn't set this whole thing up not to play, did you?"

No.

I set this whole thing up because I'm a needy fucker, it seems. And now that I've woken up these intense feelings for one particular woman, I can't seem to think straight.

"Well, if you need a partner, I can be that person for you," Everly says. "I'm just going to apologize in advance."

"She sounds like she's not great, which makes her a great partner," Polly says. "Come on, watch me and Ken beat you two."

I let out a sigh. "Sure, but let me warm up with Everly for a bit first."

"Not a problem—Ken will be doing the same." With that, Polly walks away, leaving me alone with Everly.

I turn toward her, deciding to push down my emotions and focus on the task at hand: beer pong victory. "Time to practice. Let's get you a drink, because you need to loosen up."

"I need to loosen up?" she asks, pointing to herself. "You're the one who didn't say hi to me."

"No time to argue," I say, taking her hand in mine. "We have a tournament to win."

"That's it," I say, feeling so much pride as Everly sinks another ball into a cup. "You're doing amazing."

She smiles brightly up at me. "Thank you. I really think the two fingers on the ball is better for me, rather than the three...even though I prefer three, if you know what I mean." She waggles her brows and jabs me with her elbow.

Yeah, I know exactly what she means.

And talk about making me sweat from the thought of it.

She picks up her drink and downs the rest of it before setting it on the table. "So I don't have to drink beer, and we can set our cups up with our drink of choice?"

"Yes," I say.

"Perfect, because I'm not much of a beer girl."

"You're not?" I ask as I finish off my beer.

"No, never been a huge fan."

I set my empty glass down. "Back in my day, we didn't have fancy seltzers or Moscow mules to drink for cheap. It was beer or inexpensive vodka that gave you the worst hangover ever."

She smirks. "Back in your day."

"I beat you to it before you could say it."

"Who's to say I would have mentioned your youthful years?" She leans against the table, looking so fucking good with her hair flowing over her shoulders. I've never been a hair man, but hell, Everly's hair does something to me.

"Please, you take any opportunity to mention them," I say.

"You're right." She winks. "I probably would have." She glances over my shoulder where the tournament is happening, almost the entire party gathered around the beer pong table that is covered in another plaid tablecloth. Polly has a pink feather boa that she stole from one of the garlands draped over her shoulder and is casually tickling Ken with it every few seconds. "So when do we have our first game?"

"Polly told me they have us on the board, and when it's our turn, we'll be called up."

"So what do we do until then? Practice more?"

I shake my head. "No, I don't want to wear you out. There is a certain point when you practice too much and lose that newcomer magic."

She chuckles. "Is that really a thing?"

"Oh, for sure it is," I say just as Maple walks up to us.

"Hey, was just over at the bar and thought I'd bring you guys some more drinks." She drops off two Moscow mules. Then she sets down four Jell-O shots in front of us as well.

"What are those for?" I ask, seeing right through her tactics.

"From Ken and Polly. They expect you to keep up." Maple winks and then takes off.

Now, these could be from Ken and Polly.

Or...these could be from Maple, who is trying to play matchmaker, to loosen things up between me and Everly. And talk about loose: This is a side of Maple not many people get to see. Drunk Maple. Not so reserved, doesn't hold back, just goes for it.

I glance down at the Jell-O shots and back up at Everly. "Ever do one of those?"

"A Jell-O shot?" she asks. "My God, Hardy, I'm young, but not that young."

"I don't know." I chuckle. "Just asking. Are you going to do one?"

"Probably not. I should be working this event."

And as if she's listening in on the conversation somehow, Maple reappears as if by magic. "Polly said you are relieved from your duties and you are to now celebrate with us."

Everly startles, clutching her chest. "Oh, Maple. I didn't see you there."

She chuckles. "Just forgot to mention that, so…" She wiggles her finger at the Jell-O shots. "Catch up." Then she's off again. Not that I'm surprised at all, but Maple walks right up to Polly, high-fiving her and indicating that Polly is now in on this as well. Maple probably told her what was going on, and now they've made it their mission to get me and Everly together.

God, they're going to make this so obvious. I just hope that Everly remains naïve to the situation.

"Looks like you don't have a choice," I say.

"Seems like it." She glances over at Maple and Polly. "This is weird for me because I really don't take part in the party. I monitor. I don't enjoy."

"Well, you should know at this point that when it comes to Polly and Maple, if they want you to enjoy their drinks, they won't accept anything less."

"Yeah, I'm getting that feeling." She sighs and picks up a Jell-O shot. "I hope this doesn't get me fired."

"Who would fire you?" I ask. "Maggie? Not going to happen. And like Maple said, you've been relieved of your duties."

She studies me for a moment. "You know, Hardy, it almost seems like you want me to drink, to get drunk."

"What? No," I scoff. "Why would I do that? I need you primed and ready as my partner."

"But maybe it would be easier to talk to me," she says, calling me out.

"No, that would require *me* to drink more."

She hands me a Jell-O shot. "Then drink, because I hate this uncomfortable, awkward aura about you."

"I'm not awkward and uncomfortable."

"Oh my God." She laughs. "Hardy, please. You can barely look at me, and I have no idea why."

Because if I look at you, I'll stare, and I don't want to be caught staring.

"I'm looking at you right now," I say.

"Because I told you to."

"Fine," I say. "I won't take my eyes off you." I lift my Jell-O shot to my mouth, keeping my eyes on her the entire time.

"Oh my God, don't do that," she says, playfully pushing at my head. "That's creepy."

"You're the one who ordered full eye contact."

"No, I'm ordering you to be normal," she says as she picks up our drinks and shots and carries them over to a couch. I follow her and we both take a seat. She sets the drinks on the coffee table in front of us and turns toward me. "Admit it, you ignored me when you got here."

"Ehhh, *ignored* is a strong word," I say before taking down my Jell-O shot in one smooth slurp.

"It's the correct word whether it's strong or not." She runs her tongue along the edge of the Jell-O shot, making me sweat, and then she pops the gelatin into her mouth. After setting the empty cup down, she looks me in the eyes. "Can we just be normal? Can we go back to having matching shirts and mugs?"

"I didn't know we went astray from matching hats and mugs," I say, even though that's a blatant lie. I know what I've done, and the fact that she's asking to "go back to normal" lays a heaping pile of guilt right on my chest.

"We are. We're very astray."

"Well, that makes me sad," I say as I lean back on the couch and bring my drink up to my lips.

"You're sad, I'm sad. If Maple didn't ask about the dips, I think I would have gone home tonight and tossed my mug in the garbage."

I gasp. "You wouldn't."

She slowly nods and picks up the other shot. "Yup, that's how bad it's gotten. You've done this to us."

"Well, fuck, we can't have you throwing out our matching mugs. Because that would be really sad."

"The saddest." She tips back the Jell-O shot into her mouth.

"So what do we do to avoid the throwing away of the matching mug?" I ask, feeling lighter, most likely from the alcohol I've consumed prior to this moment.

To my surprise, she scoots in closer so her leg that she's pulled under her is barely caressing my leg. She puts her elbow on the back of the couch and leans her head into her hand. "I think we get it out in the open. Just say what's been bothering you."

Ha.

Not going to happen.

"Nothing's bothering me."

"You're lying," she says, leaning in even closer. I can smell her perfume. It reminds me of something woodsy, but clean and feminine—I can't quite place it, but it's doing all sorts of things to my head, making me feel fuzzy and delirious at the same time. "How about this, I guess why you've been avoiding me."

Well, that doesn't sound like a good idea. Then again, it's better than the truth at this point, so I'd rather have her guessing than me telling the truth. I don't think I can handle the repercussions of the truth.

"Sure," I say. "Good luck because nothing is bothering me."

"Liar." She pokes my arm and then sips from her drink. "Okay, I have a theory. Are you ready for it?"

"You're coming up next," Polly shouts over to us with a point of her finger. "Get ready."

I bring my attention back to Everly, who worries her lip. When her eyes meet mine, she says, "Sorry in advance if I tank your game."

"You're not going to tank it."

"We shall see, but back to my theory. I think you're awkward around me because you're embarrassed."

"Embarrassed about what?" I ask.

"That your plan to win Maple back didn't work," she says. "But there's nothing to be embarrassed about. Sometimes life just works out like that. You gave it a try, I gave it a try, and I think we just move on from here, you know? You don't need to tuck your tail between your legs."

"You think that's why I'm being awkward?"

"Ah-ha." She points at me. "You admit that you're acting awkward."

Uhh…oops.

"No, I was just repeating what you said."

"Don't bullshit me, Hardy. There's been definite weirdness between us, and it happened after you went to talk to Maple. So, care to share with the group? Me being the group?"

"Nothing is—"

Her hand lands on my thigh and every muscle in my body seizes as she leans in even closer.

Jesus Christ.

How is this happening to me?

I went from being friendly with this woman, to friends, to now being mentally consumed by her. And overnight too.

I went to being able to kiss her on the cheek as a greeting, to freezing when she touches me.

I can smell her everywhere.

I can see her smile when I close my eyes.

I can hear her laugh when it's dead quiet in my apartment.

From the moment Maple pointed it out, I've been consumed, and right now, with a few drinks in me and her leaning in so close, it's making me think stupid things...like taking her hand in mine.

It's making me want to do stupid things, like tug her onto my lap.

It's making me want to say ridiculous things, like *will you go on a date with me?*

"See, like right now," she says. "You've gone all stiff on me."

Stiff in more places than one...

"What did I do?" she asks.

"Nothing," I say, downing the rest of my drink and then setting the empty cup on the table.

"There has to be something that I did," she says. "You're going to drive me nuts if you don't tell me."

"I think you're driving yourself nuts," I say, just as Polly and Ken clap loudly, announcing their win. "Looks like we're up. Are you ready for this?"

She glances over at the table, exhales, and then downs the rest of her drink. "Yeah, I'm ready."

I stare down at the knot around my ankle and then back up at Maple. "Is this really necessary?" I ask her.

"New rules from Polly and Ken, and we do what the bride and groom want," she says.

"This is...new," Everly says as she shifts next to me, right up against my side with her ankle tied to mine, causing a wave of goosebumps to spread across my skin.

Maple has gotten herself into some next-level meddling. I thought Everly was intense with helping as my undercover bridesmaid, but Maple is giving her a serious run for her money. But what is even more impressive is her ability to clearly work with Polly on the fly and create a situation where I'm not only teamed up with Everly…but also tied to her.

"Yeah, I've never played beer pong like this before," I say, staring at Maple.

"It's the wedding way," Maple says. "Since Polly and Ken are tying the knot, they thought it would be a fun nod to their wedding."

"Hmm, maybe I'll take note of it for future events," Everly says, once again completely clueless.

And that's what's making this incredibly hard, because if she realized Maple's clearly trying to push us together, then maybe I could talk to her about what's going on in my head. But really, she has no idea, which makes me think she's put me firmly in the friend zone.

Clearly, Maple misread Everly when she said she was interested. *Friend-zoning is not interest.*

"Okay, are you ready?" Polly asks as she holds up a ping-pong ball. "Because we're ready to smoke you."

I lean in close to Everly. "Heads-up, the trash talk is very embarrassing."

"I gathered that already. Figured it was an elderly thing." She smirks up at me.

"Funny," I say just as Polly shoots off her first ball, missing the pyramid completely.

Oh boy, this might be easier than I thought.

"Whoa, damn," Polly says, "that was not quite accurate."

"Baby, that was the opposite of accurate," Ken says as he lifts his hand and takes a shot for himself, sending the ping-pong ball right at my chest, hitting me directly on the nipple. The ball falls to the ground, but the damage has been done because immediately my nipple goes hard, pointing against the thin fabric of my T-shirt.

And my drunk friends, of course, don't let it go unnoticed.

"The nipple," Polly says, pointing. "You did it, Ken, you erected the nipple."

Ken narrows his gaze, leaning forward to take a good look. And when he notices what he's done, he claps loudly. "I got the nipple! I got the nipple."

Jesus.

Christ.

Everly now leans forward to look at my chest.

"Oh wow, that's a hard nipple," she says.

"He has the best nipples," Polly says, picking up her drink. "The most sensitive nipples you'll ever see. Just from a light breeze, his nipples will be erect. We could predict when a storm was coming in by the way one nipple would get hard and the other wouldn't."

Ken leans on the table and looks Everly in the eyes. "His nipples predicted the weather more accurately than the weather app."

"Is that right?" Everly says. "What a fantastic attribute to have."

"When we graduated from college, I was lost," Ken says. "A storm would roll in and I was completely caught off guard."

"His nipples once predicted an ice storm that no one saw coming," Polly says. "Saved our cars from sliding down the hill." She slowly claps. "Love those nipples."

"Okay," I say, rubbing my nipple to calm it down. "That's enough."

Polly leans in. "Did I mention he's sensitive about them?"

"Very sensitive," Ken says. "Maple even once said that he likes—"

"I said that's enough," I say quickly before my drunk friends can spill any more information about my likes and dislikes.

Just makes me realize that I need to end this game quickly.

I pick up the ping-pong ball and without even having to focus, I shoot it forward, scoring it in the top spot.

"Damn it," Polly says. "I forgot how good he is."

"I didn't." Ken puffs his chest. "Why did you think I went for the nipple, to try to distract him."

"It didn't work," Polly says.

"I'll try again. I'll go for the left next time."

Everly chuckles next to me.

"Don't humor them," I say. "They're drunk."

"I think they're pretty amusing," she says as she picks up a ping-pong ball and raises her arm. My arm gets in the way since we're tied together. "Why is your body so big?" she asks as she tries to get situated.

"I grew it that way," I answer, which causes her to pause and look up at me.

"That was…a perfect response."

I smirk. "Thank you."

"Now, what are you going to do about this body that you've grown?" she asks. "Because I can't get a good shot with you plastered to me."

I think about it for a second.

Well, Polly and Maple planned it this way, for me to get closer, so I might as well take advantage—I'm just tipsy enough to be okay with this decision.

"Hold that thought," Maple says as she comes around to the table. "More Jell-O shots, and you can't say no because this is a request from the bride and groom."

She hands out little syringes this time—ones you'd use to help babies take their medicine—but these are full of Jell-O. I haven't seen these in a really long time. Maple collected them from her mom who was a nurse and made Jell-O shots inside, so all you'd have to do is shoot it directly into your mouth.

I give her a look, and she just shrugs.

"Partners have to shoot the shot into the other person's mouth," Polly calls out.

"You realize how suggestive that is?" I ask.

Polly chuckles but doesn't say anything. Instead, she squeezes the Jell-O shot in Ken's mouth and he does the same.

Knowing I'm in a vortex of my friends trying to push me closer and closer to Everly, I just go with it because there's no escaping this. The only way this will end is if I leave the party, and I think we all know I can't do that.

"Open up," I say to Everly.

"What?" she asks.

"I have to squirt in your mouth."

Her eyes widen before her lips turn up in a beautiful smile. "You want to squirt in my mouth?"

"The Jell-O," I say. "I want to squirt the Jell-O."

"That's not what it sounded like to me," Maple says, walking by.

Jesus Christ, is she just floating around, sticking her head in our business every chance she gets?

"Yeah, squirt in her mouth," Polly yells.

"Squirt hard," Ken yells with a fist pump.

"Christ," I mutter, which causes Everly to laugh.

"Go ahead, Hardy. Squirt it hard in my mouth." Then she parts her lips and stares up at me.

And motherfucker, the sight of her like that makes my skin crawl with need.

I bring the syringe to her nude-painted lips and squirt the Jell-O shot inside her mouth. She swallows it and then brings the syringe to my mouth. "Open wide." Rolling my eyes, I open my mouth and she squirts the strawberry liquid inside. When she's done, she pats my chest. "Good boy."

"Yeah, Everly!" Polly shouts. "You tame that beast over there."

"How the hell is she taming me?" I ask, realizing my mistake the minute the words leave my mouth.

"Oh, she controls you," Ken says. "I can see it in your eyes. You... liiiiiike her."

Jesus.

Fucking.

Christ.

I drag my hand over my face as Everly laughs next to me.

"Oh yeah, he sure does," she says sarcastically as her elbow bumps into mine. "Now, move out of the way so I can get a clear shot."

Is she serious right now?

Ken just let the cat out of the bag. And yet she doesn't believe him. She blew right past the comment without blinking an eye.

Didn't even consider it for a second.

It was practically laughable to her.

And I'm not the only one bowled over by it, because Polly and Maple are both giving me confused looks.

See...

Friend-zoned.

This is exactly what I've been talking about. It's what I've been trying to say.

This is why I've been awkward around her.

Why I've been a nervous, sweaty wreck because she doesn't see me like that.

"You know what?" Maple says, walking up to us, making me nervous with what might come out of her mouth now. "I think I have a solution for the large-bodied man next to you."

She walks up behind us and nudges Everly's body forward and mine backward, then she wraps my arm around Everly—not being obvious at all—and places my hand on her opposite hip.

"There," she says. "Problem solved."

Jumping in on the position, Polly says, "Ken, look, that's genius, we need to copy them." And then just like that, Ken has his arm wrapped around Polly as well.

"Oh, this is a good position," Everly says, clueless—no pun intended. "Look at the range I have now." And then to my surprise, she shoots the ball, it bounces on one cup but then lands in another.

"Ahhhh!" she screams as she raises her hands in the air and turns toward me. "I did it."

Laughing, I say, "You did."

"Eeeeeep." She squeals right before wrapping her arms around me and hugging me.

In that exact moment, I make eye contact with Maple who winks obnoxiously at me.

"Oh my God, I'm not failing you," Everly says when she pulls away.

Awkwardly, I reply, "I knew you could do it."

"Don't we get to shoot again since we both made it?" Everly asks.

"Yup," I reply.

"Fantastic. Toss those balls over here," she calls out to Polly and Ken. They do, and we both grab one. "Now put your arm around me again, it was good luck. Really hold me tight. We're taking the bride and groom down."

CHAPTER TWENTY-TWO
EVERLY

"EMBER," I WHISPER INTO THE phone as I keep my eyes on Hardy, who is talking to Maple on the couch by the pool. Polly and Ken are in the middle of the dance floor making out, while others mill about playing beer pong, eating food, and cheering on the bride and groom who are still tied together.

"What?" she asks. "Are you whispering?"

"Yes. I don't want anyone to hear me." I glance around again, making sure no one is near.

We are on red alert, people. Things have happened at this party and not just things, but...*things*.

There has been touching.

Smiling.

Dare I say...flirting?

God, imagine a world where Hardy Hopper would actually flirt with me. I can't. I can't fathom it, that's why I'm calling my sister. I need help!

"Okay...what's going on?"

"I'm at the party and I'm slightly drunk, not too drunk, but drunk enough that I feel like I don't have my faculties together, and I know you're going to say I'm losing my mind, but I don't think I'm losing my mind—I think I'm right, and I know you're going to say I'm wrong, but I need to talk to someone about it or I might just do something really, really stupid."

"Uh, okay, take a breath for a moment. Does this have to do with Hardy?"

"Yes, and I have only seconds here, so just listen. He asked Maple out and she said no, not interested—insane if you ask me, but her choice. He's been weird with me, and I don't know why—he won't say—but at the party, he's been pretty normal, at least after I told him he was ignoring me, but that doesn't matter...some things have been happening."

"Uh, okay. What's happened?"

"Well, there's been talking, and touching, and looking, and... and his friends have mentioned Hardy likes me. Like, blatantly said he likes me and I naturally laughed it off, but alcohol must make my brain sticky because I haven't been able to shake off the thought of him potentially having feelings for little old me. *So*, my question is does he really like me? I mean he's been looking at me differently tonight, Ember. With...uh...heady eyes? Hungry eyes? Potent? One of those. Either way, it's making me feel nutty inside, a little turned on, and slightly unhinged to the point that I worry. I worry that I'm dreaming this up in my head and out of nowhere because I want him so bad I'm just going to randomly grope him. Hand to crotch. To penis. To junk. Right there, my palm to his—"

"I get it," Ember says, sounding exasperated. "First of all, don't grab his penis. Men have the right to grant permission too."

"I know. I know. I wouldn't really grab his penis." I know I said it, but it doesn't sound convincing.

"I don't believe you."

"I don't believe myself," I say. "Ugh, help me, Ember."

"I'm trying, but you're talking so fast and slightly erratically."

"Because I'm scared someone will hear, or he'll wonder why I'm taking so long in the bathroom."

"Oh God, you told him you were going to the bathroom?"

"Yes, that's why we are on borrowed time."

"We must make haste then—can't have him thinking you're spending too much time, if you know what I mean."

"I do," I say in a panic. "So help me!"

She chuckles. "Well, do you think he likes you?"

I glance out the window to where Hardy and Maple are chatting. "I don't know, I feel like the tables have been turned."

"And what do you mean by that?"

"I think I'm no longer the bridesmaid undercover…" Whispering, I add, "I think it's Maple."

"What? This is so confusing."

"I've never felt clearer," I say. "Oh my God, Ember, I think he likes me."

"Whoa, whoa, whoa. Hold on, before you get ahead of yourself and do something like…grab his penis, can you just take a few deep breaths and remind yourself where your head was at a few weeks ago? You're crazy about him. I don't want you dreaming up fallacies in your head when in reality he's just being a nice guy."

I pause because, wait…is he just being a nice guy?

His niceness can be considered flirting when he doesn't mean to flirt.

Which means…has this entire night just been one of those instances? Where he's just being a nice guy?

"Are you there?" Ember asks.

"Yes, sorry, just thinking."

"I know you're not in a clear state right now, but I just want you to be careful, okay? Before you make a move, before you jump right into head over heels in love with the man, remember to just…look for signs. And signs that aren't just him being nice."

"Right, okay, and what are the signs again?"

"Well, if he touches you in more intimate places."

Keeping my voice low, I say, "Like…between my legs?"

"Dear God, no, Everly. Like on your thigh."

"Oh." I giggle. "Right."

"And read his body language, watch him watch you. Listen to his words and if you think it's all there, then just go for it."

"Sooo," I drag out, "you're giving me permission to proceed?"

"You don't need my permission."

"You were against this," I counter.

"Because he was interested in someone else," she says. "But now that being with that other person is not an option, and he's available, then yes, go for it."

"Wow, okay." I prop my shoulders back. "So I'll just go for it."

"If he likes you."

"Right, if he likes me," I repeat. "An important factor." I let out a deep breath. "I can't believe I'm falling in love tonight."

"Jesus Christ," Ember mutters. "Please, Everly—"

"Ooop, I got to go, he's looking around, and I don't want him thinking I got stuck in the toilet. Love you, sis. Thanks for the advice."

"Everly, wait—"

But I don't wait, instead I hang up the phone, stick it in my back pocket, and stare out the window one more time, watching him interact with Maple.

There's distance between them. She's not leaning toward him, and from here it seems like he's not leaning toward her. But then again, I could be wrong.

Ugh, am I reading him wrong? Is he into me? Is he into her?

I twist my lips to the side. If only it was as easy as walking up to him, tapping him on the shoulder, and point blank asking, "Dear sir, are you into me?"

But I would never.

No, I have to go about this a different way.

If there is a move being made, then I'm going to do the work.

Which means we need food! Food is the universal way to see if someone is into you. Will they share with you?

Will they feed you?

If the answer is yes, they're into you.

Food will give me my answer.

And it might not hurt to soak up some of this alcohol...

————————

"Who's hungry?" I announce to both Maple and Hardy as I walk up to them.

While I was piling dips on a plate, my phone buzzed several times in my pocket, letting me know that my sister was attempting to get in contact with me, but I refused to answer because I don't need her help. I've got this.

When Hardy looks up at me, a lazy smile passes over his lips. "I could eat something. Let me go grab a plate and join you."

"Oh, no need," I say. "I piled a lot on this plate. We can share." I glance at Maple and then quickly add, "If that's okay with you, Maple. I mean, I can get another plate if you want. I have some meat on this plate, but I can make a pure vegetarian one."

She smirks and stands from the couch. "I was actually about to make my own and grab some drinks. Should I bring over another round of Moscow mules?"

"I can grab them," Hardy says as he attempts to stand, but Maple stops him again.

"Nope, I got it. Enjoy some food with Everly."

"You sure?" he asks, and for a small moment, I fear the way he's looking at her is a signal to not leave him alone with me. A crazy thought? Maybe, but he's being adamant about helping. If anything, it adds a hit of insecurity to my plan, which is probably what I needed in the first place.

"Positive, I can grab the drinks. You two enjoy," Maple replies, before taking off.

I glance down at Hardy and smile while holding up the plate. "You don't have to eat with me. I can go over by Ken and Polly, have some dinner and a show."

Hardy chuckles and pats the seat next to him. "Take a seat, Plum. You can have a dinner and a show from here too—might get a good look at some solid tongue action at this angle."

"Ooo, and I thought I would have to pay extra for that." I take a seat next to him and to my surprise, he drapes his arm over the back of the couch and turns toward me, bringing one leg up on the cushion.

Okay…okay…be cool.

This is body language, right? This is what Ember was talking about.

If I were to do the green line test…or is it red line? Either way, I can do the line test right now and the result would be positive and in my favor.

Approach with caution though, you are drunk. You don't want to do something brash because he is slightly leaning toward you.

"Dip?" I ask, holding the plate between us.

"Don't mind if I do," he says as he picks up a cracker and dunks it into the buffalo chicken dip.

I watch him pop the entire cracker in his mouth and then get lost in the way his jaw moves back and forth as he chews.

And then the swallow…

Never been a neck girl, never even thought about the neck in a sexual way, but by God, seeing him take that food down…it catapults me into another world of lust.

I could watch him swallow for hours.

"Is there something on my face?"

I wish it was my lips.

"Uh, no, why?" I ask.

"Because you seem to be looking at me strangely."

"Am I?" I ask. "I didn't realize. Would you like me to look elsewhere?"

He chuckles. "Yeah, I would prefer for you to stare at my shoe."

"Your shoe?" I ask and then shrug. "Well, your wish is my command,

Henrietta." I direct my attention to his shoe and stare at it for probably no more than three seconds before I feel his finger on my chin.

He slowly brings my gaze back to his, and when our eyes meet, my nipples go hard.

Yup, hard as stone.

Because this is an intimate touch, right?

A chin lift, that screams intimacy. I've seen it in every romantic comedy I've ever watched. Two fingers under the chin with a slight lift up, letting the girl know that he wants those eyes on him.

Well, they're on him, and with every breath that goes by, my chest grows heavier and heavier with need.

"I'm kidding, Everly. I don't want you staring at my shoe."

"No?" I ask, swallowing a lump that's forming in my throat. "What, uh, what do you want me looking at?"

"Preferably my face."

I chuckle awkwardly. "Your face, huh?"

"Yeah." He smirks. "My face."

"Cool, yeah, isn't that what faces were made for? To be looked at?"

"I think that's exactly what they were made for. Housing the eyes, nose, and mouth was a secondary thought."

"But what a great secondary thought," I say as I scoop some taco dip onto my chip.

"Might be a good slogan for a shirt. Eyes, mouth, and nose, just secondary to the face."

I feel my nose crinkle. "No one would buy that."

He scratches the side of his cheek, his fingers running over his beard. "Yeah, you might be right, but speaking of shirts, I saw one the other day that made me think of you." He picks up a carrot and takes a bite out of it with a snap.

"You were thinking about me?" I cheekily ask.

His eyes connect with mine, the blue so brilliantly bright under the dim twinkling lights above us. "Seems like I've been thinking about you a lot lately."

Dear God.

I think...I think that's another sign.

I mean, it sounds like one, but then again, am I willing these signs into existence? Am I hoping and praying that he's sending me these vibes that I'm just assuming anything he says to me is a sign?

I want to believe that's not the case, but this all feels too good to be true.

HARDY

Come on, Everly, can't you see that I'm trying here?

I'm sending her all the signals, all the tools in my box, and she doesn't seem to be taking the bait. And sure, what do I expect her to do? Climb on my lap and tell me that I'm the one she's been waiting for? That would be amazing, but I'm just looking for her to lean into me.

I'm looking for any sort of non-friend movement from her, and I'm getting nothing.

"Here are your drinks," Maple says as she comes up to us with two Moscow mules. "Enjoy. The caterers just put out the desserts, and I want one of those chocolate donuts before they're all gone."

With that, she sets our drinks down on the coffee table in front of us and hurries back inside.

"So," Everly says as she picks up her drink, "what did this shirt that made you think of me say?"

*You're the one I croissant...*but not sure I can fucking say that. Given my friend-zone track record today, it seems like that would fly over her head as well. So maybe I should settle for something simpler.

"It was of a crab," I say. "And the crab was holding a paint brush and was wearing a beret."

"Okay," she draws out with a smile.

"And under the crab, who was looking pretty mischievous if you ask me, like he just painted something naughty, it said, 'Leonardo Da Pinci.'"

Everly snorts and covers her nose at the same time. "Oh my God." She laughs some more. "That is...that's an amazing shirt."

I lift a quizzical brow. "You like 'Leonardo Da Pinci,' but you can't get on board with a fish coming out of a top hat?"

She shakes her head. "It makes no sense, Hardy." She sets the plate down on the coffee table and scoots in close. "Why would the fish be coming out of the top hat? The saying is if you fish upon a star, which is a play on words from *Pinocchio*, right? So if there's a top hat involved, then you would think that the fish would be wearing a top hat like Jiminy Cricket."

"I..." I pause, as her reasoning swirls in my head. "You know..." I chuckle and rub my palm over my beard. "I can see why there might have been some confusion about the shirt. It would make more sense for him to be wearing the top hat."

"Thank you," she says as she leans back against the couch. Because I have my arm draped behind her, she's almost leaning into me, which of course makes my pulse kick up.

This is progress.

"But, just to put this out there, did you ever think that maybe the hat is acting as a fishbowl so he doesn't shrivel up and die? Because how can you wish upon a fish if the fish is like a raisin in a dish?"

She studies me for a moment, those green eyes looking back and forth between mine. "Did you add the dish part to rhyme?"

"I did." I wince. "Did it work?"

"A little." She chuckles. "And I don't accept your hat theory. I think the designer missed the mark."

"Okay, how about this," I say, feeling slightly confident as she leans into my arm. "I saw another shirt that made me think of you."

"Oh yeah?" She crosses one leg over the other, which angles her body closer to me.

I want to put my hand on her thigh.

I want to twirl her hair around my finger.

I want to pull her on my goddamn lap and give Ken and Polly a run for their money.

But I hold back because baby steps.

Ease her out of the friend zone and right into the *let's make out* zone.

"Yeah," I answer as my hand itches to touch her hair.

"What was on it?"

"First of all, it was red."

"Okay, how does that have anything to do with what's on the shirt?"

"Because red looks amazing on you," I say, looking her right in the eyes.

But she doesn't hold my gaze, instead, she looks away. Not wanting to lose her in this moment, I decide to continue.

"And on the shirt were two croissants, one looked like Danny Zuko from *Grease* and the other was a dead ringer for Sandra Dee. We're talking blond wig and black sideburns."

She chuckles. "Who doesn't like croissants dressed up like Danny and Sandy? What did it say?"

I smirk. "'You're the one I croissant.'"

A slow smile tugs on the corner of her lips. "That...that's amazing."

"I knew you'd like it. It had a heart between them as well. I could see you wearing it, possibly walking through the zoo with me—I'd be wearing my fish top hat shirt, of course."

"You wouldn't have gotten a matching one?" she asks.

"I mean, I considered it." I take a chance and snag a piece of her hair. The silky strand wraps around my finger, and I marvel in the way her cheeks flush from the small touch. "Would you have worn it with me? Grabbed a cup of coffee? Maybe gone for a walk?"

Her teeth pull on the corner of her lip. "Is that what you would have wanted? To go on a coffee walk with me?"

Yes...and so much more.

I lean in an inch closer. "Yeah, Everly, I would have wanted to do that."

EVERLY

Dear God in Heaven.

Is this...is this what it's like to be wooed by Hardy Hopper? Because if so, I want this. I want all of this.

The close proximity.

The intimate conversation about matching shirts.

The compliments.

The way he's twirling my hair around his finger.

I want to commit this all to memory.

I want this to last forever.

I want this to be real.

Please...please let this be real.

"Everly?" The catering manager comes up to me, pulling me out of my Hardy-induced haze.

"Yes," I say, pulling away from him and trying to seem professional despite the alcohol swirling through me.

"We are going to start cleaning up. It seems like everyone is done with the food."

"Oh sure," I say as I get up. "Let me help you."

"No, we got it, but just wanted to let you know. Also, it's a quarter to eleven. I know curfew is going to hit soon."

"Right," I say. *Christ, Everly, you have a job to do, and it isn't to make a move on Hardy Hopper.* "Um, I can start getting people to leave."

"We spoke with Maple, and she said she's already started moving people along. She said we could clean up and just make sure to shut the door behind us because it will automatically lock with the keypad."

"Uh, yeah," I say feeling my body sway. "Let me help though."

"No, that's okay. We got it. That's why you paid us. Just wanted to let you know that we're done with service."

"Well, thank you. You were wonderful."

"Exceptional," Hardy says as he stands beside me and to my surprise, places his hand on the nape of my neck. "Really great service, from the drinks to the food."

"Thank you. We appreciate it."

Just then, Maple walks up to us with a smile. "I can handle this from here on out. Why don't you two take off?"

"Oh no, that's okay," I say. "I can help out."

Maple places her hand on my arm. "Seriously, you've done so much already. Let me take care of this part, okay?" When I don't answer her right away, she adds, "Please."

I don't like it, but I also know that I'm drunk right now, and I'm not sure I have much fight in me to stay. "Okay, but only because you said please."

She chuckles. "Thank you. Now, why don't you and Hardy grab an Uber?"

"Oh, I'm sure he doesn't want to do that," I answer. "He's probably sick of me by now."

His thumb caresses my neck as he leans in and says, "Impossible. I could never get sick of you."

Goose bumps spread down my arms and legs from the feel of his words so close to my ear.

"We'll grab an Uber together," he adds. "Want me to request it?"

"No," I nearly shout. "Uh, I mean, I can handle it. Let me just run to the bathroom quickly and then we can take off, share an Uber, because you know, saving the environment with carpooling." I fist pump the air and then without looking back, I hurry toward the house and straight to the bathroom.

Thankfully, no one is occupying it.

I swiftly take care of business, wash my hands, and then pull out my phone to shoot a quick text to Ember.

> **Everly:** Red Alert! There was leaning, touching, and things that he said that have led me to believe that he might want to make a move. I am telling myself that this is not a delusional moment, that this is real. He even…*whispers* he twirled my hair and touched the nape of my neck.

Ember is quick to answer, as her blue dots appear on the screen letting me know that she's answering right away.

> **Ember:** He touched THE NAPE?
>
> **Everly:** The nape, Ember. He touched the nape.
>
> **Ember:** Well, that's…that's all the indication you need.
>
> **Everly:** You think so?
>
> **Ember:** I know so. I think this is your moment.
>
> **Everly:** Oh God, I think I might faint. He's sharing an Uber with me. What if…what if he asks to come up to my apartment?
>
> **Ember:** Do you think he would?
>
> **Everly:** He TOUCHED THE NAPE!
>
> **Ember:** Fair, but that could just be intimacy. We're talking asking to go up to your apartment, which is a whole other level. That's… "he ran his hand up my ribcage and connected with side boob" level. Did he do that? Did he connect with side boob?
>
> **Everly:** There was no side boob connection.
>
> **Ember:** Tough to say then. I guess just share the Uber and see where it goes.

Everly: You think I should share the Uber?

Ember: The NAPE, Everly. He touched the nape. Share the Uber.

Everly: You're right…the nape has spoken.

HARDY

We watch Everly disappear in the house, and the entire time, I can feel my heart beating faster because I think I broke through to her.

At least that's what I'm hoping.

But I did the universal move: I held the nape of her neck.

That should indicate to her that I claim her.

That I want her.

That I want so much more than this friendship we've created.

And if the neck contact doesn't prove that to her, then I don't know what else to do.

Well…I know what I could do. I could tell her. I could kiss her. I could really throw it all out there. But without knowing exactly where she stands, it's too risky. I don't want to lose her, lose our friendship.

Maple grips my shoulder and turns me toward her, startling me out of my thoughts. Her eyes are crazed, and her grasp on me is strong. "Listen up, Hopper. I have worked my ass off this entire party to get you two together. Don't make me be the only one putting in the work."

"I've put in the work," I say, offended that she thinks she's the only one working on this.

"Sure, you have, but I've set up the scenarios in order for you to shine." She's right about that. Left to my own devices, I probably would have been too awkward to talk to Everly all night. "Now, this is your moment. Seize it. When you arrive at her apartment, you offer to walk her up to her place like a gentleman. And when you say goodbye, if you don't kiss her, then...then you're going to have to sing 'Lady in Red' at the wedding, and we both know how terrible you are at singing." "Lady in Red," where the hell did that come from? "So close the deal, get the job done, and get yourself out of the friend zone. Understood?"

I swallow the lump in my throat. "But what if she doesn't want to kiss me?"

"She does."

"How do you know that? I seriously can't read her to save my life."

"I think she's nervous. Slightly oblivious. Make her aware in that car. Obviously don't cross boundaries without permission, but a light graze here and there, hell, hold her hand on the way out to the street. Do anything to clue her in that all the freaking things we've said tonight, all our hints and all your touches were actually directed at her. Got it?"

I nod, feeling slightly pumped up. "I think so."

"Don't let me down, Hardy. I'm counting on this."

"Can I ask why? Because it seems like you're very into this coupling."

"Because I know you. We *were* different people in college. Young kids, really. And as much as I was wary about coming back to San Francisco and seeing you again, tonight has been good for me. You've reminded me why we were such good friends." She's not wrong. I've also remembered the fun we used to have—the late-night hangs and inside jokes—especially when we spent time with Ken and Polly.

"We really did have some good times."

She smiles. "We did, and now that I think we've crossed that bridge into friendship, I just want you to be happy. Everly is so wonderful, and I'd be sad if you didn't get your shot with her. So like I said, don't let me down. Got it?"

I chuckle. "No pressure or anything. This is all for you."

"I'm glad you see it that way." She lets out a heavy breath. "I think I need another Jell-O shot."

Still chuckling, I stand just as Everly returns. "I plugged an Uber request in my phone. They'll be here in six minutes."

"Okay," I say and then look around the backyard. "Uh, I don't see Polly and Ken, and I don't think I want to go looking for them."

"Probably smart," Maple says. "I'll let them know you guys said bye."

"Thanks," Everly says. "Okay, we should get outside. I don't want the driver to ruin my perfect rating because we showed up late."

That's a very Everly thing to say, and I love it.

"Then let's get going," I say.

I glance at Maple one more time. She mouths "hold hands," and I offer her a curt nod as Everly and I start to walk away.

Okay, this is your chance, Hopper, make the most of it. If you're going to make a move…now's the time.

CHAPTER TWENTY-THREE
EVERLY

BE COOL, EVERLY.

Yes, he held the nape of your neck, but you need to remain calm and continue to assess the situation.

"Then let's get going," Hardy says, his eyes beaming down at me.

Are they really beaming?

Or is he just intoxicated?

Regardless, the way he looks at me gives me a trembling, nervous sensation that I haven't felt in a very long time.

We both offer Maple a hug goodbye, and then together, Hardy and I head back into the house.

"So," he says when we reach the kitchen, which has already been cleaned by the catering company. Man, they're fast. "Did you have fun?"

"I did, it was such a good—" I start but pause in the middle of my sentence as I feel him gently take my hand in his.

Um, what?

Confused, I look up at him, searching for an answer, only for him to casually say, "Don't want you tripping after all of those Jell-O shots."

"You had just as many—what if you fall?" I ask, not even mad about this hand-holding. Actually, quite happy about it. His hand is so large that it completely encompasses mine, making me feel oddly protected. Like nothing can happen to me as long as my hand is in his.

"Why do you really think I'm holding your hand?" he says with a wink that makes me chuckle.

"And here I thought you were trying to be my knight in shining armor."

"Hell, I was hoping you would be mine."

I laugh again. "That can be arranged."

Because the house is on a hill, we take the stairs down to the street slowly, but when we make it, I expect him to let go of my hand now that we're safe and on even ground, but instead…he doesn't.

He keeps me close.

"What car are we looking for?" he asks.

"Umm…" Still holding his hand, I look at my phone screen. "A black Tesla S. It's one minute away."

"Good." He glances down at his shirt. "According to my nipples, a storm is coming."

I don't know why, but it makes me laugh hard.

It's so ridiculous.

So stupid.

But I love this side of Hardy. This side that I'm not sure if he shows a lot of people, but with me, it seems to come naturally. This goofy, down to earth guy. Not the man in the suit, but the man in the fish shirt looking for a good laugh.

This moment just adds to that.

Not to mention, it feels like he's back to his normal self, and I couldn't be happier about that. No more ignoring me. No more awkwardness. Just him.

"What kind of storm?" I ask. "Are they pointing in a certain direction, letting us know where the front is coming from?"

"I think a rainstorm from the west."

"From the west is a dead giveaway," I say.

"You knocking the legitimacy of the nipples?"

I smirk. "If I was knocking them, I think you would feel it, and according to Ken, you'd like it."

Hardy rolls his eyes. "Oh my God, don't listen to a thing he said tonight."

Not a single thing?

Meaning...the things he said about Hardy liking me?

No, don't do this, Everly. Don't start overthinking.

"Oh, is that the car?" Hardy asks as a black Tesla pulls up. I check the license plate and nod.

"That would be it."

When the car stops, Hardy opens the door and helps me in first. I settle up against the far side and then to my surprise, he slides his large body in as well, all the way to the middle so he's plastered up against me.

That's...new.

"Hey, man," Hardy says as he places his hand on my leg. "How's it going?"

Yes, hand on my leg.

We went from nape-touching to hand-holding to hand on leg.

"Good," Vinnie, the Uber driver, says. "You guys comfortable?"

Um, well, you see, Vinnie, this man has his hand on my thigh, and I'm not sure what to do with that.

"All set," Hardy says casually as he leans back against the seat before man-spreading, getting himself nice and comfortable.

I'll be honest with you, my breathing has made a complete one-eighty.

It's sharp, short, and ragged.

And if we're mentioning hard nipples, all I can say is, guilty. But whereas Hardy's predict the weather, mine are attempting to predict his next move.

Does he like me? Does he not?

I've never been more confused. I have no idea what's going on, and I'm becoming more and more tense.

After a few seconds of silence, Hardy says, "What did you think of the syringe shots?"

"Interesting," I say as his thumb rubs along my leg, making me gulp. "Never took a shot like that before."

"It's a Maple special. It took me right back to college when she pulled them out—then again, that was the theme of the night."

"It was. I hope everyone, especially Polly and Ken, enjoyed the party."

"I know they did. You did an amazing job," he says and then squeezes my leg.

"Thank you," I squeak out.

"Are you going to the wedding next weekend?" he asks.

"Uh, I don't think so. I think I was just here to help Maple get through these parties."

"Shame," he says as he removes his hand from my thigh and then drapes it over my shoulder, pulling me in tight to his chest. Warmth and yearning spread through me. "Would have been fun to have you there."

"Oh?" I ask, not much of a conversationalist as my body processes his touch, the feel of him so close…his masculine scent.

"Yeah, we could have danced together."

"Are you much of a dancer?" I ask.

"With the right partner, I am."

"And what makes you think I would be the right partner?" I ask.

"Because I like you, so that makes you a good partner," he answers, making my stomach tumble and somersault with butterflies.

He means like you as a friend.

Nothing more…right?

Ughhh, I don't know!

"Are you a good dancer, Everly?" he asks as he twirls a lock of my hair around his finger.

Don't hyperventilate, Everly, keep it together.

"Uh, what kind of dancing?"

"All kinds," he says.

"Well, I can catch a tune," I say like a dweeb.

"Catch a tune?" he asks, his chest rumbling with a chuckle. "Is that what the young'uns are calling it?"

"As a matter of fact, yes," I say.

"Uh, I don't think they are," Vinnie from up front says.

No one asked you, Vinnie!

"How old are you, Vinnie?" Hardy asks.

"Twenty-five," he answers.

"Hmm, pretty close to your age, Everly. Seems like he might be right."

"I know I am," Vinnie says. "No one is saying they're 'catching a tune.'"

"I think the girls just say it," I reply.

"Nah, I have a sister two years younger than me, and she's not saying it," Vinnie says. "Seems to me like you're nervous and just saying things. Are you on your first date?"

"No," I say—as Hardy says, "Yes."

I look up at him, confused, and he just smirks.

"Ooo, looks like you two have some details to work out," Vinnie says. "But if I were you, miss, I'd be saying yes. Looks like your boy is quite the catch."

"Thanks, Vinnie," Hardy says.

"Anytime, Boss," he answers.

And then because I'm awkward and don't want to listen to Vinnie lecture me...or call me out again, I spend the rest of the drive to my apartment looking out the window while Hardy continues to twirl my hair and stick very close to my side.

Finally, when we arrive, I start to say bye to Hardy, but instead of offering me a wave, he scoots across the seat and gets out of the car. He holds his hand out to me, and, confused, I take it and allow him to help me out.

And when I think he's going to get back in the car, he says, "Thanks, man."

"Sure thing," Vinnie replies as Hardy shuts the door, and before I can ask what's going on, the car drives off, leaving me on the sidewalk alone with Hardy.

Uhh…that was his ride home.

Was he aware?

I'm about to ask when he nods toward my building. "Aren't you going to invite me up?"

"Uh…" I blink a few times. "Do you want to be invited up?"

"Only if you want me to come up."

"Well, my apartment isn't much," I say. "I'm sure your place is much bigger so I think it would be less than impressive to you, not much to see, so—"

He tilts my chin up with one finger, so I have to look him in the eyes.

His blue to my green.

Our gazes lock under the cloud-covered sky.

And in a dark, dreamy voice, he says, "I'm not asking to see your apartment, Everly."

Oh, dear God.

My legs tremble beneath me.

My mind spirals with questions.

My heart tumbles with yearning for this to be true.

"Wh-what are you asking?" I say, my nerves getting the better of me.

His hand cups my cheek, and his thumb passes over my skin. With his eyes intent on mine, he says, "Isn't it obvious?"

"Not really," I say on a gulp.

His eyes bounce back and forth between mine. His grip on me grows tighter, more possessive, and when he steps in closer, leaving no space between us, my breath hitches in my chest.

"I want you, Everly."

Is this a joke?

This can't be true.

Am I dreaming?

Did someone put him up to this?

I've dreamed of this moment for so long, and I never thought it would actually come true.

"You...you're drunk, Hardy," I say. "I don't want you saying things that aren't true."

His expression grows stern. "Why would you think this isn't true?"

"Because you like Maple, and you're probably sad about that—"

"I'm not sad about her. Nothing is going on there."

"I saw you two," I say. "I saw—"

"What you saw was Maple helping me figure out a way to be with you," he replies. "She was trying to get me out of the friend zone. And the reason I've been weird around you? Because I fucking like you, Everly. Ken said it twice tonight. Polly and Maple were pulling out all the stops to try to get us closer, to give me a chance."

"A chance?" I ask as I pull away, my mind reeling. "You want a chance with me?"

"Yes," he says, exasperated. "Fuck, Everly, you didn't for one moment even question my intentions tonight?"

"I...I mean, I thought maybe, but it was such a far-off possibility that I didn't think... Last week, you wanted Maple. So I didn't believe you would want to be with someone like me."

"What the hell is that supposed to mean?" he asks, looking angry that I insulted myself.

"It's just...you have history with Maple, and you were—"

"I was trying to resurrect something that was never there to begin with," he replies. "And while I was doing that, I was developing a relationship with someone else, someone I can't stop thinking about." He takes a step closer. "Someone I look forward to hearing from every day." He takes my hand in his. "Someone I crave, who I want to hold...to touch... to kiss."

I swallow the lump that has formed in my throat as he closes in on me.

"Tell me you don't want this, Everly, and I'll go home. I'll call an Uber right now. Vinnie's probably still close, anyway. Send me away if this isn't for you."

"I...I don't know," I say, confused, truly unable to process what's happening, unable to believe this could be real.

But my response pauses him.

His hand drops, and he takes a step back, his expression concerned, not angered.

"Shit, I'm sorry," he says. "I, uh...I thought that maybe there was something there, but...yeah," he says softly as he pulls his phone from his pocket and taps his Uber app.

Panic surges through me because even though I've wanted this for so long, I'm still unsure I can accept that it's happening—but I don't want him to leave.

His hand tugs on his hair, his posture defeated and when he says, "Fuck, I'm really sorry, Everly," I move toward him.

I place my hand on his phone to stop him from calling an Uber and then loop my hand behind his neck right before pulling him in close. He pockets his phone, places his hand on my back, and has just enough time to cup my cheek before my lips brush against his.

It's subtle.

A whisper of a kiss.

But instead of pulling away, I remain still, our noses touching, our breath mixing.

"Please tell me you want this," he whispers as he presses a gentle kiss to my cheek, his hand growing tight on my back. "Please tell me I'm not the only one feeling this energy between us."

"You're not," I say and then I press my lips to his again, but this time, there's no pulling away.

Instead, our lips meld together in a slow, heady way that steals all of my breath.

His hand slides up to my neck, and then is in my hair where his fingers tangle with the thick strands. His grip, his possessive behavior, sends chills all the way up my thighs, giving me a brief preview of the kind of control he can have over me.

And when our lips part at the same time, his tongue caresses mine, gentle...slow.

There's no urgency in his kisses, in the way he holds me.

There's patience and exploration that's building the temptation inside of me. The temptation for more. The temptation to drag my hand up his shirt.

The temptation to peel his clothes off.

To kneel between his legs and explore every inch of him.

"Fuck," he mutters when his lips leave mine and move up my jaw.

I lightly moan as my hand falls to his chest, his thick, brawny chest.

"Everly," he says. "I need...fuck, I need to leave before this gets out of hand," he whispers into my ear before kissing back down my jaw and finding my lips again. We mold them together, caressing, tangling...drinking in the raw magnetism between us.

When he pulls away, more panic sets in—I don't want this to end.

So I take his hand and tug him toward my apartment, but he stops me.

"Everly, you don't have to—"

I kiss his jaw and whisper, "I need to."

His eyes turn dark, hungry, as he wets his lips. A thrill shoots up my spine because I know in this moment that what's about to happen will easily be the best experience in my life.

Without letting him second-guess anything, I bring him into my building, up the stairs, and as I unlock my door, his hands are on my hips, his lips on my neck as he pushes my hair to the side. *This. This is what I wanted him to do last night.* And it's better than I imagined.

When we enter my apartment, he slams and locks the door, and then pushes me up against the hard wood.

A small breath escapes me right before his lips find mine and I melt into his touch.

"Fuck," he says as he takes my hands and raises them above my head, pinning them against the door. "I want you, Everly. I want to fuck you. I want to hear you moaning, begging, screaming my name."

Chills break out over my skin as he kisses down my neck and then back up to my jaw. Wanting more, so much more, I say, "I want your shirt off."

He pulls away to look me in the eyes as he reaches behind his head and tugs his shirt up and over, tossing it to the floor. My eyes fall to his impressively built chest, his rock-hard pecs, his well-developed abs...the cut V that's just above his low-hanging jeans.

When my eyes return to his, I can't help myself. "You're so hot."

He smirks and then brings his hands to my pants where he undoes them and then pushes them down my hips. I kick them off and then stand in front of him in my bodysuit.

He drags his hand over his mouth right before he spins me around, revealing that I'm wearing a thong bodysuit.

"Fuck...me," he says quietly before his hands fall to my ass, and then to my waist. He leans in his large body, brings my chin to my shoulder where he finds my lips again and kisses me, but this time he grinds against me, his hard length to my ass.

I groan and then take one of his hands and guide it up my stomach, right to my breast.

He moans into my mouth and moves in even more as his hand cups my breast, his thumb passing over my nipple.

My head falls back, which exposes my neck where he moves his other hand, pressing his thumb along the column as he continues to kiss me.

His tongue swipes at my lips, and I open for him, matching his every stroke, letting him explore and getting caught up in the feel of him until my body is buzzing, begging for more. So I reach down and unsnap my body suit before hiking it up around my waist and exposing my bare ass. I then press into his erection, and he moans in my ear.

It's so deep, so guttural, that it causes me to turn in his embrace and look him in the eyes.

His breath is uneven, his expression is wild, and his hands inch up my sides, pulling my bodysuit until he tugs it all the way up and over my head, leaving me in a strapless bra.

His teeth roll over his bottom lip as he casually takes a step back and peruses my body.

He drags his hand over his mouth again as I undo the front clasp of my bra and let it fall to the floor, leaving me completely naked.

"Fuck," he draws out.

I move to him and run my hand along his thigh and cup his impressive erection.

Keeping his eyes on me, he sensually wets his lips and undoes his jeans, pushing them down to the floor.

My heart hammers in my chest, my skin goes hot, and when he slips his boxer briefs down, I experience a full-body shiver when he grips his length and starts pumping it right in front of me.

Oh my God...he's so fucking hot.

And he's all mine.

I guide him through my small apartment, straight to my bed where I sit him down. I kneel in front of him, spread his legs, and move in between them.

"Everly," he says softly as my hands crawl up his thighs, my fingernails digging across his skin. He leans back on both hands, watching me the entire time as his chest rises and falls, anticipating my mouth.

I lower to one of his thighs and press kisses along it, moving closer and closer to his cock, but pull back, letting my hair caress it instead. His length bobs, yearning for my touch, anything to ease the tension we've created, but I wait. Instead, I move to his other thigh and kiss his warm skin, working up, past his erection and to his stomach where his abs are crunched.

I let my hard nipple brush against his thigh as I tongue each individual ab.

"Shit, Everly," he says as my lips move close to his cock. But instead of taking him in my mouth, I move back up his chest where I lap at his nipple. He hisses and grips his cock, giving it a few pumps as I suck his nipple into my mouth, loving the way he's reacting. "Your mouth… fuck, Everly. I want…" His head drops back when I nibble on his nipple. "More," he says. "I want more."

Satisfied, I move over to his other pec, and as he pumps his cock, I work his nipple with my mouth. Nibbling, sucking, licking, playing with how hard it gets. It's so sexy, seeing him unravel beneath my touch, hearing him moan, hearing the friction of his hand against his length.

When I pull away, I stop his hand and push it to the side, then I drag my tongue back down his chest, across his abs, and right next to his length. I pause, watching as he strains, wanting my mouth so fucking bad. I push my hair to one side and then lower my head down, taking his cock in my hand and bringing the tip to my lips where I gently start sucking and pumping him at the same time.

"Fuuuck," he groans, his head falling back again. "Jesus…so good, Everly."

Pleased, I move my mouth farther down his length, stretching it uncomfortably, which oddly turns me on. *I can't wait to feel him inside of me.*

I continue to pump him, short concise strokes while taking him into my mouth and sucking, sucking so hard that his hips lift off the mattress.

"Jesus Christ," he whispers when I release him and take him all the way to the back of my throat. He groans loudly and then brings his hand to my hair where he fists it and guides me over his length.

Up and down.

Up and down.

I take him all the way back, gagging, and as I pull off him, I suck.

It's a repetitive process that has his hips thrusting toward my mouth, his breath becoming labored, and his possessive hold on me growing erratic to the point that when I lift up one more time, he pulls me away, removing my mouth completely.

With a dazed look, he says, "Going to come…got to stop."

He lies flat on the bed, catching his breath, but I don't let him. Instead, I bring my mouth back to his cock, and I continue to suck him in.

"Everly…fuck," he says out of surprise, but I keep going. I take him to the back of my throat, I move my hand between his legs and cup his balls, playing with them. I then run the thumb of my other hand over his nipple.

His body tenses beneath me.

His groans grow louder.

And his legs part just before he thrusts up into my mouth and lets out a feral sound.

"Fuck…" he shouts.

His hips still, his muscles contract, and then on a final moan, he's coming in my mouth. I swallow as he rides out his orgasm until his hips relax and he melts into my mattress, and that's when I release him.

I crawl up his body as he catches his breath and kiss along his neck, along his jaw, to his lips, and then to his ear where I whisper, "I want your tongue."

When I lift up, his eyes meet mine and he says, "Then sit on my goddamn face."

Then to my surprise, he lifts me up and makes me straddle his chest. He grips my ass as he encourages me farther up his body until I'm directly over his face.

"Mmm, you smell amazing," he says right before he presses his tongue against my clit.

"Oh fuck," I say.

"Shit, you're so wet." His tongue makes another swipe and then I'm transported to another place, a place where only he and I exist, and this pleasure lasts forever. "Play with your tits, Everly."

I cup my breasts.

"No," he says. "Tease them. Circle your nipples, barely touch them. I want you torturing yourself, throbbing, so fucking needy."

I feel another wave of arousal hit me from his command. I can already feel the sweet torture, the moment when he's going to let me fall over. I know it's going to be so good.

I do as I'm told and lightly circle the tips of my fingers around my nipples just as he starts to stroke his tongue over my clit.

I let out a hiss as my hand falls forward and I press it against the wall, propping myself up.

"Oh my God, Hardy," I say, my stomach clenching.

A few strokes, that's all it took.

A few fucking strokes and I'm already so close.

"You going to come?" he asks, almost sounding confused.

"I'm..." He strokes my clit again. "Fuck, I'm...I'm sorry," I say feeling my short trigger ready to fire off.

He pauses, his breath warm on my arousal. He lets me catch myself, allowing the yearning to grow and as I continue to circle my nipples, playing with them gently, my inner walls start to contract, without him even touching me.

"Fuck," I say as my eyes squeeze shut. "I don't...fuck, I don't want to come."

I try to take deep breaths.

I attempt to settle my brain, to get away from anything but this moment, but it's useless.

I keep playing with my nipples.

I keep feeling his mouth so close to where I want it.

The throbbing between my legs grows.

"God," I say as my body hums, climbs…edges so close. "Hardy, I—"

His mouth closes around my slit and he sucks on me, making my eyes shoot open and my orgasm immediately rip through me.

"Oh my God," I yell as my body seizes and his tongue flicks over my clit with fast, short strokes, urging my orgasm to continue, my body shaking and shivering. "Ohhhhhhh…" I slap my hand against the wall, my stomach quivering, my pelvis riding over his face as I seek out more pleasure until there is nothing left to gain.

That's when I slow down, let out a deep breath, and then fall off to the side and land on the mattress, my body feeling completely weightless.

I bring both of my hands to my eyes, humiliated that I came so quickly, but they're removed and when I open my eyes to see Hardy hovering over me, his gaze still hungry, the embarrassment starts to slide away.

"I'm…I'm sorry," I say.

"On your stomach," he says.

"What?"

He lifts me off the bed and flips me to my stomach. Then he takes a pillow and props it under my pelvis.

"This ass is perfect," he says right before his hand connects with my right ass cheek.

"Oh fuck," I say while he smooths the sting away. "Oh my God, Hardy."

"You like that?" he asks.

"Y-yes," I say, surprising myself.

"Good," he replies. "Because the fucking things I want to do to you." He spanks me again, this time twice in a row, causing a fresh wave of arousal to travel up my spine. A feeling I wasn't expecting so early, not after coming so hard.

"I want this ass. I want my dick inside of it." He spanks me again. "I want my dick in your mouth again. I want you gagging as I fuck your throat." He spanks me two more times. "I want your greedy cunt squeezing my cock. I want to fill you up with my cum." He spanks me one more time. "I don't want you thinking about anyone but me."

"I haven't," I say. "For a long time."

I feel him pause for a moment. "How long?"

"From the moment I first met you," I admit.

He leans his body over mine and turns my head so I can meet his eyes. And then he captures my mouth. I taste myself on his tongue as he molds our lips together, dances his tongue across mine, makes out with me to the point that I'm gasping for air.

When he pulls away, he says, "You never said anything."

"Too nervous," I say.

"You should have," he says. "Now I have to make up for lost time." He lifts up and spanks me one more time before pressing his fingers along my wet pussy. "Do you get turned on for other men like this?"

"Never," I say. "You are it."

He growls and then lowers his head. He spreads me and then slips his tongue in my hole, surprising me and creating a new sensation I've never felt before.

A sensation that has me sweating with need.

A sensation that brings me right back to where I was a few seconds ago, longing and searching for release.

"Hardy," I groan, as my fist curls against the mattress. "Close."

"Fuck," he says as he pulls away. "Everly, that's so hot." He runs his hands over my ass, caressing, smoothing his warm palms over my skin. "I want inside of you, but I want you bare. Can I take you, all of you?"

I feel his cock run over my crack and the anticipation of him being inside of me nearly breaks me in half.

"Yes," I say. "I'm on birth control and I'm clean."

"I'm clean too," he says in a strangled voice. "So, I can have you? All of you?"

"Take everything," I say as he growls out his appreciation.

Then I feel him at my entrance, his cock poised and ready.

"I can already tell you're going to be so goddamn tight." He lets out a deep breath, spanks me, and as I moan, he enters me, his cock stretching me just like I thought he would.

"Oh my God," I yell as he pushes in farther.

"Need you to relax," he says. He strokes my ass, running his hand soothingly over me. "Come on, Everly, relax for me."

"I…can I…can I see you?"

He pauses behind me and then slides out before helping me flip over. When our eyes meet, he smirks down at me before leaning forward and taking my mouth with his. Loving how this man can ease me with just his mouth, I sink into the mattress as I wrap my legs around his waist and my arms around his neck. He thrusts his cock over my slit as we make out, and it helps me to relax some more so I release him, bringing his cock back to my entrance, and let him slowly insert himself.

His chest ripples with tension.

The muscles in his neck strain.

And his abs tighten with every inch he pushes inside me.

His eyes grow heavy as he looks at me again and wets his lips. "Your cunt is fucking incredible." Then he pushes the last few inches, bottoming out, and causing us both to moan in tandem.

From there, he doesn't move, he just allows me to adjust, but I feel so full, so aroused, so needy that I keep my legs wrapped around him and encourage him to thrust.

"Hold on, Everly," he says. "I want to give you a second."

I shake my head. "No. Need you to fuck me."

"Christ," he says as he lowers his hands to the mattress and leans forward. "I want to keep this slow."

"No, please, Hardy."

But he doesn't listen. He bends and laps at my nipples. "You have perfect tits," he whispers. "Fuck, they're so hot. You're so hot. I could get lost here for hours." He sucks one of my nipples into his mouth and releases it, then sucks it back in and nibbles, then releases.

I'm clawing at his back as he repeats the movement, causing my entire body to throb, to yearn, seeking the friction between us.

He keeps me feeling so incredibly full while he plays with my breasts.

How can he have such control?

I'm losing my mind.

I'm ready to explode.

To beg and plead for anything.

"Hardy, please," I say again. "I want you to fill me with your cum."

He pauses and lifts his head just enough to look me in the eyes. "Say that again."

I think I hit a nerve, so I wet my lips and say, "Fill me with your cum."

His eyes go dark, and something switches inside of him. The teasing is gone. The control has slipped.

He lifts up, grips my hips, and starts pounding into me.

He's relentless.

His pace is out of this world.

And with every thrust of his hips, I lose my breath, making me gasp.

I've never been this thoroughly fucked, but I'm loving every second of it.

I'm becoming addicted to the press of his fingers into my hips.

The thickness of his cock sliding in and out of me.

The guttural groans that fall past his lips.

"Fuck, your pussy is so tight. God, too fucking good."

His hand presses down on my lower abdomen, creating a deeper wave of friction. It feels incredible.

Impossible, almost.

Nothing should feel this good. This amazing.

Nothing should light me on fire like this, bring me to the edge so fast.

"Hardy, shit, I'm...I'm close."

"Same," he grunts out and continues to pound into me, over and over, bringing me closer and closer, edging me to the point that my legs fall to weightlessness.

My stomach bottoms out.

And my muscles contract.

With one final thrust, he sends me into a tailspin of white-hot pleasure, my orgasm zinging through me, pulsing through my bones.

"Oh fuck," I scream as I contract around his cock, squeezing him to the point that he straightens, stiffens, and then I feel him spill inside of me.

"Fuck…me," he yells.

He doesn't move, instead he rides out his orgasm as I contract around him.

"Fuck me," he repeats, this time muttering it.

He looks down at me and a smile crosses his face before he lowers and presses a slow, deliberate kiss to my lips. When he pulls away an inch, he says, "You just made me black out."

I chuckle and run my hand over his beard. "Same, Hardy."

Freaking same.

"I can get my own drink, you know," Hardy says from where he lies in my bed.

"I know, but I'm up."

"And covered," he says in a disgruntled tone.

I glance over my shoulder and smirk. "You think I'm just going to walk naked around you now?"

"I would prefer that, thanks."

I feel my cheeks go red as I turn away from him and grab a glass from my cabinet.

Hardy Hopper and I just had sex.

Full-on, he came inside of me, big-time sex, and I am still considering this all a dream. I think any minute now I'm going to wake up and this amazing, mind-alternating feeling I'm experiencing is going to be taken away from me as if it never happened. I have no trust in something so monumental happening to me.

And yet, when I look over my shoulder, at my bed, there he is, staring at me, watching my every move, making me feel like I'm the only woman he's ever cared to look at.

I turn away from him again and fill up a cup of water to share, the entire time a smile is plastered across my face.

When I bring the water over to him, he takes my hand in his and pulls me down on the bed so I'm resting against the wall, and he's propped up on an arm. I pass him the water, and he takes a sip before handing it back to me. His hand falls to my thigh, and he stares into my eyes, making me blush all over again.

"What?" I ask, feeling shy.

"Nothing," he says.

"You keep staring at me."

"Do you want me to stare at the wall?" he asks. "Because right about now, I'll do pretty much anything you say."

"Anything?" I ask.

His hand slides up my thigh as an evil grin spreads across his lips. "Anything."

I set the water down on my nightstand and then slide down the bed, so my head is resting on the pillow and I'm looking up at him. His hand finds the hem of his shirt I'm wearing, and he slides it under, making contact with my hip.

His thumb teases my skin as he rubs back and forth, igniting a burning ember that never went out.

"You're so beautiful," he says, his eyes scanning my face.

Once again, my cheeks heat up. "Thank you," I say as my teeth pull on the corner of my lip.

"I love it when your hair is down."

I bring my hand to his beard. "I love it when your face is between my legs."

His brow lifts. "Wow, that got dirty very quickly. Here I was complimenting you on your beauty and you went there."

I shrug. "Just telling you like it is."

"Well, you could have started out slow, maybe complimented me on my nostrils. You went on and on about Tomothy's, but I've got squat over here."

I let out a low chuckle. "I'm sorry." I clear my throat. "Oh Hardy, you have the sexiest nostrils that I've ever looked upon. The cleanest air tunnel award goes to you."

His hand slides higher up my hip, straight to my ribcage where his thumb rests just below my breast. "Probably one of the best compliments I've ever received."

"Then people aren't complimenting you enough," I say as I smooth my hand over his beard.

"Well, I've been hanging out with you a lot, so maybe I should be pointing the finger at you. Where have my compliments been?"

I wet my lips. "Bottled up because I wouldn't dare say what I really thought."

"Why not?" he asks as his thumb strokes the underside of my breast. The light touch makes my skin tingle.

"Because you were trying to get with someone else," I answer honestly.

"Yeah, and look who I'm with now," he says.

"Because you want to be?" I ask, my voice full of insecurity. "Or because we might have had a few too many drinks and Jell-O shots?"

"Because I want to be. The drinks just gave me the courage I needed."

"You didn't need the courage," I say as I bring my hand down his chest and then nudge him to lie down on his back. He complies, and I sit up and remove the shirt. His eyes immediately fall to my chest as I straddle his body. "I've been waiting for my turn," I say as I press my chest to his and cup his face. "I've wanted you for so long."

His hands run along my back and then over the curve of my ass.

"Fuck," he whispers as I start rocking over his lap, loving the feel of him growing hard beneath me.

I bring my mouth to his and devour his lips, letting my passion fuel the fire that's building inside of me. I don't ever want this to end. I want him, all of him, every day. I want to show him how much I depend on his smile, his laughter, his understanding.

I want his encouragement.

I want these private, intimate conversations.

I want these long, naked nights.

I want warm, smiling mornings.

I want none of this to end.

"Christ, Everly," he says as I slide over his cock, my arousal evident. "You're so wet."

"Because I want you," I say.

He wets his lips and his eyes lock with mine. "Then have me." He scoots me back, grips his cock, and then says, "Fuck me."

The arrogance in his stare.

The confidence in his smile.

It's a lethal combination that has me throbbing for release, so I lift up on my knees, move over him, and then slowly slide down over his cock. He places both hands behind his head, and bites down on his lower lip while I take him all the way in, until I'm completely full.

"Fuck," he whispers, his voice gravelly, which sends shivers all the way up my legs and to my clit.

Hands on his chest, I start to rock over him, taking it very slow and allowing myself to feel the friction we create, the way his large cock feels inside of me, touching places I've never experienced before.

It's filling.

It's addictive.

It's dangerously captivating.

"That's it, Everly," he says. "Use my cock."

My fingers curl into his chest as my speed picks up, the friction too great as my clit rubs against him, each pass like a shockwave to my system. The telltale sign of my orgasm starts to build at the base of my spine.

"Your cock is so good," I say as I move even faster. "Fuck, Hardy."

He groans and grips my hips, encouraging me to move faster, harder. Guiding me to grind down on him, which increases the pleasure for me.

"That's it, Everly. Fucking use me."

I release my hands from his chest and lean back, letting my grip fall to his thighs as I continue to rock over him, the new angle hitting me in a completely different way. My mouth falls open and a long, drawn-out moan leaves my lips.

"You're so fucking hot," he says as he runs his hand up my stomach and to my breast. He cups me first and then with every roll of my hips, he swipes his thumb over my hardened nipple. A hiss escapes me as every touch ignites me even more to the point that my legs start to tingle, my core starts to constrict, and my body prepares for another orgasm to rock through me.

"Fuck, I'm close," I say, and I pause, not wanting to fall over just yet. I take a few deep breaths, but he doesn't let me catch myself, because he grips my hips and starts thrusting up inside of me. "Hardy, I'm...I said I'm...fuck...I'm there."

"Good. Come on my cock."

I fly forward again and position my hands on his pecs. My head falls forward, my hair blocking my vision as I rock hard on him.

Over and over.

My hips flying.

My stomach bottoming out.

My breath gasping.

Everything inside of me tightens, and it feels like the room stills as my mind focuses on one thing and one thing only—the way my clit rides over him.

"Oh God, Hardy," I cry out as the first wave hits me.

Then the second.

And before I know it, my entire body is seizing as my orgasm rips through me, sending me into a convulsing mess as I search out all the pleasure.

My hips are wild.

My moans are feral.

And my fingers dig into him as I come all over his cock.

"Holy fuck," he says right before he flips me to my back, spreads my legs, and starts pounding into me—the strength of his thrusts brings me right up to the surface of the wall where I brace my hand. "Fuck, so good. Your pussy is so fucking good," he shouts right before he stills, and I feel him come inside of me for the second time of the night.

And it's so sexy.

Every muscle in his chest and stomach fires off.

His eyes are squeezed shut.

And his teeth pull on the corner of his lip right before he releases his tension and collapses onto me.

I wrap my arms and legs around him as he presses sweet, gentle kisses to my neck.

"Fucking hell," he mutters right before lifting up to look me in the eyes. He doesn't say anything—just stares at me in disbelief, and I do the same, because right here, in this moment, I know for a fact that I have found my person. His humor, his kindness, his sexual drive, his intelligence, his love for my comfort—*the way he not only anticipates my needs but also provides for them*—his passion. *This is the man for me.*

He lowers his mouth to mine and lightly kisses me. I thread my hands into his hair and kiss him back, never wanting to let go.

Oh.

My.

God.

My vagina feels phenomenal.

And I don't say that lightly.

I mean, this girl is absolutely, without a doubt, one hundred percent satisfied.

There's an ache between my legs.

My breasts feel sore in the best way possible.

And the clarity in my mind right now almost feels unreal.

There is not a single person on this planet that can tell me Hardy was not made for me.

Because he was.

His body, the perfect size.

His penis, even better.

And his knowledge on how to pleasure me, out of this world.

Waking up has never felt this amazing, and there is one person to give credit to: Hardy Hopper.

Smiling, I stretch my hands above my head and then flutter my eyes open, looking for the man who just convinced me that I've found my happily ever after. I glance to the right where he fell asleep and when I come up short, with no man next to me, concern takes root in my gut.

My eyes fall to the floor where his clothes were but are now gone.

And I sit up, nervous that he left, just as the bathroom door opens and he pops out.

I quickly cover up my breasts with my blankets, even though he spent the night sucking on them, and smile.

"Oh…hi," I say as I take him all in. Why is he dressed?

He scratches the back of his head, his eyes locked on me. "Hey," he says, his voice coming out all scratchy.

"Are you, uh…leaving?" *Please say no, please say no.*

He thumbs toward the door and says, "Yeah, was going to take off."

"Oh, sure, yeah." I worry my lip.

Why is he leaving so early? I thought…well, I thought that maybe we could have spent the morning together.

"Have an early start to the day," he adds.

A sense of panic hits me as I read his body language. Someone who had an intense night and enjoyed it probably wouldn't be slowly leaning toward the exit. My assumption would be he'd be cupping my cheek, kissing me, and telling me how much he enjoyed the night before.

Did I read this wrong? All his words of how much he wanted me, of how I was perfect in his arms. Beautiful. Was it all…was this just a drunken night for him?

A way to blow off steam?

Was it all meaningless?

"Of course," I say, feeling all kinds of awkward. "Work, work, work."

"Yup, got to love that work," he replies, looking away.

"So much work," I say because, oh God, this is awful.

"All the work," he mumbles.

He's avoiding me.

I fell asleep last night thinking that what we just shared was the start of something amazing.

And I've woken up to the gut-wrenching feeling that I'm the only one who thought that.

Don't be clingy, Everly. This was probably just one night, and he used all the right words so that you'd feel wooed. *Well, it worked.* But now, I just feel stupid. *Fooled.*

A tense silence falls between us as I stare down at my sheets. "Yeah." Feeling so vulnerable but not wanting him to leave without making sure I didn't cross a line, I stutter, "I, uh, I hope I didn't do anything wrong."

His eyes quickly flash to mine. "No, you didn't. It was...last night was...phenomenal. Really fucking great."

Relief washes through me because, yeah, it was great.

Better than great.

It altered me in a way, and I don't think I can go back to who I was before.

"Yeah, it was."

"The best," he says.

"Easily," I reply.

"Like, my world is different now," he says, surprising me. *Because yes, same, Hardy. Freaking same.* Although somehow, I don't think he's being sincere, especially when he says, "Well, I should be going."

I feel my expression fall because I thought that maybe he would stay. "You don't, uh...you don't want any coffee or anything?"

He shakes his head as he grabs his shoes and slips them on. He's bolting, but why? "Nah, I'll pick something up. But thanks."

"Okay." I worry my lip, my mind spinning a million miles a minute. It's like he can't leave fast enough.

"So, yeah, thanks for last night, but I'll, uh, I'll see you around, I'm sure."

See me around?

He'll see me around?

After he just said that last night was phenomenal, now he's just going to casually *see me around*? How does that make sense?

The truth is it doesn't.

"Yeah." I divert my eyes away from him because I can't look at him right now, not when I feel myself clawing desperately for any sort of wisdom to help make this make sense. Because he said things last night, intimate things. He made me believe that what we shared was special, so what am I missing? "Um, before you leave, not sure how much alcohol took over last night, but…you said some things…"

He passes his hand over his face. "Yeah, there was lots of alcohol, huh?" he says. "People say weird things when alcohol is involved."

So is that what it all was?

An alcohol-charged night?

If so, then why didn't it feel like it? Why did it feel like there was so much clarity, like both of us were more focused and present than filled with alcohol and bad choices?

Maybe I read him wrong.

Maybe I've read this entire situation wrong.

Maybe he doesn't even want me.

Maybe I was just a way for him to let out his frustration.

His frustration over not going home with Maple.

Maybe I'm the consolation prize. The second choice, the one who said yes at the right moment.

The mere thought of that makes me feel physically ill. I don't want to believe it, but from the way he's got one foot out the door, it's hard not to believe.

"Okay, yeah, I get it." I softly smile, and when I meet his eyes, I feel dead inside. Like the conversation stole the life from me, and I'm just sitting here, naked and on my bed, soulless. "You know, I still think you have a chance with Maple. I saw you guys talking, so, you know, if you want me to still try to make that happen, I can."

He doesn't answer right away. He looks away and shifts on his feet, as if he really needs to think about his answer.

Come on, Hardy, stop pretending, I think we both know what you want.

You got some relief with me, but the real prize is the girl you didn't take home last night.

Finally, he says, "That, uh, that would be awesome."

Just what I thought.

Any remaining joy or hope that was left inside of me that was holding out completely vanishes as I turn into an empty shell.

He used me.

He told me what I wanted to hear and then took what he needed.

That's not what friends do.

That's not what nice men are supposed to do.

All that trust we built, the friendship we created, it's all shot to hell now.

Torn down.

Buried.

And as I sit here, the feel of his beard burn still prickling between my legs, I stare up at him, lifeless. "Okay, well, see you."

He pauses, and for a split second, I think that maybe he's going to take back everything he said, that he's going to tell me that this is some cruel joke he was put up to, but instead, he raises his hand in a wave and says, "See ya," before exiting my apartment.

The click of the door shutting behind him rings through my small space, indicating his departure. I can finally let go of the tight hold I have on my emotions.

I slide down to my pillow, curl into the scent of him, and I cry.

CHAPTER TWENTY-FOUR
HARDY

FUCK, I HAVE TO GO back in.

What the hell was I thinking?

I don't want to get back together with Maple, and I definitely don't want Everly thinking she needs to try to mend the bridge between me and my ex either. That ship has sailed.

I want Everly for myself.

Ever since I spoke with Maple, and she's opened my eyes to what I've really been feeling, I know for certain that Everly is the one for me. And after last night, that thought was solidified.

But…fuck, Hudson is right.

I can't possibly be with her.

Not when she works with Haisley.

Not when things are rocky with our dad.

Anything, and I mean anything he finds out about us that is less than pristine, he'll find a way to expose it. Sleeping with one of our employees is definitely one of those things, and beyond that, sleeping with my sister's partner is just a terrible idea.

But I can't stand here and let her think that last night didn't have the impact on me that it so clearly had.

No fucking way.

She deserves to know the truth. And at least with that, maybe there's a chance we can still be friends—hell, do I even want to be friends? Trying to act like I don't have feelings for this girl, that we're just buddies? Not sure I want that either.

But either way, she deserves to know the truth.

On a deep breath, I walk back to her door and without even thinking about knocking, I let myself in—only to find Everly curled on her bed...crying.

I feel all the color drain from my face as she looks up at me, tear-stained cheeks, a wobbly lip, and watery eyes staring back at me.

Fuck.

Me.

She quickly wipes at her eyes. "Did you...did you forget something."

Yeah...you.

I forgot you.

I forgot to kiss you.

To tell you how much I want you.

Heart heavy in my chest, my stomach twisting in knots, I walk up to her and take a seat on the edge of her bed.

For a silent breath, I stare at her, at the pain I've caused her, the turmoil I've put us both through, and I can't stomach it. I can't sit here and act like everything is fine when it's not.

"Hardy..." she whispers, her voice soft, weak.

It's too much and before I can stop myself, I pull her up to a seated position, letting the sheets fall between us. I keep my eyes trained on hers as I cup her cheek and bring her mouth to mine.

She exhales softly while her wet cheeks momentarily press against mine, our lips tentatively kissing.

But the timid imprint of her lips against mine is not enough.

It *should* be enough.

I should pull away right now and not get lost in this moment with her, but for the life of me, I can't.

Instead, I move my hand to the back of her head and deepen my kiss, sinking into the feel of her.

The taste of her.

The sound of her sweet moans as I swipe at her lips with my tongue, begging for entrance.

Her mouth parts and I take advantage of it, slipping my tongue against hers, letting them tangle, as our lips mold together.

Fuck, this is heaven. Right here. Her warm, naked body next to mine, her mouth on mine, her tongue dancing with mine. Everything about this. I don't want to let it go. I don't want to give it up.

I want this.

I want her.

But in the back of my head, I can hear my brother telling me to stop. Yelling at me to stop.

Begging me.

And it's just enough to make me reluctantly pull away, and when those bright green eyes stare up at me in confusion, I have to warn myself of the repercussions.

Don't, man.

Don't break.

Don't lay her on the bed and press kisses up and down her body, revel in tasting her, spreading her legs wide, and taking what you so desperately want.

Hold strong.

I tug on my hair, frustration careening through me like a bomb ready to explode. "I'm...fuck, Everly, I'm sorry."

Her beautiful, watery eyes search mine. "Sorry for what?" she asks.

"Sorry for walking out of your apartment, making you think you're not the one I want. Because you are. You're the one that I want to take out on dates, the one I want to get to know better, the one I want to spend evenings and mornings with. You, Everly."

"But you said—"

"I know what I said," I reply. "And it was a lie."

She sits back, confusion laced through her brow as she brings the sheet up to her chest to cover herself up. "I don't understand."

Time to go with the truth. It's the only way she won't hate me. The only way I won't hurt her.

"This is complicated. I fucking like you, Everly. The reason I've been weird around you, it's because I realized that I like you and it—*fuck*—it threw me for a loop. The day I went to go see Maple at the zoo, she pointed out my feelings to me. She opened my eyes and showed me that she isn't the one I actually want, that the person I'm supposed to be dating is you."

Still confused, she scoots away, but I don't let her get that far. I close the space between us as she leans against the wall behind her. "I don't understand, Hardy."

"I know. I'm not making sense. I've just been blind to the way I feel about it, and Maple helped me see it. Then last night, the entire party, Polly, Ken, and Maple were all working overtime to get us together. And why didn't I just ask you out myself? Well, I was worried that you had put me in the friend zone, and that's why I was being weird. Why I was avoiding you and distancing myself. I was fucking nervous you didn't feel the same feelings as I do, and I didn't want to make you uncomfortable."

"But...I *was* feeling the same way," she says quietly, which just cuts me deeper.

"I know that now," I say. "And last night, well, I took a fucking chance, and it was the best chance I ever took. I can't tell you how amazing it was. I...I got lost in you." I push my hand through my hair. "I still feel lost in you."

"Then...then why leave? Why make me believe that you want someone else? Why did you try to hurt me this morning?"

I look away, hating myself. "I wasn't trying to hurt you, Everly. I was... ugh, fuck, this is complicated. Hudson texted me this morning. I guess I texted him last night and told him how amazing you were at kissing and how much I liked you." She doesn't move, barely blinks, doesn't offer me any sort of reassurance that what I'm saying is making any sense. "Well, this morning, he pointed something out to me that I overlooked, something that's important." I look into her gorgeous eyes and hate every goddamn second of this. "Since you technically work for us but more importantly for Haisley, I can't, uh...I can't be engaging in anything romantic."

"Oh." She looks away, still not giving me any indication of where her head is.

"Yeah, and it's a long backstory, but Hudson reminded me that Haisley is very serious about us, as in her brothers, not getting romantically involved with anyone she works with."

She slowly nods. "I get it."

"Trust me, Everly, if I had it my way—"

"No, I get it, Hardy," she says with an edge to her voice, the first indication of what she's feeling. And then to my surprise, she rises from the bed, letting the sheets slide off her body.

"Everly, you believe me, right?"

"Yeah, of course," she replies, even though her voice is not convincing at all. She goes straight to her robe that is hanging on the back of her bathroom door. For a brief moment, I let my eyes travel down her body, my mind taking me back to last night when I had my mouth all over her silky, soft skin. But before I can fully start to reminisce, she slips the robe on, cinches it tightly around her waist, and then goes to her kitchen.

Fuck.

Not wanting her to get too far away from me, I walk up to her. "Why does it seem like you don't believe me?"

She pulls down a mug from the cabinet and then turns to face me. "Why don't I believe you? Uh, I don't know, Hardy, maybe because you just gave me several reasons why this can't work out between us."

I grip my forehead. "Yeah, I know, it wasn't—"

"How about this. Just tell me that it was a one-night thing for you and walk away, because that would be a whole lot easier. And it wouldn't string me along."

"I'm not trying to string you along," I say.

"You're not?" she shouts. "So then you just tell me all of these things last night about how much you want me, how much you like me. How beautiful I am, how you've held back from kissing me. Then you nearly leave my apartment without saying goodbye—the only reason you spoke to me was because I woke up. Then you give me some shit excuse about work, then tell me you want to be with Maple again, and *then* kiss me after sending me into a tailspin of asking myself what I did to make you bolt. You made me feel used, unwanted, not good enough. Do you see what I'm dealing with here, Hardy? You're all over the place, so I'm sorry if I don't sound convinced that you really mean what you're *now* saying."

"But I do," I say, growing in frustration with myself. "I meant those things that I said."

"Well, you sure have a funny way of showing it."

"Everly, listen, I didn't handle things well this morning, but I promise you this wasn't a one-night thing for me," I say.

"So then you want to be with me?" she says, hand on her hip.

"Yes, I do."

"But…" She waves her hand, knowing exactly what I'm going to say next.

"Fuck." I pull on my hair. "I…I can't."

"That's what I thought." Staring at me, her eyes welling up, she shakes her head and says in a calmer tone, "Hardy, please. If you even remotely care about me, even a little, just leave, okay?"

"Everly—"

"Leave, Hardy. I can't take whatever wishy-washy story you have to tell me." A tear rolls down her cheek. "Please…just leave."

I hear what she's saying.

I can see the way my presence is hurting her.

But fuck, I don't want to leave and let her think that I'm not choosing her, because I want to choose her. I just can't.

"Can you just listen for one second?" I ask. "Let me explain."

"You've explained enough," she says as she walks over to her front door and opens it. "Now, please leave, and if you don't, I'm going to make sure everyone in this building knows you're not listening to me."

Fuck.

My hands turn into fists as my frustration grows even more intense.

This is fucked.

I fucked this up so badly. I should have just told her the truth in the first place. I never should have left her apartment without a real explanation. I never should have bolted out of bed.

I should have been a fucking mature man rather than an idiot asshole who has now confused the situation so much that I don't even know what I've said anymore.

But I don't want her causing a scene for her building, more for her since she has to live here than for me, so I move toward the door. I don't want to make this harder on her, and I want to respect her wishes. But before I step outside her apartment, I look at her from over my shoulder. "This was not one night for me, Everly. If you hear one thing from me today, please hear that this was not just one night—this was so much fucking more."

And with that, I take off, my chest heavy and my heart feeling like it's in shambles.

"What the fuck were you thinking?" Hudson says as he strides into my office and shuts the door.

I've spent the weekend avoiding all calls from my brother. I didn't even let him in my apartment when he tried to come by. I blocked out the world, lay on my couch, and let the Game Show Network play in the background as I stared up at the ceiling, regretting every second of my interaction with Everly that morning.

I should have been truthful from the beginning. I shouldn't have tried to sneak out. I shouldn't have blamed work. I shouldn't have gone back in, kissed her, and then tried to tell her the truth—which she didn't believe anyway. It's all a fucking mess, and there is only one person to blame. Myself.

That doesn't mean I wanted to hear it from my brother though.

Unfortunately, we are jam-packed with meetings today, which means I'm in the office. I considered going out to the farm and checking on the almond trees just for the hell of it, maybe to find some peace even though I know operations are running smoothly. I was desperate for an excuse to avoid the sharp, cunning eyes that are staring daggers at me right now.

I lean forward, elbows on my desk as I grip my hair. "Can we not?" I ask.

"No, we're going to fucking talk about this. And since you avoided me all weekend, we get to do it in the office." He takes a seat across from me. "Please tell me you ended things with Everly immediately."

My eyes meet his. "Yeah, I fucking ended it, okay? Now if you could please leave my office, I would appreciate it."

But of course, why would he listen to me?

"Why the fuck would you even start something with her? What happened to Maple?"

"Maple wasn't interested."

"So you just move on to the next female you see? Jesus Christ, man."

"I didn't just move on to someone else," I say in a stern tone. "I...I developed feelings for Everly. I didn't realize it until it was pointed out to me. And fuck, the minute it was, it felt like a tidal wave crashing down on me, leaving me no chance to breathe."

"Feelings?" he asks with a quirked brow.

"Yeah, *feelings*. Do you remember what those are, Hudson? The direct response your body or brain experiences when exposed to images or objects, or people."

"Don't be an ass," he says.

"Well, don't come to my fucking office and lecture me about a girl that I like," I nearly yell. Thankfully my office door is shut.

Hudson pauses and leans back in his chair. I can feel him studying me, that brotherly stare trying to read me, to understand where I'm coming from.

After a bout of silence, he says, "I didn't know you liked her that much."

"Yeah, well, neither did I." I lean back in my chair as well, feeling that emptiness inside of me that's been gnawing at me all weekend. Because there's no solution to this. I like Everly, and she's off limits. Simple as that.

The anger in Hudson starts to fade as the concerned brother appears. "Hardy, you know...you know this isn't a good idea."

"I know," I say as I drag my hand over my beard.

"I don't want to look like the dick here—I'm just trying to protect everyone."

"I know, Hudson," I say, and this time I look him in the eyes. "You're not to blame here. I am."

He slowly nods and after another bout of silence, he asks, "Are you going to be able to work with her and be okay with this? Because I was talking to Maggie, and she's going to have Everly head up some events for us. Is that going to be a problem?"

"No, it won't be."

"Are you sure, because I can get someone else to plan them, mainly an event coming up that we're putting on for some possible partners."

"No." I shake my head. "Don't take the job from her. It'll be fine."

"Are you sure?" he asks.

"Yeah, positive," I say as I swallow the lump in my throat. "Everything is fine."

"Okay," he says skeptically. "Because I'm going to need you to work on this event with her."

"What?" I say, shooting him a glare. "Why me?"

"Frankly," Hudson says, "because you're the one who has the most time. Jude is too busy with renovations, between the pop-up shops with Brody and Haisley's rentals. And I'm busy juggling everything else, not to mention I'm going to be down in LA for a week working with Huxley Cane on a few things. You're not going to have to work hand in hand with her, just shoot over a few emails, let her know what we need, make sure the guest list is set, that kind of shit. Unless, like I said, this is going to be a problem for you."

I feel my teeth grind together. "It won't be a problem."

"You sure?"

"Positive," I say.

"Okay, because I'm counting on you, Hardy."

"I know you are," I say.

"And I don't want you to think I'm being a dick."

"I know you're not. We stepped out and took on this new venture together, and I don't want to let you down. I don't want to let Haisley or Jude down. This thing with Everly…it came out of nowhere, and I wasn't expecting it. We got close while planning the bridal shower and the bachelorette party for Polly and Ken, and then, well…yeah, that closeness turned into so much more. You don't need to worry about it though, okay? It's shut down."

"Thanks for letting me know and for what it's worth, I'm sorry, man."

"No need to apologize."

He stands from his chair and starts heading toward my door. Then he looks over his shoulder. "If she means that much to you, you could always talk to Haisley about it."

"No." I press my lips together and wake up my computer. "She'll feel obligated to say it's okay when I know it's not. It's fine, man, seriously. It'll take me a second to readjust my thinking, but it's seriously fine."

When I think he's going to leave, he doesn't. "Give Haisley some credit. She's married, in love… She may have loosened up these past few years, and she very much might understand."

"I don't know," I say.

"Just give it some thought."

"I thought you didn't want me to get romantically involved with someone we work with?"

"I don't," he says. "But I've also never seen you like this before, and it makes me feel uneasy. Makes me think there's more there than I thought." He grips the doorjamb. "I don't want to be the one who stands in the way of a real relationship." Then with that, he takes off. When the door clicks shut, I exhale sharply and bury my head in my hands.

What a fucking mess.

I don't know what to fucking do.

Of course I have to work closely with her on another party. Why wouldn't I have to do that? Because that seems to be my shit luck.

And what's going to suck about that is that I'm going to have to act like everything is fucking fine between us when I know goddamn well it's not. She'll probably put on her professional face and work through the details because that's what she's good at. But me, I'm not good at masking that shit. I'm going to want to talk to her. Explain what happened, try to convince her that I wasn't trying to use her, that I really was telling her the truth. If only she would listen to me.

I know nothing could come of this, that if we talk and she does believe me, it's not like we can go back to that night, but I don't know, maybe we can go back to being friends because after this weekend, fuck, do I miss talking to her.

I miss her text messages.

Her emails.

Her smile.

Fuck…maybe I should talk to Haisley.

Maybe I could plead with her.

And if I'm a lucky motherfucker, maybe I'll get the chance I want.

But if Haisley says no, then maybe I can at least have a small piece of Everly. Maybe I could have my friend back.

I grab my phone and shoot off a text.

Hardy: Hey Haisley, you free to meet up? I need to talk to you about something.

"Hey, sis," I say as I pull Haisley into a hug before I follow her into her house.

She and Jude share a quaint bungalow on the top of a hill, offering them a view of the bay. They're in the middle of renovations, so there are tarps hanging from doorways and painting tools gathered in a corner, but I know once they're done, it's going to be the perfect starter home.

"Hey," Haisley says. "Come on to the backyard and out of this dust-covered house."

I follow her to the back where the living room opens up completely to the backyard. Ten-foot bushes flank both sides of the yard while the back overlooks the beauty of the bay. The bushes cut them off from their neighbors, affording them a great deal of privacy despite how close the other houses are, and the view offers them tranquility. I know it's one of the reasons they loved the space so much, that and the charming characteristics of the bungalow style.

Since I've been here, they've updated the pool with a new liner, added more foliage, and some new outdoor furniture. There's no doubt in my mind that this is where they escape to.

"Place looks great, Hais," I say as I take a seat at their outdoor dining table. Being the ultimate host, she has set out some drinks, pretzels, and hummus.

"Thank you. It's a work in progress and has been slower to come together given Jude is working all day on the other properties and I refuse to make him work overtime. But that's okay, we kind of enjoy the chaos."

"You're a good wife," I say, not trying to butter her up, but you know, never hurts.

She grins at me. "Uh-huh, and what exactly did you say you wanted to talk about?"

I point to the lemonade on the table. "Is that lemonade up for grabs?"

"Are you nervous—is that why you need it?" she asks with a smirk.

"No." I awkwardly laugh and then touch my throat. "Just a little parched."

"Uh-huh." Seeing right through me, she shakes her head and pours us each a glass of lemonade. When she hands me my glass, she sits back and crosses one leg over the other. "So, Hardy, why did you need to come and talk to me?"

Just like Hudson, always getting right down to business.

"Well, I want to preface this by saying I need you, and I'm going to emphasize *need* you to be upfront and honest with me. I don't want you bypassing your thoughts and feelings to accommodate me, okay?"

"Wow, that's not loaded or anything." Her brow furrows. "Is this about Dad?"

"No."

"Because Hudson was telling me about the possible lawsuit. Is that still happening?"

"I have no idea. He's made threats, said a lawsuit is coming, but he hasn't cashed in on them yet. I wouldn't put it past him to move forward on the threats though."

Haisley shakes her head in disappointment. "I don't get him," she says. "I know there was a point in our lives where he was proud of us, but what happened? It's like all of a sudden he became this overbearing monster. I still don't think he likes Jude. I think he just accepts the fact that we're in love."

"Good thing you don't need his approval," I say. "You only need Hudson's and mine." I wink, which makes her laugh.

She takes a sip of her drink. "So, is that why you're here? For approval?"

"What makes you think that?" I ask.

She gives me a look. "Come on, Hardy. When do you ever want to meet up to ask me a question? And then tell me to be honest about my feelings and not accommodate you?"

"When I think our siblingship needs a little shake-up."

She nudges my leg with her foot. "Be serious. Why are you here?"

I shift uncomfortably. "I wanted to talk to you about something that has happened, and before I get into it, I want to apologize first, because when everything was happening, I didn't have you in mind—but, well, this affects you."

"Okay," she draws out. "What is it?"

I run my hands over my thighs, feeling really fucking nervous. "So, I've developed feelings for someone."

"Feelings?" she asks. "Like, real feelings?"

"Yeah."

"Okay, how does this affect me?"

"Because it's Everly," I say, letting her name just hang out there in the open.

"Oh," Haisley says as she sets her drink down on the table.

"And I want you to know that I wasn't pursuing her at all. She was actually trying to help me get back together with Maple and, well, we got really close, and…I sort of fell for her." I let out a deep breath. "Not that you really need to know this, but the other night, we slept together."

Her eyes widen, and I can see this is all a shock to her, so I just keep going. I'm not sure she's going to respond any time soon.

"Hudson found out and lectured me about how we shouldn't get involved with anyone who works with you. For the record, Everly had no idea you felt that way. And, well, I fucked up the entire situation with

Everly. I hurt her, and now I'm trying to create a situation where we can go back to being friends—but in all honestly, Haisley, I don't want that. I don't want to be friends. I want so much more than that with her. I realized very quickly how much she's become my best friend. How much I want her in my life. How much I depend on her. And on top of that, how much…well, how much I enjoyed the romantic side of things, without getting into details and freaking you out. When I spoke to Hudson about it, he said to talk to you. And that's why I'm here, to feel you out. And like I said, if this is a no-go for you, I completely understand. I fucked up, and I take responsibility for that, but if there is the slightest chance that maybe you're okay with me pursuing her, please let me know because I want nothing more than the opportunity to make things right and maybe even have a future with her."

Haisley pulls her legs into her chest and hugs them as she looks off to the side, her face unreadable.

I can feel my hope draining with every silent second that goes by.

I'm on the verge of telling her to forget I even said anything when she finally looks up at me. "Do you know what happened when I told Dad about Jude?"

"He didn't want you being with him, right?"

She nods. "He didn't think Jude was good enough. He thought Jude was just a construction worker with no ability to make anything of himself. But I saw it completely differently. It wasn't about what Jude could offer me monetarily—it was what Jude could offer me emotionally and physically. It was the love and protection, the undying support he gave me. When I turned my back on Dad's wishes, I know that was the start of the feud that we're living through now. I know it. Because we were always *yes kids*. And do you know what I learned from that?"

I shake my head. "No."

"I learned that it will never be anyone's business who I love. And no one will ever get in the way of that." She softly smiles. "Hardy, if you like Everly, if you have feelings for her, who am I to stand in the way of that?"

I feel all the air escape my lungs from sheer disbelief. "Are you serious?"

"Yes." She scoots in and takes my hand in hers. "Hardy, I appreciate you worrying about how this would affect me and the business, but what it comes down to is I want us all to be happy, and if that's being with Everly for you, then I want you to be happy. All I ask is that you don't hurt her."

I wince. "Well, a touch late for that."

Her eyes narrow. "That you don't hurt her *again*."

"Now that's something I can do," I say and then exhale deeply. "Fuck, Haisley, I don't think you understand how much I appreciate this. When Hudson reminded me of how you freaked out when he tried to ask out one of your employees a few years ago, I thought it was done. I told Everly it was over before it even began. That was after a few other less than ideal things I said and, well... let's just say I have a lot of making up to do."

"Seems like you do—because if she hates you, that's on you, not me. You two idiots should have asked me first before reacting."

"Yeah." I grip the back of my neck. "Probably should have done that."

"Now you have an uphill climb, don't you?" she asks.

"A big one."

"Well, better get wooing. If I know anything about Everly, it's that she's very serious and doesn't give in easily."

"I've noticed." I let out a sigh and catch Haisley smiling at me. "What?" I ask.

"You know, I never thought I'd see the day when you fell for a girl."

"I was with Maple for three years," I remind her.

"You were with her, but let's be honest, if you were truly into her, you would have followed her to Denver."

I rub my eye, because Christ, everyone keeps saying that.

"Yeah, I know."

"Tell me this, if Everly was moving somewhere else, would you follow?"

I look up at her and ask in a panic, "Why? Did you hear something?"

She chuckles and shakes her head. "No, it's just hypothetical."

"Jesus." I lean back in my chair. "I mean, I don't think we're at that point of moving in and shit. Hell, I haven't even taken her on a proper date. But if she were to move, I'd attempt a long-distance relationship until we got to a point where we were thinking about more serious things."

"If you're not serious, then what's with the panic?"

"I mean, I'm serious about how I feel about her right now, but at the moment, she's not talking to me. She's hurt. She doesn't want to talk to me, and I haven't even been able to ask her out properly. Would I consider her one of my best friends? Yes. And after the other night, I'm suffering from the silence. So, I'm right there. I want to explore this. I want more. But I need her to be on the same page, and she's far from it."

Haisley smirks and nods.

"You know, you almost make it seem like you get joy out of my pain."

She holds up her fingers and presses them together like some sort of supervillain. "Maybe a little."

I shake my head at my sister. "Wow, Haisley."

She chuckles and then nudges my leg again. "What's the plan? How are you going to win her back?"

"Good question. I'm going to try to talk to her first, text her, warm her up. And if that doesn't work, I'm moving on to plan B."

"And what is Plan B?" she asks.

"Using our work event to get close to her again."

"Ooo." Haisley shakes her head. "Low blow, Hardy. Low blow."

I shrug. "I'll do whatever it takes."

CHAPTER TWENTY-FIVE
HARDY

Hardy: Hey Everly, how you doing? Stupid question, I know. You're probably not happy with me and I get that, but as someone who isn't afraid of rejection, I was hoping that maybe you would consider giving me a chance to explain myself to you. Do you think you could be open to that?

One day later…

Hardy: Yeah, I didn't think you were going to want to talk to me. I get it. I'm not sure I would want to talk to me either. But if you would just give me a chance to explain everything so we can go back to being friends, I'd be really grateful.

Another day later…

Hardy: Okay, I know how that sounds—being friends after everything that happened that night—but I think that's all we can be and, well, Christ, I'm messing this up too. I'm second guessing everything I say to you and making it all a mess. What I'm trying to say is that I miss you, Everly. Can you please just text me back, at least let me know that you're okay?

Another day later...

Hardy: Everly, please, I need to talk to you. Just give me ten
  minutes, that's all I need. Please.

Well, texting is not working. Moving on to plan B.

To: Everly Plum
From: Hardy Hopper
Subject: Party for Partners

Hey Everly,

*I know I'm bombarding you, but Hudson has informed me that
I'm going to be working with you on a party that we're throwing
for some future partners. I'd love to meet up so we can discuss
the details, and I'd also like the chance to properly apologize to
you again.*

  I miss talking to you.

  Let me know when and where works for you, and I'll be there.

Thanks,
Henrietta—at least I still hope so.

To: Hardy Hopper
From: Everly Plum
Subject: RE: Party for Partners

Hardy,

Please send me your thoughts on the party—what you're think-ing for the menu, the drinks, and the setting. I have attached three of my top venues that might work, as well as one of Brody's more moody pop-up shops for consideration.

I will need your thoughts no later than EOD. No need to meet. I can gather everything I need through email.

Everly

To: Everly Plum
From: Hardy Hopper
Subject: Please…

Everly,

I'd really like to go over the details in person. Please reconsider your thoughts on the matter. I want nothing more than to prove to you that I didn't intend to hurt you.

I miss you.

Hardy

To: Hardy Hopper
From: JP Cane
Subject: Save the Pigeons

Dear friend,

*It's been a while since we last spoke. I'm afraid I've been busy
with a lot of endeavors, but I will tell you one thing I'm never too
busy for, and that's saving the pigeons.*

*Recently, the pigeon adoption agency I've been working with
has encountered some hardships with being short on staffing
and foster homes, which is why I'm reaching out to you. Have
you ever considered fostering a pigeon? Now is the time to give it
some good thought. They are excellent companions, offer a great
deal of entertainment, and are beautiful to look at.*

*We are looking for a few individuals with safe homes to take in
a few of our pigeon friends. If you're interested, please click here.
Please open your heart and home and help us save the pigeons.*

Your friend,
JP Cane

From my car, I stare at the Magical Moments by Maggie storefront and
contemplate if I should go in or not.

I did drive all the way here with the intention of going inside the store,
but now that I'm here, I'm second-guessing that decision. Because what
am I really going to say to her? She asked me to leave, she's ignored my text
messages, and she denied me any meetup for the party we're throwing
together. She clearly—and understandably—doesn't want me around,
and I handled the entire situation completely wrong.

And yet here I am with a box of matcha Oreo cronuts, ready to fucking
beg her to forgive me.

If I'm going to try to win her back, to get her to listen to me, I'm going to have to go about this in a different way. Because here's the thing, I think we all know I messed up the morning after. No, I didn't just mess it up—I destroyed any possible hope of making that night magical.

I tainted it with my idiocy.

Therefore, if I walk into the office with a cheery disposition and say, "Hey Everly, guess what? Haisley said I can date you. So, when would you like to go out?" I think we all know that's not going to go over well.

I think her exact words would be "Oh, so your sister says we can date, so now it's okay?"

See the mistake in there?

She doesn't want permission.

She doesn't want excuses.

She wants to be wanted, and that's what I have to show her. She needs to know that I'll never want another woman the way I want her.

She's it for me.

That has become clearer with every day without her.

So that's why I grab the box of cronuts and head toward the storefront, knowing full well that this could go two ways. She could be excited to see my face but be upset—which is ideal because that I can work with. Or she could hate me with every fiber of her being and tell me to leave, only to toss the cronuts at my retreating back.

For some reason, I have a sinking feeling it's going to be the latter.

When I reach the door, I open it and let myself in.

The space is quiet, and thankfully, it seems they don't have any guests at the moment, so when I hear the telltale sound of high heels clicking across the cement floor, I steel my nerves.

It takes a second, but when Everly peeks around the corner, my breath gets caught up in my chest because fuck, it feels like it's been months since I've seen her even though it's been mere days.

And to my fucking surprise, her hair is down, curled into soft waves. Her hair is never down.

Ever.

So, it feels like she's already got a leg up on me—well, I already knew she did, but this makes it drastically worse.

Not to mention she's wearing a simple purple dress that clings to her curves and black high heels that I know she hates wearing around the office. She's put-together, beautiful as always, and looking razor sharp and ready to kill.

Ready to kill...me.

"Hardy," she says flatly. "What are you doing here?"

Now's the time to try to win her over, make her your friend again, man.

Woo her in any way possible.

Hand her the cronuts.

Sweeten her up first then go in for the kill.

"I brought you cronuts," I say, holding out the box.

Her eyes fall to the box and then back up to me, completely unimpressed. "I don't want your cronuts. Now if that's all, I'm going to get back to work." She turns on a dime and without another word, slips into her office.

Uhh...okay.

Wasn't expecting that.

I thought the cronuts would at least soften her a touch.

Well, worst case scenario, she takes the cronuts, kicks me in the shin, and walks away. At least if she accepted the cronuts, she'd think about me writhing on the floor while eating them.

Knowing this probably isn't a good idea—going into the bear's den—I continue forward and walk up to her office door. Without knocking, I let myself in and find her sitting behind her desk, staring at her computer screen.

"It's worrisome that you don't know how to take no for an answer," she says as she keeps her eyes trained on the screen in front of her.

"You forgot to take the cronuts."

She continues to type. "I told you I don't want them."

"Afraid they're poisoned?" I ask. "Because for future reference, that's not my brand."

"No, I don't want to accept your pity cronuts."

"They're not pity cronuts," I say, getting slightly frustrated. I don't pity her.

I like her…a lot. And I need her to see that.

"I don't have time for this, Hardy. I have a lot on my to-do list, and that list doesn't include listening to you try to come up with another explanation for what happened the other night."

Well…fuck.

This is going to be a lot harder than I thought, and with that last comment from her, I feel my nice guy persona slipping.

I want to woo her. I want to show her how much I want her, how much I need her in my life, and I'm not sure this soft, loving approach is going to work, not when she's matching my energy with a frosty bite.

I think…fuck, I think I'm going to have to step it up to the same energy.

I might have to fight ice with fire. I guess there's only one way to find out.

I set the cronuts down on her desk. "I brought you something, so the kind thing to do would be to accept it."

She sits back in her chair and picks up a pen before meeting my eyes. "Are you really going to lecture me about being kind?"

The bite in my voice must have caught her attention. Hell, I think I might be onto something. Not the approach I'd usually want to take, but at least she's looking at me, engaging with me.

"When you need it, yeah."

"What I need is for you to leave."

Not going to happen. I see the challenge in her eyes. If she wants to play games, I'll play, because I will do just about anything to get her to talk to me, even if it's like this.

So, despite her, I take a seat in front of her desk and get comfortable.

Her eyes narrow, and it's almost comical to see her like this.

Putting up a front.

Slipping out of her professional self and showing me her true colors. I fucking like it, even though I shouldn't.

That sass and spice is on full display and only makes me want her that much more.

"What do you think you're doing?" she asks.

"Getting comfortable. What does it look like I'm doing?"

"Being a nuisance," she says. "I told you to leave."

"Yeah, and last time I listened to you, I ended up not hearing from you, so I think I'm good with just sitting here until you want to talk."

"Fine, then I'll leave," she says as she stands from her chair and walks around her desk, attempting to move past me.

Big mistake on her part.

Before I decided to dip into this battle of wills, I would have let her walk by and just followed her, but the approach has changed. The heat has turned up, and there is only one way to win this…

Before she can retreat, I grab her wrist, stopping her in place and forcing her to pause.

With a turn of my head, I drag my eyes up her arm to her face. She's looking down at me as if she can't believe I'm holding her back. "What the hell do you think you're doing?"

Taking a chance, I rub my thumb over her wrist, wanting to warm her frosty exterior. And from the way her lips part, I can't tell if she's insulted that I'd even consider touching her or if it's the right move.

"Sit down, Everly," I say sternly.

"Do really think that tone is going to work on me?"

"I don't know," I say. "Let's see." And then I tug on her hand, throwing her off balance, and guiding her onto my lap.

"What the hell, Hardy," she says in shock. She whips her head around, her hair brushing up against me right before her eyes fall to mine. "What are you doing?"

"I told you to sit down, and when you don't listen, I have to take matters into my own hands."

"Jesus, you don't own me."

"Not what you said the other night," I say, causing her mouth to fall open in shock. Yup, this is the right approach. At least I'm garnering a reaction from her. I can work with this. I can slowly soften her this way.

"Not once did I say you owned me."

"You didn't have to say it," I reply. "Your moans did all the talking for you."

Her eyes narrow. "Yeah, well, I faked it."

That makes my head fall back as a guttural laugh flies out of my mouth. "There is no way in hell you faked that."

"Don't give yourself so much credit. It's easy to fake it."

"Says the girl whose pussy clenched around my cock so hard that you made me black out."

"It's called Kegels," she says in defiance.

"Bullshit," I say. "Don't even try to lie to me." I run my hands up her hips to her sides as I softly say, "There was nothing fake about the way you kissed me, the way you sucked me off, the way you screamed out my name, and the way your slick, wet pussy contracted around my cock."

She twists her lips to the side as I move my hand up even higher, just below her breasts.

"Just like right now," I whisper. "There's nothing fake about the way you're reacting, the way your breath is hitching, the way your eyes try to avoid mine because you know if you look at me, you'll be tempted. You want me, Everly. You just wish that you didn't."

Not sure how pushing her buttons is going to pay off, but she's still on my lap and despite my loosened grip, she hasn't attempted to stand or walk away.

After a few short seconds, she finally says, "You were a decent fuck, Hardy. That's all it will ever be."

Not going to lie and say that didn't sting, but I also am well aware of the wall she's erected between us—the one protecting her from getting hurt one more time—that means she'll say and do anything to keep me at a distance. It's my job to tear down that wall brick by brick, until I reach the point where I can tell her what Haisley said. Until then I will use any means necessary to woo her.

"Just decent?" I say. "Hmm, interesting, because you came back for seconds."

"Because you didn't satisfy me the first time," she says. "Thought that maybe I could try again."

I chuckle—the lie is so ridiculous, it's the only reaction I can muster.

"Uh-huh, and what happened that second time?" I ask.

She shrugs. "Like I said, decent." And then she turns away from me so her back is to my chest. I take that moment to place my hand on her stomach and pull her back against me. I wait for her to try to lift off my lap because I would let her. I would let her get up. I'm not about to hold her back against her will, but when she doesn't make the attempt, I know I've got her.

She might have erected that wall as high as she can make it, but she can't deny the fact that she still wants me. That she feels the attraction pulsing between us and wants to indulge.

And if that's the way to get her to talk, then that's what is going to have to happen.

"Maybe I need to prove to you that I'm more than decent," I say as I move my other hand down her leg, to the hem of her dress and then slip it under. I pause, waiting for her to stop me, but she doesn't. So I drag my hand up farther, pulling the tight hem with me until it's up and around her waist. I run my hand over her inner thigh, letting my thumb drag over the seam of her underwear. That elicits a small, almost silent gasp from her.

"Say the word, Everly, and I'll stop," I whisper.

But she doesn't.

She stays silent, just the sound of her labored breath filling the air.

So I take that as the green light to keep going as she leans back against my shoulder, and I know in this moment I've got her. So I slip my other hand under her dress and drag it up to her breasts. When I notice that she has another front-clasp bra on, I smile to myself as I unclasp it, letting it fall open. She shifts her body, her hips lifting up against my hardening length. Once again, she softly groans—a sound I've committed to memory.

I've missed this. I know I only had her for one night, but that was enough. That was all it took to know that I was going to need so much more. And right now, it's just solidifying that idea in my head.

"I've missed these tits," I say as I cup both breasts, feeling the weight in my palms and growing even harder.

I swipe my thumbs over her already hard nipples and love how she moans from the touch, so I decide in that moment to tease her. Since her neck is exposed, I press a few soft kisses to her skin and to my surprise, she moves her head to the side, giving me more access, and as I run my mouth up and down the column of her neck, I draw slow circles around her nipples. It's a whisper of a touch, so gentle that the only thing it's doing is ramping up her need for me to deepen it.

When I find her jaw with my lips, I kiss closer to her mouth, but she doesn't turn in my direction, and I'm not going to force her to kiss me. I want her to give in willingly like she has with the rest of this position, so I bring my lips back to her ear and whisper, "Are you wet?"

I catch her bite down on her bottom lip, keeping her mouth quiet, not wanting to give away exactly how turned on she is.

"I bet if I slipped my hand between your legs, I'd find out."

Her chest rises and falls more rapidly, and her legs spread just an inch. If I wasn't paying attention, I might not have seen it, but I'm reading her like a book. She doesn't want to seem desperate, but she wants it. *She wants me.*

I go back to kissing her neck, sucking on the juncture near her shoulder, and when I lightly nibble on her skin, I take that moment to pinch her nipples.

"Oh fuck," she says, shifting against my erection and causing me to smile.

So I repeat the sensation. I nibble and pinch.

Nibble and pinch.

Driving up that need for me until her hand grips the back of my neck and she starts rocking her ass over my erection.

Fuck.

Me.

I grind my teeth together, telling myself this isn't about me; this is about her.

But shit, that feels so good.

Everything about this feels good.

It feels right.

It feels like this is where she belongs, and I need to prove that to her.

Focusing on her, I start circling her nipples again and with every circle, I make one pass over them, loving how sensitive she is.

After a few more swipes, I drag one hand down to her pubic bone. While I bring one of her nipples between my fingers, rolling it, I slide a finger over her underwear and down her slit. It's a quick pass, but it's just enough to feel her arousal through the fabric and to garner a moan from her.

Smiling, I drag my hand back up her stomach, letting the tips of my fingers create a burning need within her.

When I start circling her nipples again, she grinds against me and whispers, "Fuck." Then she spreads her legs wider, and I smile to myself.

"Where do you want my fingers, Everly?" I ask her while passing them over her chest, up to her collarbone, and across her breasts again. "Do you want them here?" I play with her nipples. Her breathing turns even heavier. "Or here." I drag them across her stomach. "Or here," I say as I dance them across the waistline of her underwear.

When she doesn't answer, I say, "Well, I guess you want them up here." I start to move my hand, but she stops me and slips my hand under her underwear and right to her soaking arousal. "Fuck, Everly," I whisper. "You're so goddamn wet."

Again, she keeps her mouth closed but when she encourages my hand to play with her, I listen. I bring two fingers to her clit, making slow circles over the sensitive nub.

"Yes," she whispers before lifting my other hand to her breast. I bring her nipple between two of my fingers and start rolling it.

"You going to fake it again this time?" I ask her. "You going to pretend like you're wet for no reason? That you're not turned on by me? That I didn't bring you to this point?" When she doesn't answer, I say, "Because I can stop."

And I do just that. I pause my hands.

"Don't," she says, her voice barely above a whisper. "Don't stop."

"Ahh, so this is real. The orgasm that's building inside of you, it's real." When she doesn't say anything, I whisper in her ear, "Answer me, Everly."

"It's...it's real," she says.

I continue circling her clit as her pants grow heavier. "And the other night, when I was deep inside of you, bottoming out with every goddamn stroke, that was real."

She wets her lips and nods.

"No, I want to hear you say it. That was real."

She threads her fingers through the short hairs on the back of my neck. "It was real."

"And when your tight pussy contracted around my cock, that was real."

"It...it was all real," she answers.

"Good, never lie about that again," I say as I remove my hand from her underwear, causing her to cry out in frustration.

But I'm not done with her. I lift her off my lap and push her back onto her desk so she's leaning back. Her keyboard crashes to the ground, but I don't care as I reach for her underwear and pull it off. For a moment, I consider unzipping my pants and taking what I so desperately want, but I maintain control and spread her, kneel on the floor, and bring my mouth between her legs.

With one swipe of my tongue, she's trembling. So I spread her even more and suck on her clit.

"Oh my God," she says as her feet, still in their high heels, land on my shoulders. "Oh fuck, Hardy."

That's it. That's my girl. That's what I want to hear.

I roll her nipple again while I make short, tight flicks with my tongue over her clit.

Her legs squeeze around my head.

Her breathing becomes erratic.

And her body starts to shake as her pelvis tenses.

She's right there.

So I keep flicking.

And flicking.

And flicking until she tugs on my hair and then with one last flick, she's moaning and coming on my face. I let her ride my tongue, seeking out every ounce of her orgasm and, when she finally starts to slow down and gain her composure, I lift back up to my feet and lower her legs.

When her heady eyes meet mine, I feel a pull in the pit of my stomach, a pull so great that I know she's not done. She wants more.

I want to keep this about her, but I think...I think she needs that connection between us. I think she needs to know how out of control she makes me feel.

How she in fact owns every aspect of me.

So, keeping my eyes on her, I pull my wallet out of my pocket and secure a condom. I grip it between my teeth while I undo my pants. I watch her intently the entire time, making sure she doesn't give me a sign that she doesn't want this. But she never does. Instead, she wets her lips and watches me take my cock out of my briefs and sheath it with the condom.

Ready, I move in closer and take one of her legs by the ankle where I press a kiss along her already heated skin and then prop it up against my shoulder, opening her up more to me.

Hand on my cock, I press the tip to her entrance, waiting to see if she stops me. But when her teeth roll over the corner of her mouth, I take that as a green light from her and slide all the way inside of her.

Her head falls back on a moan while I bottom up, grinding my teeth together from just how perfect she feels wrapped around me.

Nothing has ever felt better.

Fucking nothing.

And I need to let her know that.

"You're...fuck, Everly, you're perfect."

I grip her hips, my fingers digging into her skin as I begin to rock in and out of her. Her pussy is still slick from her orgasm, which makes our connection that much more electric because I know I brought her to that place and I'm going to bring her there again.

"So good...so fucking good," I grind out as my hips start to pulse faster. I look her in the eyes and catch her staring up at me, so I take that moment to say, "I'm addicted to you. I need this...you." Then I pull out, lift her hips and drive back in.

Her head falls back, and a feral moan falls past her lips.

"This pussy is mine, Everly."

Her eyes meet mine again, and when I think she's going to deny me that claim, she doesn't. Instead, she releases her leg from my shoulder and then pulls away. I'm about to protest until she flips her body, so her stomach is resting on the desk and her ass is propped up, waiting for me.

"Fuck," I grumble as I smooth my hand over the round globe.

I kick her legs apart, giving me better access, prop my cock at her entrance and then slide right back in. When I'm fully inside, to the hilt, I glide my hand up her back and right to her undone hair. I gather it together with one hand and then twirl it with my fist, making her head slightly bend back. I lean forward and with my other hand, I gently run it up her exposed neck and I press a light kiss to her cheek and whisper, "This pussy…is…mine."

I want her to know that.

I need her to know that.

And she seems to understand, because there's no protest as I stand back up and hold onto her hair as I stroke in and out of her, letting my body take in every tug and pull from her constricting walls.

It feels all too perfect.

Every aspect of having sex with her.

Like I finally found the missing piece to my life. She's been sitting there all along, writing emails to me, laughing with me, showing me that it's not Maple I want, but her. It's been her all along.

It's been this connection.

It's been me and her.

And I'll be damned if I let her slip through my fingers.

As I pick up my pace, letting her sweet moans fill my mind, fill my memory, I say, "It's you and me, Everly."

I pump into her.

"You and fucking me."

My hips fly, my thighs slamming against her legs.

"I want nothing else."

My muscles fire off, my orgasm building.

"Just you…"

I pump even harder, her body stiffening beneath me.

"And me."

Her hands claw at the desk to anchor herself as her walls start to constrict around me.

"Fuck, Everly. Give me this…give me you."

I release her hair, letting her head fall against her chest as I grip both her hips now, angle her up, and rapidly drive into her. Her desk shakes, the pens in her pen cup rattle, and papers on her desk fly off from the sheer momentum we're producing.

"Fuck," she whispers, her hands curling.

"Come for me, Everly. I know you want to."

"God," she mutters as her back arches. "Fuck…fuck…" She pounds the desk with her fist, almost in frustration, right before she lets out a loud cry and her body spasms beneath me, her pussy clenching around my cock in one large wave as I pulse inside her, catching her orgasm just at the right time to send me into a frenzy.

I feel my hips take over as my mind blacks out.

I thrust harder…deeper…my orgasm tiptoeing up my back until it clutches around me, seizing me.

I still as I roar out my pleasure, my cock swelling right before I spill inside of her.

"Fuck, Everly," I say as I catch my breath, my body trying to come back down to Earth, but that feels impossible as her pussy continues to lightly clench around my cock.

It takes us a few seconds, but when we're both settled, I remove myself from her, pull off my condom and place it in her trashcan. I adjust myself back into my pants and when she tries to sit up, I stop her.

Instead, I grab her thong from the floor and slide it back up her legs. "I'll let you keep these this time, but next time, they're mine."

After I adjust her dress, and she sits up, turning to face me, I catch her heady eyes. "Who says there will be a next time?"

Did I wish this would have fixed our problems? Yes.

Did I know it was a slim chance? Absolutely.

But that doesn't mean it's not the first step. She wants to be desired and wanted. Well, what we just did showed exactly that.

I smirk and take her hands in mine before helping her up to a standing position. I straighten out her dress for her and then tip her chin up with one finger. Moving in close, I whisper, "If I have anything to say about it, there will be a next time." And then I press a soft kiss to her lips.

It's short, but it's just enough to hold me over.

I step away and head to her office door. I'm about to tell her to enjoy the cronuts when she follows me with the box. "You're forgetting these."

"They're yours, Everly."

"I don't want them."

"So you'll take the orgasms but not the cronuts?"

Her eyes narrow. "What game are you playing, Hardy?"

"I'm not playing any game—you're the one being difficult."

"Difficult?" she says with a raised voice. "You're the one who hurt me and then you just come in here thinking you can...you can play around with me and make everything better?"

"I don't, actually," I say as I turn to face her. "I came here to show you what you mean to me. What I did the other morning was not only wrong, but pretty much unforgivable, I get that. But I'm not too proud to make sure you know that I'm sorry, because I am. And that I want you, because I do. The cronuts were a gift, the orgasms were to help you feel just as desired and worthy as you deserve." I want to tell her that the orgasms were to thaw out her iciness, but I understand that she's in self-protection mode. Still, she needs to know I'm not done. "Maybe next time I run into you, you won't be as icy."

Then with that, I walk out of her office with the taste of her still on my tongue and another plan brewing in my mind.

Hardy: Can you invite Everly to your wedding? I know it's last minute, but maybe say you need help with something.

Polly: What did you do?

Hardy: Let's just say the morning after wasn't my finest moment.

Polly: Oh Hardy.

Hardy: I know, okay? I don't need to hear it. I've already beaten myself up about the whole thing. I need some help and I would really appreciate it if you could get Everly to the wedding. Maybe she can be a second bridesmaid.

Polly: You know, George, Ken's cousin, was bitching the other day about not being a groomsman.

Hardy: Perfect, add him to the mix and then hire Everly, I'll pay for it. Does she need a dress? I'll pay for that too.

Polly: Maple is just wearing a formal black dress, so Everly can do the same.

Hardy: Great! Then it works.

Polly: For you, but now I have to explain to the moms why I'm changing things two days before the wedding.

Hardy: Want me to talk to them?

Polly: No! You've done enough.

Hardy: Ooo, I have an idea!

Polly: Oh God, what now?

Hardy: Can you pull together a shopping trip for a dress tomorrow? Have her meet you, tell me where to go, and then say you need to leave, so I'll help her instead.

Polly: Do you want her to hate me?

Hardy: Please, Polly. **insert puppy eyes** Please. Please. Please.

Polly: Can you enlighten me? How does this benefit me?

Hardy: I'll throw in a few excursions for free on your honeymoon. You choose, I'll cover the cost.

Polly: Now we're getting somewhere.

CHAPTER TWENTY-SIX
EVERLY

"THANK YOU SO MUCH FOR doing this for me," Polly says as she greets me with a hug.

"Of course," I say. "I'm glad I had the weekend open so I could help you."

That's a lie.

In fact, I'm *not* glad I had the weekend open.

And I'm *not* glad I could help her.

Because I can see right through this little set-up.

Let me lay it out for you from the night of the coupling, so you can understand where my mind is at.

You ready?

First, the bachelorette party. There was a lot of confusion, a lot of drinks, and a lot of sex.

A night where dreams were made.

Where fantasy became a reality.

He told me he liked me, I fawned, swayed...swooned and then had the best sex of my life.

Flash forward to the morning, when I woke up feeling like a well-satiated goddess only to make a complete one-eighty and spiral through a dark tunnel of despair, feeling like a discarded turd.

Hardy tried to sneak out the morning after, but I woke up and caught him, forcing him to fumble around and tell me he had to leave for work—on a weekend. Yeah, a freaking weekend!

It was awkward. I knew he was lying, but I went with it because that's the kind of girl I am. I will discard my own feelings to make other people feel better.

Fast forward to the awkward goodbye where he agreed that me helping him still try to hook up with Maple was the way to go.

Once again, not the narrative I thought we were going with. I assumed after he said he liked me that perhaps there was a future for us.

Apparently not.

I was the one-night girl, and that was it.

He left, I cried.

Then, a crazy miracle occurred because he came back in and kissed me.

Okay, great, we were kissing again. It was unexpected, but it was so much better than sitting in this pit of disappointment.

Then he pulled away, told me he liked me, but he couldn't be with me.

He used Haisley as an excuse.

At that point, I completely blacked out and shut down.

Because what kind of roller coaster was that? He likes me, he doesn't. He likes me, but he can't. Jesus Christ, that's not the kind of mental anguish I signed up for.

I mean…if you just wanted one night with me, then fine, take the night with me and move on.

But the many excuses—three to be exact—as to why he couldn't be with me were just too much. Like, if you have to say it three different ways, I get the hint. I'm not the girl you want. Just move on, because I am.

Well, at least that's what I told myself.

And then the text messages, the emails…can you see the trend here?

It feels very toxic to me. He likes me but can't be with me. *Oh, I miss you, but I can't be with you. Talk to me but I shouldn't be talking to you.*

Pardon my French, but *fuck off, man.*

And then…this is where my temper flared. This is when I was ready to knock him right in the nuts.

That's right, ladies, the old one-two pow-pow to the junk.

He waltzed into my work and tried to bring me cronuts.

The freaking nerve!

The audacity.

As if I would eat his cronuts.

Sure, I might have let him touch me and go down on me, among other things, but that's neither here nor there. I was caught up in the moment. The minute he tugged me onto his lap, I was a goner. Can you blame me? The best sex, remember? The best freaking sex of my life. I couldn't pass that up.

Doesn't mean I don't still hate him.

Actually, after that round of him making me come on my desk—twice—I actually hate him more!

That's right, I'm at that level of hate.

We went from acquaintances to friends to one-night lovers to… mortal enemies.

If he thought my knife hand to his throat in the car was suffocating, wait until he gets a load of what else is in my arsenal.

And I see the game he's playing. I see him trying to get near me. Using a work event to see me in person. Pathetic.

Coming to my work with cronuts. Equally pathetic.

Using his friend's wedding to force me to be near him. Positively desperate. *I mean, seriously, man, these are all moves you made to get closer to Maple.*

For all I know, Polly is going to disappear during this try-on session, and lo and behold, he's going to swoop in and help me.

No, I don't trust him with my heart.

My body, well…once again, let's not go there.

"Would you like any champagne?" Darla, the shop owner, asks as she comes up to us. I've known Darla for a while, and when Polly said I needed an elegant black gown, I knew exactly where to go. Darla will let me rent because she knows I'll take great care of the dress and return it in pristine condition.

"I'm good," Polly says. "Maybe some water though."

"Water is good for me too," I say just as Darla ducks into the back and the door to the shop opens.

From the way Polly's eyes dart to the front, I have a sneaking suspicion I don't even need to look to know who it is.

"Oh, wow, Hardy, you're here," Polly says in the least convincing tone I've ever heard.

Surprise. Surprise.

I turn to see Hardy walk toward us wearing a maroon suit with a black button-up shirt underneath. I know how much he hates wearing his professional clothes, but even I have to admit how good he looks in them.

And that's the only nice thing I will say about him.

"Yeah, Ken told me about the last-minute change, and I thought I should help out any way I can," he says as he presses a kiss to Polly's cheek in greeting. When he turns toward me, I hold up my hand.

"Come any closer and I'll knife-hand you in the neck like I did in the car."

Luckily, he's smart enough to realize a real threat when he hears it, and he keeps his distance.

"She seems spicy," Hardy says. "Is that the bridesmaid you ordered?" He sticks his hands in his pockets and gives me a long once-over. "Hot too."

Oh, fuck off, Hardy.

I don't need your offhand comments.

"Well, this seems uncomfortable," Polly says, and then she turns toward me, a look of apology in her eyes. "He made me do this."

"I'm not surprised," I say to Polly. "Just disappointed that you went along with it."

She presses her hands together. "He promised me paid-for excursions on our honeymoon. I couldn't pass it up."

I nod. "I get it—I don't blame you. I blame him."

"That's fine with me," Polly says. "Now, as he planned…" She clears her throat and then grips her forehead. "Oh no, I seem to have come down with a migraine." Her voice is monotone and incredibly unconvincing. "Whatever should I do? I want to help pick out a dress, but dear heavens, the pain. Oh, the throbbing pain."

"Oh, I know," I say, playing into the ridiculousness of this scene. "Why don't you go home, and Hardy can take your place?"

"Wow," Polly says. "You know, I never would have thought of that. Hiring you was one of my best decisions ever."

"I expect that same sentiment in a glowing review," I say while I fold my arms over my chest.

"Oh, I can't possibly say anything else." Then she turns to Hardy and adds, "Dear sir, do you think you could take my place? The pain is just so excruciating. Ouchie wah wah."

Hardy's expression flattens. "Ouchie wah wah?"

Polly shrugs. "Thought it really expressed the type of pain I'm in."

"You sound like a fool," he says.

"Really? Insulting the person who's helping you out?" Polly asks.

"You're right." He clears his throat. "Why, of course I can help out, Polly. Anything you need. I can undress Everly and help her into her dresses."

"Not necessary," I say.

"Well, I have no problem checking her out and making sure the dresses fit correctly on her. Now, do you want something revealing? No back? Maybe a deep V in the front?"

"God, you're annoying," I say as I walk over to the dresses.

"Whatever she's comfortable in," Polly says.

"Then that will be a turtleneck dress," I shout over to her.

"That's fine with me. Thanks for doing this."

"Anything for the bride," I say and then she takes off, leaving me alone with Hardy and Darla who arrives just in time to bring out water.

"Oh, where is the bride?" Darla asks.

"Came down with a migraine," I say. "Luckily, the best man is here to help. See how that worked out?"

"Oh, wonderful," Darla says, missing my sarcasm completely. "Would you like me to start pulling dresses?"

"Actually," Hardy cuts in. "I think we can pull some, but we'll let you know if we need any help."

"Oh, okay," Darla says, looking slightly confused. Technically, it's her job to pull dresses but from the command in Hardy's voice, I can see she has no intent to challenge him. "Well, do you know how long this will take? I have a meeting in half an hour."

"I can lock up for you," I say to Darla. "I remember the routine from when I helped out last summer."

"You don't mind?" she asks, twisting her hands together.

"Not at all. You know I'm just grateful you're letting me look around on such short notice."

"Oh, you know I would do anything for you and Maggie—you've brought me so much business."

I smile kindly at her. "We are happy to help. If you want to lock up the front and I can use the pin pad in the back, then we will be good to go."

"Great. Thank you," Darla says. "And if you do need help with any-thing, just text me, I'll have my phone. Leave the name and style of the dress on the notepad for me, and I'll process it in the morning."

"Not a problem," I say.

Darla hurries off and leaves me and Hardy in the store, alone. I'm sure this is more than ideal for him.

"So," he says, after Darla has locked up and clearly taken off, "crazy you're going to be in the wedding, huh?"

"Yeah, insane how that worked out. Here I thought I wouldn't have to see your face again, and lo and behold, I'll be spending the weekend with you."

"Very coincidental," he says.

I roll my eyes dramatically and head over to the black dress section. Luckily, Darla has made it incredibly easy to find dresses in her store. She has them sorted by color, then by length. Since I'm going for something elegant, I head over to the floor-length black dresses and start looking through them. Darla has a large assortment, and lucky for me I'm sample size, so anything I might like that fits well, I'll easily be able to rent.

"Want me to pick some dresses out?" he asks as he comes up behind me, his large body taking up all of my personal space.

"I'd prefer you stick your head in a trash compactor, but not sure I'm going to be that lucky today."

"Unfortunately not," he says as his chest presses against my back and his arm reaches out in front of me. He grabs a black silk dress that's practically backless, only held together by a few thin ties. The front is a loose cowl neck which seems to dip low, exactly what he wanted. "This looks like it would be perfect."

"Of course, you would say that," I reply. "It barely has any fabric."

"Which is perfect," he says. "Even a long slit up the front."

I study the dress and I feel a smile pass over my lips as I say, "You know what, that dress very well might be perfect."

"Yeah?" he asks, looking hopeful.

"Yeah, Polly informed me there would be some single and very attractive men attending her wedding. It would be the perfect dress to garner some attention."

His expression flattens and it almost makes me bust out in laughter, but I keep it together.

"The more I think about it, the more I'm liking the idea of showing more skin," I say as I pluck a few dresses from the rack that are nothing I would ever wear for a work event, but I think we all know this isn't really a work event. I can see right through this whole farce.

"That dress?" he asks me as I gather a dress that looks like just a bunch of straps of black fabric.

"Yeah, I think this is the one I want to try on first." I hand him the rest of the dresses and say, "Pick some more while I try this one on."

I leave him by the dresses as I work my way to one of the dressing rooms. I'm going to tell you right now, I plan on showing this man what he could have had with no intention of handing it over.

And why?

Because I am a strong woman who doesn't appreciate a multitude of excuses as to why I can't be with someone.

You either want me or you don't.

I don't need excuse after excuse.

So I am going to be strong and I'm not going to let him convince me otherwise.

snorts steam emoji

I hang the dress on the hook in the dressing room and close the curtain behind me. Do I wish it was a door? Absolutely, but I will take what I can get. And because I came fully prepared for this moment, knowing damn well what this group of friends is up to, I showed up with no bra—only a thong as an undergarment. He thinks he can mess with me? Ohhhhh no, I'm coming in hot and he's going to regret it. Cronuts be damned!

I strip down to just my thong and take the strappy dress off the hanger. The thing about Darla's store is that the dresses she carries are for all occasions. Normally this is not a dress that you would see offered to a bridesmaid, but because I am choosing to be vindictive—don't be mad at me, be mad at the game he's playing—then I am going to make him sweat with this outfit.

It takes me a few seconds to get the straps fixed correctly and to be situated properly in the dress without being exposed, but once every scrap of fabric is in the right place, I take a second to look at myself in the mirror.

Dear God in heaven, I would *never* wear this to a wedding. Never. It's like the green J-Lo dress, you know the one that stole the show at the Grammys? But instead of long sleeves, there are no sleeves at all. Just two thin straps that barely cover my breasts, but my entire stomach is out in the open. There is nothing left to the imagination, and the only place I see this dress being appropriate attire is at a strip club.

But do you think I'm going to let him think that?

Oh no.

I'm going to march out there, let him believe this is a solid contender, and see what he has to say.

Before I leave though, I reach behind my head and undo my hair from my bun, letting the long black strands fall into waves around my shoulders. I adjust my part to add more to my right side, fluff it up, and then smile into the mirror because I know how much he loves it when my hair is down.

If he's going to mess with me, he'd better be prepared for me to come at him harder.

On a deep breath, I slide the curtain open just in time to catch Hardy walking toward me with an arm full of dresses. The moment his eyes land on my body, his lips part and his expression falls flat.

"What do you think?" I ask as I turn around, letting him see my bare back. "I sent a picture to Polly. I think she might like this. She said to pick whatever I'm comfortable in, and this dress is all airy."

"Because it has no fabric," he says as he sets the other dresses on the couch and walks up to me.

"It has fabric," I say as I tug on one of the straps. That's when I notice how hard my nipples are.

I think he notices at the same time because his eyes turn dark, and he wets his lips as he closes the space between us. When he gets only a few inches away, I take a step back and hold out my hand.

"Personal space, please," I say, my hand connecting with his strong, thick chest.

"You're not wearing this," he says as he attempts to reach for me, but I step back again.

"Sorry, sir, but you have no right to an opinion."

"Yes, I fucking do," he says, moving in close again. "I'm the best man."

"Well, pin a rose on your nose," I say, crossing my arms over my chest, which of course draws his attention. "But the last time I checked the wedding handbook, the best man's opinion is pretty low on the pecking order."

His brows crash. "You're not wearing that."

"You know, I hear what you're saying, but I don't really care."

"Don't fuck with me, Everly. You know damn well you're not going to wear that to Polly's wedding, because if you do, you're the one who is going to have all eyes on her, and not the bride."

"How little you know about the people coming to the wedding," I counter.

He moves in another inch, so I scoot back, leaving me directly in the dressing room and then to my chagrin, he steps in close again and draws the curtain shut behind him.

Oh boy.

I've seen that look in his eyes before.

I've noticed the way he wets his lips.

There is one thing on his mind right now, and it's me—and most likely, I'm naked.

Not going to happen.

He closes in on me even more and then places his hand on my hip. "You're not wearing this, and if I have to change you myself, I will."

"As if I would let you see me naked," I say.

"Babe, I've sucked on your tits and your clit—there isn't an inch of your body I haven't seen bare."

"And what's your point?" I ask him. "Just because you've seen it before that doesn't give you the right to see it again."

"All I'm saying is you're not wearing this dress."

"And what I'm saying is you have zero right to an opinion." I shoo my hand at him. "So you can leave now."

He studies me, his eyes going back and forth between mine, ready to snap.

But he doesn't move.

He doesn't give me my space.

His gaze just turns darker, his shoulders grow larger, and his presence turns more commanding.

"Uh, I said you can leave now."

He wets his lips as his fingers slowly drag up my right arm, sending goose bumps all along my skin. When he reaches my shoulder, he gently tugs on the strap, sending it down my arm. I quickly wrap my arms around my breasts so I don't show off anything.

"What do you think you're doing?"

"Not falling for it, Everly."

"Falling for what?" I ask.

"For your game of trying to make me jealous."

I scoff. "I have better things to do with my time, Hardy, than attempt to make you jealous."

"Uh huh," he says skeptically. "If that's the case, then walk out of this store right now with that dress as your choice for the wedding. Prove me wrong."

God, he's annoying. I can't even have this.

I raise my chin. "Out of fear that Maple might be wearing the same dress, I think I'll pick something else." I scoot past him, but he doesn't let me get far as his hand connects with my exposed stomach, stopping me in my place.

"I can help you take it off."

"I'd rather have a rabid dog lick it off me." I push past him and out to where he deposited some dresses on the couch. I paw through them, not finding anything that I would ever wear.

When I straighten back up, I catch him out of the corner of my eye, leaning against the wall of the dressing room, arms folded across his chest, watching my every move.

"Why don't you be helpful," I say. "You're not doing anyone any good by just staring at me."

"Not true. I feel pretty good about it."

I roll my eyes and move toward the rack of dresses again, this time searching for something that would actually be appropriate to wear. The idea of making him jealous quickly backfired, so I'm on to plan B—get out of here as quickly as possible.

Because I'm nervous that if I don't…I will make bad choices.

There's something in the air, something that…that I can't seem to control when he's around.

When I look at him, I have this deep-rooted irritation at him. I'm mad at him.

Angry.

Frustrated.

And yet whenever he seems to come near me, touch me, I can feel that anger and frustration temporarily fade away as my mind wanders back to that night.

A night when I felt cherished and appreciated…desired. When I assumed I was the one he wanted. When he slept next to me all night, naked, occasionally waking me up with his mouth, his soft lips pressing against my warm skin.

As much as I hate to admit it, I still think about that night. I still think about the way it felt to be held by him, touched by him, kissed by him. What it felt like to have him spread my legs and rock in and out of me, demanding more. How I quickly fell victim to his pleasure, his dirty mouth, his unkept promises. That night, he offered me a drug, a high that I seem to keep chasing even though I don't want to.

And that high…it's heavily present right now.

I can see it in his eyes.

Hear it in his voice.

Observe it in the length of his strut and the sturdy set in his shoulders.

He's out to get me again.

He's hungry, and I'm his prey.

And I know I should run away. I should take off at a gallop, get as far away as I can, but there's a nagging voice in the back of my head, a devil on my shoulder, whispering…just one more taste, just one more fuck. Let him give you what you want just one more time.

No.

I'm not.

I'm not going to give in.

It will only hurt me in the end.

So with my chin held high and my mind set on hurrying this along, I sift through the dresses, looking for a simple neckline that won't reveal too much and something classy that I could feel proud representing the business in.

After a few minutes, I find three dresses that I know will work. I just need to check the sizing. So I drape them over my arm and turn toward the dressing room where Hardy is still standing, waiting for me.

"You know, I really have this covered if you want to take off," I say.

"Yeah, that's not going to happen."

I sigh and look him in the eyes. "Hardy, seriously, we all know why you're here and it's not going to work, okay?"

"Why am I here?" he asks as I make my way into the dressing room where he continues to stand.

"To…you know…"

"Uh, I don't, but I would love to hear what you have to say," he says with an annoying smirk.

I hang up the dresses and turn toward him. "To do things…like you did at my office."

"Bring you cronuts?" he asks as he sticks his hands in his pockets. "No, not here for that. After you wouldn't take them the first time, I was insulted. I was here for Polly. Can't imagine what a change it is to add someone to the wedding party on such short notice. So being the best man, I just want to try to make things as easy as possible."

"Which is why you bribed your friend into asking me to be a part of the wedding?"

"Uh, you being a part of the wedding was for George—he wanted to be a groomsman. I'm over here making dreams come true."

"Actually, you're over here making nightmares become reality."

He frowns. "You know, when you say things like that, they hurt."

I roll my eyes and push at his chest, sending him out of the dressing room, only to snap shut the curtain on him.

"You don't need help getting into those dresses?"

"No," I say as I slip out of the barely there dress and into a more suitable mermaid satin dress with a tasteful slit and off the shoulder sleeves. When I turn toward the mirror, I can already tell this is going to be the one. It floats along my curves, hits me in all the right places, doesn't show off too much skin, and most certainly won't steal the show.

The only problem is I'm having trouble with the zipper.

I need to know if it's going to fit, and I'm out of options for help. I part the curtain open to find Hardy hasn't moved. I thought that perhaps he would be on the couch, but instead he's standing right in front of me, and I don't miss his reaction to the dress as his eyes travel the length of my body, pausing every once in a while, until he meets my gaze.

"That's uh…that's a nice dress," he nearly croaks.

I catch his Adam's apple bob.

I take note of the way his hand strokes his beard.

And I can't help but notice the way he tentatively wets his lips as if he's preparing to devour me whole.

They're all desirable signs that I probably would have killed for a week ago, but now...now they're testing me.

They're making me lower my defenses.

They're nudging me, reminding me of just how much I liked this man—well, how much I still like him.

That crush isn't just going to go away. Especially after the night we shared.

I would be lying if I said I didn't think about him every day.

Because I do.

I think about what it would have been like if I woke up that morning and he brought me coffee, a cup we could have shared while I curled into his chest, breakfast being delivered because neither of us really wanted to leave the bed. I think about what that day could have been like. A lazy Saturday with him, taking a shower together, maybe holding hands and taking a walk in the park across from my apartment. The smiles, the laughter, the long, languid moments in bed.

It was what I so desperately wanted and yet I was met with something else.

Something pain-inducing.

Something that has altered the way I perceive this man.

But despite that perception, there are little moments like this where that night, that very special and memorable night, feels so real again.

"You're...you're beautiful, Everly," he says softly, his eyes gazing into mine. Washed away is the sarcasm, the antagonizing behavior, and in its place is only appreciation.

The type of appreciation that's breaking down my thin, poorly constructed wall.

But there's still some resilience in me, so I turn my back toward him. "Can you zip this up for me, so I can make sure it fits?"

"Yes," he says as he steps in closer.

I look up into the mirror in front of me and catch the way he gently gathers my hair and drapes it over my shoulder before gliding his hands down to the zipper and slowly dragging it up.

The air around us is so quiet, so still that I can practically hear and feel every tooth of the zipper as it moves up the chain until I'm fully secured in the dress.

And then he looks into the mirror as well, our gazes locking as he rests his hands on my hips.

I feel my breath start to slow as the room falls silent.

His fingers press against the dress, creating an imprint on my skin.

And when he wets his lips, I can feel my resolve slipping.

No, Everly. Don't.

Don't fall for his awed expression.

Don't fall for the way he holds you.

Don't fall for his words that make you feel desired and wanted.

"I don't think you need to try on anything else," he says, his voice hoarse. The catch in his throat weakens me.

I press my lips together, my body tingling with desire despite my mind telling me otherwise.

"Yeah, I think this will work," I reply softly.

His eyes remain on mine as we continue to stare at each other in the mirror. The electricity bouncing between us makes the vibe feel so heady, so strong that I fear it might take over. That it might create a bad scenario that I'll regret, so before I can let myself slip into decisions I'll end up regretting, I say, "Can you unzip it for me?"

"Yeah," he says quietly. He brings his hands to the zipper of my dress and through the reflection of the mirror, I watch his intense stare as he slowly...and I mean *slowly* unzips my dress, all the way down.

I cup the front so it doesn't fall off me and then take a step away from him. "Can you shut the curtain?"

He hesitates. I can see it in his expression that he doesn't want to, but he offers me a curt nod and then shuts it. I let out a sigh of relief when I'm alone.

Okay, that was intense.

More intense than I prefer.

For a second there, I thought there was a chance we were going to have a repeat of what happened at the office.

And even though I'm so angry at him, I wouldn't have been surprised if I gave in, because despite the way I feel about him and the way he treated me, I still feel this clawing attraction toward him.

I still very much like him...

On a heavy sigh, I slide the dress down my body, step out of it, and then gather it by the hanger loops. I bring it up to the hanger and carefully situate it just as I hear Hardy's voice right next to the curtain.

"Want to hand me the dresses you're not getting so I can hang them up?"

I gulp, because having him that close when I'm wearing nothing but a thong has my body tingling, very aware of his presence.

"Sure," I say as I gather the few dresses in the dressing room.

I hand him one, pushing it past the curtain, and he takes it.

I do the same thing with two more and as I pass him the last one, the curtain parts just enough for his eyes to catch mine.

I bring my arm up around my breasts to stay covered up, but I don't have to worry—his eyes never stray from mine.

They stay steady.

Fixed.

Like he's locked in, unwavering, communicating with me through his gaze.

He wets his lips.

My eyes fall to his mouth.

He sets the dresses down.

My heart stumbles in my chest.

He parts the curtain open.

My body shivers.

And when he takes a step forward, closing any possible space between us, I feel a tap on the defensive wall I've tried to keep up when I'm around him. A tap just light enough to cause a crack.

So when his arm wraps around my waist, I don't stop him.

And when his hand tilts my chin up, I wet my lips.

And when his mouth descends upon mine, I press my hand to his chest to brace for impact.

His lips meet mine in a fever of a kiss.

A demanding kiss.

A kiss so hungry that I can feel it all the way down to my toes as our mouths mold together, him stealing my breath as he threads his hand into my hair.

"Fuck," he whispers as he pulls away just enough to remove his shirt and drop it to the floor.

My worries, my reservations, they are completely tossed away as I slip into this dreamlike state, where this is real. His feelings for me are real. Into a world where he never hurt me. Where he never made me question my worth. Where he wanted me that morning...wanted me just like he wants me right now.

Gripping my hips, he gently moves me up against the dressing room wall where he lifts me up, and I instinctively wrap my legs around his waist, anchoring myself right over his bulge.

His hands move up my sides as he continues to kiss me with deep hunger, and all I can do is try to match his intensity or give in and let him take over.

When his thumbs land right below my breasts, gently swiping under them, I know there's only one thing I can do...let him take the lead.

Because this is too much. This is too overwhelming.

This feels far too incredible to not get lost.

And that's what's happening—I'm getting lost.

Lost with every kiss.

Every stroke.

Every grunt that falls past his lips.

I'm getting lost in him…

CHAPTER TWENTY-SEVEN
HARDY

SHE TASTES SO GOOD.

She feels amazing.

She smells unbelievable.

I have never wanted a woman like I want Everly, and with every press of my mouth to hers, my body becomes more and more out of control with need.

Was my intention when I came here to get her naked and sink myself deep inside of her?

No.

But the minute she started trying on dresses, it was hard not to want that.

Not to want her.

And I tried.

Fuck, did I try.

Might not seem like it, but it was a Herculean effort not to strip her down after that first dress. But the second…the second was my undoing.

She was stunning.

Breathtaking.

She short-circuited my thoughts and what I was trying to accomplish.

I couldn't think of anything past the fact that I wanted to taste her lips again. I wanted to hear her soft moans. I wanted to feel her grip me with such force that my eyes have no other option than to roll in the back of my head as I drive into her.

It's why I can't stop myself, why my hand inches over her breast, and why I feel total satisfaction when she moans while I squeeze her, allowing my thumb to slide over her nipple while my mouth devours hers.

"God," she whispers as her back arches and her chest presses into mine.

I release her lips and kiss up her jaw, to her ear where I quietly say, "You unravel me, Everly." I roll her nipple between my fingers, causing her to gasp. "You unnerve me." I pinch her nipple, only to release it, letting her feel pleasure in the pressure. "You make me feel mad, insane, so fucking needy that I can't think straight."

I drag my lips down her neck, across her collarbone and to her breasts where I lap at her nipple with my tongue.

Her hand sifts into my hair, tugging, pulling, creating a tingling sensation along my scalp as I continue to play with her breasts, soaking in every second of this bliss.

When I first kissed her, I half-expected her to pull back and tell me to stop, and I would have.

When she didn't, I felt my mind snap, my urges take hold, and now I want it all.

I keep her pinned against the wall, bring my mouth back up to hers, and then work my hands between us so I can undo my pants. But to my surprise, she moves my hands away and does it herself. It takes a bit of finagling, but when she's done, she pushes them down just enough for me to take over the rest, leaving my cock stretching between us.

She groans when she feels me at first, and then to my utter surprise, she grinds against me, letting me feel how wet she is through the fabric of her thong.

Fuck.

"Uhhh," I exhale. "You feel so good, so wet." I slide my hand between us again and move her thong to the side, letting her slick pussy drag along my length. "Fuck, Everly," I whisper. "I need to be inside of you."

She continues to thrust her slick center along my length, every stroke shooting waves of pleasure through me, lighting me up inside to the point that I start to sweat with desire.

Her pace picks up and so does her breath as her arms loop around my neck, grounding her better.

"Uhhhh God," she says as she curls in closer, her body moving faster.

"That feel good, Everly?" I ask. "You getting close?"

"Yes," she whispers as she continues to stroke herself, using me for her own pleasure, which only makes this that much better. I want her to use me. I want her to find her pleasure. I want her coming apart in my arms.

"Then ride me, Everly. Fuck me. Get off. Come all over my fucking cock."

"Fuck," she yells as she moves even faster, her hips flying, her grunts so fucking pure, so fucking sexy that I can't do anything but watch her pleasure play out. I hold still, being the anchor for her so she can use me.

"Fuck...fuck," she says. "Ohhhhhhh fuck," she yells just as her warmth spreads over my cock, and she starts coming. Her head flies forward, her mouth landing on my shoulder as she bites me, her orgasm rocking her so hard that she breaks skin.

But I love it.

I fucking live for it.

I stay still, my hard-on throbbing, begging for more, begging to feel her contract around me, but I let her ride out her pleasure until she rests her head against the wall, her body sinking into bliss as it slowly climbs down from the clouds.

That's when I make my move.

I lower us both to the floor. I kick off my shoes and pants and boxer briefs and then take a seat on the floor, pulling her back on my lap.

She's dazed, smiling, marred from my coarse beard rubbing all over her silky soft skin.

It only makes me that much harder.

I grab my wallet, pull out a condom, and slip it on quickly before I bring my mouth to hers again by looping my hand to the nape of her neck and pulling her in close.

And she comes in easily, but now her kisses are more frenzied. Not languid.

Her hands are passing over my heated skin. Not timid.

And she lifts up on her knees, positioning me at her entrance. Not shy in the slightest.

She teases me, lets me feel a hint of her warmth, but doesn't let me enter. She just poses me there, driving me crazy.

"Everly, fuck, take my cock."

But she doesn't listen; instead she strokes my length with her hand, not giving me what I want.

I want her heat. Her warmth.

"Babe," I say, unable to control myself. "I need that cunt."

But she doesn't sit down on me.

She removes her hand and circles her hips, just letting me tease her entrance.

"Uhhhhhhh, fuck," I moan. "Everly, pl—"

I don't get the words out because within a second, she sits down on my cock, fully inserting me, so deep inside that I see fucking stars.

"Mother-fucker," I groan as my stomach bottoms out and every muscle inside of me seizes. "Everly, I…" Fuck, I'm going to come fast.

Her hands smooth up my chest, up my neck, and right to my face before her lips descend upon mine. Her tongue runs over my mouth and then inside where she dances it across mine.

It's an onslaught of sensations, pulsing through me and driving up my desire to the breaking point in seconds.

Her hips drive over my cock.

Her hands keep me locked in.

And she pulses over my length, squeezing me so goddamn tight that I have no other option than for her to take control.

"You're going to make me come," I say when she pulls her mouth away and brings those devilish lips to my neck.

Her hands move to my chest, her fingers right to my nipples where she plays with the hard nubs.

"Fuck, yes, that's it, baby," I say as I thrust up into her when she pinches my nipples. "Christ, Everly."

She brings her mouth back to mine where she kisses me again, her tongue desperately playing with mine, the urgency between the two of us climbing to a frantic rate.

I need more.

I need deeper.

I move her off my lap and place her on all fours on the floor of the dressing room and then I get behind her, position my cock at her entrance and then drive into her with one giant force.

"Hardy...fuck," she yells as her head falls forward, and she presses her hand to the wall, bracing herself so I don't fuck her right into it.

I'm mad with desire.

Frantic to come.

So goddamn turned on that I can feel every nerve in my body zeroing in on my orgasm that is building on the base of my spine.

I want her coming with me, so I take her breast in my hand and start massaging it, playing with her nipple, pinching just enough to force her to contract around me.

And it's just what I need.

That warm, wet pussy squeezing me so goddamn tight.

It's heaven.

So I keep playing with her nipple and every time I squeeze, I thrust inside of her, seeking out that contraction. It's a drug, a feeling so fucking desirable that I'm chasing it every chance I get.

"I fucking love this pussy," I say as my pace picks up. "You make me come so fucking...hard." I grunt out the last part as the early signs of my orgasm start to tighten my balls. "Fuck, Everly, I'm there."

I bring my hand to her clit where I spread her and play with the aroused nub. I still my hips, wanting to bring her to completion so I can feel the sweet tightening of her walls.

I lean forward, pressing kisses between her shoulder blades, over her back, holding off on my orgasm, waiting for her, driving her forward, wanting to experience this together.

"Fuck," she whispers, indicating she's getting close. "Ohhhh yes, right there, Hardy. Right there." Her back arches, her stomach hollows, and her breath catches in her throat. "Right...there."

I swirl my fingers over her clit a few more times, her body tensing, tightening, and then her pussy starts contracting around my cock as she shouts out my name.

I keep circling her clit, prolonging her orgasm as I begin driving into her again, riding out every pulse.

My muscles tense, my back stiffens, and my cock swells as I spill inside of her, my orgasm ripping through me in seconds.

"Yes, baby," I grunt as she continues to contract around me.

And I revel in it.

In every goddamn second until there is nothing left to take.

That's when I pull out, but not before placing another kiss on her back.

I stand up and remove the condom, tying it off. I quickly slip on my briefs and then walk through the empty store and straight to the bathroom where I wrap the condom in some toilet paper and toss it in the garbage to go undetected. I take a second to wash my hands and then I walk back to the dressing room where I find Everly already dressed and adjusting her hair.

Well...fuck.

When her eyes meet mine in the mirror, I can feel the distance in that one gaze, as if she just shut the door on her soul, leaving not even the barest glimmer of what lies inside.

I walk up to her, but she moves past me and strides over to the couch, sitting down to put on her shoes.

Yup, she's shutting down.

Quickly, I get dressed in silence, trying to think of a way to close this gap, to make things right. The desire is there. The attraction is there...I fucking know for certain the connection is there. I've never connected with a woman like I've connected with Everly.

Now I just need to figure out how to break through the mistake I made and prove to her that I won't do it again. I was hoping the sex we just had would have warmed her up, but from the tension in her shoulders and her pursed lips, I could be incredibly wrong about that.

I bring my shoes over to the couch as well, and when I take a seat, she starts to stand, but I take her by the hand and tug her back down.

"Everly, can we talk?"

"There's nothing to say," she says.

"Uh, I think there's a whole lot to say."

"No, Hardy. There's nothing to say. Once again, that shouldn't have happened, we should have—"

"Shouldn't have happened?" I tuck my finger under her chin and bring her eyes to meet mine. "Everly, there's a reason why that keeps happening, and I think that's something we should talk about."

"No." She shakes her head. "There's nothing to talk about, because... because there's nowhere to go from here. We just need to get through this weekend, through this work event. Then we can go our separate ways, and I would appreciate it if—"

"Go our separate ways?" I feel my stomach sink, and I realize immediately that this approach is not working either.

Sure, she probably feels desired.

Possibly satisfied for a moment.

But it's not breaking down the wall she's erected between us—the wall I forced her to build.

Which means this is going to be my last-ditch effort.

I have to put it all out there and hope for the best.

"Yes, Hardy. Go our separate ways," she repeats.

"I don't want to do that," I say, my nerves clawing at me as I stare into her beautiful eyes. "I don't want to lose you. My life…" I gulp. "My life has felt empty since that morning. I miss our emails, our texts, our conversations. I miss seeing you and listening to you tell me about your day. I miss our jokes and our dinner dates and the way you smile whenever you see me." I take her hand in mine, and she stares down at the connection. "I miss you, Everly. You're…you're all I think about. Constantly. Night and day, you're on my mind. And I was a fucking fool that morning. I should have…fuck, I should have handled things differently. I should have—"

"It doesn't matter," she says, freeing her hand from my grasp. And when her eyes meet mine, I can distinctly see the dissociation in them, like the words I'm saying aren't even coming close to clicking in her head.

"Everly," I say, my voice nearly shaking as panic grips me. "It does matter." She attempts to look away, but I turn her head, practically begging her to look at me. "This, *us*, it matters, and I will do anything…and I mean anything to fix things between us."

"Why?" she asks. "You told me there can't be anything between us. So what's the point? I can't…" Her voice catches in her throat, and it brings me to my goddamn knees. "I can't sit here and act like we're just friends. I can't hang out with you and pretend like I don't have feelings for you… or…had feelings for you." The use of past tense guts me. "It's too hard. And I'm sorry that you miss me, and you miss our friendship, but I'm not in a position where I can just ignore this…this physical connection we have. And honestly, I have no idea why you think it's okay to just…to fuck me and then ask to be my friend."

"I'm not asking you to be my friend, Everly," I say, desperation heavy in my voice. "I'm asking for so much more."

"But why? You yourself said you can't be romantically involved with me because of your sister, and yet you're putting me in situations where you're feeding into this desire—and for what?" Her voice is rising, becoming shakier as she stands. "So you can just fuck with my head, Hardy?"

"What? No," I say, realizing that she doesn't know I had a conversation with Haisley. I'd been waiting for the perfect time to tell her that we have Haisley's blessing, but now I've just tangled things up even more.

Jesus Christ, I've fucked this up so badly.

"Just stay away from me," she says, moving past me and grabbing her dress.

"Everly, wait," I say as I stand as well. "It's not like that."

"I don't want to hear it." She picks up the dresses I didn't put away and brings them over to the rack, where she hangs them up.

I watch her angrily make sure everything is in place and when she's done, she heads toward the shop's back door, and I follow closely behind.

"Everly, can I just explain?"

"No," she snaps. "I never should have let you touch me in the first place. I swore to myself that I wouldn't. That I wouldn't give in, and then, God, one look from you and I'm breaking every rule in my head. I'm such an idiot."

"You're not," I say as she opens the door and steps out with her dress draped over her arm. "Everly, this is all just one big mistake."

"Yeah, tell me about it," she says as she ushers me out of the store and shuts the door. She presses a few buttons on the keypad, and the lock clicking into place fills the silence between us.

And with that, she heads toward her car, which is parked on the street behind the store.

"I didn't mean it like that," I say, pushing my hand through my hair. "I meant how I handled all of this."

"Yeah, well, it was probably best so I didn't get too attached. Breaking me on morning one was the way to go, Hardy. Now I just need to stick to that broken spirit and stop believing there could be more."

"But there could be," I say, moving in front of her so I can look her in the eyes. When her watery gaze meets mine, it feels like a gut punch so deep that I can feel the pain all the way through every nerve ending. "I spoke with Haisley, Everly. She said...she said she just wants us to be happy."

A lone tear rolls down Everly's cheek and before I can brush it away for her, she wipes it herself.

"Is that supposed to make me feel better?" she asks. "Is that supposed to make me throw my arms around you and celebrate?"

"I...well...no," I say with a pinch to my brow. "But I thought—"

"You thought what, Hardy? That I was going to automatically forget about everything else? And if she wasn't going to stand in the way of anything happening, then why would you once again fuck around with me? Why not just tell me?"

I drag my hands down my face as frustration engulfs me.

Not frustration with her, but frustration with myself.

"Because I thought that I could warm you up first, show you that I wanted you and then, I don't know...tell you that we could be together."

She shakes her head. "Wow, Hardy, and here I thought you were a smart man." She takes a step back from me. "You realize the kind of torment I've been putting myself through, right? I hated myself the day you came into my office because I wanted nothing to do with you, and then there I was, wanting you so badly, giving in to temptation and comfort— the same comfort you gave me that night. But at what expense? You should have told me then that everything was cool with Haisley."

"I didn't think you would believe me, that you would accept that answer. I wanted to show you that I wanted you, that you were the person for me regardless of my family or work or anything else."

"By continuing to mess with my head? You're playing games, Hardy, and I don't want to and won't be part of it." She turns on her heel and walks toward her car.

"Everly, wait," I say as I jog after her. When I touch her shoulder, she spins on me, her finger going right to my chest.

"Don't," she says in a stern tone. "Don't touch me. Don't come near me. I'm not kidding when I say whatever this was…is…it's over. After this weekend, I will be asking Maggie to move me off any events with the Hoppers and the Canes. I'll have Scarlett take them over because I'm done. I don't want this." She looks me in the eyes. "And I don't want you."

Her words slice right through me as she turns away, opens her car door, shoves her dress in and then slams the door shut.

I stand there, stunned, gasping for air as I realize just how badly I fucked this up.

How I lost her because of my own dumb choices.

How I probably won't recover from this, because the girl I'm supposed to be with, the girl I've fallen for…my girl…she's driving away with no intention of ever seeing me again.

———

"I know my dad's speech was a bit boring," Ken says, coming up to me at the bar. "But I didn't think it was so boring that it would make the best man seem like a depressed sack of potatoes."

A sack of potatoes on one of the fanciest rooftop bars in San Francisco—not sure that's what Ken and Polly's parents were going for with this rehearsal dinner. And I attempted to tuck myself away from the romantic ambience—with the twinkle lights shining above the soon-to-be-married couple, the soft instrumental music pouring through hidden speakers setting the mood for friends and family to pair up and peacefully sway together.

But it looks like I've been found.

Leaning my forearms against the bar counter, I stare down at my glass of water—far too depressed to even consider alcohol. "Sorry, man. I swear I'll get it together for tomorrow."

Though I have no idea how I plan on doing that, since I'll have a hard-as-fuck time not staring and pining after Everly during the entire wedding ceremony and celebration.

I half expected her to show up tonight to the rehearsal, but Maple said that she had another event she had to tend to, which I don't fully believe. I think she's skipping out on tonight to avoid me. Polly was okay with Everly missing the wedding rehearsal because it's not like Everly needs practice walking down the aisle; she's the one who tells people how to properly do it.

"Want to talk about it?" Ken asks.

"Not really," I say as I lean back in my bar chair.

"Well, I don't think you have a choice."

"Why do you say that?" I ask.

"Because Polly and Maple are on their way over here, and they don't look happy."

"Christ," I mumble just as they walk up to us, both of them standing on my right-hand side, arms crossed.

"He doesn't want to talk about it," Ken says, and I'm grateful he's taking the lead.

"And I don't want a moping best man at my rehearsal dinner, so it looks like he doesn't have an option," Polly says.

I let out a huff and drag my hand over my mouth. "Can we just…not? I promise I'll be good for tomorrow, and if you want me to leave early tonight, I can."

"Leave early? You're my ride," Ken says.

Oh…right.

Jesus, I really need to get it together.

Sitting up, I shake out my shoulders and then spin on my barstool to face my friends. "Okay, right, I'm sorry." I slap on the fakest smile I can muster. "So, those oysters, they were…slimy, huh?"

"They were," Polly says with a skeptical look in her eyes. "But we didn't come here to chat about my mother's poor taste in hors d'oeuvres. We came here to see why the hell Everly is avoiding the rehearsal dinner when you had a chance to patch things up yesterday?"

"Those tuna tartare bites though," I say, ignoring Polly completely. "They were great."

"I had five," Ken says, patting his stomach.

"Kenneth," Polly snaps at him. "We are not engaging in his topic avoidance. We are getting to the bottom of this Everly thing."

"Right." Ken clears his throat. "Sorry, dear." Then he nudges me with his elbow. "I get to marry that spitfire tomorrow."

That seems to soften Polly only slightly, but just enough for her to say in a calmer tone, "Okay, what happened?"

I sigh, knowing I'm not going to avoid this conversation. "It's just... not going to happen between us. I fucked up too many times. Hurt her too many times. She's done with me. Said it to my face, and honestly, I think I should just let her be. She was...she was really upset yesterday, and I don't like seeing her upset. I want her to be happy, and if moving on without me makes her happy, then that's what I want."

"But how did you mess up?" Maple asks gently. "I thought everything was good with Haisley."

I slowly nod. "Yes, it is, but I didn't tell Everly that until yesterday and that was after, well, I won't go into detail, but let's just say we did some things in that store."

"Dear God," Polly says. "So you fucked her."

"For lack of a better term," I say.

"And you didn't tell her about Haisley until after that?"

"When she was trying to walk away from me."

"Oh my God," Maple says, disgust in her voice. "What is wrong with you?"

"I don't know." I toss my hands up in the air. "That's an amazing question because I honestly have no idea what's wrong with me. I have never in my life made this many mistakes consecutively. It's like I've lost all ability to act like a normal human and have transformed into the epitome of a dumbass."

"I'm not going to argue with that," Polly says. "I thought you were going to make up with her yesterday, so you could spend the wedding together, dancing and having a good time."

"Yeah, that would have been ideal, but seems like I don't know how to fix my mistakes when it comes to her." I shake my head. "It's best if we just drop it."

"But do you want to drop it?" Maple asks. "I thought you liked her."

"More than like her," I say softly.

"Oh. My. God," Polly says, gripping my shoulder. "Do you love her, Hardy?"

"I mean...I've fallen for her pretty damn hard, and I think...I think that's why I've been such an idiot." I shoot Maple an apologetic look. "No offense, but I don't think I've ever felt this way for another person before."

Maple nods. "None taken. I know that it wasn't that deep for us. I understand the stakes are higher here, and it makes sense. Our relationship was easy, simple, predictable. But with Everly, it goes so much deeper, and because of that more intense connection, you don't know how to function without her in your life."

"Exactly," I say. "It's like I'm panicking every time I see her, afraid that I'm going to mess up because I don't want to lose her. I don't want to lose what we have. But all that panic just hindered me, and I still ended up losing her." I pick up my glass of water from the bar and stare down at it for a moment. "She really wants nothing to do with me. Trust me when I say there's no chance of rectifying this."

"Are you sure?" Polly asks. "I feel like there has to be a bridge we can mend."

I shake my head. "No, she was very clear last night. I hurt her, badly, and she wants to move on. She doesn't want to give me another chance.

So please don't even try." I look at both Maple and Polly. "Seriously, don't try."

Polly slouches against the bar, blowing out a heavy breath. "Well, this is stupid. Now I'm depressed."

"Not something a groom wants to hear his bride say the night before their wedding," Ken chimes in.

"Aren't you depressed?" Polly asks. "Your best friend has lost his chance at an epic ending of a friends-to-lovers romance."

Ken glances at me and then back at Polly. "A what?"

Polly groans. "Ugh, you're irritating." She then turns toward me, desperation on her face. "Are you sure it's over? Like, absolutely positive?"

"Yes," I say, looking her dead in the eyes. "It's over. There's nothing left to do other than let her be…"

And admitting that hurts possibly even more than losing her.

I'm never one to give up, but I know when I'm fighting a losing battle.

And this battle with Everly? It's over.

CHAPTER TWENTY-EIGHT
EVERLY

Hardy: I know you told me to leave you alone, but I wanted to send you a text to let you know I'm giving you space at the wedding. Don't worry about having to dodge me. I want you to be comfortable and have fun, so I'll keep my distance. Thank you for being there for Ken and Polly. I appreciate it.

I STARE DOWN AT HARDY'S text as I sit in my car in front of the hotel where I'm meeting Polly, tears filling my eyes.

I turn my phone over and lean my head back against the headrest, taking deep breaths to calm myself.

You're a professional, Everly.

You can do this.

You can get through this wedding without crying.

Without thinking about him.

Unfortunately, that's what I tried to convince myself of yesterday when I was supposed to go to the rehearsal dinner, but since I couldn't get it together, I cancelled on Polly, letting her know I had another event.

Well, that other event was actually a sobfest put on by yours truly. I spent the entire night in my apartment, crying into my pillow while I inhaled the lingering scent he left behind from our one night together.

So freaking pathetic.

But that can't be me today.

I have a job to do…and though it may be a phony job, I am still a professional and will see through my commitments.

I will get through this wedding, take pictures, smile at the reception, and after dinner is served, I will slip out, knowing my duties are done.

Simple as that.

I can do this.

I was made to get through tough things, this being one of them.

Taking a deep breath, I fold down my car visor, open up the mirror, and wipe at my face, attempting to brush away my sadness and put on a bright smile for the bride.

When the lump in my throat has dissipated and the redness in my cheeks has calmed down, I gather the bag that's next to me as well as my dress, and I exit my car, ready to take on this challenge.

If anything, I've always enjoyed a good challenge, and this is no exception.

I'm going to walk into the bridal suite, show just how ready I am for this wedding, and be the best bridesmaid ever to be hired.

Shoulders held back, I walk into the opulent conservatory and make my way toward the beautiful old garden, one of my all-time favorite venues here. Once a botanical garden open to the public, a new owner took over and has turned the glass conservatory into a wedding venue, hiring a twenty-four-hour garden staff to maintain the stunning plants, and turning the inside of the conservatory into a paradise for parties. It's on the smaller size, so there is just enough room for a group of one hundred and fifty, along with a dance floor. But when the San Francisco weather cooperates, the conservatory's attached courtyard offers more space and is surrounded by native foliage, botanicals of vibrant colors, and water features that set a beautiful, serene ambiance for any event, especially a wedding.

Today, we will be having the ceremony in the courtyard and hopefully getting inside just before the rain is supposed to start. There's a small window, so I hope we can make it.

And because the owner was thinking about the conservatory with weddings in mind, they turned two of the garden sheds into bride and groom suites, each on opposite ends of the venue.

I'm headed toward the bride's suite.

My feet crunch against the gravel of the path that leads to the back of that suite, not needing to stop and talk to anyone because the whole staff already knows me here. I glance over at the courtyard where white chairs are lined up, the archway opening up on a shrub maze covered in beautiful pink, purple, and white flowers. Just stunning.

Polly and Ken's moms did a beautiful job picking everything out. From the votives lining the aisle, to the choice in flowers and venue, this will be a wedding they will never forget.

As I near the bride's suite, I remind myself that I am smiling, keeping it together, and being the consummate professional.

I can do this.

I plaster on a smile, knock on the door, and when I hear Polly call out "Come in," I open it and step inside to find Polly in a chair getting her hair styled, and Maple sitting across from her, getting her makeup done.

And for some stupid reason, seeing their welcoming faces, it…it does something to me.

It reminds me of the night of the party, the night Hardy and I got together, and before I can stop myself, my emotions get the better of me.

My lip quivers.

My eyes well up with tears.

And my stomach heaves in embarrassment as I let out a feral sob.

"Oh my God," Polly says as she gets up from the chair and comes up to me, pulling me into a hug. Holding me tightly, she turns toward the makeup and hair artists. "Can you give us a moment?"

"That's not necessary," I say, snot forming in my nose.

"It is," Polly says and then brings me over to the couch that's a focal point in the room, a place where mothers of the bride usually sit and watch their daughters get ready.

I hear the makeup and hair artists leave the room just as Polly and I sit on the couch, Maple coming to sit right next to me as well.

"I'm sorry," I say as Polly hands me a tissue. "This wasn't supposed to happen. I came here with every intention of being professional and not bringing my personal issues into this wedding…but the moment I saw you two, I was just…reminded. I'm sorry." I dab at my eyes. "Just give me a second."

"You don't need to apologize," Polly says. "I'm the one who pulled you into this mess. If you need to cry, then you cry."

"No, it's your wedding day." I take a deep breath and swipe at my eyes with the tissue. "I'm not going to sit here and cry. We are going to celebrate."

Maple places her hand on my leg. "Everly, we are not going to bypass the fact that you're upset. You've helped us so much these last two months, and now it's time for us to help you."

"Seriously, it's not—"

"He's fallen for you," Polly shouts over me.

"Huh?" I ask.

Maple stands and walks over to Polly's side where she takes a seat on the arm of the couch, so I can look at them both at the same time. With a serious tone and a sincere expression, Maple repeats, "He's fallen for you."

"What…what are you talking about?" I ask, even though I know exactly what they're talking about.

"Hardy," Polly says. "He has fallen for you. He told us last night at the rehearsal. He's miserable, pathetic, and beyond regretful for how he treated you. He was a real downer last night and told me he promised to be better today, but I know the minute he sees you, he's just going to return to the depressed state he was in last night."

"Depressed state?" I ask.

Polly slowly nods. "Yes, Everly. When I say I've never seen him like this, I'm not lying. He's so far gone where you're concerned and truly believes that he's lost any chance at being with you."

"Has he?" Maple asks.

I look between the both of them, their hopeful faces making me feel sick to my stomach. "Uh...I just...I can't." My eyes well up again and I hate myself for it. *Come on, Everly, get it under control.*

"You can't what?" Polly asks. "Talk about it or be with him?"

"Both," I say while Maple hands me another tissue.

Silence falls between us as Polly gently rubs my back.

After a few seconds, she says, "Well, that's...that's unacceptable."

"What?" I ask, wiping away another tear.

Polly shakes her head. "This is not what I signed up for. This...this pursuit, it can't end like this."

"What do you mean it can't end like this?" I ask.

"She means you're supposed to be with him. Simple as that," Maple puts in. "All of this happened for a reason—you trying to help him to get close with me again, when in reality you two were forming a deep bond. This wedding brought you two together. I saw it with my own eyes the night of the double date. You have a connection that is unlike anything I've seen before, and he knows it. He feels it. He wants it. It just can't end like this. You and Hardy belong together."

"You do," Polly adds. "And I know he hurt you. We are *not* forgetting that part because your feelings are valid, but...he apologized, right?"

I slowly nod. "He did."

"And even with that apology, you can't forgive him?"

I twist my hands in my lap. "I'm just...I'm scared," I admit and then look up at both Polly and Maple. "You don't know this, but I've liked Hardy for a while now." I clear my throat. "Uh, was crushing on him hard when he asked me to help him get back together with you, Maple."

"Wait…really?" she asks with a concerned expression. "You were helping him get close with me when you were crushing on him?"

I nod again, more tears flowing down my cheeks. "When he initially asked me to help, I thought he was asking me out. It was sort of a blow. Either way, I said yes, and the more time I spent with him, the more I hoped and wished that he was going to maybe see me for who I was, not just the girl helping him get back together with his ex. And then when he finally did see me, it was…" I dab at my eyes with the tissue. "It was everything I hoped for, an actual dream becoming reality, only for the reality to come to a crashing halt. I was so hurt, so damaged that it scared me. It still scares me because I like him so much. I can't stop thinking about him, but I don't want to feel that pain…this current pain. I hate it."

Polly takes my hand in hers and rubs her thumb over my knuckles. "I'm so sorry, Everly. We had no idea."

"That makes me so…sad. I wish I'd known," Maple murmurs.

"It's fine," I say as I continue to wipe away my tears. "No one really knew besides my sister. It was why I was trying to date other guys, because I was trying to forget about him. But it was impossible. So after everything that happened that morning when he told me he couldn't be with me… three different ways, it was like a dagger to my soul, crushing and heart-breaking. This man that I've wanted for so long, trying everything in his power to let me down gently. It just…it—"

"It wasn't his truth," Maple says. When I look up at her, she gives me a kind smile. "That wasn't his truth. Was he a dumbass in that moment? Yes, but it wasn't how he felt. He wanted nothing more than to be with you. But his brother got in his head, and given the situation with his father and not wanting to damage the family any more, Hardy would have done anything to keep his siblings close, even if that meant giving up what he wants."

"She's right," Polly adds. "Hardy is very loyal, and if Hudson put up a fight, then he would have stepped back to make sure he didn't hurt his siblings."

"He's never fought like this before," Maple says. "I know because he didn't fight for us, and I'm okay with that—we weren't supposed to be together. I like to think that my relationship with Hardy was a pathway for you two to find each other. I know you're scared, and I know he hurt you, but it wasn't intentional. Hardy would never do that. He's a good guy, a solid guy, the kind of guy that you want in your life. He'll be good to you, Everly. He'll be a partner—someone you can rely on. Please don't block him out of your life because he was an idiot the morning after, or an idiot in handling this whole situation."

"And he owns up to being the idiot. Last night he told us all about it and how he wishes he could take it all back, have a do-over." Polly looks me dead in the eyes. "I think he's in love with you, Everly, and if you don't let him back in, if you don't allow him to have another chance, then you're going to be missing out on a great man."

My lip quivers.

More tears build behind my eyes.

And I lean back against the couch, letting out a deep breath as I stare up at the ceiling.

"I think I'm in love with him too," I say, surrendering to these feelings that won't stop racing through me no matter how hard I try to block them out. "And I don't think I can stop it from happening."

"You're not supposed to stop love, Everly, you're supposed to embrace it." Polly tugs on my hand, forcing me to look at her. "It will be okay, I promise. He won't hurt you again, and if he does, I'll be first in line to hurt him."

Maple holds up her hand. "Second."

I chuckle and cover my face with my hands. "Ugh, this is not why I'm here. This day is about you."

"In that case," Polly says, "I demand that you make things right with Hardy."

"Polly—"

"I'm serious. It's the least you can do for putting me ten minutes behind on hair and makeup." She smiles softly. "Seriously, I have an idea, a way to seal the deal on this romance you two have been working through."

"I love ideas," Maple says. "Especially when they're demanded by the bride, because you have no other choice. If she demands it, you have to do it."

"Precisely," Polly says. "So...are you ready to make things right with Hardy?"

I look between the two of them and despite the nerves bouncing through me, I say, "I hope I can trust you two."

A large smile spreads across both of their faces. "Oh, you can trust us," Polly says. "We were the ones who made the night of your dreams happen...it's only poetic this comes full circle now."

HARDY

Smile.

Breathe.

Smile...

Breathe.

Two words and two words only have been on repeat in my head since the moment we started taking pre-ceremony pictures.

I've been chill all morning, hanging out with Ken and a very excited George who bought us all matching socks because he was so thrilled to be a groomsman. I've kept my mind on my friend and not the impending photo session and ceremony, where I knew I'd have to see Everly. I did a good job, but fuck, the moment I saw her in that dress, I felt my heart crash to the ground.

The dress is hugging her in all the right places but not showing off too much. When she walks, the slit shows off a glimmer of her leg, reminding me of how they felt wrapped around my waist. And her hair, sleek and curled on the ends, hangs like a black velvet curtain over her shoulders, tucked behind her ears so her heart-shaped face is on display. And those lips, painted in a simple rose color, shine against the light of the day, tugging on my heart, reminding me of how much I lost.

She is stunning.

So goddamn beautiful that I've had a really hard time keeping my eyes off her.

And I think I've held it together for the most part. I've kept my distance like I promised. I've stolen glances when she hasn't been looking—well, she's only caught me staring twice. But now, as I stand next to Ken, him reciting his vows to Polly, the clouds rolling in, ready to downpour any second, I can feel this ache so deep in my soul that I'm not sure how I'm going to make it through the reception.

"It is with the greatest pleasure…" the reverend says, but I tune him out as I glance over at Everly for the hundredth time since the ceremony started.

I catch the tears in her eyes, the joy in her expression.

Even with everything I put her through, she still can look past that and see the love between two people, really feel and celebrate it.

It makes me want her that much more.

The crowd cheers, knocking me out of my thoughts and reminding me that I need to participate, so I clap as well while Ken and Polly start heading down the aisle.

Thankfully I'm paired up with Maple, so we meet in the middle of the aisle, she loops her arm through mine, and we follow behind Ken and Polly all the way into the conservatory. When we stop in the middle of the dance floor, I grow confused, because from what the wedding planner said yesterday, we were supposed to branch off and take more pictures. Did plans change?

"Are we supposed to be doing something?" I ask, my back toward Everly. "I thought the wedding planner said we were taking family and bridal party photos?"

"No, we took enough," Polly says. "We actually want to get into first dances."

"Oh," I say with a nod as the guests start to filter in as well. Isn't there supposed to be a happy hour or something? This seems so...odd.

"Let's get out of the way," Maple says, tugging me to the edge of the dance floor as Ken wraps his arm around Polly. And then as if everyone was instructed, no one takes a seat. Instead, all the guests circle the dance floor, and the lights dim, thunder strikes in the distance, and "Thinking Out Loud" by Ed Sheeran starts playing through the speakers surrounding us.

I couldn't have picked a better song for my friends.

Keeping my eyes on them, I catch the glimmer in Polly's eyes as she stares up at her now husband. I see Ken's tight grip as he holds her close. And as they slowly move over the dance floor, the group surrounding them is captured by the love they have for each other. It's undeniable, and all I can think about is how much I wish I had that with Everly.

How I wish I never fucked things up with her.

How I wish that instead of us keeping our distance, her arm was looped through mine.

This evening would be so much better with her by my side, her hand in mine, safe in the knowledge that I wouldn't be going home alone tonight, but instead I'd be going home with my girl.

"You're tensing up," Maple says next to me.

"Am I?" I ask, not noticing.

"Yes, you're squeezing my arm."

"Oh, sorry," I whisper back.

"Everything okay?"

"Yup," I say, even though I'm the furthest thing from okay. "They look great, don't they?"

Maple glances over at Polly and Ken and then back at me. "They are amazing. I'm...I'm proud of them for finding their way back to each other. When they broke up, I almost couldn't believe it. I knew they were meant for each other, so being here at their wedding and witnessing a start of a new chapter, it brings me a lot of joy."

I smile at that. "Me too. They're going to have a beautiful marriage."

"To everyone out there, friends and family, the couple would like you to join them on the dance floor if you're willing," the DJ says into the microphone.

Of course, the older couples are first out on the dance floor, Ken and Polly's parents not being shy in the slightest.

I turn toward Maple. "Do you want to dance?"

"No," she answers flatly.

Okay. Wasn't expecting that answer or an answer so abrupt.

"Not a problem," I awkwardly say just as there is a tap on my arm. I look to the right and feel my entire body seize as my gaze locks in on Everly's green eyes.

A lump immediately grows in my throat, and I can feel all the air escape my lungs because this is how much she affects me.

"May I have this dance?" she asks, holding her hand out.

Uh...is she serious?

She knows she's asking *me*, right?

When I don't answer right away, Maple nudges me. "Of course, he would love to dance with you." And then she pushes me toward the dance floor.

Confused and nervous all at the same time, I turn toward Everly, unsure of how to handle this. "I, uh, I was giving you space," I say awkwardly.

"I know," she replies as she takes my hand in hers and wraps my arm around her waist. "But I'm not looking for space right now."

What?

Before I can ask her what she means, she leads us in a gentle sway, her hand landing on my shoulder, near my neck.

So many thoughts, so many questions are running rapidly through my head, but for once, I don't open my mouth because I don't want to scare her away. I don't want her to regret this decision to dance with me. Because I might not be able to have her, but I can at least have this small moment with her.

After a few seconds of swaying back and forth with her, I can feel her eyes land on me, peering up, looking for a return in her stare. On a deep breath, I look down, and when she smiles up at me, I become weak in the goddamn knees.

"Everly," I say, my throat choking up, but I don't get to finish my sentence because the music stops, and everyone starts clapping.

"The bar is open, and appetizers will be passed around. The bride and groom want you to mingle and enjoy," the DJ says.

Sad the music is over, I let go of Everly and take a step away from her. "Uh...thanks for the dance." I stick my hands in my pockets out of pure survival, because if I don't, I can see myself grabbing her, pulling her into my chest and running my hands through her luscious hair.

"Hardy?" she says, taking a step forward, closing the space I put between us.

"Yes?" I gulp.

Her eyes search mine, and when she grabs my hand, lacing our fingers together, I try not to close my eyes from the feel of it, the connection I so desperately want. "Can we talk?"

I nod. *Please, fuck, let this be a good talk.*

She weaves us through the crowd and toward the front of the conservatory where the lobby opens up to public restrooms and a miniature fountain feature, which helps drown out the echo the tall ceilings and glass walls provide.

She tugs me over to the side, to a bench that is tucked in the corner, near an old gift shop that is now used as a coat check.

When we sit down, she turns toward me and takes both of my hands in hers.

Please let this be good.

Please, fuck, let it be good.

Her thumbs rub over my knuckles, and when those green eyes stare up at me, I can see my future. She's in it. We're wearing matching shirts, holding hands, and sharing a large chocolate cake that we have no intention of finishing but are talking a big game about how we're about to own the sugary confection. I see lazy mornings in my bed, late nights in her apartment sharing a meal, long conversations about nothing and everything. I can feel the love she gives me every day, the affection she bestows upon me, and the comfort in knowing that I have a partner in this life.

"Hardy," she says, her voice sounding nervous.

"Yes?" I ask.

She wets her lips and says, "I was wondering if maybe, uh...you would like to go out on a date with me."

All the air escapes my lungs as I tug her even closer. "Are you serious right now? Please don't be joking—I don't think my heart can take it."

She smiles softly. "I'm not joking. I wouldn't do that."

"I mean, yeah, Everly. Of course. I...fuck, I want nothing more than to take you out, to...to have so much more with you. I..." I feel my words catch in my throat, my thoughts jumbling in my head out of pure excitement. "I didn't think you were interested. I was...I was giving you space."

"I know," she says quietly. "But I don't want space, Hardy." When her eyes meet mine again, I watch, hope welling in me, as they tear up. "I'm falling for you and there's nothing I can do about it. There's no amount of space that can stop it from happening. It just...is."

"Fuck," I say as I bring her hands up to my mouth. I press a kiss to her knuckles. "Everly, I…what…why did you change your mind? I hurt you, and I don't deserve this—I don't deserve you."

"You do," she says with a tilt of her head. She runs her hand over my beard. "And I deserve you. I just needed some people to put that into perspective for me."

"Some people?" I ask with a raise of my brow. "Would those people be Polly and Maple?"

She nods. "Yes, they told me what you said to them last night and, well, they swore you would never hurt me again."

"Never," I say far too quickly. "Fuck, never, Everly. I'm…I'm so sorry about everything. About that morning, about not telling you about Haisley, about how I handled every aspect of this. I've been out of my god-damn mind, unable to figure out how to handle these feelings because…" I look her in the eyes, holding her captive. "Because I'm falling for you too, and I've never felt this way before. Not that it's an excuse, but I handled these feelings terribly. I hurt you, and I swear I will never fucking do it again. I want you, Everly. I want everything about you. I want your charm, your sass, your notes in your notebook. I want to be able to touch you, kiss you, hold you without some sort of ulterior motive. I want your mind, your jokes, your shameless attitude about wearing matching shirts." She smirks. "And I want your heart, to hold in my hands, where I can protect it and never let anything bad ever happen." I tug her toward me, and she slides onto my lap as I cup her cheek. "I want this, us, and I will do everything in my power, if you will let me, to prove to you that I'm the man you deserve."

Her hand presses to my chest. "I already know you are, Hardy. I've known for a long time and there's no changing that in my mind, no matter how hard I try."

"Well, please don't try anymore," I say. "Please be mine."

She grins and presses her forehead against mine. "I'm yours."

"Fuck," I whisper and nuzzle my nose against hers. "I'm so sorry, Everly. So fucking sorry."

"I know," she whispers back and then brings her lips right above mine, a whisper away. "I know."

And then her mouth meets mine. Immediately, I shift my hand behind her head, holding her in place as I part her lips with my tongue and find that deep connection I so desperately desire with her.

She matches my strokes, her hands closing around the lapels of my jacket, her sweet moans bringing me back to that night...the night where I felt my entire life change.

The night I realized that I hadn't truly experienced life in its full technicolor until her lips met mine.

And now that I get to have her in my arms again, I get to hold her and claim her, that feeling is in full effect—I can hear louder, see clearer, smell every last flower in this conservatory. Life is brighter, bolder with her in my arms, and I'll be damned if I ever let her go again.

It's me and her...my best friend, my girl.

"Woooooo!" Clapping and cheering sounds off in front of us, and I pull away just enough to catch Maple, Polly, and Ken standing a few feet away, huge smiles on their faces.

Everly looks over her shoulder and when she sees them, she curls in closer to me.

"You two are perfect," Maple says, clasping her hands in front of her.

"You better not hurt her," Polly calls out.

"I won't," I say. "Never again." I kiss Everly's bare shoulder and when she looks back at me, I know for certain there isn't a chance in hell I will ever hurt her again.

She's it for me, and I will spend every last second of my life proving that to her.

From an acquaintance, to a bridesmaid undercover, to a best friend, to my girl, that's how it will stay.

EPILOGUE
HARDY

"ARE YOU ALMOST DONE IN there?" I call out to Everly who is in her bathroom, finishing up her shower.

"Yes," she calls out just as the door opens and I catch sight of her in her silk robe, her hair wet and draped over her shoulders. "Is dinner ready?"

"Yup," I say as I set two bowls of tomato bisque soup on the table along with some bread that I warmed in the oven.

She walks up to me, the cinch on her robe entirely too loose, and she presses her hand to my chest before standing on her toes and kissing my chin. "Thank you for making dinner."

"Anything for you," I say as I lift her chin and kiss her on the lips. When she returns the kiss, I wrap my arms around her waist and pull her in even closer. And when she moans, it's like music to my goddamn ears.

Her hand slithers under my shirt, her fingers dancing along my abs as she deepens the kiss. A few more seconds like this will lead to her robe on the floor and me feasting on her pussy rather than the soup I made… just like last night…and the night before and the many nights before that.

But not tonight.

I pull away and put my arms on her shoulders, giving us some distance.

"Hey," she says with a pout. "I was just about to stick my hand down your pants."

I chuckle. "As amazing as that sounds, hold that thought, because we are having dinner tonight the way I want to have dinner."

"And that doesn't entail my hand being down your pants?"

"No." I shake my head and then bring her over to her seat. As she sits down, I hand her a spoon and add, "Now eat."

"That's very demanding of you," she says.

I take a seat across from her. "It's not, when I've been wanting to have a normal dinner with you so we can talk about your day."

When her eyes meet mine, I see the soft expression that passes over her features in understanding. It was one of the things that stuck out to me when Everly and I first started getting to know each other: wanting someone to come home to, someone to share a meal with, someone to talk to at night. After the wedding, I swore to myself I will be the man she wants, the man she desires, and that means being there for her when she gets home from work, ready to welcome her and spoil her. But it seems like I can't get a hold on this simple task, even after two weeks of being together—every chance we've had, I've fallen for a quick kiss and turned it into so much more.

Not tonight.

Tonight, I will give her what she wants...at the dinner table and then on top of it.

"So, tell me about your day," I say.

She crosses one leg over the other and tries to hide her smile, but I can see it clear as day. "Well, I was planning an event I'm working on with one of my bosses and ended up getting bent over his desk instead."

"Everly..." I raise a brow at her.

"What?" she says with a smile. "It was a highlight of my day. If only he would do the same right now."

"Great things come to those who wait."

"I waited long enough for you. I should be able to have you whenever I want."

Did I mention she's insatiable?

Did I mention...so am I? Hence the *bent over the office desk* sex we had today.

"After dinner, promise, but I want to hear about your day first. Humor me." I offer her a wink.

She sighs. "It's cute that you're doing this. It does not go unappreciated. I want you to know that."

"Thank you," I say.

"But I got a new toy in the mail today, and I really want to use it."

I gulp because a new toy means a lot of moaning and biting in my future, something I can't fucking deny.

"Then eat fast and tell me about your day even faster."

She laughs. "Honestly, the best thing about it was seeing you in your office. I know it was a rough day for you, so being able to put a smile on your face really made my day."

"You always put a smile on my face."

She leans across the table, looking for a kiss, so I give her one but pull away quickly.

"We also landed a big event with the Fog Horns' children's charity, which is amazing. Scarlett will be heading it up. She's been a huge asset to the team. And then I worked on some centerpiece ideas for a wedding Maggie is in charge of — she was struggling, so I came up with some ideas. Then I came home to you making soup, and everything is right in the world."

She reaches for another kiss, and I give her one.

"Are you ready to talk about why you were in such a bad mood earlier?" she asks.

I pick up a piece of bread and tear off a bite. "Hudson and I were served today—by our father. Wasn't sure it was going to happen since he was taking so long, but he went through with it." I let out a sigh as Everly gets up from her chair and sits on my lap. She wraps her arm around my shoulder, keeping herself in place as my hand goes to her bare thigh. "It's really fucked up, and Hudson is taking it pretty hard. I know he's trying to act like everything is okay, but I know it's not."

"I'm sorry," she says as she rubs my chest. "Does he have any leg to stand on—your dad, that is?"

I shake my head. "Our lawyers don't think so. It's a frivolous case that will just be a waste of time, but it doesn't take away from the fact that he went through with it."

"I know," she says softly. "I'm sorry. You both deserve so much better than that."

"Thank you," I say as I run my hand up and down her thigh slowly. "I worry about Hudson though. He's been staying late at the office, working and not taking much time off. He's so determined, so set on not being our father, on proving him wrong, that I think he's getting lost. When I ask if he wants help, he just shakes his head and tells me to go home to you. I'm afraid he's taking on so much and not giving himself a chance to breathe. And today did not help."

"Have you talked to him about it?" she asks.

"Not yet, but I will. He's also been working Jude's sister hard too. She stays late with him."

"She has?" Everly asks.

I nod. "She's always there."

A small smile passes over Everly's lips. "What if there's something there between them?"

"Between Hudson and Sloane?" I ask incredulously. "Yeah, no fucking way."

"What? Why not?"

"Uh, first of all, Sloane is Jude's little sister—there is no way in hell Jude would ever approve. Second of all, she's Hudson's assistant, and he would never be with anyone he worked with, especially that closely. Third of all, she's way younger than him, and I don't think they have anything in common."

Everly shrugs. "You never know, they could be opening up to each other. They could be getting to know each other over late-night dinners in the conference room."

"This is your little romantic mind going off on tangents. Trust me, they are not together."

"And what if they were?"

"If they were?" I ask. "Then…hell, what would you want? I would give you anything."

"How about those three little words I've been looking for?"

I smirk. "Everly, you don't have to make a bet with me to hear me say I love you."

Her expression grows into one of full joy.

"Because I do," I say as I unknot the belt of her robe and push the fabric off her shoulders. "I love you more than anything."

She straddles my lap, her nearly naked body wrapping around me. "I love you too, Hardy."

"You mean that?" I bring my hands up her sides, to her breasts, only to lightly massage them as her eyes try to focus on mine and not roll to the back of her head.

"I more than mean that," she replies as I lower my head to her breasts and suck on one of her nipples. "Oh, Hardy," she moans. "Mmm, I thought we were having dinner."

"You convinced me that eating you would be so much better." And then I lay her down on the floor in front of me, spread her legs, and feast.

DISCOVER MORE MEGHAN QUINN WITH A SNEAK PEEK INTO HER CANE BROTHERS SERIES

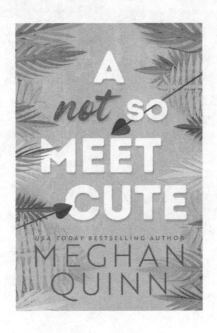

PROLOGUE
LOTTIE

"HEY, GIRL."

Hmm, I don't like the cheeriness in her voice.

The smirk on her lips.

The overuse of her toxic, throat-choking perfume.

"Hey, Angela," I answer with wary trepidation as I take a seat at the table in her office.

With a flip of her bright blond hair over her shoulder, she clasps her hands together, her body language conveying interest as she leans forward and asks, "How are you?"

I smooth my hands over my bright red pencil skirt and answer, "Doing fine. Thank you."

"That's so wonderful to hear." She leans back and smiles at me but doesn't say another word.

Ohh-kay, what the hell is going on?

I glance behind me to the row of suited men, sitting upright in chairs, folders on their laps, staring at our interaction. I've known Angela since middle school. We've had one of those on-again, off-again friendships, me being the victim of the intermittent camaraderie. I was her main squeeze one day— the next it was Blair, who works in finance, or Lauren, who works over in sales, and then the friendship would come back to me. We're interchangeable. Who's the bestie this week? I'd always wonder, and in some sick, demented way, I'd have a hiccup of excitement when the bestie card landed on me.

Why stick around in such a toxic friendship, you ask?

The answer is threefold.

One: when I first met Angela, I was young. I had no idea what the hell to do during such a vibrant roller coaster ride. I just gripped the handles and held on for dear life, because frankly, hanging with Angela was exciting. Different. Bold, at times.

Two: when she was nice to me, when we were deep into our friendship, I had some of the best times of my life. Growing up in Beverly Hills as the poor girl didn't lend its hand to many adventures, but with the rich friend who looked past your empty wallet and welcomed you into her world—yeah, it was fun. Call me shallow, but I had fun in high school, despite the ups and downs.

Three: I'm weak. I'm confrontation's bitch and avoid it at all costs. Therefore (raises hand) here I am, doormat, at your service.

"Angela?" I whisper.

"Hmm?" She smiles at me.

"Can I ask why you called me in here and why the FBI seems to be lined up behind me?"

Angela tilts her head back and lets out a hearty laugh as her hand lands on mine. "Oh, Lottie. God, I'm going to miss your humor."

"Miss?" I ask, my spine stiffening. "What do you mean, *miss*? Are you going on vacation?"

Please let that be the case. Please let that be the case. I can't afford to lose this job.

"I am."

Oh, thank God.

"Ken and I are headed to Bora-Bora. I have a spray tan scheduled in about ten minutes, so we need to get on with this."

Wait, what?

"Get on with what?" I ask.

Her jovial face morphs into something serious, the type of serious I don't see very often from Angela. Because, yes, she might be the head of her lifestyle blog, but she's not the one who does the work—everyone else does. So, she never has to be serious.

She sits taller, her jaw grows tight, and through her thick fake eyelashes, she says, "Lottie, you're a true pioneer for Angeloop. Your mastery behind the keyboard has been positively unmatched by anyone in this company, and the humor you bring to this thriving, money-dripping lifestyle blog has made this trip to Bora-Bora a reality."

Did I hear that right? Because of me, she's able to go on her vacation?

"But unfortunately, we're going to have to let you go."

Hold up...what?

Let me go?

As in, no more job for me?

Like a bolt of lightning, three of the men come up behind me, two on either side, flanking me like security. With their heavyset shoulders blocking me in, one of them drops a folder on the table in front of me and flips it open, revealing a piece of paper. My eyes are too unfocused to even consider reading what it says, but taking a simple guess, I'm thinking it's a termination paper.

"Sign here." The man holds a pen out to me.

"Wait, what?" I move the man's hand away, only for it to bounce back right where it was. "You're firing me?"

Angela winces. "Lottie, please don't make this a thing. You must know how difficult this has been for me." She snaps her fingers, and an assistant magically pops up. Angela rubs her throat and says, "This conversation has truly taken it out of me. Water, please. Room temperature. Lemon and lime, but take them out before you give it to me." And like that, the assistant is gone. When Angela turns back around, she sees me and clutches her chest. "Oh, you're still here."

Uhhh...

Yeah.

Blinking a few times, I ask, "Angela, what is going on? You just said I make you a ton of money—"

"Did I? I don't recall making such a statement. Boys, did I say anything like that?"

They all shake their head.

"See? I didn't say that."

I think… Yup, mm-hmm, do you smell that? That's my brain smoking, working overtime, trying to not LOSE IT!

Calmly, and I mean…calmly, I ask, "Angela, can you please explain to me why you're letting me go?"

"Oh." She laughs. "You've always been such a nosy little thing." The assistant brings Angela her water and then rushes away. Sucking from an unnecessary straw, Angela takes a long sip and then says, "Your one-year anniversary is on Friday."

"Yes. That's correct."

"Well, per your contract, it says that after a year, you're no longer under restricted pay, but instead receive your actual salary." She shrugs. "Why pay you more when I can find someone to do your job for less? Simple bottom-line thinking. You understand."

"No, I don't." My voice rises, and two large hands land on my shoulder in warning.

Oh, for fuck's sake.

"Angela, this is my life. This isn't some game you get to play. You told me when you begged me to work for you that this job was going to be life-changing."

"And hasn't it been?" She holds her arms out. "Angeloop is life-changing for everyone." She glances at her watch. "Oh, I have to get naked in five. Spray tans don't wait." She twirls her finger at the guys beside me. "Wrap it up, boys."

Two sets of hands grip me and help me up from my chair.

"You can't be serious," I say, still not quite grasping what's going on. "You're having security drag me out of your office?"

"Not by my choice," Angela says, the picture of innocence. "Your hostile attitude is making me use security."

"Hostile?" I ask. "I'm hostile because you're firing me for no reason."

"Oh, honey, I can't believe you see it that way," she says in that condescending voice of hers. "This is nothing personal. You know I love you and still plan on your monthly invitation to brunch. This is just business." She blows me a kiss. "Still my bestie."

She's lost her goddamned mind.

I'm pulled toward the door, but I dig in my two-seasons-ago Jimmy Choo heels. "Angela, seriously. You can't be firing me."

She looks up at me, tilts her head to the side, and then presses her hand to her heart. "Ahh, look at you, fighting for your job. God, you've always been scrappy." She blows me another kiss, waves, and calls out, "I'll call you. You can tell me about your horrible boss later. Oh...and don't forget to RSVP to our high school reunion. Two months away. We need a head count."

And just like that, defeat whips through me, my heels let up in total shock, my body goes limp, and I'm dragged by my underarms through the offices of Angeloop, the most idiotic and absurd lifestyle blog on the internet, a place where I didn't want to work in the first place.

Peers watch me.

Security doesn't skip a beat as they drag me all the way through the tall glass front door.

And before I can take my next breath, I'm staring at the obscenely large Angeloop sign outside of the office, a box of my office things in hand.

How the hell did this all happen?

ABOUT THE AUTHOR

#1 Amazon and *USA Today* bestselling author, wife, adoptive mother, and peanut butter lover. Author of romantic comedies and contemporary romance, Meghan Quinn brings readers the perfect combination of heart, humor, and heat in every book.

Website: authormeghanquinn.com
Facebook: meghanquinnauthor
Instagram: @meghanquinnbooks